A... :

'The Malazan franchise is fighting fit in the
hands of its co-creator'
SFX

Dancer's Lament

'Brilliant . . . filled with rooftop knife fights,
devastating magery and underworld evil, this book
hits all the right notes at all the right times'
FantasyBookReview

Deadhouse Landing

'Has all the hallmarks of great epic fantasy . . . an
essential read for Malazan fans, new and old'
CriticalDragon

Night of Knives

'I had a blast reading *Night of Knives* . . .
I highly recommend it'
FantasyBookCritic

Return of the Crimson Guard

'Everything you expect of a Malazan story . . .
epic and relevant . . . nail-biting and anything

Stonewielder

'A terrific read . . . impossible to put down
and highly recommended for all fans of
The Malazan Book of the Fallen'
FantasyHotlist

Orb Sceptre Throne

'The finest Esslemont novel so far, and a super
Malazan novel in its own right'
Drying-Ink

Blood and Bone

'Compelling . . . his best book to date'
SFFChronicles

Assail

'*Assail* by Ian C. Esslemont had a lot to live
up to. And boy did he pull it off . . . one of
my favourite books of the year'
FantasyBookReview

ABOUT THE AUTHOR

Born in Winnipeg, Ian Cameron Esslemont has studied and worked as an archaeologist, travelled extensively in South East Asia and lived in Thailand and Japan for several years. He now lives in Fairbanks, Alaska, with his wife and children. He has a creative writing degree and his novels are all set in the fantasy world of Malaz that he co-created with Steven Erikson. *Kellanved's Reach* follows *Dancer's Lament* and *Deadhouse Landing* and continues the story of the turbulent early history of this great imagined landscape. To find out more, visit www.malazanempire.com / www.ian-esslemont.com

KELLANVED'S REACH

Path to Ascendancy
Book 3

Ian C. Esslemont

BANTAM BOOKS

TRANSWORLD PUBLISHERS
61–63 Uxbridge Road, London W5 5SA
www.penguin.co.uk

Transworld is part of the Penguin Random House group of companies
whose addresses can be found at global.penguinrandomhouse.com

Penguin
Random House
UK

First published in Great Britain in 2019 by Bantam Press
an imprint of Transworld Publishers
Bantam edition published 2020

A CIP catalogue record for this book
is available from the British Library.

ISBN
9780857502858(B format)
9780857504395 (A format)

Typeset in 10.75/13pt Sabon by Jouve (UK), Milton Keynes
Printed and bound in Great Britain by Clays Ltd, Elcograf S.p.A.

Penguin Random House is committed to a sustainable
future for our business, our readers and our planet. This book is made
from Forest Stewardship Council® certified paper.

MIX
Paper from
responsible sources
FSC® C018179

1 3 5 7 9 10 8 6 4 2

To A.P. Canavan

ACKNOWLEDGEMENTS

Once again, thanks to Gerri and the boys for their support and patience with my strange calling. Continued thanks and gratitude to Simon and all the people at Transworld Publishers, and the dedicated readers at the Malazanempire.com site.

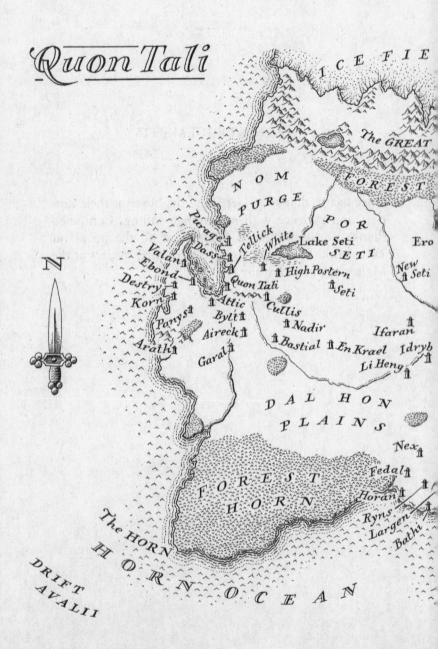

Quon Tali

N

ICE FIE

The GREAT

NOM

PURGE

FOR

The GREAT FOREST

Ero

Purage

Dass

Tellick

White

Lake Seti

SETI

New Seti

Valan

Ebond

Destry

Korn

High Postern

Quon Tali

Seti

Attic

Cullis

Panyst

Bylt

Nadir

Ifaran

Aireck

Bastial

En Krael

Idryb

Arath

Garal

Li Heng

DAL HON

PLAINS

Nex

FOREST

Fedal

HORN

Horan

Ryns

Largen

Bathi

The HORN

DRIFT

AVALII

HORN OCEAN

LDS

COLONNUS
SEA

WICKAN
PLAINS

FALARI SEA

FENN RANGE

FENN

Voron

Baran

D'avig

Habal

Athrans

Thades

Jurda

Balstro

Lake

Rath

Nita

Gris

Thade

Unta

Haljhen

Bloor

Fools

Telo

Estawn

Netor

Drim

Sentry

Larent

BLOOR SEA

Ipras

Cawn

Layes

Yellows

Shedry

Satar

Gast

Kartool

Aska

Halas

Bris

Nure

KARTOOL
ISLAND

Feng

Marl

Aythan

Borid

Carasin

Buld

NAP

REACHER'S

Traly

Then

SEA

Nap

OCEAN

Ijor

Itko Kan

Pryl

Laeth

NAPAN

Wal Tes

ISLES

Malaz City

Wal Fend

MALAZ
ISLAND

GENI

DRAMATIS PERSONAE

Of Malaz

Kellanved	New ruler of the isle of Malaz
Dancer	A notorious assassin
Surly	A Napan aristocrat
Cartheron Crust	A Napan captain
Urko Crust	A Napan captain
Choss	A Napan admiral
Tocaras	A Napan archer
Dassem Ultor	A Dal Hon swordsman, whom some name 'Sword of Hood'
Tayschrenn	A renegade mage of Kartool
Dujek	A recruit
Jack	A recruit
Nedurian	A veteran, and mage

Of Nap

Tarel	King of the Napan Isles
Lady Elaina	Head of the Ravanna line
Torlo	Of the Torlo Trading House
Lord Kobay	Head of the Medalla line
Karesh	High Admiral, lord of all Napan fleets

Of the Bloorian League

Gareth	The king of Vor, and a principal of the League

Styvell	The king of Rath, and a principal of the League
Hret	The king of Bloor, and a principal of the League
Leah	A corporal of the Yellows Regiment
Teigan	A sergeant of the Yellows Regiment

Of Gris and its Allies
Malle	Ruler of the city state of Gris
Ranel	Baron of Nita
Ap-Athlan	Court sorcerer of Gris

Of Nom Purge
Elath Lallind	High General of Nom Purge
Ghenst Terrall	Baron of the Coastal Provinces
Jeral	Prevost (captain) of Purge forces

Of Orjin Samarr's Troop
Orjin Samarr	A mercenary commander
Terath	A lieutenant
Arkady	A Wickan scout
Orhan	A fighter of possible giant blood, perhaps of Fenn
Yune	A Dal Hon shaman

Of Itko Kan
Leoto	Head of family Kan, the Kan of Kan
Jadeen	A feared witch of the south
Iko	A Sword-Dancer guard to the king

Of the Crimson Guard
| Courian D'Avore | Commander of the Guard |
| K'azz D'Avore | His son, whom some name the Red Prince |

| Surat | Champion of the Guard |
| Cal-Brinn | A mage, and adviser to Courian |

Others

Gregar	An apprentice stonemason
Haraj	A prisoner
Heboric	A priest of Fener
Hairlock	A mage

Prologue

AS IT DID EVERY TIME, THE ODIOUS IDRYN MUD sucked at his boots – touching, even, the hem of his fine midnight blue (not black, mind you!) silk trousers, though he'd pulled them up as high as he could as he tramped the river shore to find Liss. Halfway, amid the stink and disgusting sewer filth, he paused, and he raised his eyes to the sky to entreat the gods. Why must you punish me so? Where did I transgress? Was it those curvy Leparia twins? If so, have I not endured enough?

Silk, city mage of Li Heng, lowered his gaze. Perhaps not. Those two had been so very delicious.

He spotted her then, in her dirty rags, among the pilings where they stood exposed, for this had been a dry summer, and the Idryn was low.

Once again Silk reflected that were it not for his strong suspicion that this hag was far more than a mere crazy witch, he would most certainly not be here.

Sighing, he slogged onward until he was within hailing distance, and he set a hand to his mouth. 'Hello! Crazy catfish lady? You called?'

She straightened and turned his way, pushed snaggled tangled hair from her dirty face – which brightened. 'Pretty boy! Decided to grow up, have you?'

1

Silk rolled his eyes. 'What is it you want, Liss? I'm a busy man.'

'Oh yes! So much posturing and self-indulgence to pursue! Where indeed to start?'

Silk peered about at the northern waterfront, the raised boardwalk and the inns and bars that fronted it. 'You know, I could leave in any direction. Shall I choose?'

Liss straightened among the rags heaped over her shoulders, her mocking smile falling, and Silk was momentarily taken aback to see that she was even taller than he – and he was considered a rather tall fellow. 'I see a storm approaching, Silk. One you may not weather well.'

'Really? A storm? You can't do better than that? A storm?' He laughed, shaking his head. 'Any cheap Dragons Deck reader on any street corner could do better than that! You do realize that's a cliché, don't you?' He slapped at the drying mud marring his fine trousers. 'I can't believe you dragged me here for this.'

The old hag's pinched mouth drew down and she cut a hand through the air as if to say, *Very well!* 'I see a time of great upheaval approaching. One that may cost you in particular a great deal.' She cocked a brow. 'Dismiss that – if you will.'

Silk crossed his arms. 'Fine. Brass tacks, as they say. What sort of upheaval?'

The old witch turned away, hunching once more. She probed the mud before her. 'Ancient,' she murmured. 'Very ancient. That is all I can say, to my peril.'

'Peril? You mean whatever this is – it threatens even you?'

She turned upon him, suddenly, peering about. 'Oh yes. Everyone. Even the Elders. None can escape this.'

Despite his scepticism, Silk retreated a short distance from the woman. 'Elders? You mean, even the . . . Tiste?'

The hag shambled off. 'I can say no more. It may come. Beware. That is all I dare say.'

Silk remained – ankle-deep in the muck – watching the old witch as she wandered off. Madness perhaps? A sad need for attention? Nothing more? Or so much more than that? Who could say?

He set his hands to his hips and let out a great breath, nodding to himself.

Fine! Time to talk to Ho . . .

Chapter 1

DANCER SLIPPED SILENTLY INTO THE MAIN RECEPTION hall of Mock's Hold and peered round. It was night and only the torches in their sconces lit the broad empty chamber. Turning, he nodded to Surly and indicated the stairs. 'He's in his rooms,' he mouthed as quietly as possible.

Surly, a Napan woman bearing the characteristic blue hue of those isles' natives, turned to the two men hanging back, also Napans. Cartheron Crust and Urko Crust were brothers, but as unalike as night and day, since Cartheron stood short and wiry while Urko bulked as wide as an ox. 'No one comes down or up,' she ordered.

Cartheron nodded, while his brother smacked one meaty fist into the other palm. Dancer and Surly glared at the loud slap of flesh and he grimaced, muttering, 'Sorry.'

Surly started up. Her bare feet were silent on the polished stone. Dancer glided with her almost as if he were floating up the steps. Together, they reached one particular door in the hall and took up positions to either side.

They nodded in unison, then Dancer took the latch and threw open the door. Both stormed into the chamber.

5

An aged, dark-skinned Dal Hon native snorted at the interruption, feet up on a desk, arms crossed over his paunch. He blinked, surprised, then frowned his displeasure. 'So,' he announced, 'it has come to this.'

'You leave us no choice, Kellanved,' Dancer answered. 'If you cooperate we'll make it quick.'

The wizened elder twisted up his lips and turned his face away. He crossed his arms. 'Never. You wouldn't dare.'

With a gesture as graceful as his name, Dancer invited Surly forward. She leaned up against Kellanved's desk. Crossing her arms, she cleared her throat and began, 'Let me see . . . Nom Purge remains in perpetual warfare with Quon Tali. Dal Hon is currently probing a weakened Itko Kan's borders. The Seti continue to attack anyone other than travellers who enters the central plains. The War Marshal of the Bloorian League, in secret connivance with Unta, is steadily isolating Gris from its surrounding principates and allies, while the city state of Cawn sells arms and provides mercenaries to all sides.'

The wrinkled ancient had pressed his hands to his ears and was shaking his head. 'No! Stop this horrible babble – you're killing me!'

'Then how are we to proceed?' Dancer demanded. 'Tell us what you have in mind. For once.'

'Never! The element of surprise . . .'

'Surprise our enemies,' Dancer pleaded. 'Not us!' He nodded for the woman to continue. 'Surly here has spent a great deal of time thinking about Nap.'

The ancient mage rolled his eyes. 'Oh, please. Who cares about Nap now? Dancer, a much more profound errand beckons . . .'

The assassin glared a warning. 'Hear her out, at the least.'

Kellanved groaned and let his head fall to the desk.

Ignoring this, Surly went on, 'We should approach Dal Hon for an agreement exempting their shores and merchants from all attacks. We could ask for twenty ships with crews – or funding to the equivalent. For if we take Nap we will be the sole raiders of the Southern Seas. And they know this.'

Kellanved's head snapped up. 'We? What is this *we* business?' He eyed Dancer narrowly.

Dancer pressed a hand to his brow in frustration. 'That's all you take away from that? This is sound strategy. I think we should listen.'

The mage set his elbows on the desk and steepled his fingers before his chin. He regarded Dancer with some scepticism. 'And just which *we* are we talking about here?'

'You, me, us – whoever! Just listen, dammit all to Burn!'

Kellanved pursed his lips and bounced his steepled fingers from them then lowered his hands to grip the desk. 'Very well. I shall reveal my plans! They are as follows . . . we shall take all our ships, attack Dariyal, and take Nap!' He thrust a bent finger into the air. 'Ha!'

Surly and Dancer eyed one another, appalled. Dancer pulled a hand down his face. 'Gods have mercy,' he muttered, and turned away to pour a drink.

'That's just what Tarel would expect,' Surly explained, rather acidly. 'The same thing's been tried again and again for hundreds of years.' She pressed her hands together, almost at a loss for words. 'Nap invading Malaz, Malaz invading Nap. It always fails in the end. We need an alliance. I suggest Dal Hon.'

Kellanved waved that aside. 'I need no damned allies. Duplicitous betrayers! Two-faced turncoats! I curse them all.'

'Then what exactly do you suggest?' Dancer demanded.

'Exactly what I just outlined.'

Dancer sipped his wine. He eyed the mage over the glass. 'Haven't you been listening?'

Kellanved nodded. 'Yes I have. I hear that my plan is exactly what Talen and his admirals would expect of a new impetuous leader such as myself.' He cocked a brow at Surly. 'Yes?'

Now the Napan raider frowned, uncertain of the man's tack. 'Well, yes . . .'

Kellanved gave a curt nod. 'Excellent. Because said invasion will be a diversion to draw their forces out of the capital. The real attack will come from the landward side. I myself shall transport a small force on to the island, led perhaps by our friend Dassem, to take the palace and replace its ruler.'

Surly snapped up a hand. 'Agreed – so long as you swear to leave Tarel to me.'

Kellanved inclined his head. 'Agreed.' He waved, shooing Surly from his chambers. 'Very good. Now, make the same offer to Itko Kan and Cawn in secret. But we will renege on those – yes?'

Dancer and Surly turned to eye one another, their brows rising: neither had thought of that.

Kellanved waved Surly off. 'Go on! Make the arrangements. Dancer and I have things to talk over.'

Surly did not move. Her gaze slid between the two, suspicious. 'If you disappear again how can I count on you being where you need to be?'

'Tayschrenn should be able to contact us,' Kellanved supplied, untroubled. 'And in any case, I see your point. We shan't be leaving for some time.'

She backed away to the door. 'Very well. But how can we know you'll be there . . .'

He fluttered a hand. 'We shall. Do not worry.'

She pulled the door open, and could not help but add a last, dark, muttered, 'You'd better be.'

The Crust brothers met her at the bottom of the stairs and Cartheron asked, 'So? How'd it go? What's the plan?'

She eyed the upper rooms and ran her fingertips over the ridged calloused knuckles of her other hand. 'Remind me to stop underestimating that damned fool mage.'

* * *

Baron Elath Lallind, Sentry of the Seti Marches and High General of Nom Purge, was very pleased with his prosecution of the campaign against Quon Tali to date. He'd taken over from General Yellen of the Agar family – now stripped of all rank and disgraced – two seasons ago, and since then had proved victor far more often than the reverse. The most recent retreat of Quon Talian forces had brought the contending armies to the very border of Quon lands, at the shore-side plains of Sighing Grasses. A victory here would open the way to the rich northern provinces of their traditional enemy, and not too inconsequentially seal his name as the greatest leader in the history of Nom Purge. So it was that confidence was high and the mood one of barely suppressed glee at this last meeting of his command staff before battle.

'We will finally break them here and retake our ancient lands,' Elath announced to the nobles, captains and aides gathered in his command tent. 'So ends the last legacy of their vaunted hegemony.'

All glasses rose in a toast. 'To the general!' All save one, Elath noticed, a young captain of heavy infantry, risen to prominence for his personal skill in battle.

Hugely broad he was, and blunt-faced. An uncouth commoner with a thick length of prematurely grey hair.

Elath lowered his glass, his satisfaction souring. 'You are concerned?' he asked this leader of one of their foreign contingents.

The fellow rubbed a heavy paw over his jowls and let out a breath of unease. 'It's not like these Quon Talians to be so unprepared. Where are their reinforcements?'

'Our sources tell us this is all they can muster at this time.' He offered a shrug. 'Quon and Tali are not what they once were.'

'And they no doubt have sources among you who tell them you believe this.'

Elath's mood was now positively darkening. 'And you are . . . Orjin Samarr? Yes? Well, come out with it, Captain Samarr. What is it you are suggesting?'

The swordsman pointed to the east. 'These deep wooded valleys flanking the plain. You could hide a whole army in there. I don't like it.'

Elath turned a raised brow upon Baron Ghenst Terrall of the Coastal Provinces. The baron bowed. 'The woods are clear, lord marshal. My own personal scouts searched them.'

Elath returned his attention to the foreign swordsman. 'There you are. The baron assures us they are clear.'

'Just the same, I'd feel a lot better if I could send a few of my own lads and lasses to—'

The marshal snapped up a hand for silence. 'Captain . . . if a noble of Nom Purge says something is so, then it is so. A gentleman does not question another gentleman's word.'

Many of the gathered nobility smirked at this particular phrasing, while the foreigner's thick brows clenched as if he were too dense to parse the hidden insult behind the words. He nodded then, bowing to the general. 'Too much drink, perhaps.' He finished his cup and picked up the battered iron gauntlets on the table before him. He saluted the marshal, 'To a glorious victory, sir,' and brushed aside the heavy tent flap, exiting.

Outside, in the cold damp wind off the deeps of the Western Sea, he muttered to himself, 'But whose?'

Four figures rose from a fire nearby. A scarred Wickan with a wild, wind-tossed mane of tangled hair, wearing a long studded leather hauberk; a towering pale fellow, bald, in an iron cuirass; a woman in a full-length coat of mail, twinned Untan duelling swords at her sides; and a squat, very black Dal Hon elder in a cloak of multicoloured rags and patches.

'He's not attacking, is he?' the woman demanded.

Orjin sighed; tucked his gauntlets into his weaponbelt. 'He's attacking.'

'And the woods?' the bald giant asked.

'Baron Ghenst Terrall assures us that the woods are clear.'

'There are horses in the woods,' the Wickan muttered. 'I can sense them.'

'And what would you know about horses?' the Dal Hon ancient cackled. 'That is rich! You, Arkady, a Wickan without a horse!'

The Wickan answered slowly, through tightly clenched teeth, 'I told you . . . I swore a vow.'

Orjin waved a hand for silence. 'Spread the word – everyone stick close to me. We may have to carve our way out of Hood's own grasp tomorrow.'

The four nodded, answering, 'Aye, captain.'

It was probably Orjin's impolitic honesty at the staff meeting that saw his command stationed at the rear of the dispositions for the coming battle, in the reserves. He and his would see no glory this day, but that suited him just fine. He wasn't in it for the glory; leave that to the nobles bred on war and battle. He was here for . . . well, he really couldn't say why he was here. It all happened kind of by accident. He'd left Geni, a small backwater fishing isle famous for nothing, and set out to win a living by the only thing he seemed to have an aptitude for – swordplay. And over the next few years he'd found himself with a growing name and a growing set of followers attracted to that name. Now he was a captain, if only unofficially, as his troop was no formal mercenary force, rather more like a large warband such as the chieftains of ancient times used to lead.

So it was that at dawn he and his command stood waiting with hands at belts, or, in the case of the bald giant Orhan of Fenn, leaning his seven-foot frame on a twelve-foot-tall halberd.

As the rising sun burned the fog from the plain and warmed him, the light murmur of contact reached even here, far to the rear.

'Skirmishers are feeling each other out,' Terath supplied, her gauntleted hands clasping and reclasping the worn leather grips of her duelling swords.

The Wickan, Arkady, grunted his agreement.

'You know,' offered Orhan, 'in battles the view I'm used to isn't the rumps of the officers' horses.'

'We must be *really* far back,' Arkady grumbled.

The swordswoman had set to rubbing her teeth with a willow twig and now she tossed this aside, spitting. 'You know what we say out east in Unta about this interminable Purge–Tali war?'

'What, Terath?' Orjin answered, distracted, focused

12

upon the growing clamour of battle ahead – the lights and mediums must be closing upon one another.

'Everyone says that the war with Nom Purge is just the Talians keeping in practice.'

The giant Orhan's chuckle was a deep bass rumble. 'That is a good one. I like that.'

Orjin rubbed his chin, listening even more keenly now, and muttered, 'I think you're right in that, Terath.'

A roar washed over them at the rear, sweeping down from the battlefield – the largest cohorts colliding, mostly medium infantry. Among these two armies the cavalry was mainly the officer corps and their staff, for visibility and mobility rather than actual fighting.

'Now or never . . .' he breathed aloud.

But it came not as he'd expected it – an explosive burst of despairing shouts and screams – rather, all the Nom Purge mounted officers in view slewed their horses over to the forested east and Orjin knew that the rest of the Quon Talian forces had just revealed themselves. And done so too far from the engagement.

'Ready weapons!' he bellowed to his troop.

The impact of the charging Quon Tali forces came as a menacing roar and a shudder beneath their feet. Orjin knew the Purge forces still had a chance – as long as they held fast and resisted. One break, or routed company, however, could very well crack the entire dam. He and his force awaited the outcome, whichever it may be, in the rear.

After a good twenty minutes of pitched battle back and forth, Nom Purge infantry appeared, running past them, some even throwing down their weapons as they went. Orjin sought out the company mage, the Dal Hon shaman, Yune, and gave him a nod. The hunched old man pounded his raven-feather-strung staff to the ground – once. That blow communicated itself to all Orjin's forces, its meaning prearranged: *Tighten up.*

Mounted Nom Purge nobles then appeared, battered and bloodied, pushing their horses through the milling infantry to charge past Samarr's unit.

'Where is Elath?' he yelled as they thundered by. 'Dammit! What's going on?' All ignored him. Orjin spotted a harried and wild-eyed Baron Ghenst Terrall among those abandoning the field and charged towards him, pushing aside fleeing soldiers as he went. He waved the nobleman down.

'Out of my way, damn you!' the baron shouted.

'Rally the troops – while you can!' Orjin shouted back.

Ghenst attempted to yank his mount around him. 'Word of this must reach the queen, dog!'

'And what of the woods?' Orjin demanded. 'The Quon forces came out of the woods!'

For an instant their eyes met, and the baron glanced away, his face flushing. Stunned, Orjin let his arms fall. 'You Hood-damned *bastard* . . .'

Ghenst took that moment to spur his mount past.

Orjin's troops found him there, motionless, still peering after the diminishing figure of the fleeing nobleman. They surrounded him, using the flat of their blades to push back a rising tide of refugees from the front, all clamouring for protection among Orjin's tight unit. The giant Orhan came wading through the press. 'Orders?' he rumbled.

Blinking, coming to himself, Orjin gestured to the east. 'Make for cover in the woods – as a unit!'

Orhan inclined his bald scarred head. 'Aye, aye.' He waved his great halberd overhead in a circle, ending the arc to point east. As one, the chevron of mercenary heavies began marching, with Orjin at point.

As they pushed through the rout, Orjin spotted a staff messenger, bloodied from a head blow, staggering almost aimlessly. He broke ranks to take hold of the woman's shoulder and give her a shake. 'What happened, dammit to Hood!'

'We held them,' she murmured, dazed. 'We held . . . but there were too many. Too many . . .'

'And Elath? What word?'

'Fallen.' She wiped a wet, bloodied hand across her face. 'We are lost.'

'Only if you break,' Samarr snarled, pushing her to the rear. 'Never break.'

They marched onward. Quon Talian forces now appeared, harrying the broken Purge mediums. Among these came grim-faced heavies in long surcoats that bore a black field adorned by a simple silver crown. The famous sigil of the Talian Iron Legion.

These men and women simply struck a guard, allowing Orjin's troops to pass; after all, the day was already theirs. Why pursue unnecessary hard knocks?

Orjin answered the salute and continued onward, flanked by Terath and Orhan. In this manner they made cover among the woods and here Orjin waved his lieutenants to him.

'What now?' Terath demanded. 'Our contract was with Elath.'

Orjin shook his head. 'Technically, our contract is with the queen.'

Orhan rubbed his wide jaw. 'If Purage falls, we don't get paid.'

Orjin sent him a glare. 'I know! With Elath's expeditionary force broken the passes are open to Tali.'

'The old keep at Two-River could contain them,' Yune supplied.

Terath laughed her scorn. 'That pest-hole? A crumbling stone tower and a wooden palisade! Indefensible!'

Orjin looked to the distant north-east highlands. 'That's about two days' march from here.'

'Two *good* days,' Terath appended.

Orjin gave a curt jerk of his head, pushed back his long grey hair. 'We'll march straight through. Beat them there. The Purge forces must be rallying somewhere – it's the obvious strong point.'

'A hundred years ago maybe,' Terath grumbled, and she slammed home her blades.

'None the less. We march.' Orjin raised a hand and signed *Move out*.

* * *

Crouched on his haunches, Tayschrenn squinted into the dark gap that remained between the twin monoliths lying lengthways one above the other, and reflected that, as far as instruments of execution went, this was a most ingenious one. Crushing the condemned between two immense slabs of stone – elegant in its simplicity.

This victim, however, refused to cooperate. So far, at least.

Sighing his distaste, the mage sat and idly brushed the night's flying insects from his face. Too bad; now he would actually have to talk to the fellow. He patted the top slab of granite. 'Hello?' he called. 'Still with us?'

He waited patiently. The night wind rose, hissing through the tall grasses of the surrounding savanna foothills of these Itko Kan–Dal Hon borderlands. Eventually, a voice snapped from within the darkness of the gap – a

16

space no wider than the outstretched fingers of one's hand, thumb to pinky.

'Fuck off. Kinda busy right now.'

'I should say so,' Tayschrenn agreed affably. 'I can feel your Warren sizzling just from here. Weakening, though.' He added, conversationally, 'Not much longer, I should think.'

'Listen.' The man hidden within spoke again, his voice clipped and breathless. 'Are you naturally this much of an asshole, or are you making an extra special effort?'

Tayschrenn patted the top granite slab once more. 'Actually, I'm here to offer a deal.'

'A deal? Really? Hardly fair, don'tcha think? I'm in a tight spot right now.'

Tayschrenn shrugged, then realized the fellow couldn't see him. 'Regardless. The deal should be obvious. Your life for your service.'

'To you?'

Grimacing, Tayschrenn brushed the rock dust from his hands. 'My employer, actually.'

'Ah. And who is he or she?'

Tayschrenn raised his eyes to the starry night sky, twined his fingers together at a knee and rocked back and forth. 'I really don't think you're in a position to ask any questions.'

'How do you know?' answered the hidden victim. 'Maybe I always wanted to lose some weight.'

Tayschrenn made levelling motions with his hands, as if smoothing a cloth. 'You wouldn't lose it. It would just be more . . . spread out.'

'Asshole!'

'Regardless, time is running out. You are not the only minor talent I could approach.'

'*Minor!*' the fellow burst out – then gasped as the top

17

granite block dropped a finger's width. 'Fucker! If I was out of here I'd tear you apart!'

'Hardly. Your Warren's flickering. You are almost spent. And in any case, if you were such a fearsome warlock how did the townsfolk get you in there?'

A sullen silence radiated from within the thin gap. 'I have something of a weakness for the pleasures of the flesh – wine and women, as they say.'

'So they drugged you.'

'Yeah.'

'Well . . . let this be a warning.'

'Won't happen again.'

'Do we have an accord then?'

'Fine. Yes! An accord. I'd shake on it but I have my hands full right now.'

'Very well.' Tayschrenn gestured and the huge block flew off, spinning through the air to crash to the ground in a shuddering impact.

The little man revealed beneath peered in that direction. 'Show-off.' He rose, shakily, and brushed at his fine rich shirt and trousers. Tayschrenn merely gave him a nod in greeting.

'So who's our employer, then?'

'A mage of Meanas, named Kellanved.'

The young man – though young in appearance only – raised a quizzical brow. 'Not the mage who's got all the talents up in arms as Shadow cards are jumping from their decks and doing jigs on the tables?'

Tayschrenn showed a pained expression. 'The same.'

'Hunh. And you are?'

'Tayschrenn.'

The slim youth nodded. 'Calot.'

* * *

Gregar Bluenth groaned and regained consciousness. He rubbed his head, only to wince at the numerous raised welts, and swallowed the taste of old blood. He pushed himself up from the pile of rotting damp straw he lay upon and surveyed his surroundings: the sight was not promising. The only light cascaded down from an opening hidden in the stone ceiling far above. The dim glow revealed that he'd been thrown into a prison cell.

He staggered to the stout iron-bound door and banged upon it. 'Hello! Anyone there? Hello?' He kept banging.

After a very long time – half a day, perhaps; he had no way of telling but for the gradual waning of the natural light filtering down into the cell – heavy footsteps sounded from the hall outside the door. 'Hello?' Gregar called once more. 'Who's there?'

'Oho! Awake, are you?'

He sighed his relief. 'Yes. Where am I?'

'They always ask that,' said his interlocutor in a tone of wonder. 'Thought it must be obvious.'

Gregar kicked the door. 'Yes, yes. In prison in Castle Gris – I just wanted a second opinion. Thank you. Now that you've had your joke you can let me out.'

'Out? Out you say, lad? Whatever for?'

'What do you mean, "whatever for"? I've done nothing wrong. Let me go, dammit!'

'Nothing wrong? You assaulted the Grisian guard. Sent many to the healing wards, so I understand.' The shambling, heavy steps came closer. 'You even boasted of meaning to join the Crimson Guard – and you know those criminals are outlawed here in Gris.'

Gregar let his head touch the cool damp wood of the door. Yes, he remembered that boast. 'Fine. I'm sorry, okay? I repent. I'm an apprentice stonemason here at the castle. You can let me out now.'

'Sorry, lad, but this is your third run-in with the guard. You're bound for labour in the quarries.'

The quarries? As a mason Gregar knew about the wretched lives of those sent to break rock in the quarries. It was no better than a death sentence.

'Look – I recant. I'd been drinking, okay? Haven't you ever had a little too much?'

'Oh, yes,' answered the hidden jailer. 'Many times. But it's not up to me. By the way – I say sorry, but I'm not. Not at all. I just say that to quieten you fellows down. Farewell!'

'Wait!' He banged on the door. 'Wait, dammit to Hood!'

The heavy dragging steps diminished into the distance, accompanied by a mocking chuckle.

He slid down the door to the stone floor and lay there up against the wood, cursing. In time, he must have fallen asleep again, because he imagined himself clawing at the wall. He scratched, pulled, seemed even to be digging – as at the promised quarry, perhaps – pushing at the stones, desperate to escape.

And when he awoke once again the light was different. Flickering sallow lamplight illuminated a narrow stone hallway. He jumped to his feet, unbelieving. The fool of a jailer must've left the door unlocked! Gregar ran.

After numerous intersections and doors – always choosing the upwards path, be it stairs or a sloping hall – he found himself in the lower kitchens of the great stone fortress that was ancient Castle Gris. Fat cauldrons steamed over charcoal fires, and wide counters held fowl waiting to be plucked and butchered piglets awaiting dressing. The scent of food made him almost faint and he went to the nearest cast-iron pot. A wooden spoon rested nearby and he dunked it into the dark roiling fluid.

'I wouldn't eat that if I were you,' warned an amused voice nearby, and Gregar jumped backwards.

What he'd taken for a pile of rags and bones now stirred, revealing a painfully skinny figure all angles and protruding joints. A pale skull limned by greasy lank hair rose as its owner regarded him.

'Why?' he demanded.

'Because that's lye in there.'

'Lye? Doesn't smell like it.'

'Been boiling for days. Ready to treat the hides now.'

Gregar flinched away. 'Isn't there anything to eat here? Isn't this a damned kitchen?'

The emaciated lad – if it was a lad; Gregar couldn't really tell – chuckled.

'This is the sub-sub-kitchen. If Castle Gris has a basement, this is the shithole beneath. Not much food here. Just the worst cast-offs and leavings.'

'There's a lot beneath here,' Gregar answered. 'I've seen it.'

The eyes, huge and luminous in the lean fleshless skull, somehow became brighter. 'You've come from below? How?'

'I escaped.'

'Escaped?' The figure repeated the word as if mouthing it for the first time. 'Escaped . . . how?'

'Never mind! I need food.'

'No. How. Tell me how.'

Gregar eyed the three open approaches to the kitchen and the one locked door. 'Fine. The jailer left the door to my cell unlocked and I escaped. There. Happy? Now – where's something to eat?'

An etiolated hand rose and long crooked fingers extended to point to the far cauldron. 'Ham hocks rendering. Try there.'

Gregar used the spoon to fish out a pig's knuckle to gnaw on. 'Who're you?' he asked, as he eyed the openings and considered his chances in the upper halls.

'Never mind me. Escaped, you say? From the cells? What did you do?'

Gregar shrugged, rather self-consciously. 'I had a fight with the guard.'

'Last night?'

'Yes.'

'Ah! So that was you the servants were talking about. They said you beat down an entire watch of the guard while armed only with sticks. And that you meant to join the Crimson Guard. Is that true?'

Gregar looked away. 'I suppose so. Can't really remember.'

'Then how did they capture you?'

He sighed, spat the knuckle to the floor. 'I passed out.'

The figure, who had been lying or crouching, now rose to stand, and Gregar was appalled by the state of its emaciation, and the filthy rags that hung from its skeletal frame. He was also rather unnerved by the brightness that flamed in its huge eyes. 'What is your calling?' the figure asked.

'Calling?'

'What do you do?'

'Oh. I'm an apprentice mason.'

'Mason.' The figure nodded to itself, thinking. Gregar now noted a collar and chain that ran from the poor slave's neck to a ring set in the wall nearby. 'Have a way with stone, do you?' it asked, suddenly, as if struck by a thought.

Gregar gave a curt jerk of his head. 'Aye. Always. Comes natural to me. I can just see it.'

'See it? See what?'

Gregar shrugged again. He fished out another pig's knuckle. 'Where to strike. The stresses and strains running through any rock. It's all obvious to me. Plain as day. The north tower, for example – it needs shoring up. The foundations are eroding.'

The sickly lad smiled now – a corpse's grin of yellowed teeth against sunken cheeks. He grabbed hold of the chain securing him to the wall and held it out. 'Break this,' he demanded.

Gregar waved him off. 'Thanks, but no thanks. I'm for the higher halls.'

'You won't make it ten paces.' The lad's fevered pale eyes were blazing with a new light. 'I, however, know all the upper halls. I can get you out of Castle Gris.'

Gregar waved him off. 'Sorry, but I can't break that chain.'

The lad lifted his chin, revealing his collar. 'What of this?'

It was a plain length of leather riveted about the boy's neck. Gregar thought even this fellow ought to be able to break it. 'That's our deal then, is it? I release you and you get us out?'

The young lad nodded, very sombrely. 'Oh yes. And we join the Crimson Guard.'

Despite himself, Gregar laughed his disbelief. 'Really? I was just boasting.'

The slave edged his head from side to side in all seriousness. 'You break this collar and we will join the Crimson Guard.'

'Really? Just like that?'

The young slave nodded. 'Just like that.'

Gregar laughed. 'You sell a good line, whoever you are. But I'll give it a try.' He reached out to the poor fellow's neck. A yank and the leather band parted. He handed the broken length to the lad. 'There you are. Don't know why you couldn't have done that yourself.'

The slave stared for a time at the leather band in his pale, long-fingered hands. Then his gaze rose in wonder to Gregar. 'My master ensorcelled these bonds so that I couldn't break them. Only a certain sort of person could.'

At the word 'ensorcelled' a cold sickness took hold of Gregar's stomach. 'Your master?' he breathed.

The skinny lad nodded. 'The sorcerer Ap-Athlan. High Mage of Gris.'

Gregar resisted the urge to cuff the youth across his head. 'Why didn't you say so, dammit! I thought your master was just the cook or something!' Realizing he was shouting, he lowered his voice, hissing, 'I don't want any attention, in case you hadn't noticed.'

The lad – in truth, perhaps no older than himself for all he knew – raised his eerily long-fingered hands in reassurance. 'I know, I know. And I can get us out. Guaranteed. Then we'll join the Crimson Guard.'

Gregar rubbed the back of his neck while the lad limped about the kitchen, digging out a cured ham, a wedge of cheese, a skin of wine, and throwing all into a burlap sack. 'Ah, about that joining up thing . . . I was drunk. It was just a damned boast . . . I really don't think that's gonna happen . . .'

The lad raised a hand once again. 'Don't worry. It will. They'll take both of us. I'm sure.'

Gregar laughed, shaking his head. 'Well, kid. As I said: you talk a good line – I'll give you that. What's your name, anyway?'

He raised his hands to study them once more. 'Dog, he called me. My master. I did . . . *things* for him. Things I do not want to think of. But now that I am free – I can forget him. So, I will use my old name, Haraj. And you?'

'Gregar Bluenth.'

The lad pulled a face. 'Gregar Bluenth? Really. Have to do something about that . . .' He limped to a heavily bound door that Gregar knew must lead closer to the rear chambers, and possible freedom.

'That's locked,' he warned. 'No point trying that.'

The lad pressed his hands to the door. He brushed and rubbed his long fingers over the iron lock. Then, with one extended finger, he gave the door a push and it creaked open. He flashed an evil boyish grin to Gregar. 'No it's not.' He crooked a finger, inviting him onward. 'Let's go.'

Chapter 2

THE DAY AFTER HE, SURLY, AND KELLANVED HAD their strategy talk, Dancer was in the upper chambers of Mock's Hold when Kellanved entered and carefully shut the door behind him. The mage, now permanently appearing as a wrinkled, black-skinned Dal Hon elder, beckoned Dancer close and whispered, hushed, 'Are we alone?'

Dancer shrugged, a touch mystified. 'Well, yes. I imagine so.'

'Good. Then let's go.'

'Go? Go where?'

The grey-haired ancient raised his eyes to the ceiling in frustration. 'Our research. The stone! We follow the stone!'

For the last month Dancer had heard nothing but this and so he pulled a hand down his face, exhausted by it. Their first trip chasing up a lead regarding ancient weapons from the Fenn mountains had been an utter disaster and they'd barely escaped with their lives – yet again. He'd hoped that would've been enough to quell the lad's ambitions, but apparently no setback, no matter how dire, could in any manner rein in this one's plans. 'Right. The spear-point. You mean this very moment?'

'Of course!' The mage drew himself up straight and

pronounced, 'If not now, then what? If not where, then who?'

Dancer stared at him, his brows crimping. 'What?'

The mage threw a finger in the air for a pause. 'Wait!' He stroked his chin, thinking furiously. 'If not where . . . then why . . . no, that's not it. If not what, then who?' He shook his head. 'No. Wait . . .'

Dancer waved that aside. 'Not now. We have to prepare. Water, food, the proper gear.'

'Fine!' Kellanved pointed to a candle inscribed with lines. 'One segment – an hour.'

Dancer nodded his agreement. 'Okay. One hour.' He headed to the door. 'We'll meet here.'

Downstairs, in the main hall of the Hold, he found Surly. She was leaning up against a long feasting-table, her arms crossed, the usual sceptical and disapproving scowl on her hard face. 'You're off disappearing now, aren't you?'

'Yeah, we're leaving.'

She raised a hand to inscribe a languid circle as if encompassing the Hold. 'And what makes you think all this will be here waiting for you when you return?'

He raised his shoulders, dismissive. 'I don't assume any such thing – if that's what you mean.'

'Really? Then why all this? Why do any of it?'

'This? The Hold? The isle?' He waved a hand. 'I care nothing for this. It's a by-product only. I don't need it.'

Now Surly raised a brow, extremely doubtful. 'Really. A by-product . . . of what?'

'Of me challenging myself.' He inclined his head. 'Now, if you will excuse me – time is short.' He headed off.

'What if you do not return?' Surly called after him. 'Then what?'

Turning, he bowed, while retreating. 'Then do with it what you will.'

An hour later he pushed open the door to Kellanved's chambers then kicked it shut behind him. He now wore his customary armoured vest beneath his shirt and pocketed jacket. Knives of all lengths and weights were thrust into sheaths sewn into vest, shirt and jacket. Further weapons were secreted at his neck, in his boots, and round his waist. A coiled rope was at one shoulder, and a pack containing a drinking skin and dried food. A pouch inside his jacket held a selection of miscellaneous coins, a tinderbox, lengths of drawn wire, a few fine tools, and two beeswax candles.

Kellanved he found once more behind his desk, feet up, snoring.

In three long strides he was across the room to kick the desk and Kellanved fell from his chair, arms flailing. His head appeared from behind the desk, peering about in wonder. 'What was that?'

'An earthquake.'

'Really? Imagine that.'

'Yes. Ready to go?'

'Already?'

Dancer righted the candle, indicated the remaining scribed lines.

The mage frowned, then shrugged. 'Hunh.' He stood and straightened his vest. 'Very well.'

'All set, are you?' Dancer enquired sweetly. 'Got everything, have we?'

The ancient-looking Dal Hon fluttered a hand. 'Well, I imagine you've taken care of all the mundane details.'

'Thank you so very much . . .' His acid comment trailed off as he found he was no longer in the mage's chambers in Mock's Hold. The two now stood on a vast plain of volcanic black dust and ashes, a sky of roiling dark clouds shot through by blasts of lightning above. 'That was ... very smooth,' he managed, secretly quite impressed.

'Why thank you,' the little mage answered, with all his usual smugness. 'It's coming so much more easily now. Almost as if I never really leave, you know?'

Dancer didn't know, but he nodded. 'If you say so. This isn't Shadow, clearly. The Scar?'

Kellanved nodded. He waved his walking stick about and headed off. 'Yes. More private, don't you think?'

Personally, Dancer didn't like it. He was uncomfortable in this wasteland region, or Warren, or whatever it was. He felt as if he were always being watched. And there was also the atmosphere. Melancholy was the best word he could come up with to describe the aura this place seemed to exude. It unnerved him. But at least nothing was actively trying to kill him – nothing he knew of, at any rate.

He turned his attention to the crabbed, hunched, falsely aged mage at his side. 'As if I never leave,' the fellow had said. Dancer thought that inadvertently revealing. Once more he tried to make sense of what the Tano Spiritwalker had confided to him that day in the far-off Seven Cities prison. That this mage may inhabit more than one plane or Warren at any one time. That having been engulfed by a storm of Otataral dust, his essence had been annealed, or translated, across more than one location: the mundane physical plane, the Warren of Shadow, and this strange artificial dimension – be it whatever it was.

And if this were indeed so – he glanced aside to the mage as he sauntered along swinging his walking stick – it may be that this fellow had become rather difficult to kill. For it may be that his spirit would persist in those other Realms.

Dancer rubbed a temple, almost wincing. Whatever. Not his area of expertise. Suffice it to say he had a resourceful partner he could trust, and so it was time to push himself as far as possible to see just what he could accomplish.

Kellanved fished in a vest pocket and brought out the stone – the infamous knapped broken spear-point – which he jiggled in his palm. 'Nothing,' he announced. 'Thought not. The influence, or connection, that bears upon it does not extend to this Realm.'

'So we return.'

'Yes.'

'Where?'

'North. Somewhere north.'

'Not Heng, please,' Dancer said, laughing.

Kellanved offered a weak smile. 'No indeed.' Then he frowned, thoughtful. 'But it came to me there, didn't it?'

Dancer's half-amused smile fell. 'Not that town.'

The mage offered an ambiguous shrug. 'Who knows? I swear, Dancer, I mean to avenge myself upon those mages. Eventually.'

They paced onwards for a time; a thin, wind-borne scarf of ash and dust preceded them. Dancer could not shake his discomfort, his sense that the Realm was somehow haunted. 'I dislike this place,' he announced to Kellanved, who nodded, not surprised at all.

'Yes. It has that aura. A great crime was perpetrated here, I believe. Long ago.'

Finally, Dancer could endure the wait no longer, and he asked, 'Now?'

Kellanved paused, peered round. 'Well. I suppose we could see where we are . . .'

In a moment Dancer found himself in sudden night, amid a plain of tall windswept grasses. He peered round, crouching, now quite used to these transitions. 'Northern Dal Hon,' he offered, cocking an eye to his companion.

The mage glanced about, distaste upon his wrinkled features. 'Sadly so,' he agreed. He studied the stone in his hands, then announced, 'This way.'

Dancer followed, hands on his heaviest weapons, for hyenas, leopards and other beasts stalked these grasslands. After a time, the wide, bright bridge of the gods arcing overhead, he suggested, 'We should bed down for the night.'

The wizened Dal Hon native had been slashing his walking stick through the grasses as he went. 'Really?' he answered. 'Are you tired?'

Dancer considered. Was he tired? He realized that he was not. The walk through the ashen Warren had only been a few hours, after all. Yet it was night here. Had it been a half-day, or even two? He had no way of knowing until they reached a settlement that kept a decent record of the days – beyond that of the traditional 'close to harvest', or 'soon after the solstice', or whatever.

Not that it mattered. Days and years came and went. There was no pressing need to keep count. Why bother, after all? Only pinched dry historians argued over what happened in the third year of king so-and-so's reign. It was all over and done with to him. Not of the moment.

Setting aside his musings, Dancer looked to his companion and realized that he was uncharacteristically sombre and quiet this night. 'You are troubled?' he asked.

The little fellow shrugged his thin shoulders as he swatted at the grass. 'Unhappy memories.'

Dancer smiled to himself. He thinks *he* had a difficult childhood?

31

'I was beaten and mocked and belittled all through my youth,' Kellanved began, unbidden. 'Dal Hon tribes value martial ability, you see. Fighting. Strength. Athleticism.' He motioned to his skinny form. 'I possess none of these qualities, as you see. So I was the mongrel dog, the runt of the litter, that is the target of all abuse. Further, there seemed some darker motive behind it all. Some deliberate dislike or dread. At the time I knew nothing of this – all only became clear later.'

Dancer listened quite astonished; this was the first time the lad had opened up regarding his background.

The mage swatted anew as they paced along. 'Eventually, useless as I was judged for warfare, I was taken in, reluctantly, by a neighbouring tribal shaman. I was overjoyed at first. This would be my calling! It seemed to fit so very well. But soon I found myself suffering even worse abuse at the hands of this fiend. Every degradation, every humiliating and disgusting task he set me, seemed deliberately designed to drive me away. And so, in time, he succeeded, and I ran away from my apprenticeship, out into the wilds, quite alone. Of course slavers captured me almost immediately.' The lad swatted ferociously at the grass. 'I will never forget the torture I received at their hands!

'So I languished for a time, a bound servant in their camp. Then, one day, a man picked me out and took me away to serve him in his tower on the Itko Kanese border. He was a mage and he revealed to me that he'd picked me out because I, too, was touched by talent. There my real journey began.'

Dancer nodded. All this sounded not too dissimilar from his experience. 'He trained you,' he offered.

The lad nodded. 'Yes. The rudiments. But nothing more. Stingy, he was. Never revealing quite enough to allow me to stand on my own. Eventually I realized the damned fellow intended to keep me perpetually in his service, if he could. And so I ran again.'

Dancer nodded. He, too, had also fled his master.

The lad raised his walking stick to the stars. 'Then it happened. A revelation in the wilds. As you now know, mystic legend has it that ancient Shadow, Kurald Emurlahn, was shattered, broken into countless shards. In these very grasslands, I stumbled upon, or was washed over by, one of those shards, and at that moment everything became clear. Shadow! That was my home. All the dark insults and muttered asides directed my way during my youth were explained: such a fragment had happened to pass over, or through, the village during the moment of my birth.'

The mage halted, and Dancer drew up short, surprised, as Kellanved faced him. 'That is why Meanas does not trouble me, you see. It is my home. I was born in it. All this,' and he gestured about, 'all this is an impediment; irksome. I loathe it. It is in Meanas that I feel most whole. It is my centre. I was formed within its influence. Do you think it mere chance that the Hounds responded to me? No. My soul, my essence, belongs there. It took a while – but they recognized a kindred spirit.'

Dancer let out a breath, nodding. *Well . . . that explains a lot.* 'I . . . see . . .'

Kellanved continued on. 'For a time I bounced from scholar to scholar, mage to warlock, ever pursuing more knowledge of Shadow. Everything since has been an effort to return there for ever. And I shall.' He thrust the walking stick to the night sky. 'I shall!'

'I do not doubt it,' Dancer murmured.

The mage now set a finger to his lips as he eyed the silvery monochrome landscape before them. 'I judge we are some three days south of the Idryn. Must we walk it?'

Dancer considered the alternatives – neither of which he judged desirable. 'Sorry,' he answered, 'but we really ought to.'

Kellanved sighed, his thin shoulders falling. 'Really? Must we?' He raised a finger in warning. 'Fine! If we must. But I tell you, once I come into my own there'll be no more of this tramping about, I promise you!'

Dancer smiled his approval. 'Agreed. Once the benefits outweigh the hazards.'

* * *

Nedurian walked the cobbled main road that led out from Malaz City to cross the isle. Once he'd passed two wayside inns, an informal market ground, a blacksmith's, and a shop dedicated to building and repairing the local heavy slate roofs, he entered fields and market-gardens where produce, pigs and chickens vied for space among low hedges and ancient, crumbling fieldstone walls. Past these he came to long fields of grain such as barley, millet and wheat that ran in narrow strips out from the road to a distant hidden stream. These rural farmers – crofters, some named them – lived relatively independently of the city just a few hours' walk, though something of a world, away.

His left leg started to ache then, as it always did when called upon to cross more than a few rods of journey. It was an old injury. A summoned demon had taken a chunk out of his thigh and nicked the femur; a military churgeon had reached him in time to save his life, but the leg had never been the same. Thankfully, not so far

34

ahead, among the windswept hills, he spotted what surely must be his destination.

It was an old local burial field, abandoned now, but rumoured to be haunted, of course. Shunned by the locals. Yet here fresh new canvas tents snapped and shuddered in the wind while long thin banners of black rippled above – sigils of the cult of Hood, resurgent here on the isle due to a personage now accruing a near worldwide reputation among the faithful. Dassem Ultor, Mortal Sword of Hood, god of death.

Nedurian limped onward, entered the field and traced his way through the tents to where adherents and the faithful were gathered, some kneeling, others standing as they prayed. He tried to push past the crowd, only to have his way barred by armed cultists.

'Yes, brother?' a woman demanded, her arm out.

'I am here to see the Sword.'

'As are we all. Yet he is praying and not to be disturbed.'

'He'll see me.'

'Oh? And why is this?'

'Because I'm here with a message from the woman he works for!' Nedurian snapped, rather irritated. 'That's why.'

The cultist dropped her arm. 'Ah. The Sword has left instructions. You may pass.' Yet the arm snapped up again, a finger thrusting. 'But the Sword does not *work* for this woman. They merely share obligations to the master of Shadow.'

Nedurian had been about to slap the woman's arm aside, but her words startled him enough to make him pause, blinking. 'The master of *what*?'

'Shadow, of course. There are those among us who

share allegiance to that faith as well. They wear the colours of twilight grey.'

Now Nedurian could not stop himself rolling his eyes to the sky. *Gods!* These religious people and their love of pompous self-important titles and hierarchies of power. Personally, he thought it insane – but, after all, he was just a soldier at heart. Give him comrades in arms, a warm fire and plenty to drink, and life was good. Who needed more than that?

So he shrugged, mumbling something like 'Pissant fools', and shouldered his way through.

The centre of the field was empty; a measure of the respect, and perhaps dread, in which the Sword was held. Nedurian passed simple cairns of piled stones to a larger structure, a sepulture of dressed black volcanic rock. Here the Dal Hon lad who was held to be the living embodiment of Hood's will sat cross-legged, meditating – or dozing, depending upon your level of reverence.

'Stay like that and you'll stiffen up,' Nedurian growled.

A smile crooked the lad's lips. 'Spoken like an old campaigner.' He raised his dark, so very dark blue eyes and even Nedurian, sceptic and veteran, felt a shudder. *As if he were looking through me to something else. Something so very far away.* 'What may I do for you?' the lad asked.

Now Nedurian smiled, despite himself. No false pride or haughtiness here! Just two veterans hunkering down for a chat. And so he crouched to his haunches, picked up a rock and studied it, saying, 'Got us a lot of raw recruits in need of training . . .'

The lad's face clouded, and he nearly winced. He dropped his gaze. 'Death comes to us all.'

Nedurian fought to hide his impatience with this sort of easy youthful fatalism. 'That's true. But it could come a year later just as easily – so who's to decide? You?'

36

A half-smile ghosted the lad's lips. 'Touché, my friend. Nedurian, is it?'

'Yes.'

'And veteran of the Iron Legion.' The lad's penetrating gaze rose and Nedurian had to look away. 'Officer, yes?'

He nodded. 'Of the Old Guard. Before the legion was broken on the fields of Commor before Unta.'

'The Untans take credit for that victory.'

'They shouldn't,' Nedurian answered, rather testily. 'It was the Bloorian and Gris heavies. They sacrificed themselves to turn the tide. It was a slaughter, but they weakened the lines just enough. The Untans came swanning in later.'

'You were there,' the lad said – and it was not a question.

Nedurian jerked a nod, his gaze lowered. 'Yes. I was there.'

The Dal Hon youth was quiet for a time, then he asked, quietly, 'What is it you want of me?'

Nedurian flung his arms open. 'Training, man! At least give them a chance to survive the first sword stroke!'

Dassem glanced away. 'I'm not a soldier. Nor do I pretend to be.'

Nedurian swept that aside. 'Don't worry about that. We'll take care of the soldiering. You just handle the swordsmanship.'

The lad considered, his head cocked. Then he gave a slow nod. 'Very well. If that is our agreement. But I am no soldier or general. Remember that.'

Nedurian gave a curt nod of agreement in answer. 'Whatever. So long as our lads and lasses have a better chance. That's all I ask.'

'You?' Dassem demanded sharply. 'Or this woman, Surly?'

37

'Does it matter? So long as we can help these recruits?'

The Dal Hon smiled in answer, almost as if rueful. 'She sent you, didn't she?'

'She asked that I speak to you,' Nedurian admitted. 'Yes. Why?'

The lad shook his head. 'Never mind. It's just that she knew. She knew that out of everyone you had the best chance of ... well ...' He shrugged. 'What's done is done. Very well. I will return.' He extended a hand, indicating that they were finished. 'Tell her I will return.'

Despite his natural scepticism and irreligious bent, Nedurian bowed his head, rising. 'Thank you. It will mean a lot to the ranks, I'm certain of it.'

Dassem inclined his head in acknowledgement of the compliment. 'Thank you. Now I must reflect upon this. I must consider if this is the right path for me.'

Nedurian straightened, wincing at the jabbing pain from his left leg, and massaged his hip. 'Well, we'll see you at the wharves tomorrow, yes?'

The Dal Hon youth waved him off. 'Tomorrow.'

He limped away, clenching his lips against the ache of his old wound. Well, if he'd just secured training from the foremost swordsman of their age for his boys and girls, then he didn't give a tinker's damn how much this furthered or served the woman Surly's schemes.

* * *

Tayschrenn returned to Malaz City via the hidden Warren Kellanved had found and revealed to him. Not that he feared a renewed confrontation with any D'rek priests – it was just perhaps prudent to avoid notice for a time. Also, though it was personally crushing to admit, he'd failed his god and wanted no more reminders.

This new mage who pretended to be a youth, Calot he called himself, should follow along shortly. Tayschrenn did not consider himself naïve in allowing him time to finish his personal matters; he'd asked him for a small item, in this case a rag used as a handkerchief, and told him that should he fail to appear Kellanved would give this as spoor to the Hounds of Shadow, and they would chase him down no matter where he hid and tear him limb from limb.

Tayschrenn knew he was not the best judge of people's social signals and body language, but the mage had seemed appropriately alarmed.

On his return, Tayschrenn went straight to Smiley's. He found the Hold irritatingly distant from the ships that came and went daily with their news of distant lands; it was such news that interested him most, while he suspected that prior occupants of the Hold had been far too uninterested – to their ruin.

This disruption of the cult of D'rek, for example; were there whispers or vague rumours of similar upheavals among cults in other lands? The priests of Hood, say, or the Enchantress? Poliel? Or any other god or goddess? The phenomenon troubled him for reasons he could not yet firm up in his mind.

So it was that he entered, tapping a finger to his lips, his mind elsewhere, not paying particular attention to the common room until a gruff voice called out, 'Hey, skinny – you work for the Dal Hon mage, Kellanved?'

He paused, blinking, drawing his mind in from its wanderings, and glanced over to see a very squat, sun-darkened older man gesturing at him from a table. He drew himself up to his full height and peered down his nose at the bald sweaty fellow. 'And you are . . . ?'

'Fucking irritated to be kept waiting like this, kid.'

'How very unfortunate for you.'

A broad, frog-like smile cracked the man's face and he pushed back his chair to cross his thick, muscular arms. 'No. Unfortunate for you, 'cause I was invited by Kellanved to join him here. So, my question to you is . . . who the fuck are you?'

Though quite taken aback, Tayschrenn controlled his features; he glanced about the common room and saw several of their Malazan hires lounging about, all armed, and all eyeing this stranger.

'I have been asked to organize a mage corps,' he answered. 'And so I must ask again. You are . . . ?'

The fellow's dark gaze moved about the room also, his smile becoming, if anything, even more evil. 'Oh, I see. *You're* organizing a mage corps, are you? Well, we'll see about that. Name's Hairlock, and I've already seen some action with your Dal Hon friend. Up north. Seven Cities way.' He hooked his thumbs at his tight belt. 'So maybe I'll just hang about till he shows up.'

Tayschrenn lifted a brow. 'I was unaware that Kellanved had been to Seven Cities.'

The mage – for it was clear to Tayschrenn that this fellow was a fairly powerful mage – deliberately turned away to peer out of the dimpled glass of a slit window. 'Oh, he gets around, he does. You'd be surprised.'

Privately, Tayschrenn was coming to the conclusion that nothing involving that mage of Meanas ought to surprise him at all; yet he shrugged. 'As you please. We are recruiting, of course. Our aim is to place a talent with every military unit.'

The fellow barked a harsh laugh. 'Slog through muck and dust surrounded by a pack of dimwitted knuckleheads? No thank you. Not for this mother's son.'

Tayschrenn waved his dismissal. 'Very well. We need

people who aren't afraid of a little discomfort,' and he turned away.

A Malazan guard at the stairs motioned to him and he stepped close. 'Yes?'

'She wants to see you.'

He nodded and started up the stairs. He allowed himself one quick glance back to see Hairlock scowling savagely as he stared out the window.

At the top he knocked on the door to what was once Kellanved's office, but had since been taken over by Surly as her headquarters; like him, she found the Hold too . . . high profile.

The door opened and he faced two guards in blackened leather armour. A more divergent pair one would be hard-pressed to find: a Dal Hon woman, surprisingly tall, with extraordinarily long thin arms; her partner, a man of swarthy shading, perhaps of south Itko Kan, squat, bearded and barrel-shaped. Yet both shared the same flat evaluative gaze as they studied him in silence.

Tayschrenn couldn't remember having seen either of them before. But then, he wasn't around much.

'Let him in,' spoke a hidden Surly from somewhere further within.

The two parted, hands on the knives at their belts. Curious, Tayschrenn also noted the glint of identical brooches at their chests: silver tokens that resembled birds' feet. Some sort of order, or brotherhood?

Beyond, Surly stood, chin in one hand, peering down at a swath of papers spread out on the hardwood floor before her. Two aides, or scribes, knelt before her, arranging the pages. Seeing him enter, the two hurriedly turned each sheet face down.

He glimpsed copious notes and numerous long lists.

The blue-hued Napan woman turned to him, rubbing her eyes, which shone bloodshot and bruised.

'You appear to be in need of rest,' he told her.

A half-smile ghosted her lips. 'Ever the smooth flatterer and courtier, Tayschrenn.' She added, musingly, 'Rather like me,' then, more forcefully, 'thank you for coming. How goes the recruitment?'

'It proceeds.' He glanced to the guards. 'As yours appears to be. Where are your old crew? Urko? Tocaras?'

'They are far too busy these days. Urko is off raiding the coast, as is Tocaras.'

'Raiding? I thought they were preparing for the—' He caught himself before saying anything specific aloud, even here, and finished, 'ah, the attack.'

The lean woman nodded, gestured for the scribes to turn back the pages, and resumed her study. 'They are. We need weapons, stores, supplies. Raiding is the quickest way to amass them.'

'Ah. I see.' He waved to the papers. 'And these?'

'Reports. Estimates. Correspondence with . . . assets . . . in the coastal cities.'

The two scribes now eyed him warily, as if he were about to snatch up a handful of the pages and race for the door. He nodded instead. 'Intelligence. Very good. We are on track, then, for the . . . ah, the plan?'

She spared him a sharp glance. 'Are we?'

He tilted his head, thinking. 'Speaking for the mage corps – no. We are not. We are far behind my first expectations. Surprisingly, recruiting here on this island has been poor. To say the least.'

'I thought you told me the island was rife with talents.'

'It was – is. However, none appear interested in leaving. They seem content to remain. Which, as I say, is surprising. I assure you this is not the usual case.'

The Napan woman nodded, her attention refocusing upon the reports spread before her. 'Very well. Continue your efforts.'

The conversation – or interrogation – was over. He inclined his head and turned away. He knew that another person might be insulted by the curt treatment, but somehow he and she seemed to understand one another; each considered themself a professional in their field, untroubled by such petty concerns as feelings or ego. And each seemed determined to out-professionalize the other.

Exiting the bar, he turned uphill, his feet taking him whither they would, as he set loose his thoughts. Surly's questioning reopened the mystery of why this island's fecund pool of talents should be so reluctant to leave. Quite frankly it did astonish him that almost none were willing to join Kellanved's forces. Perhaps some personal animosity or dread? But no, he was given to understand that such had always been the case. And all the more unlikely was it, given that this isle's crop of wax-witches, hedge wizards, wind-callers, card readers and sea-soothers was the densest anywhere. Above almost every cottage door there hung a sign proclaiming readings, healing or an apothecary, or showing the candle of a wax-witch.

He brooded upon the mystery for a time as he walked, hands clasped at his back, until, looking up, he realized he'd left the town far behind and had climbed one of the low and bare inland hills. Here, lichen-dappled granite rocks protruded through the grasses as little more than stubs – a circle of ancient standing stones.

The hill afforded a view southwards, over further blunt hills. Unseen beyond lay the southern seas. The Strait of Storms. Said to be haunted by the so-called Stormriders: alien beings that terrorized the waters and allowed no trespass. He remembered reading third- and fourth-hand transcribed legends of attacks upon this isle by the Riders.

He pressed his fingertips together and brushed them to his lips; something. He'd touched upon *something* – he felt it. There was a mystery here. But one so very much larger than he'd first imagined. It was as if he had entered some shepherd's sod-roofed hut only to find a multi-roomed mansion.

But what was it? What was hidden here on this island?

'You are looking for recruits?' someone called, startling him.

He turned. A woman approached, tall and thin, in bedraggled simple peasant's tunic and trousers, her feet bare and dirty. As she neared, he became uncertain as to her ethnicity; her hair was hacked short, dirty brown, her eyes very large, her face long. He couldn't quite place where she might hail from. She walked stiffly, using a cane, one hand across her front. It seemed she'd suffered some sort of injury recently.

He nodded to her. 'Yes. You are interested?'

'Yes.'

He attempted to sense her aura only to find himself blocked – this in itself startled him. Few possessed the power to so fully forestall any probing from him. 'You are shielding yourself,' he observed.

'As are you.'

He allowed himself a thin smile. 'True enough.'

'You hide from the priests of D'rek.'

Now he frowned, irked. 'That is not your—'

'That is wise,' she said. 'I am of the same mind as you. Some taint has contaminated that cult. It is a worry.'

He waved a hand to dismiss the subject. 'You say you are willing to join. Why?'

44

'This mage of Shadow. He ... interests me.'

Tayschrenn now understood. 'You mean you sense he has found power and you wish to learn his secrets for yourself.'

She shrugged her thin shoulders. 'Have it that way if you wish. Is that not why he fascinates you?'

He laughed, a touch unnerved by her strange frankness, and insight. 'From a purely academic stance only, I assure you.' He shook his head. 'I do not think anyone could wrest away those powers he has demonstrated. I believe it all to be part of him. Of his essence.'

The woman nodded. 'I sense this also.'

'Very well. You are ... ?'

She inclined her head a fraction. 'You may call me Nightchill.'

Chapter 3

A COLD, LONG-FINGERED HAND CLASPED ACROSS his mouth woke Gregar and he flailed for an instant before realizing who it was; then he nodded. Haraj released him and raised a single digit to his mouth to sign for silence.

They lay in a half-fallen-down old barn, close by the rutted road north to Balstro, along the River Nye. It was early morning and soldiers were tramping about outside; he could glimpse them through the slats. They wore the sky-blue livery of Gris.

Gregar held himself as still and quiet as possible.

After an agonizing wait, a gruff woman's voice called out: 'We know you're in there! C'mon out.'

Gregar shot an angry glare to Haraj, hissed, 'You said they wouldn't bother!'

'I got us this far!' he hissed back.

'I had to carry you half the way!'

Haraj flapped his hands, dismissive. 'I'm not used to all this walking – who knew it'd be so fucking far?'

'You coming?' the woman barked. 'Hurry up! Haven't got all day.'

Gregar shot Haraj another glare.

'Maybe they don't know we're here,' the lad whispered. 'Maybe they'll just go—'

He shut up as thrown brands came arcing through the open doorway to land amid the scattered straw and rushes. A tossed splash of oil followed and immediately burst into flames.

Gregar shook the fellow. 'Magic us out of here!'

The lad hugged himself. 'I'm not that kind of mage . . . but I have an idea.'

Gregar released him, coughed into a fist as the smoke thickened. 'Fine! What? What is it?'

Haraj ran for the entrance and jumped the flames, his hands held high, shouting, 'I surrender! Don't kill me!'

Gregar threw wide his arms. 'That's it? That's the plan?' He shook his head then picked up a harvesting scythe – the only decent weapon he'd come across – and followed.

Clearing the smoke, he paused, blinking, then threw down the scythe; the soldiers held crossbows trained upon him. In front of him, Haraj was kneeling on the ground, arms out.

The fat female sergeant swaggered forward and tied their hands together behind their backs with leather thongs. 'All this fuss just to get caught again,' she growled, and clouted Gregar across the head. 'That's for all the trouble you caused me, y'damned wretch of a stonemason. And you,' she shook Haraj like a rat. 'Your master bent my ear warning me how tricky you are, so I'm gonna keep a close eye on you!'

The soldiers yanked them to their feet and marched them down to the road, where a caged prison wagon waited. Gregar growled to Haraj, 'Some plan.' Yet his companion didn't appear the least bit troubled by what was happening; he was even smiling as they were thrown in, and he offered Gregar a broad wink.

The sergeant slammed and locked the cage door then

returned to her troop. There she bellowed orders for them to set to work to contain the fire; it seemed she was having second thoughts about burning Grisian property so carelessly.

Gregar threw himself down on the dirty straw. The quarries for him. Or just plain execution for escaping.

The wagon rocked beneath him and he raised his head, complaining, 'What in the name of Hood are you doing?'

But the fellow wasn't in the cage. In fact, the door now hung open and Haraj was on the roof, clambering like a human-sized spider for the front, and the driver's plank seat.

'Grab the reins!' Gregar urged, coming to the front bars.

'What're they?'

'The reins! The leads!'

The lad thumped down into the driver's seat. 'These strappy things?'

'Yes! Snap them. Snap them and yell!'

Haraj gave the reins a pathetic shake. The two horses, sad old beaten-down animals, merely turned their heads to give him an amused look.

'Mean it, dammit!' Gregar snarled.

A bellow of alarm sounded from the direction of the burning barn.

Haraj snapped the leads as hard as he could and he may also have yelled something, but it was swallowed by the curdling scream Gregar let loose. The horses reared, startled, and took off up the rutted mud way – northward, fortunately.

Once the horses were spent, which didn't take very long at all, they came to a slow stall amid deep woods and Haraj and Gregar jumped from the wagon. With a mere flick of his wrist the strange lad loosed Gregar's bonds. Then he peered up at him and asked, 'Now what?'

For an instant Gregar was tempted to free the horses of their tack and try riding them, but being a mere commoner and apprentice stonemason he'd never even been on one before, and so he eyed the surrounding woods instead. 'We should take off through the forest.'

Haraj winced. 'Really? I mean, the road would be easier going . . .'

'They'll send riders after us – or you, really. It's you they want, isn't it? They don't give a damn about me.'

The lad hunched from him as if expecting a beating, and the sight of this brought a wringing pain to Gregar's chest. He looked away, blinking, and muttered, 'We should get moving.' He headed into the trees. 'Follow me.'

They walked through the forest for a time, or rather Gregar walked and Haraj crashed, tripped, cursed, broke branches, and shook brush as he fell. Gregar just sighed and waited for him to catch up. As the evening darkened into night Haraj cleared his throat to offer, tentatively, 'Ah . . . we have no food . . .'

'Noticed that, did you?'

'Or water.'

'Yeah.'

'So . . . what've you got in mind?'

'Can you hunt?'

'Ah . . . no. Can you?'

'Nope.'

'Ah. Well. That's a problem.'

Gregar started off again. 'Yes it is. But it's not one we can solve by standing around.'

Haraj followed along, stumbling and breathing loudly. 'What about tonight? Sleeping and all?'

'What do you mean?'

'I mean . . . what about wolves and such?'

Gregar turned to offer him a smile. 'We're the wolves now.'

This mollified the lad for a time, though as the night darkened he spoke again. 'But you do *know* where you're going . . . don't you?'

Gregar halted to point roughly northwest – or at least what he was fairly certain was northwest. 'I'm heading for the lines.'

Haraj blinked at him uncomprehendingly. 'I'm sorry . . . what lines?'

Gregar couldn't help but gape at the fellow. 'Are you a fool? The lines! The Bloorian League is trying to encircle Gris! Surely you've heard about it.'

The skinny fellow winced and ducked, writhing almost as if in agony, his head lowered. 'I've *heard* about it, of course. But I've never – that is, I was never let . . .' He cleared his throat, and finished as if in apology, 'I didn't get out much.'

Again Gregar had to look away. He took a long breath, squinting at the surrounding dark woods. Finally, after some time, he said quietly, 'Something will turn up, don't you worry.' He gestured north once more – at least what he hoped was north. 'Let's go a bit farther.'

Some time later, exhausted, and, Gregar suspected, possibly lost, they halted next to a giant oak, gathered up armfuls of leaves, and covered themselves to attempt to sleep.

Gregar woke first. The sun glared down in a dappling pattern about him through gaps in the boughs above. For a time he watched the sleeping curled form of his companion, then he scanned the woods. Let him rest a while longer. He was obviously completely unused to any physical exertion. Gregar had seen dogs raised in cages. Released, the poor pathetic things couldn't even straighten their legs. They were cripples. Unable to walk.

But to do that to a boy. To raise him in such a way.

A burning heat clenched Gregar's chest and he found he had to wipe his eyes to clear them.

This Ap-Athlan had a lot to answer for.

Noises in the underbrush caught his attention. Animals running. A forester would imagine that meant . . .

Shapes now moved through the brush, upright. Gregar caught glimpses of pale sky-like blue amid the bushes. Grisian soldiery.

A loud snapping of branches jerked Haraj awake, gasping and flailing. Gregar tried to calm him but the nearby figures halted. A step sounded next to him and he spun to peer up at a Grisian infantrywoman in mail, her surcoat torn and bloodied. She held a sword on him.

'Here!' she called.

Gregar's shoulders fell in despair. They'd been found.

The figures closed. 'Who is it?' one called.

'Don't know,' the woman answered, studying them with something like distaste. 'Outlaws, looks like. Wretched runaways.'

Gregar felt his mouth open, but no sound emerged. *Outlaws?*

The surrounding brush parted and a number of Grisian heavy infantry now squinted down at them. One waved a dismissal. 'We don't have time for this. Just kill them.'

'Righty-o,' the woman answered, and raised her sword.

For a fraction of an instant Gregar simply stared upward, completely paralysed by disbelief. Really? This was happening? He was to be murdered. Just like that?

Then he reacted, and suddenly everyone about him seemed to be moving in slow motion. Rising, he pushed his back into the woman, and taking her descending arm used his strength and the techniques of years of heaving stone blocks, and threw her to spin head over heels. She crashed amid the brush.

Now the soldiery gaped at him – then rushed. First came the one who'd ordered their deaths. His sword was raised and Gregar stepped into the swing, blocked the arm, and shoved his straightened fingers into the man's throat. Cartilage popped and snapped. The man flinched in shock and pain.

Drawing backwards, Gregar slid his left hand down the man's arm and snatched the sword from his weakened grip, then pushed him away with his right.

For a fraction of a second he admired the silvery iron length of the blade he had taken. This was the first real sword he'd ever held – not some wooden training piece he'd secretly played with until someone saw and beat him for it. Frankly, it felt too heavy in his hand; he much preferred the sticks he had practised with ceaselessly.

The next man came in, swinging. Gregar sidestepped the blow, and because they were all wearing armour and he was not, he didn't bother hacking at the extended mailed arm but slashed downwards in passing, across the back of the man's knee.

The fellow bellowed his pain and fell.

Something crashed into him, sending him flying; a shield-bash, he realized, as he staggered into a meadow of tall weeds and grass next to their hiding place. The helmeted heads of at least twenty more Grisian troopers turned his way.

Shit!

The one who had shield-bashed him now came on, thrusting and jabbing with the point of his sword – he'd obviously been watching and learning. Gregar gave ground, circling.

Capricious Oponn's luck was with Gregar then, as the fellow tripped on something: a hole, or a tangle of grasses. Gregar was immediately inside his guard, thrusting in over the shield to strike the neck and push inwards, feeling the muscle, the frail bones and ligaments parting and giving.

The man fell gurgling and clutching at his neck.

Gregar pulled back, turning in a full circle. He now faced a ring of infantry.

Strangely then, though the sky was completely clear, approaching thunder sounded, turning everyone's head.

Two cavalrymen crashed into the ring of troopers.

They swung down at the soldiery, hacking from side to side. One heaved his mount to the left, the other to the right. Immediately, Gregar was forgotten. All the Grisians closed on the mounted fighters.

The newcomers fought with astonishing speed and ruthlessness. One threw himself from his mount even while still moving; he bore a tall spear that he whipped about, slashing. A banner rippled close to its broad leaf-shaped tip. The other remained mounted, hacking with two swords in elegant figure-eight motions. Even the mounts fought, lashing out to crush chests.

Gregar stared, stunned. Each rider wore an ankle-length tabard of a red so dark as to be near black. Sinuous down the front and back writhed a long silver dragon sigil. Their mounts' livery shared this dark blood-red field and sigil.

The Crimson Guard.

The two finished off the Grisian infantry with brutal efficiency. Then the spear-bearer turned to regard Gregar, planting the long weapon. Haraj came staggering out of the brush then, attracting everyone's attention; the lad tripped over a torn bloody body, took one look, then promptly vomited, heaving and gagging in misery.

The two Crimson guardsmen exchanged arched looks. The spear-bearer inclined his head to Gregar in salute and remounted, while Haraj waved an arm, wiping the spume from his mouth. 'Wait! Wait! We want to join the Guard!'

The two shared amused smiles. 'Sorry,' answered the spearman. 'Our roster is full right now.'

'No!' Haraj insisted. 'You don't understand . . .'

The spearman pointed north. 'There are refugees in the Coastal Range. Outlaws too. They'll take you.' The two kneed their mounts and thundered off.

'No, wait!' Haraj called after them, but he let his arms fall. 'Dammit.'

'I don't think we made much of an impression,' Gregar offered.

'I'll make an impression,' Haraj practically snarled. 'What now? I'm famished and cold and wet.'

Gregar waved to the bodies. 'This lot must have something. Search them. And quickly, before more show up.'

Haraj recoiled. He shuddered and hugged himself. 'Must we?'

'If you want food and water. Myself, I might try to find some armour that fits.'

After rifling through all the bodies they came up with a few pouches of dried meat and wrapped boiled barley and assorted light weapons, and Gregar had selected a coat of mail that he believed might fit.

'Now what?' Haraj asked, burdened by seven skins of water thrown over a shoulder. 'Which way?'

Gregar had to smile. He motioned to the twinned deep sets of hoofprints.

They set off running as best they could.

* * *

54

The hamlet on the south shore of the river Idryn was so small it didn't even have a formal name. The locals Dancer had asked directions from just called it 'the town', and pointed them onward.

No formal roads. Just mud paths between a few wattle and daub mud houses, sod-roofed. Fish dried on racks while a handful of sheep watched them nervously from a pen.

He and Kellanved walked down to the muddy waterfront and peered around. Dancer eyed the mage, who raised his chin to indicate the distant shore. 'North – and west.'

Dancer grunted. This news eased his general illtemper a touch. He did not like this errand much. Not much at all. Just a few lazy days' journey east down the Idryn lay Li Heng. He did not want to see that city again.

Children played along the shore and Kellanved approached them. 'We're looking for a boat,' he called.

The mud-smeared pack halted in their game of capturing frogs to gape at them. 'Who're you?' one demanded.

'A traveller. Now, do any of you know—'

'You talk funny.'

'So do you. Now, a boat, yes?'

'No we don't.'

'Don't what?' Kellanved asked.

'Talk funny. We talk normal-like.'

Kellanved opened his arms. 'Well, it's all a matter of perspective. Different peoples—'

Dancer held out a single Hengan silver round. 'This goes to whoever can bring us a boatman.'

The children took off as a mass, straight down the shore. Dancer raised a brow to Kellanved, who huffed and rolled his eyes.

Moments later the gang returned with a stooped

elderly man whom they alternately cajoled and pulled. Once they neared, the children abandoned him to mob Dancer.

'I found him! Me!' they all shouted at once.

Dancer made a display of tossing the coin far off into the tall grasses. The kids ran off, kicking and piling on to each other.

'They'll search for ever,' Kellanved opined.

'Yes, they will,' Dancer agreed, and he showed Kellanved the coin still cupped in his palm.

Kellanved smiled appreciatively. 'I'm not the only one with tricks, hmm?'

The old man tipped his head. 'You want a boat, sors?'

'We wish to cross,' answered Kellanved.

The oldster nodded and motioned that they should follow.

The boat proved to be a leaky punt that the old fellow pushed off the strand then invited them to enter. Dancer stepped in gingerly, fearful that his foot might go right through the rotten planks. Water sloshed, filling the bottom. Kellanved rather daintily set himself down on a plank seat. The boatman set his two oars into their locks and heaved.

They barely made any headway from the shore. The boatman motioned a clawed hand to Dancer and indicated a wooden cup floating at his feet. 'Gotta bail.'

Dancer picked up the pathetic piece of carved wood and examined it incredulously. 'With this?'

The boatman spat over the side. 'What you do is you dip it into the water and throw it over.'

Dancer gritted his teeth against saying anything more – and making things worse – and started bailing.

'You city folk,' the boatman sniggered. 'Don't know nothing.'

Kellanved swept an arm to the west. 'So tell me, O stalwart wise man of the river, salt of the earth, what lies to the west?'

The boatman hawked up a mass of phlegm and spat over the side once more. 'The rest of the damned country, that's what.' And he shook his head at the astounding depth of their ignorance.

Kellanved and Dancer exchanged quizzical looks and were quiet for the remainder of the trip.

When they reached the north shore, Dancer tossed the man the silver Hengan round and the fellow grunted, unimpressed, though it was no doubt ten times anything he had ever been paid. Then Kellanved pointed his walking stick west and they set off, the mage swinging his stick, Dancer shaking his head.

After a time Kellanved observed, 'I do enjoy these earthy conversations with the local worthies, don't you? So very edifying.'

'They say wisdom comes from the country,' Dancer offered, 'but frankly I don't see it.' He motioned to the plain of the Seti grasslands ahead; rolling hill after rolling hill, the sun lowering towards them. 'Could be all the way to Quon. Even beyond the coast.'

The mage pursed his wrinkled lips. 'True . . . however, there is one particular feature ahead. One legendary for its religious and mystical importance . . .'

Dancer nodded. 'Ah, the Idryn Falls.'

'And the Escarpment,' Kellanved added. 'Where legend has it Burn herself sleeps.' He jiggled the mottled pale brown point in his hand. 'This appeared in Heng after all. Nearby.' He shrugged. 'Well, if it proves to be a false lead, then perhaps we shall have to take to the Warrens after all.'

Dancer nodded his assent as they walked.

The evening darkened into a deep purple. The insects of the night began chirping and bats flew overhead. Kellanved was waving his stick through the grasses, but suddenly he pointed it to the north. 'Am I mistaken, or is that a light glimmering there?'

Dancer rubbed his chin, and noticed the stubble growing. 'Must be a wayside stop along the trader road.'

Kellanved's thick black brows rose in delight. 'A stop? Perchance an inn? Excellent!'

Dancer sighed; he'd been hoping to keep Kellanved away from people, for the most part. Trouble seemed to follow him round like, well, like his own shadow. 'Very well. This one night.'

The little mage headed off. 'Come, come. Let us sit at the fire and hear the travellers' news, yes? News perhaps of how a certain terrifying mage haunted Heng!'

Dancer winced, following. 'Please don't try to bring that up.'

Kellanved did try to bring it up, several times. Dancer, however, interrupted each time to ask of Tali, Kan, or Unta. It occurred to him that the mage had had a good idea in catching up on happenings around the continent. Nom Purge, for example, appeared close to overrunning Quon Tali – an astounding development in their decades of intermittent hostilities. But that news was two weeks old.

Most of what preoccupied the travellers and inhabitants was local: dark scandals and wild rumours. As was the case everywhere, no doubt.

One moment of the evening struck Dancer; when talk came round to news of the nearby mines at the Escarpment, Kellanved actually started, as if shocked by something. Then he stared off into the distance for a time, thinking perhaps, and grinned wickedly.

All this told Dancer that he was scheming again – as usual.

The next day they set out west along the trader road. The poetry of this amused Dancer. Not so long ago he had come up this very road heading east, to Heng, an unproven ambitious youth. And now ... well, he was still a youth, but only in years.

Kellanved had been consulting the spear-point and now he halted, appearing rather surprised. He regarded Dancer. 'Northwest from here.'

'Really?' The assassin examined the point in the mage's hand. 'Northward? What's there?'

'Well, the mines for one thing. Which is odd, as I was about to suggest just such a detour.'

'What for?'

The little mage had got that cunning self-satisfied look on his wrinkled face that so exasperated Dancer. 'Oh, you'll see ...'

Dancer clenched his teeth as the mage set off, but followed, rubbing his chin savagely – a smooth chin, since that morning he'd taken the opportunity to shave.

Striking northwest across the plain they soon came to a road, little more than twin ruts in the grass. This they followed until it met up with a more substantial route, muddied and rutted. Already Dancer could smell in the wind the smoke and the noisomeness of trash and cesspits.

They topped one of the low smooth hills and halted, taking in the vista west, of the tall sheer stone cliff of the Escarpment itself, and the disorganized scattering of ragged tents, open pits and fenced enclosures at its base. The workings of the mines.

'The stone?' Dancer asked.

Kellanved jiggled it in his hand. 'It points northwards

of here. You don't mind, though, if we have a look. Do you?'

Dancer shrugged. 'Fine. But I don't see why.' Still, something about the mines did tickle Dancer's memory. Something about them; he just couldn't place it.

Armed men and women watched the newcomers suspiciously as they made their way between the pits – some open, others fenced. This place was notorious all across the continent for unrestrained greed, casual murder and lawlessness. The only rule here was the one of the sword and utter ruthlessness.

After a time it appeared to Dancer that his companion seemed to be looking for something. They passed numerous tall fences of planks, most overlooked by dirty and ragged men and women armed with crossbows. One, however, appeared unguarded, and this one Kellanved studied for a good while before approaching and knocking on a plank.

'Go away!' piped a high voice.

At that instant Dancer knew – he remembered – and he pressed a hand to his brow. Blessed Burn! Could it be that they were actually really still here?

The mage drew himself up as tall and straight as he could. 'Not the welcome I was expecting,' he announced.

A young girl, dirt-smeared, her hair a frightful mess, peeped over the top. Her eyes grew huge. 'Magister!' she squeaked, and disappeared.

Kellanved shot Dancer a smug look; Dancer looked to the sky. 'How is it they could still be here?' he whispered. 'Surely these gem-hunters would've enslaved them.'

'My dear Dancer,' the mage answered, 'more than half these orphans are talents. Remember that. Rashan, Thyr, D'riss, Denul – you name it. I'm surprised they're not running the entire place by now.'

The groaning of heavy timbers sounded from behind the plank door, and it opened. Kellanved swaggered in, Dancer following. The door was shut behind them.

A crowd of children had gathered; unwashed, in ragged torn clothes. More and more appeared, climbing up rickety ladders from the lower works. Dancer recognized a number of the orphans he'd seen in Heng. He reflected that perhaps it was not so surprising that they'd survived, given the abuse and brutal treatment they'd endured digging for the black market boss Pung then.

The older of the lot pushed forward, girls and boys. They inclined their heads to Kellanved. 'Magister.' Dancer noticed a number of these were actually bowing to him, addressing him as 'Master'.

'You have done well?' Kellanved asked.

All nodded. 'Rubies, emeralds, and sapphires. Burn's bounty,' one girl said.

'Very good,' Kellanved answered, as if he'd been expecting no less all this time. 'A new mission. Take what you have gathered and use it as a fund to establish eyes and ears in every major city. In Unta, in Tali, in Cawn, in Purge – everywhere. Yes?'

All bowed in assent. One boy asked, 'Even Heng?'

Kellanved nodded. 'Yes. Even Heng.' He raised a finger. 'And remember – you answer only to myself and my partner here, yes? To none other. You are mine and his. Our hands, our ears, our eyes. Do you so swear?'

All pressed hands to their chests. 'We swear, Magister.'

Kellanved nodded indulgently, smiling. 'Very good.'

Another lad straightened. 'But how shall we communicate? I know the earth, D'riss, but Leath here knows of the night, Rashan.'

Kellanved nodded once more, reassuringly, hands raised. 'Worry not. Tonight all you talents must gather

61

with me. I will show you a place where we may travel. A place that shall be ours, and ours alone.' He waved them away with a flutter of his hands. 'Go now, prepare your leave-taking.'

The majority of the youths left the main gathering, all but some twelve. These lads and lasses all stood silent, steadily regarding Dancer, who, in turn, studied them. One came forward and extended his hand, palm upwards, exposing the inner wrist. Here Dancer saw crudely tattooed, perhaps by a sharp iron point with charcoal for ink, a small arc, or curve. Anyone could have mistaken it for a sickle moon, but Dancer recognized it. A talon.

'We heard of your sigil,' said the lad. 'Will you have us?'

He did not know what to say. To agree would be to take advantage; to say no almost inhumanly cruel. He set a hand on the lad's shoulder. 'You do not have to do this. You could leave, go anywhere, do anything with your lives. The choice is yours.'

The girls and boys exchanged glances. 'All our lives we have fought for each other,' a girl said. 'Everyone we've met has tried to enslave us, beat us, rape us, sell us. We've fought everyone. Everyone but you and the magister. Only you and he treated us fair. Home is here with each other. Where else would we go? Who could we trust? Who would defend us?'

'We serve each other,' the lad affirmed. 'Give us our orders.'

Dancer nodded; this he understood. 'Very well. Join with the others. Serve Kellanved, go where you are sent. But in each city seek out the underworld, the thieves and killers. Learn your trade. And wait. A time will come when I will call upon you.'

The twelve inclined their heads in acceptance.

'What of recruitment?' one asked. 'We are few.'

Hearing the youth's voice, Dancer remembered his name. 'Baudin, isn't it?'

The lad blushed. 'Yes.'

'Wherever you go watch for those skilled and trustworthy. These may join – but it must be their choice. There can be no coercion.' He motioned to where Kellanved sat surrounded by the rest of the orphans. He appeared to be regaling them with a tale of how he personally conquered Malaz. 'Go ahead and join them.'

The twelve bowed, then slipped in among the others. Dancer propped his shoulders against the side of a crude lean-to dwelling and watched. The mage certainly had a way with mongrels and misfits . . . like himself, perhaps? Dancer thought about it. Like them both, apparently, from what the girl had revealed of their childhood.

A fire was started and a simple meal of flatbread and boiled lentils was prepared. Guards were changed at the walls, light crossbows at their hips. Then a troop of the orphans descended with Kellanved into the works below. The mage will be showing them the Scar – how to transition into it and how to move about, Dancer reflected. It would be their personal circuit of communications no matter where they may travel.

Since he was awake, he stood a watch at the wall. The mineworks stretched mostly north and south, in a thin line tracing the base of the Escarpment. Each claim was sectioned off by fences or armed guards, every one standing careful vigil against their neighbours, watchful for any attempt to steal the bounty they'd dug. Beyond this stretched a wide tent town of hangers-on, hopefuls, and those who preyed upon the miners, selling supplies, food, wine, and themselves. He wondered, idly, how these lads and lasses had come into a claim, then decided that they'd probably secretly studied them all and simply taken the richest. At least that's what he'd have done.

After his watch, he bedded down for the night. Before sleep took him he lay for a time staring up at the stars wondering just what Kellanved had in mind for the morrow, and beyond.

*　*　*

Nedurian leaned on a gritty granite battlement of the keep above Malaz City, overlooking the Inner Bailey. Just what to name the old fortress had been aired briefly, what with Mock's death and all. But the question answered itself, as everyone simply continued calling it Mock's Hold. And so it was now, formally. There were even rumours of a 'Mock's Barrow', as funds were being raised to construct one.

He watched a class of Malazan marines, mixed recruits and veterans, training under the watchful eye of their swordmaster and champion, Dassem Ultor.

It was a wonder to watch the man work. How, with a simple adjustment of an elbow here, or the widening of a stance there, he transformed men and women into far more balanced and effective fighters.

And the rankers knew it too. Nedurian could even tell when the man simply entered the training field: backs straightened, chatter died away. It was almost comical to see the youth holding forth among a crowd of scarred and grizzled veterans of decades of sea-raiding and see them all nodding sombrely at his words and taking his advice to heart.

It was a wonder. But it was also a danger.

He'd seen what such regard could do to a person. The power it offered. This man might be a favourite of Hood, but all those around him, and following him, certainly weren't. He'd seen blind worship lead a lot of people to their deaths.

He hoped this swordsman would prove able to resist its seductive call.

He shifted his stance to rub his left leg, wincing. That was not all there was to worry about. What of the Napans? Where were they? Gone off raiding, most of them, while Surly kept out of everyone's sight. With the absence of their glorious leaders – the fearsome mage and his assassin partner – just where were the soldiers to place their esteem and regard? And, dare he say it . . . their loyalty?

It was another danger.

The class below laughed then, hazing or chaffing one of their number, and he smiled, remembering such comradeship. He shook his head at himself; gods above, he was becoming quite the gloomy old duffer, wasn't he! Searching for trouble everywhere he looked.

No, he should keep his thoughts to his assigned job – setting up a cadre system of mages among the army such as had been instituted in the old days among the Talian legions.

So he studied every set of recruits just as carefully as Dassem. And, just as Dassem admitted he was surprised by the depth of the fighting talent offered up by the island – as almost every family was the selected product of generations of raiders – so, too, was Nedurian again surprised by the depth of true talent. Nearly every day's lineup saw at least one witch or warlock or talent of some order. Sometimes as many as four.

Again, it was astonishing to him that this tiny insignificant island could possibly churn out so many touched by the Warrens. True, the vast majority were minor hedge wizards only, or wax-witches, or wind-callers, or sea-soothers, or minor clairvoyants. But still – so many!

And this was after Surly's own sorting through the pick of everyone for her own unit of specialized recruits. He suspected that he'd missed out on a number of talented youths in this regard and this irked him, but there was nothing to be done about it, as in Kellanved and Dancer's absence the Napan aristocrat pretty much ran everything.

This afternoon he watched while the Dal Hon swordsman ran down the line of men and women all eager to enter Malazan service – many from elsewhere drawn by the reputation of Dassem himself, plus the fearsome tales spreading of Kellanved's prowess – fed, no doubt cynically, by Surly's agents on the mainland and elsewhere. This day, as Dassem walked down the line of hopefuls Nedurian eyed each in turn as well, and when the Dal Hon came to one particular young woman, an obvious Seti girl, in leathers, with a bone-handled blade thrust though her belt and her long auburn hair tied in a single thick braid, he tapped his dagger's hilt on the stones and Dassem glanced back to nod.

This girl Dassem spoke to in low tones and sent to him.

She met him with her head thrown back and scorn in her brown eyes. 'And who are you?' she demanded.

Inwardly, Nedurian smiled, remembering his own youth and his own assurance of immortality and supreme talent. He crossed his arms. 'Name's Nedurian. I'm organizing a special element among the Malazan forces. A cadre of mages to serve in the combat units. Are you interested in fighting?'

The girl snorted her impatience. 'Of course! That is why I am here, fool.'

'Yes, you have come a long way. Why?'

She curled a lip. 'I am disgusted. The elders of my people are fat and lazy. They refuse to see what is coming – or are blind to it.'

'And that is?'

'Destruction. The loss of our way of life. We are bounded in, surrounded. With each day our land is smaller. The trend is obvious.'

Nedurian nodded at this and rubbed his neck, thinking. 'But isn't the cult of the White Jackal fighting this? Why not join it?'

The girl's brows rose, as she was apparently quite impressed by his knowledge. 'The cult of Ryllandaras has always been with our people. Traditionally he is regarded as a threat, a scourge. I, personally, am not comfortable with his worship.'

Nedurian nodded his understanding. 'I see. So here you are, forced to fight among foreigners.'

'As my own people will not, yes.'

'And your name?'

'Thistle.'

Nedurian cocked a brow, wondering whether she was named after her character manifested itself, or whether she just grew into the name. 'So you agree to join the cadre?'

'Not if it means some sort of special treatment, or being taken from the ranks.'

Nedurian smiled, encouraged by her reaction, though others might have thought it insolent. 'No. As I said, you will remain in the ranks.'

'I answer to you?'

He smiled again, amused by how she somehow managed to make every statement a challenge. He shook his head. 'No. There is no hierarchy among the cadre. Each squad mage is equal to any other. All may have their say in tactics or strategy.'

This claim obviously surprised her. She frowned, thinking, then she threw back her head, sneering once more. 'And what of this Kartoolian magus I hear so much of? This Tayschrenn?'

Nedurian nodded, rubbing the bristles of his growing beard. 'He is in charge of the formal cadre. Those who mostly don't wish to serve among the ranks. Who think they are above it. Or those who wisely know they'd be of no use in the field.'

Thistle's scowl deepened. 'They will consider themselves above *us*.'

His smile turned wry. 'Well, they can think that all they want – can't they?'

An answering smile grew on the girl's lips, and she laughed. 'Very good. May I return to the ranks?'

'Yes. Just come to me if you have any questions.'

She inclined her head, then jogged off.

Nedurian watched the slim, vibrant young girl go and wished, for however brief an instant, that he was a hundred years younger.

Chapter 4

IT WAS COLD, RAINING, AND DARK WHEN GREGAR and Haraj came across an army encampment at the edge of the woods. Fires burned fitfully in the thin misty rain and troops moved between a jumbled patchwork of tents. Horses nickered from somewhere across the crowded field.

Gregar looked to the skinny mage; the lad's black hair lay flat and dripping, and as he wiped his nose, sniffling, he let the bundle of equipment he carried fall at his feet.

'Where's the shield?' Gregar asked.

'Dumped it. Too godsdamned heavy.'

Gregar swore under his breath.

'I'm cold,' Haraj complained, stammering. 'Can't sleep out in the rain again – it's fucking winter!'

Gregar nodded. Neither of them knew how to survive outdoors. The wretched few scraps of food and water they'd looted from fallen Bloorian troops wouldn't sustain them; they needed shelter. He couldn't even feel his fingers or toes any more. Another night in the open might finish them – his sickly friend especially.

He kept nodding, disgusted. 'So, we turn ourselves in just to survive.'

Haraj's answering nod was a puppet-like jerking shiver. 'Welcome to how things are for most nobodies.'

Gregar gestured to the belt-wrapped bundle. 'Fine. Pick it up and let's go.'

'Take it? Whatever for? Don't need it no more, do we?'

Gregar was already pushing his way through the low brush. 'It's a bribe now.'

'Who are they, do you think?' Haraj asked, following.

'Doesn't really matter any more, does it?' But Gregar made a quick last check to make certain neither of them was wearing or carrying any colours or sigils – of any troop or side.

They had to stand in the open for some time before one of the spear-carrying pickets noticed them through the rain. The skinny girl jumped and raised her spear. 'Halt!' she squeaked out, the spear quivering. 'Raise your arms! Who – who're you?'

Gregar nudged Haraj, murmuring, 'Raise your arms.' He called out, 'We've come to join!'

The girl, in ragged old leathers, her long dark hair twisted high on her head, gaped at them. 'Sarge!' she called over her shoulder.

Moments later a squat, fat-bellied fellow in leather armour came stomping through the rain. A sigil – a strip of cloth tied about his arm – was dark and soaked; Gregar couldn't tell its actual colour. 'What in the name of Hood's bony balls is this?' the sergeant bellowed as he came.

The picket motioned her spear to them. 'These two want to join up.'

The soldier raised an astonished tangled brow at this. He looked them up and down, and what he saw, or believed he saw, made him sneer even more. 'Useless deserters. Big bad world too mean for you, hey? Come crawling back hungry and wet.'

Gregar and Haraj – both dropping their arms – exchanged a look, then hung their heads.

'Sorry,' Gregar mumbled, and pushed forward.

The sergeant held out an arm. 'Not so fast.' He waved them closer. 'Now look here – I'm supposed to report such things to the captain, but I don't want to get you lads in hot water. What do you say, hey?'

Gregar and Haraj sent one another bemused looks. Gregar shrugged. 'I suppose so . . .'

The sergeant clapped him on the shoulder. 'Excellent. That's the spirit. So hand over that gear and such.' He gestured to Gregar's mail shirt.

'But it's mine . . . been in the family . . .'

The sergeant looked skyward. 'And maybe I should report this to the captain . . .'

Gregar let his shoulders fall. 'Fine.' He started undoing the leather straps.

'Don't fit you no how,' the sergeant observed. He also gestured for Haraj to drop his bundled gear. 'That too.'

'But that's all we got!' Haraj complained.

'What you get is your freedom and your lives. So drop it all. Even that,' he added, pointing to Gregar's belted shortsword.

Gregar ground out a breath, but let it fall.

The sergeant waved them away. 'Now gawan with ya.' He pointed to the girl. 'Take them to your squad, Leah.'

'What!' the girl answered, outraged. 'They're useless.'

'Go!'

The girl, Leah, snarled under her breath, then waved them onward. 'This way.'

Leah's squad, it turned out, occupied a floorless tent, a brazier banked at its centre. Haraj and Gregar crowded round the brazier, warming their hands. The rest of the squad lay asleep on the ground. Leah set her fists on her hips and eyed them, her disapproval obvious.

'Dumbasses,' she finally concluded, and, shaking her head, threw herself down on her own bedding.

Gregar ventured, 'Ah . . . what's the pay, anyway?'

The woman rolled her eyes. 'Sarge would know. He's gonna draw it.'

'*What?*' Gregar choked out, nearly spluttering.

The girl's laugh was mocking, but sadly so. 'Just discovered life's not fair, hey?'

'And just who,' Haraj asked, 'are we with?'

'You're with the Yellows' Fourth – the Seventh Lights,' she drawled from her tattered horse-blanket. 'And if the Bloorian League can be said to have an anus – you're stuck in it.'

Haraj and Gregar exchanged another look and Gregar shook his head. 'Wonderful.'

The next morning, after a hot meal that was hardly more than mere warmed broth, they mustered in the pattering rain. He and Haraj were issued spears, which they held straight up beside them as their sergeant – Teigan – walked up and down the lines heaping abuse on them. Though still fuming, it was all Gregar could do not to burst out laughing. It was all so clichéd and stupid.

'Are we gonna fight?' Haraj asked, dread in his voice.

'Naw,' Leah answered. 'It's raining, innit? Them Bloorian nobles won't fight in the rain. Gets their fancy bird-feather helmet plumes all droopy.'

Gregar snorted a laugh.

Sergeant Teigan rounded on him. 'Oh! The ingrate new recruit thinks this is all just hilarious!'

Gregar struggled to contain a new bout of laughter. Closing nose to nose with him, Teigan yelled, 'Maybe the new recruit would like the honour of being the colour-bearer!'

Gregar had no idea what to say to that. 'Well,' he began, 'if you think—'

'*Shut up!*' Teigan bellowed. 'That's yes sir!'

Showing great restraint, Gregar merely clenched his lips. 'Yes,' he ground out, 'sir.'

'Hand the colours over!' Teigan yelled.

Another of the skirmishers came running bearing a tall spear from which hung a limp yellow silk banner. Teigan thrust it at Gregar. 'There you go.'

A touch befuddled, Gregar took it. 'Yellow? Really?'

'March!' Teigan yelled, and the troop set off.

As they went, Gregar murmured to Leah, 'I don't understand. Isn't this an honour? Bearing the colours and all?'

Leah just smirked. 'The Grisians think it great sport to collect regimental colours. They think it's noble and courageous or some such rubbish to ride down a farmer and take the flag. We go through two or three colour-bearers every battle.'

Gregar shared another look with Haraj. 'Wonderful. Fucking wonderful.'

* * *

Having finished his immediate orders recruiting a number of potential cadre mages, Tayschrenn found himself between duties and so sought out the Napan aristocrat, Surly, who – if anyone – was actually getting things done.

He had to push past numerous bodyguards and layers of security in Smiley's bar before gaining entry to the second floor. And by the time he did it appeared to him that the bar seemed more a nest of spies, assassins and agents provocateurs than any drinking establishment.

Upstairs, he was allowed, with some reluctance, to

edge past a final layer of bodyguards and enter the presence of the woman herself.

Standing, a sheaf of vellum sheets in her hands, Surly lowered the reports to eye him, a touch impatiently. 'Yes?'

'Timetable,' Tayschrenn offered, being deliberately obscure.

The faintly bluish-hued and quite muscular woman eyed him for an instant without comment. Then she allowed one curt nod. 'Proceeding.'

'And what of our glorious leaders?'

She shrugged. 'Irrelevant.'

Tayschrenn gave her a sceptical look. 'Really? The plan calls for—' He paused here to peer about the room, crowded as it was with the woman's bodyguards, staff, and various agents.

'These are the people executing said plan,' Surly explained.

Tayschrenn coughed into a fist. 'Ah. I see. Well, the plan calls for—'

'I know the plan,' Surly interrupted, not bothering to disguise her impatience. 'Your point?'

Tayschrenn decided that she was trying to goad him, so he clamped down on any reaction and eyed her impassively. 'What if Kellanved does not show?'

'Then a vessel will land the assault party outside the city and you will proceed from there.'

'You? I mean, me?'

'Yes. You will be among the party.'

He peered about the room, searching for smirks or laughter, as if at a joke at his expense. 'Me? Whatever for? There is nothing I could possibly contribute to such a mundane, ah, errand.'

She gave him a hard stare, from one eye. 'You *are* a mage . . . are you not?'

Now he felt rather flustered. This curt woman was frankly intimidating him. 'Well, yes. Of course. Just not *that* kind of mage.'

'What kind? The useful kind?'

Instead of slipping into anger or withering beneath such scorn, Tayschrenn stepped back from the conversation to study it from afar. *Why such hostility?* If this was hostility – perhaps this was the woman at her most people-friendly. He simply did not know. One thing he did know, or suspect, was that some sort of contest was being acted out here; one he had heretofore been unaware of. And there could only be a contest between rivals.

And there he had it. If she could be said to be the head of her branch of this nascent organization they were pulling together here on this wretched island, then so too was he.

They were, quite frankly, rival department heads, and their battles would be over what was always at stake: resources and prestige. And so he inclined his head in agreement. 'You, however, will not be with us, I take it?'

She scowled at this, unhappy. 'No. It has been decided that I remain offshore and only come in when the situation has been stabilized.'

'I see. Very well.' He gave a faint bow. 'You are busy. I will leave you to it.' He turned and walked away without waiting for her reaction.

When he reached the door she called out, 'Tayschrenn . . . if you are not that kind of mage, then bring one who is.'

Facing away, he gave the slightest inclination of his head as he pulled the door open and went out.

* * *

75

It was night, and as was her habit Iko walked the open-sided halls and colonnaded walkways of the rambling palace at Kan. Finest silk hangings of pink and pearl-white shimmered in the lamplight, all to celebrate the passing dusting of glittering frost. The wind brushed through the surrounding orchards and gardens; night insects chirped, and bats swooped in to feed upon them. The only unnatural sound was the shush of the fine mail coat hanging to her ankles where it hissed as she paced.

She turned a corner of the open-walled colonnade and paused, half meaning to go back, as ahead came a gaggle of the local courtly Kan 'ladies', tittering and gossiping among themselves as they closed. She opted to remain still, and bowed as they neared. They passed, whispering to one another behind their broad fine brocaded sleeves, and laughing, eyeing her sidelong.

She sighed. From among *these* her ward Chulalorn the Fourth was to choose a mate? She did not know whom to feel more sorry for. These spoiled cloistered creatures, or her ward who would have to put up with them.

Still, she, captain of the select bodyguard, the Sword-Dancers, must no doubt appear as strange and exotic to them as they did to her.

She started off again on her meditative walk, hands at her belt, head cocked as she listened to the sounds of the night. Two turns later she paused once more and turned back. Far up the hall a young servant now closed, her bare feet only faintly slapping the polished marble of the hall. The servant bowed to her. 'M'lady. You are called to council, if you would.'

'It is not m'lady,' Iko corrected her. 'You are new here, yes? I am not noble born. It is captain.'

The servant bowed once more. 'Yes captain, m'lady.'

Iko let out a hard breath. 'Council you say? At this hour? The king?'

'Safe, ah . . . captain.'

'Very well. I shall attend.' The servant hurried off ahead to pass the word.

For her part, Iko remained still for a time longer. She attempted to regain her sense of calm oneness with the gardens and the night, but the mood was broken. She hoped this was not word of some new border transgression from Dal Hon. The last thing Kan needed now after the losses at Heng was a war. Any war. Unfortunately, her enemies knew this also. So she adjusted the whipsword at her back and headed for the council chambers.

The guards admitted her, opening the broad double leaves of the gilded doors. Within, she saw Mosolan, the regent, as expected, but she was surprised to find a newcomer, a rather striking figure. Tall she was, her hair a bunched silvery mane that reached all the way down to the back of her knees. This woman turned, and regarded her with captivating, equally pale-silver eyes. Her mouth, however, soured the striking effect, pulled down as it was in a lined frown. *Bitch face*, Iko had heard this sort of resting expression named.

Mosolan extended an arm to the woman. 'The Witch Jadeen. Iko, Captain of the Guard.'

Iko's brows rose in astonishment – and a touch of alarm. *This* was the terror of the south? The mage who many said kept the Dal Hon shamans in line? From her sour mouth alone Iko could almost believe it. She nodded a greeting; the woman did not deign to respond.

'You will speak with us,' Mosolan told Jadeen.

The mage threw back her head, her spectacular mane of hair tossing. 'I am come to demand action.'

'What sort of action?' Mosolan enquired. The old

77

general, now regent of Itko Kan, crossed an arm over his chest and rested the other upon it to hold his chin. Iko knew enough of the man to know he was taking this meeting very seriously.

The witch was about to speak when the doors opened again and in swept a tall middle-aged man in a silken robe, sashed at the waist, his long black hair loose. 'What is this?' he announced. 'A council meeting without the nobles' chosen representative?'

'This is a consultation only,' Mosolan answered wearily. Yet he extended an arm in introductions: 'Leoto Kan, of family Kan. Leoto Kan – the Witch Jadeen.'

Leoto flinched at the name, while Iko noted how the witch's scowling mouth drew down even more in evident satisfaction at the response.

'You were saying . . .' Mosolan prompted Jadeen.

She nodded, then tilted her head back, glowering imperiously. She slammed a fist into a palm. 'You must crush Malaz Island. Now. Destroy it.'

Iko almost missed her words in her surprise at seeing the woman's nails were long, pointed, and entirely black.

Yet Mosolan nodded, all seriousness. 'Malaz Island? Why?'

'A disturbing set of powers are gathering there. I have foreseen they could threaten the mainland. Threaten Itko Kan.'

Iko cudgelled her brain to even recall that particular island to mind. All she could remember were tales of a pirate haven. She snorted. 'Sea-raiders are no threat to the kingdom.'

'Shut up, Sword-Dancer,' the witch snarled. 'There is more here than you can grasp.'

Iko let out a hissed breath, but held her silence: Mosolan was regent, not she. She also noted a smirk of satisfaction similar to the witch's earlier pleasure quirk the noble Kan's lips.

Mosolan had raised a hand to intervene. 'Iko here was at Heng. She is not to be dismissed.'

The witch tossed her mane once more to show what she thought of that. 'I do not travel here and give my warnings lightly, regent. Do not dismiss *me*!'

Mosolan raised a placating hand once again. 'We would do no such thing, Jadeen. Your wisdom is appreciated.' To Iko's eyes the witch was in no way appeased. 'Yet,' Mosolan continued, 'for such drastic action – what evidence can you provide?'

A snarl twisted the woman's thin lips even more and she glared. 'I am not used to having to justify my advice, regent. But if you insist . . .' She crossed her arms, grasping her black-nailed hands on either arm. 'The Dragons Deck warns of the end of the Chulalorn line.'

Iko was before the witch in an instant, her whipsword half drawn. 'What is this!'

To her credit, Jadeen did not so much as flinch; her gaze remained fixed upon Mosolan. 'You are warned,' she announced, and spun upon her heels to march from the chamber.

When the door closed, Councillor Leoto coughed lightly into a fist. 'Well, regent. I must attend your consultations more often. They are certainly not boring.'

Iko slammed home her whipsword and turned upon the aristocrat. 'Shut up, Leoto.'

The head of family Kan offered her a cold smile. 'A pleasure as always, Iko.'

Mosolan paced the marble floor before the empty throne of Itko Kan, now draped in royal green silk. 'Malaz?' he wondered aloud. 'A gathering of powers that could worry Jadeen?' He shook his head, almost in wonder. 'She warned against the Third's march north, you know. And before *that* she gave warning of the Dal Hon invasion to the Second.' He turned to regard them, amazement upon his features now. 'I never imagined I would be the one to hear a prediction from her.'

Iko cut a hand through the air. 'She senses a rival to her influence in the south and would have us do her dirty work for her.'

'Perhaps,' Mosolan allowed.

'Question,' Leoto put in, raising a finger. 'What sources do we have on that worthless island?'

Mosolan turned to face them, clasped his hands at his back. It looked to Iko as though the Witch Jadeen's words had affected him far more than her; the man had already been old – practically retired – before the burden of regency had fallen to him. Now he appeared positively exhausted, his lined features marked by the cares of his office. He sighed. 'Not a one.'

* * *

The so-called 'fortress' at Two-River Pass occupied a wide gravel wash between the two braided arms of the river that gave it its name. After a series of falls the Two-River lost its way in the lower northern valley of the pass, and here the fortress guarded the road to Tellick on the coast.

Orjin Samarr's troop descended the pass in the night, their way lit by a clear and bright starry sky. In the pre-dawn light they forded one arm of the river, the frigid rushing waters rising to Orjin's waist, and marched up the gravel strand of the mid-channel island.

Vegetable plots planted in the rocky soil surrounded the fortress's outer timber palisade. Within, peeping above the sharpened logs, rose the top of the inner tower, built of mortared river stones. He noted multiple watches on the walls pointing their way and shouting down within. The twin leaves of the palisade gate stood open, and as Orjin and his immediate lieutenants – who considered themselves something of an unofficial bodyguard – approached they were met by a cordon of Purge regulars barring the way in a shield-wall. An officer pushed through to meet with them; a tall and lean woman in a coat of leather armour, cut as overlapping scales. Eyeing them, she announced to the gate guards, 'More survivors from the battle. You are?'

'Captain Orjin Samarr.'

She extended a gauntleted hand, 'Prevost Jeral.'

Orjin knew 'prevost' to be an ancient rank equivalent to captain. He took her hand and she nodded, then pulled off her helmet to reveal four long braids that bounced about her shoulders. She waved him onwards. 'You are free to join us, though we are ordered to withdraw.'

'Withdraw?' Orjin replied, startled. 'This is the last fortress between the pass and Purge lands . . .'

'I know.' She drew off her gauntlets and waved them towards a file of wagons, incompletely loaded with supplies and materiel.

'Who gave the order?' Orjin asked.

'Two nights ago three noblemen came charging through on their way to Purage. They ordered the garrison withdrawn to help protect the city.'

Protect them *more like*, Orjin almost said aloud. 'Was Baron Terrall among them?'

'Aye, he was.'

Orjin eyed the half-loaded wagons. Two nights ago? 'You are still evacuating?' he asked, rather confused.

'Oh, aye,' Jeral answered, clearing her throat.

'Unfortunate shortage of mules and horses. Also, a broken axle. I've sent a messenger to Purge to requisition adequate cartage.'

Orjin rubbed his chin to hide a smile. 'I see. By regulation.'

She nodded, echoing his understanding. 'All by regulation. In the meantime,' she continued, giving him a sidelong glance, 'if the enemy appears – we'll just have to fight.'

This time he did not try to hide his smile. 'If you must. Of course.'

Orjin's troop was filing in now, and the tall leaves of the main gate were being pushed shut behind them. The prevost extended him a look. 'And what's your story?'

Almost wincing at what was to come, he drew a folded sheet of vellum from a waist pouch and held it out to the Purge officer. 'We are signed with the throne.'

Jeral examined the signed sheet, the wax seals, cocked a brow. 'Meaning?'

'Meaning – by regulation – I outrank you.'

Her mouth hardened and she handed the folded sheets back. 'Now I see. And what are *your* orders, sir?'

'*My* intention is to slow the Quon Talian advance by any means possible, prevost.'

The smile returned to Jeral's lips, and she saluted. 'Excellent, *sir.*' Searching among the troops, she pointed to a soldier. 'Sergeant – unload those wagons!'

The trooper answered the woman's smile and saluted. 'At once, prevost.'

The officer returned her attention to Orjin and shook her head, her long braids bouncing. 'So – your first command? Take a look.'

She led him on a tour of the fortress, such as it was. He did his best to hide his growing dismay; not only was the garrison shockingly under-supplied, but much-needed repairs were years behind. Rot in some sections of the palisade made it more dangerous to the defenders than any would-be attackers. The tower itself proved to be nothing more than a hollow three-storey stone circle, its interior flooring and joists long burned away over the decades of interminable border warfare. The installation had in fact changed hands more times than a Cawnese gambling establishment, leaving neither side interested in sinking any resources into it.

After the brief tour, Orjin and Jeral ended up at the south wall of the palisade, peering up at the steep and rocky Two-River Pass. She took hold of her long braids, one on either side of her head, and rested her arms in this manner, the way a man might tuck his hands into his belt. The gesture rather charmed Orjin, who had taken a liking to the straight-talking daughter of some minor Nom baronet. She leaned back against the sharpened palisade logs and regarded him. 'So, your first command. Well – looks like it's gonna be your last.'

Orjin was eyeing the steep, bare mountainsides. 'We'll see.'

'There's no way you can stop them, you know.'

He nodded. 'You're right. There's no way we can stop them.'

She dropped her arms. 'So? I won't just throw my lads and lasses away. Perhaps we *should* abandon the fort.'

'Got any locals among your troops?'

'Locals? Yeah, I suppose. A few.'

'Have them sent to me. I want to have a word.' He raised his chin to the mountain slopes then gave her a look. 'That pass – it's damned steep. Prone to slides, I imagine.'

She glanced up and set to rubbing her chin once more.

After a moment her lips crooked and her brown eyes – shot through with green – narrowed and got a sly look to them. 'Yeah,' she agreed, 'all the time.'

Orjin's lieutenants, Yune, Terath, and Orhan of Fenn, joined him and Jeral at the meeting with the local recruits – 'recruits' being a gentle euphemism for taxation as enforced service. These dirt-poor herders and farmers were used mainly as mountain guides and light skirmishers. Once the meeting was over, Orjin sat back from the cookfire they'd met around in the enclosed grounds of the bailey and eyed Jeral; the woman was clearly still troubled as she tapped a thumb to her lips. He cocked a brow, inviting her to speak. She let out a hard breath. 'Okay. I get it. We hit the supply train then raid it, if possible. But what I don't get is what about the fortress? Who'll be down here when we're all up the slopes?'

He nodded. 'I will, together with a few of my picked troops.'

She snorted her disbelief. 'Really? You'n'a few others – while I'm out runnin' the ambush, I suppose?' He nodded again, eyeing her steadily. 'You're taking a big chance.'

He just shrugged. 'I suppose that's entirely up to you.'

She looked away, sighing and shaking her head, appalled. 'Crazy fucking Hood-damned lunatic.'

He poked a stick at the embers of the fire. 'Better get going. I expect they'll be here right on our heels.'

She stood and brushed the long leather skirtings of her coat. 'We'll assemble supplies and head out within the hour.' She peered down at him for a time, her expression unreadable, then she gave a curt nod. 'Oponn be with you.'

'And with you.' He waved her off.

As he'd anticipated, Terath immediately cleared her throat loudly and drawled, 'And who's gonna be with you on this suicidal heroic last stand?'

He cast an amused look her way. 'Why you, of course.'

She snorted her disbelief, poked a finger after Jeral. 'Like the woman said – you're taking a big chance. What if she decides to withdraw after all?'

Orjin shook his head. 'She won't.'

'Oh? You think so? You know people so well, do you?'

He continued shaking his head while prodding the embers. 'No. I know soldiers. And there's no way that one would do anything that would shame her in front of her troops.'

Terath looked to the Dal Hon shaman in his robe of faded tatterdemalion rags. 'What about you, Yune? You for this?'

The wrinkled elder shrugged. 'It is for the captain to decide.'

Terath looked to the sky in her exasperation. 'Why even ask a fatalist for his opinion?' She sighed. 'Well, it'll be a great fight . . . while it lasts.'

The giant Orhan clapped her on the back and guffawed. 'That's the spirit!'

She mouthed curses under her breath and glared.

* * *

A lone traveller walked the sandy strand of the cliff-faced shore of south Quon Tali. He'd recently come from Horan, near to the Dal Hon border and the Forest of Horn, having been staying for many months with the priests and priestesses of the large temple to Poliel in that city.

The squat but powerfully built man travelled in a plain loincloth only, his arms, chest, and legs bare and sun-scorched, yet declaring to all his role and his calling, for tattooed upon his flesh, rising from his ankles to his shoulders and onward to his face and wrists, rode emblazoned the likeness of a rampaging boar: Fener – the god of war himself.

Though alone and unarmed he walked without fear. None in their right mind would dare accost any man or woman so inscribed, for everyone knew such an all-embracing display could only be granted by the dispensation of that very god. Likewise, the man carried no pack or other supplies; Fener would dispense all – or not.

And so the man did not flinch or cower when four robe-wrapped figures rose from the wave-splashed boulders of the rocky coast. He merely halted, crossed his arms, and waited calmly for Fener to reveal his purpose.

All four threw back their hoods, revealing two men and two women, all bearing similar boar-visage tattoos upon their faces, though, tellingly, not their arms or legs.

'Heboric of Carasin,' one of the men announced, 'we are sent from your family.'

A lopsided smile crooked the priest's heavy lips. He knew that by 'family' the priests and priestesses before him meant his adopted family of the faithful of Fener, not his long lost and forgotten family of birth. 'And what word from our family?' he asked.

'We are concerned,' said one of the women.

'Concerned? Concerned for what?'

'For your soul,' the other woman put in bluntly.

'And what reason have you for such concern?'

The bearded eldest of the four gestured back up the strand. 'Your consorting with other cults! And this is not the only time, either. We know you have sought out those loyal to the damned meddling Queen of Dreams and taken consultation with them! Not to mention seeking out hermits and ascetics who affect to speak for eldritch powers, such as K'rul.'

Heboric's thick lips crooked even deeper. 'Heavy are my crimes indeed.'

The priest's finger now jabbed at him. 'Do not mock your duties to Father Boar!'

'Enough!' the first woman interjected – she was the youngest of the group, and was blue-hued as a native of the Napan Isles. 'Enough, brother Eliac.' She faced Heboric. 'What of these charges?'

He shrugged his meaty shoulders. 'I have heard no charges – only an itinerary of my travels.'

Eliac spluttered his outrage; the young woman sighed and crossed her arms within their long loose sleeves. 'Very well ... the family is concerned that you are neglecting your sworn obligations to your god.'

Heboric inclined his head in acknowledgement of this well-mannered enquiry. He crossed his thick arms, the boar forelimb tattoos writhing and twisting as he did so. 'I consider myself to be pursuing those very obligations with these researches.'

Brother Eliac snorted his scorn and drew breath to speak, but the young priestess raised a hand, silencing him. Heboric was impressed – for one so young to have acquired such authority spoke of great talent. She cocked her head. 'How so?'

Heboric nodded again, pleased that the priesthood was now finally asking questions. 'Have you not noted the disturbances among the Warrens and the gods? The strange manifestations? Ripples of power from no accountable source? A peculiar restiveness among the pantheon?'

The priestess shook her head, disappointed. 'Heboric – none know of what you speak. Come back to the temple. A great honour could be yours among the family. Please.'

He gestured to his body. 'I carry Fener with me no

matter where I go. He may withdraw his presence whenever he wishes.'

The priestess appeared pained. 'Do not tempt the Boar, Heboric. Withdrawal would kill you.'

'I tempt nothing. Fener is with me. He guides my path – of this I am certain. And so the priesthood should not interfere.'

The young Napan priestess now shook her head in sadness. 'You are determined to pursue this path . . .'

'I am.'

She let out a long hard breath. 'Very well. Who are we to intercede? May the Great Boar watch over you.'

Brother Eliac pointed down the strand. '*This* path leads only to death, fool. None return from the Isle of the Cursed.'

Heboric offered up a sideways mocking smile. 'Know you not, brother, that those living there have another name for their home? They name it Poliel's Isle of the Blessed.'

Eliac shuddered within his robes. 'They are exiled. They bear the taint of the rotting flesh. Travel there and you too shall be exiled – for life.'

Heboric gave a wink. 'I, brother Eliac, trust in Fener.' And, bowing, he carried on his way. None shouted after him, and none pursued. Nor would they again, he knew. For though a place high within the priesthood of the Boar might have been his, it was this mission that possessed him. Let the others climb the dreary career rungs of the priestly hierarchy – he had been called. He felt it. And he would pursue it no matter what fate may await.

Chapter 5

I N EARLY WINTER WORD CAME TO SILK REQUESTING his least favourite duty. The bureaucrats who actually ran the day to day activities of the city, the record-keepers who granted deeds, oversaw the maintenance of roads, sewage tunnels and gutters – all the mundane administrative requirements that any large population requires – had forwarded to him a request to look into disturbances in the western caravanserai district.

Disturbances and complaints that involved an alleged local talent.

It happened once or twice a year. Either a new local talent had emerged, or someone new had come to the city who didn't know, or was defying, the rules the Protectress had set forth. In either case, one of the five city mages had to look into it and it was his turn.

And so one chilly morning he wrapped a thick cloak about himself and set forth. Of course he was also armed, as occasionally – despite his best efforts to keep things civil – these confrontations turned violent.

Those city bureaucrats had obviously dithered over this problem until the complaints became overwhelming, because no sooner had Silk entered the district than local shopkeepers and residents came clamouring. They pointed out the business – one of the many stablers serving the caravans – and recounted stories of lost sheep and goats, missing dogs, even, some whispered, missing children, all taken by this shapeshifting winged demon child who resided, apparently, above the stables.

Silk raised his hands to quell everyone, and nodded his tired assurances. He regarded the closed and shuttered building. A shapeshifter? Hardly. No soletaken was likely to come to Heng given its ages-long feud with the man-beast Ryllandaras.

He banged on the closed front double doors, now probably barred against the angry neighbours.

'Go away, damn you,' a gruff voice answered.

'It is Silk, city mage. Here on order of the Protectress. You cannot keep me out.'

Silence, then a clatter as a smaller entrance in the broad doors was unbarred. It opened and Silk stepped in. The first thing he noticed in the slanting light cutting in through gaps in the clapboard siding was that every stall was empty. Next he took in the fellow facing him: old and beaten down in a stained leather apron. Silk merely cocked a questioning eye. The man raised his chin to the stairs. 'The loft,' he ground out, hands clenched at his apron.

Silk nodded at this, then climbed. A trapdoor led to the upper loft and here he found dusty old crates and bundles of tattered horse-blankets, old cracked leather tack and other equipment hanging from rafters, and amid this jumble, hunched on a box and wrapped in one of the dirty old horse-blankets, a young girl. A tiny yellow songbird fluttered about one of her hands, alighting from one finger to the next. When he drew near, the bird shot off through an open window.

He sat next to her and sighed loudly. 'You know who I am?'

'Yes,' she whispered, her voice hoarse – probably from crying.

'You know why I am here?'

'Yes.'

Her head was hung so low he could not see her face, but in the silence he carefully raised his Warren and studied her. Her strong aura told of talent – but of a strange sort. Not drawn from any of the Warrens he was familiar with. Yet it was there. Old. And wild.

No wonder she'd avoided detection for so long – this aspect was completely unknown to him.

After they'd sat in silence for some time he asked, 'And what will you do?'

She hugged herself. 'I will go away.'

He nodded at this, peered round. Bird feathers lay everywhere yet not one bird was in evidence. Now he remembered hearing stories of some sort of bird-tamer in town. 'Where are your pets?' he asked.

'I sent them away,' she whispered, pain in her voice. 'People were throwing rocks at them.'

He nodded again. 'Ah. They'll do that.'

'They threw them at me, too.'

'I'm sorry. They're just frightened. Ignorant and frightened.'

'At first it was fine,' she said, almost dreamily. 'I made money for Father healing and taming animals.' Her voice hardened. 'But then people began to whisper against me. Claimed I'd made pacts with demons or some such stupid thing.'

'And the disappearing animals?'

She made an airy gesture. 'Hunters must hunt.'

'I see. Well . . . best you go soon.'

She nodded. 'Tonight. Father will give me a cart and a mule.'

'And where will you go? There are schools in Unta or Kan that may take you in. Help train you.'

She gently shook her head at his suggestion. 'No. There are none who can train me. I will go north.'

Silk was surprised. 'North? There's nothing to the north.'

'There are the mountains.'

'You will not survive, child.'

Her head remained lowered, but at one cheek he thought he discerned the hint of a secretive smile. 'Yes I will.'

He pressed his hands to his thighs. 'Well . . . that is your business, of course. Mine is done. Remain, and we of the Five will see you out – understood?'

She jerked a nod.

'Very well.' He stood and stared down at the young girl for a time. So tiny and frail-looking. Dare he say, bird-like? 'I'm sorry,' he said, at length, and headed for the trapdoor. Descending, he paused, peering back, and asked, 'Why north – if I may?'

Her back to him, she answered, 'I have a promise to keep to an old friend.'

At midnight of that very evening the guards of the Westward Gate of the Dusk were shaken out of their lazy dozing by the arrival of a cloaked city mage who ordered one leaf of the broad double gate opened. Shortly thereafter they eyed one another in puzzlement as a battered cart drawn by a single mule came clattering through the gate and continued onward up the Grand Trader Road.

The sleepy guards, Silk knew, did not notice the dark shapes passing overhead, but he did. An enormous flock of knife-winged silhouettes: birds of prey, and damned large ones, wafting westward high above the cart. He cocked a brow in acknowledgement – yes, this one would survive.

While he watched from the wall the cart lurched off the road and headed north along a track. The shapes lazily circling above shifted to follow.

* * *

Tayschrenn had called a meeting of the mages who to date had enlisted with the formal mage cadre, as distinguished from the minor talents who served as battle mages. Gathered here atop a grassed hill outside Malaz were he, the short and burly Hairlock, the youthful-appearing Calot, and the woman Nightchill, who he speculated must be some type of sorceress. She no longer walked with a cane, but still held an arm pressed across her front.

He mused that a troubadour might name such a meeting a 'fell gathering'; a less generous observer might call them a troop of fools. Eyeing his reluctant, mismatched collection, he was tempted to name it a cavalcade of clowns.

He did not want this task; this was Kellanved's duty, surely. However, he had – in a moment of weakness, and much to his annoyance – agreed to stand in the man's absence. And so he nodded a subdued greeting to all and cleared his throat. 'Thank you for coming,' he began.

'Where's the little feller?' Hairlock interrupted. 'Shouldn't he be here?'

'He is travelling,' Tayschrenn answered tersely.

'Travelling? What for?'

Tayschrenn drew breath to subdue his annoyance. 'I believe he is currently pursuing a mystery.'

Calot raised a hand. 'Mystery, you say? What sort of mystery?'

Tayschrenn clasped his hands tightly behind his back; gods, could anything be worth such aggravation? What must he answer? A mysterious mystery? 'One that he no doubt believes will lead to power.'

Hairlock grunted at this, satisfied. 'So, what do you want?'

Tayschrenn let a breath out between clenched teeth. A rising wind from the south cooled his back and sent errant loose lengths of his hair blowing. He drew the hair from his face. 'What we must do is organize ourselves.'

'In what manner?' Nightchill asked.

Tayschrenn nodded, acknowledging the directness and perceptiveness of the question. 'Indeed. That is what we are here to discuss.'

Hairlock cut a blunt hand through the air, scowling. 'I don't work for you. It was the fellow who calls himself Kellanved who invited me to come.'

Calot was nodding his agreement. His night-black curls blew about, and he appeared to be shivering though wrapped in a thick cloak. 'You said my arrangement was with Kellanved.'

Tayschrenn raised a hand in acknowledgement. 'Yes, yes. I serve only as his deputy here, head of this assembly, this cadre. The question, then, is . . . since we could probably never agree on any hierarchy among us . . . how do we organize?'

'We do not,' said Nightchill. 'We each answer directly to Kellanved, or you as a coordinator . . . or,' she added, thinking, 'another duly appointed representative.'

Hairlock's thick lips curled upwards in a smug smile at that addition and Tayschrenn could almost hear him thinking: *That'll be me*.

'Academic,' supplied Calot, shivering even more – he was quite slight, and seemed to be the only one of them feeling the chill wind. Or at least he was pretending to. 'Our patron is not here.'

Tayschrenn nodded. 'Fine. It will do for the moment. Now we can move on to our tasks. Once we are ready we are planning to move against Nap. An invasion of the capital, Dariyal, no doubt. Therefore our duty is to investigate what awaits us there on the isles. How strong are the talents? Do any hidden powers await us? What sort of opposition should we expect?' He cleared his throat, uncertain what reaction his next words might elicit, but continued regardless, 'I, ah, *suggest*, then, that you, Calot, and Hairlock travel by mundane roundabout means to the isles to investigate.'

Hairlock cocked a hairless brow. 'Really? Him'n'me? Why us? Why not you or this lass here?'

'I would attract too much attention,' Nightchill supplied, as if stating a plain fact.

Hairlock smiled crookedly, looking her up and down. 'You got that right, lass. There's a touch of the Elders about you . . .'

She pointed to Tayschrenn. 'And this one has announced his presence on Malaz already. Neither of you have.'

Tayschrenn inclined his head to her – she'd already grasped that salient point.

Hairlock's jaws bunched as he chewed on this, unhappy. Finally, he gave a curt nod. 'Fine.'

'Excuse me,' Calot began, raising a hand, 'but when you say "mundane" do you mean by boat and such?' Tayschrenn nodded, a touch mystified by the question. 'Then I will need a fair amount of coin, my friend, as I do *not* travel with the common masses.'

Tayschrenn fought the urge to roll his eyes at the sheer prosaicness of the request, and instead inclined his head in assent. 'You will both be given sufficient funds, of course.'

Calot shrugged within his bunched, thick cloak. 'Very well. I'll go ahead and nose around.'

Hairlock flicked a hand to indicate his agreement as well.

'Then this first conclave is over,' Tayschrenn announced. Calot hurried off; Hairlock went thumping after, hands clasped at his back, head lowered, scowling.

'And what of us?' Nightchill asked.

'We remain on guard in case Itko Kan or some other entity decides to strike before we've gathered our strength.'

The strange, almost otherworldly sorceress had been peering southward as if distracted, but now she looked to him and extended a hand, inviting him to join her. 'Prudent,' she supplied. 'And what of our patron?'

Tayschrenn fought to keep his irritation and impatience with just that party from his face, and offered, neutrally, 'If the worst comes to the worst, I will reach out to him.'

The wind plucked at his robes and thorny bushes caught at the cloth as they walked a narrow path down the hillside. The sorceress wore only thin linen trousers and a loose shirt, yet she showed no discomfort from the chill wind, though she walked haltingly, and he thought he saw her wince in pain now and then.

'And where are you from?' he asked, now that they were alone and he could focus upon the mystery that the woman posed.

'From very far away,' she answered, her voice tired and very soft.

He cocked a brow. Fine. Be all reserved and distant, then. Yet his ruthlessly analytical self could not help but whisper in his ear: *And are you irritated with her because she's better at it than you?*

* * *

It was Gregar's first taste of a foot-soldier's life and he wondered how anyone could ever be stupid enough to choose it, let alone actually like it. Of course, by now he understood that the word 'choice' wasn't even in the common soldier's vocabulary. Most of the wretched youths in this troop had no say in the matter at all: impressed or conscripted by force, or offered up by their families to perform obligatory service as taxation owed to their lords in Yellows, or Gast, or Satar, or Netor.

And he couldn't help glaring and clenching his pike-haft with white knuckles whenever these same lords came trotting past in their fine regalia of flowing tabards, plumes, and intricate painted heraldry. They went bantering and joking, trading comments about the deplorable state of this year's pike-pushers, or what fun they'd have on the field of colours against the Grisian cavalry.

Gregar didn't know whether to stab them in their fat arses, or puke; or do both at the same time.

Time passed and he and his fellow infantry remained standing at attention in the chilling rain. Haraj sniffed and shivered. The sun behind the clouds rose to midday and still none of the assembled knights and lords appeared from within their tents. The delicious aroma of cooking wafted over Gregar and his stomach rumbled.

'How much longer are we going to have to wait?' he complained to Leah.

'Till the order to stand down,' she answered from the side of her mouth.

'But this is useless. We're just standing here!'

97

'Quiet in the ranks!' Sergeant Teigan bellowed from down the line.

'We serve at our betters' whim,' Leah murmured – not without a strong dose of sarcasm.

'So we just stand here while they decide whether they want to get their expensive clothes and decorations wet?'

Leah crooked her lips. 'Now you're catching on.'

Sergeant Teigan came storming down the front rank. 'Quiet!' he bellowed, halting right before Gregar. 'You hold the colours – show some dignity and respect!'

Gregar squinted up at the wet rag hanging limp from the top of the pike. 'Know what I think, sergeant? I think you can take this spear and—'

At that moment Haraj fainted to the muddy ground. Sergeant Teigan gaped at him lying limp in the muck. 'Insulting the glorious tradition of Yellows!' he roared. 'Get up, you worthless piece of human waste! You'll stand all night for this!'

'He fell because he *can't* stand,' Gregar supplied, and he knelt to pick the lad up.

'Not you,' Teigan snarled. He pointed to two others, 'You and you. Stand him between you.'

'But f'r how long, sergeant?' one of them complained.

Teigan pulled a hand down his flushed face and looked to the sky above. 'Until the fucking Enchantress invites you into her boudoir – that's how long!'

'Now that's a long time,' Leah murmured aside to Gregar.

'Hold him up,' Teigan snarled, 'till he can stand for himself, and then he'll be out here all the night – I'll see to it!'

'He'll die of exposure,' Gregar asserted.

Their sergeant cocked a brow to him. 'And what of it? Little loss, I should say.'

Stung by such casual cruelty, Gregar answered, 'I'll stand for him.'

The bushy brows now rose, either in astonishment or sarcasm – Gregar couldn't be certain. 'Oh, you will, will you?' The fat man bellied up, nearly pushing against him. They were close to identical height, yet the sergeant stood stocky and rotund, Gregar broad and muscled. 'Well, maybe I have something to say about that!'

'Which is?'

Now the brows clenched, knotting together over the sergeant's tiny eyes, as if the man were momentarily confused by Gregar's direct response; clearly things were not proceeding in the usual manner. He pushed a stubby finger into Gregar's chest. 'Then I say you will stand! There! How do you like that?'

Gregar nodded slowly, feeling rather confused himself. 'Right . . . as I offered.'

The sergeant sniffed loudly and peered round triumphantly. 'That's right! Ha!' He brushed his hands together as if having set things well in order, and stomped off.

Gregar cast an entreating look to Leah, who was doing her best to keep a straight face.

The sergeant struck a position at the centre of the line and turned to face the assembled ranks. 'Anyone else?' he bellowed. 'Anyone else have any pressing engagements? Invitations to dine with the chatelaine of Unta perhaps? No? Extra sets of lacy underthings to air? No?' He set his ham-like fists to his hips and surveyed the troopers, nodding to himself. 'Then we wait here as ordered! And we wait until the damned hillside crumbles into the sea if need be! For we are Yellows!' Scanning them once more, he nodded to himself again, then strode onward.

Gregar leaned to Leah. 'You know, he's not half bad at that.'

'You should hear him when he really gets on a roll.'

Limp between his two supporters, Haraj raised his head just enough to peer about. 'Is he gone?' His two supports pushed him from them, disgusted, and he stood brushing at the mud smearing the yellow surcoat over his old leather jupon.

Gregar restrained himself from swatting the fellow. 'So you can stand?'

'Quite. Thought that rather obvious from the timing, hey? There you were about to commit a punishable crime.' He held out his pale hands. 'I had to do something.'

Leah was now laughing openly, though silently. 'Your friend's right. He saved your skin.'

Gregar scowled his irritation. 'Saved me? I don't see how – I'm gonna be out here all the godsdamned night!'

'There's worse,' Leah supplied. 'Far worse.'

'Such as?'

Leah's amusement fell from her and she half turned away, squinting up at the thin cold rain. 'Whippings. The stocks. Branding. Maiming. Imprisonment. Hanging.' She jerked her chin to the tents now lit against the gathering gloom of the overcast sky. 'Whatever our betters wish. We live, and die, at their discretion.'

'Not me,' Gregar growled through clenched lips. 'Not me.'

The order to stand down only came to the ranks after each and every aristocrat and knight had ambled off the field, accompanied by their bevy of aides, squires, attendants, servants and grooms. Only then were the assembled infantry allowed to file back to their bivouacs. By then it was long after dark.

All quit the field save one; Gregar remained, tall pike of the Yellows' colours in hand. Soaked through and chilled to the bone, still he did not sit and huddle for warmth, for he knew that damned Teigan would pounce and he refused to give him the satisfaction.

Standing there all alone in the broad trampled field, he eyed the pike and the limp sodden rag tied just behind its narrow dagger-like blade. It struck him then that the weapon was really nothing more than a very long stick. And he knew how to fight with sticks or staves – twinned sticks were his preferred weapons. So he began experimenting: spinning, thrusting, trying circling counters, even entire turning sideways slashes. The weapon's arc was impressive. In fact, it looked as if he'd have the reach on any mounted foe. That made him smile, and he turned to see Leah standing behind him, a bemused look on her face, and a cloth-wrapped bundle in her hand.

'What in Burn's name are you doing?' she asked in wonder.

'Experimenting.'

She cocked a brow. 'Right. Well, here,' and she held out the bundle.

'What's this?'

'Dinner.'

'This allowed?'

Her answering smile was a half-scowl that held a mischievous tilt. 'Teigan didn't forbid it . . .'

Gregar huffed. 'That fat oaf.'

Leah handed over the bundle and Gregar unwrapped it to find a half-round of coarse hard bread and a small portion of dried meat. While he ate, she rubbed her arms for warmth, saying, 'Don't be too hard on Teigan. He fights hard for us and he fights from the front – but I think yelling is the only way he knows how to soldier.'

Gregar grunted a neutral demurral. 'How's Haraj?'

'Sleeping like the dead. Why's he here? This is clearly not the life for him.'

'Long story.'

She raised her hands in surrender. 'Right. None of my business.'

'And you? What about you?'

She shrugged. 'I'm all that's left of two brothers and one sister. My parents are old. We have no money. When the baron's officers came round demanding back rents and taxes I had no choice.'

'I'm sorry.'

She shrugged again. 'That's how it is for most of us here. But not you. You're no farmer.'

His mouth full, he said, 'No. Apprentice stonemason.'

'A free craftsman? What on earth are you doing here?'

'Like I said – long story.'

She shook her head in disbelief. 'Well, you made a poor swap, that's what I think.'

'I don't know about that. Standing around isn't so bad.'

'Not tomorrow. Marching. The Grisians and their allies have moved on. We follow.'

He looked to the night sky. 'Wonderful. What are we even doing here?'

'We're the expendable fodder, friend. We're just here to stand in the way of a charge, hold some piece of ground, or protect our lords if they're unhorsed.'

'What? Protect those arses from being killed?'

Leah appeared almost shocked. 'Oh, no. Not killed. Ransomed. We get killed – lords and ladies get ransomed.'

Gregar couldn't believe it. He wiped his hands clean on his sodden yellow surcoat. 'Just when you think things couldn't be any more insulting . . .'

Leah gave him a wink and headed off back to the bivouac grounds.

Not much later Teigan himself appeared. The sergeant looked surprised to find him still standing, then sullenly waved him off. 'Get some sleep,' he growled.

Gregar saluted and headed for his group's tent; he walked stiffly, his legs numb and tingling.

* * *

Tarel, king of the Napan Isles, walked alone through the empty night-time halls of the harbour fortress that served traditionally as the ruler's palace. He always walked alone as he did not wholly trust his bodyguard, many of whom he suspected would have much preferred seeing his sister upon the throne.

In fact, he was quite certain of it.

And so this night he hurried through the damp and bare stone halls, his pace ever quickening despite his efforts to remain calm, until he reached a certain door that he yanked open and flung himself within.

He turned, blinking in the dim yellow lamplight, to face his closest allies among the ruling council of Nap. Or rather, his most browbeaten, blackmailed, foolish and servile cronies among the Napan Council of Elders. Lady Elaina of the Ravanna line, as desperate to retain the prerogatives and privileges of her aristocratic class as she was determined to retain her line's riches. Torlo of the Torlo Trading House, as bought and paid for as any of his illicit goods. Lord Kobay of the Medalla line, whose unsavoury habits had placed him under Tarel's heel. And High Admiral Karesh, lord of all the Napan fleets, a deluded pontificating fool who owed his rank, estate and riches entirely to Tarel's patronage.

Lady Elaina rounded upon him, pointing an age-spotted hand. 'What now, Tarel? You have thrown away good troops for nothing!'

'Commander Clementh has assumed all responsibility for the debacle. She is imprisoned now in the cells below.'

'She is from a noble family . . .' Lord Kobay warned, his barrel stomach making his voice a low rumble, and he making the most of that.

'Oh, shut up, you idiot!' Lady Elaina snapped.

Torlo, the eldest of the Council of Elders by far, raised a frail thin hand for silence. 'Perhaps this dark mage she has enlisted with can be bought . . .'

'I doubt it,' Tarel answered. 'From all reports all he desires is power. But you are not too far from the mark, I think, Torlo.'

'Meaning what?' High Admiral Karesh asked.

'That this mage may be a weakness.'

Lady Elaina waved her disbelief. 'How so? Everyone agrees he is fearsome.'

Tarel nodded his agreement. 'Exactly. And mages are a notoriously envious and jealous breed. Many suffer no rivals. His growing repute has won him enemies.' He crossed his arms, peering right and left – *no turning back now*. 'And one has contacted me to let me know her willingness to confront the fellow.'

Torlo's already narrow gaze slit even more, making his resemblance to a carrion bird even greater. 'Who? And how much?'

Tarel crooked a smile; of course Torlo, the canny merchant, would immediately turn to money. He raised a hand in reassurance. 'I will get to that. As to costs, no cost at all. Just permission to meet him here.'

Lady Elaina clutched her wrinkled neck. 'Here! He is here?'

Tarel worked hard to keep his annoyance from his face – he wanted to bark at the old aristocrat: *Not* now, *you stupid hag!* Instead, he said through tight lips, 'When the time comes.'

'And that time?' the admiral asked.

Tarel nodded his gratitude for the question. The one to bring him to the issue of the night. He cleared his throat. 'When my sister invades.'

All four co-conspirators displayed their disbelief.

'All the admirals agree the Malazans are far from ready,' said Admiral Karesh. 'And wouldn't invade in any case. Everyone agrees they are much more likely to raid the mainland for funds and materiel.'

'My agents on the island report those pirates are busy doing just that,' supplied Lord Kobay.

Tarel waited for them to quieten then shook his head. 'You do not know my sister. She is utterly pitiless. She will come for me – I know this. And . . .' he pointed to all four, 'she will come for those who conspired against her as well.'

Lady Elaina regarded him and sighed. 'It is time to let her go, my king. She is nothing now. She has sold herself to these evil allies – imagine, an assassin and a dark mage! She is their creature now. A slave, no doubt.'

But Tarel knew he could not 'let her go'. Nor could he possibly convince these four of what he knew of her. None of them grew up in the royal household. None of them knew that the old king, his father, would lean to Sureth and murmur a name and later that man or woman would disappear, or suffer an accident, or be waylaid and murdered by brigands.

She had been his assassin from the start. The dagger in his right hand.

Yet no one ever saw it. Only he. Only watchful Tarel. *He'd* seen through her all along.

Which was why he struck first to take the throne. He had to. It was a question of self-preservation. So long as she lived, his life was worth a basket of rotting fish.

None of these gaping fools could possibly understand any of this.

He swept a hand before him. 'She is coming, and that is that. We must prepare. Therefore . . . with your permission . . .' He clapped his hands lightly, twice, and faced a corner of the murky room. 'A visitor.'

The darkness thickened to the blackness of wet ink. Lady Elaina gasped her dread of sorcery. Lord Kobay rumbled his unease. A burst of air came then, like a gust through a window. Dust blew about the room and the glasses on the table rattled.

Out of the murk stepped an aged woman in long loose robes. Her hair was a dramatic mane of greyish silver, her lined features sun-darkened to the hue of ancient wood. Her most striking feature, however, was her eyes. They flashed a silver light as if dusted in that precious metal.

Tarel held out a hand in invitation. 'Lords and ladies, may I introduce the Witch Jadeen, terror of south Itko Kan.'

The smile the witch gave in answer to that introduction could only be described as hungry.

* * *

Dancer did not mind the actual physical walk across the central plains; the gentle hills, small copses and tall grasses were pretty, as was the enormous sky with its horizon-to-horizon fronts of massed clouds passing overhead like the fabled sky-castles of the ancients.

Fabled no more, he reflected, as they'd found the shattered remains of one such in Shadow.

No, it was the uncertainty surrounding the errand that bothered him. Were they wasting their time? Could they simply wander for ever, pursuing a will-o'-the-wisp? Had Kellanved finally slipped over the edge into obsession and madness?

How could he discover the answers to any of these questions? Whom could he ask? Certainly not Kellanved.

So for three days they walked in relative silence on a roughly northward path, tracing the ever diminishing escarpment until it lay across the landscape as nothing more than a particularly steep hill. At nights he lay back to study the starred night sky – so much brighter here, far from the lights of any city. There was a delicacy and an intricacy in their arrangements he never would have guessed at before. Perhaps there was some credence after all to the astrologers' assertion that secrets lie hidden there among such complexity.

That third night he could restrain his unease no longer, and he cleared his throat, turning his head to regard his partner who sat now, hands atop his walking stick, studying the flames of their meagre fire. 'Do you even know what you are looking for?' he asked.

Kellanved did not stir – he might have been asleep for all Dancer knew – yet he answered readily enough, 'I'll know it when I see it.'

Such unhelpful answers were the main reason for Dancer's unwillingness to ask the maddening fellow any questions.

'We really should be heading back. We have no idea how far—'

'It is close,' the hunched mock-elder snapped. 'Close. I feel it.'

Dancer raised a brow; the man was rarely so touchy. Clearly he must be sharing something of his own

disquiet. So Dancer relented; he would push no further –
for now.

As winter was coming on, morning revealed a thick
misty ground fog. The blanket Dancer slept wrapped up
in carried a silvery lacing of frost. He rose to see Kellanved
still sitting hunched, hands atop the short walking stick.
'Kellanved?' he asked.

The lad's head jerked as he came awake, blinking.
'What?' Then his gaze slid aside, probing the rolling
fog, and he faced the east, standing. Now Dancer felt it
too; though no mage, his training had raised his senses
to a point where active Warren magics played upon his
nerves.

The fog was not entirely natural.

As if now aware of their regard, whoever lay behind
the deception let it slip away and the roiling banks
parted, fading, to reveal a band of Seti horsemen and
women, some twenty or so.

Their leathers and regalia were impressive. Wolf-tails
swung from the tops of raised spears; necklaces of wolf
and cat teeth hung at their necks. The foremost, the old-
est, rode a dappled grey mount. A thick cloak of white
fur draped his shoulders, and the tails of grey-white animals adorned a stone-headed mace cradled in his arms.

'Shadow mage,' this Seti elder called to them, 'did you
think your crossing of our lands would go unnoticed?'

Kellanved thoughtfully scratched his chin. 'Actually,
no – I didn't.'

'Then you are even more the fool than you appear.
You know you are not welcome here.'

Kellanved opened his arms wide. 'We are merely passing through. That is all.'

'Passing through?' the elder repeated, doubtingly.
'Passing through to what? There is nothing here for you

outlanders. No town or settlement. Only our plains, which only we seem to value.' He pointed the mace to the north. 'But perhaps you mean to travel to the mountains yonder and the fields of ice beyond. In which case, you are welcome to continue onward and good riddance to you.'

Kellanved tapped his walking stick to the ground, tilting his head. 'In truth, we are searching for something . . .'

Now the lean elder frowned suspiciously beneath his long grey moustaches. 'Searching for something? For what? A quick death?' He motioned with the mace and the war band spread out to either side, beginning to encircle them, spears lowered. 'You are not intending to meddle here with the resting place of the Great Goddess, are you? In which case you have earned your deaths.'

Dancer set his back to Kellanved and rested his hands on his heaviest parrying blades.

'And who will have given us our deaths?' Kellanved asked.

The elder nodded at the justice of the question. He pointed the mace to his chest. 'It is I, Imotan, shaman of the White Jackal, who judges. You outlanders push in upon us with impunity. And though we do all that we can to drive you from our lands, game becomes scarce. Hunger stalks our encampments. It is not how things used to be in my forefathers' time.' He extended the mace, pointing to Kellanved. 'Push us no longer, outlander. You may not like where we go.'

Kellanved raised his arms, walking stick in one hand. 'We are not here to trouble your lands, Imotan. But we are here searching for something.'

'And what might that be?'

'This.' Kellanved flicked his raised hand and the

brown flint spear-point appeared between thumb and forefinger.

The elder shaman stared for a moment, squinting, then he did something that made Dancer thoroughly uneasy. The man threw back his head and roared with laughter. And it did not end there; he continued laughing, even pressing the mace to his side as if in pain from his mirth. The rest of the troop joined in then, adding their scorn-tinged merriment.

Dancer and Kellanved shared a bemused look.

'I'm sorry,' Kellanved began, 'but perhaps you would care to enlighten us . . . ?'

Wiping his eyes, and still chuckling, Imotan waved an invitation for them to continue onward. 'Be our guests, little ones. Do quest onwards. Your efforts will be rewarded – I am certain of that.' He circled his mace in the air and the troop pulled away as one, cantering off. Imotan followed.

'But wait!' Kellanved called after them. 'What do you mean?'

'I guess he means us to find out,' Dancer mused as they watched the Seti riders diminish across the hillside.

'Yes. But find out *what*, hey?'

'That's what's worrying me.'

Kellanved eyed the spear-point. 'Well, it can't be too far. I'm fairly certain of that.'

'I like this even less now.'

The mage stabbed his walking stick to the ground, impatient. 'Yes, yes. We'll be careful.'

You mean I'll *be careful*, Dancer answered silently.

Kellanved set off, grumbling to himself. Dancer followed, now even more vigilant – scanning the surroundings, hands on his weapons. As the afternoon waned, he warned, 'Not much light left. We should halt for the day.'

Kellanved rolled his eyes in exaggerated vexation. '*Here?* But we are close! I'm certain.'

'All the more reason to wait till morning.'

'Really?'

Dancer gave a slow stern nod. The mage's skinny shoulders slumped.

'Oh – very well.' He sat unceremoniously in the grass.

'No fire tonight,' Dancer warned.

Kellanved slanted his walking stick so that he could set his chin upon it, and regarded Dancer through one cocked eye. 'There is no one nearby. I would sense it.'

'None the less.'

The mage snorted, glaring. Dancer ignored him, and scanned a full circle of the nearby hillsides. Perhaps there was no threat. Yet why the laughter? What did Imotan know that he and Kellanved did not? It was worrying.

A chill wind buffeted him and lashed the tall dry grasses. He reflected that for all its starkness, the land did hold a certain sort of harsh beauty. It was immense, seeming to stretch on for ever. Yet he did not feel diminished by it. In fact he rather felt at home. Which was strange, as he was city bred and born.

That night he slept poorly, jerking awake to see Kellanved still sitting, seemingly staring off into the distance – or fast asleep upright. At dawn's first light he rose, stretching and circling his arms for warmth. The two of them ate a cold meal of salted meat, dried bread and watered wine, then set off once more, the mage leading the way.

Their route took them to a broad crested hill and here Kellanved paused. 'The other side, I believe,' he whispered. Dancer nodded and the pair climbed. Before reaching the top they crouched among the tall windswept grasses to shimmy forward until they could see what lay beyond.

It was a broad valley that ran more or less east–west. A dried riverbed of pale gravel and stone wended its way down the centre.

'I see no one,' Dancer said.

Kellanved grunted his agreement. 'But it's *there* – whatever it is.'

'There's nothing there.'

The mage waved for silence. 'I tell you it's there. I can sense it.'

Dancer eyed his partner dubiously. He wondered once again whether something was wrong with the lad – that is, beyond all the wrongness he knew about already.

Kellanved's beady eyes slid to him and narrowed. 'Don't look at me that way.' And he rose, brushed the dust from his travel-worn jacket and trousers, and set off down the hillside.

Dancer followed, heavy daggers drawn, circling warily.

They reached the valley floor and still nothing had risen from the rocks or bushes to attack them; nor was there any structure or ruin in evidence. Clouds of dragonflies did arise, though, as they pushed through the grasses. Dancer mused that they must be the last of the season.

He kicked up against rocks hidden by the thick brush and stands of grass. Looking down, he noticed something else lying among the stones and picked it up.

It was a small stone arrowhead, knapped of dark flint.

He was incredulous. What might be the odds? On impulse, he showed it to Kellanved and was about to speak when the mage himself bent and lifted an object from the ground: it was a leaf-shaped spearhead as wide across as his hand.

Dancer halted in wonder, his words forgotten. Kellanved's gaze rose to his, wide and brimming with not only a similar wonder, but a strong colouring of dread.

The mage staggered off as if drunk. He stooped now and then, scooping up objects as he went, and his sputtering reached Dancer: 'How ... No! ... What is this? ... What ... ?'

Dancer let his arrowhead fall. It clattered among a litter of similar weapons and tools that lay among the larger rocks like a layer of fallen leaves that carried on even to the dried riverbed, and here he wandered, picking up a scraper, or a gouge, or what might be an awl. It was appalling, but it also struck him as strangely funny.

Somewhere out of sight Kellanved screamed his frustration and rage.

Dancer sat on a particularly large rock in the ancient riverbed and kicked at the clutter of knapped objects at his feet. Most were manufactured from some sort of native flint, but others shone a creamy white, like chalcedony, while a few gleamed blue-grey.

Eventually, the crunch of footsteps announced Kellanved's approach. Dancer looked up, not daring to speak; even the smallest hint of smugness or self-satisfaction from him would arouse an explosion of resentment from the fellow.

Kellanved held his walking stick behind his back in both hands. He was staring off into the distance as if unable to look at him. After a time he dipped his head and, taking a deep breath, announced, 'Very well. You were right. Let us return.'

Dancer couldn't imagine how much that admission must have cost the man. He nodded, gestured to the trove of countless tools surrounding them. 'It seems it just wanted to join its brethren here.'

But the mage was shaking his head. 'No, Dancer. You do not understand. Every one of these arrowheads and spear-points, scrapers and gouges – all were brought here by someone like us. All like us searching for something that *is* here – but isn't.' He continued shaking his head. 'It is a mystery. And whatever it is isn't in Shadow, either. I know, I checked.'

'Then it remains a mystery.'

Kellanved nodded his agreement. 'Yes. For now, it remains a mystery.'

Dancer rose, stretching. 'Well . . . it was worth a look, my friend.'

Kellanved winced as if pained, then hung his head. 'Let us leave this place.'

Chapter 6

IN THE MAIN HALL OF MOCK'S HOLD, MALAZ CITY, a battle raged back and forth across the central dining table. It shook and echoed from the thick tarred timbers that crossed the hall's ceiling and rattled its closed and locked doors.

At the long table where so many Malazan pirate admirals and captains once sat were now gathered Surly and the Napans who happened to be on the isle that day: Choss, Tocaras and Urko, together with Nedurian, Dujek, Jack, the mage Tayschrenn and the Dal Hon swordsman Dassem.

Nedurian sat in stunned silence, his brows rising higher and higher as the fight wore on unrelenting all through what was meant to be a dinner of consolidation and organization. He exchanged a look of amazement with Dassem at his side.

'No, I will not be the commander of this military,' Tocaras emphasized for the twentieth time.

'Then who?' Surly pushed once more. 'Give me a name.'

'Amaron,' Urko supplied.

Surly looked to the ceiling. 'He is not available for that.'

Urko jabbed a finger. 'Aha! So he *is* still alive!'

Surly's already sour expression deepened even further.

Nedurian noted that so far no one had offered the position to Urko.

Surly's impatient gaze shifted to Tayschrenn. 'And what have you to report? How goes the organization of our vaunted mage cadre?'

The lean Kartoolian cleared his throat, leaning back. 'Ah . . . well, the organization is that there's no organization.'

Surly pressed her hands to the table – its wood much scarred and abused by centuries of fights, stabbings, feuds and murders. 'Clarify,' she fairly snarled.

'We have agreed that there will be no encumbrance of a hierarchy, nor the awkward delaying hindrance of a chain of command. Each elected cadre mage will report directly to Kellanved, or any one of a very few chosen representatives.'

Nedurian couldn't resist leaning to the Kartoolian and murmuring, 'I like the positive light you cast that in . . .'

Tayschrenn shot him a glare.

'And these "chosen representatives"?' Surly enquired, brow arched. 'They are . . . ?'

The mage cleared his throat once more. 'Ah. So far? Well . . . myself.'

'I see. So, as command grade of one of our departments, you need a title.'

The young mage appeared rather taken aback by the suggestion. 'Well,' he managed, 'I suppose so . . .'

Surly's sour expression crooked upwards as she considered this. 'You are the highest of the mages – so to speak. So, you are the High Mage.'

Tayschrenn lifted a brow. 'Really? *High Mage?* You're going to—'

Surly rapped her glass to the table. 'Done.'

Tayschrenn pressed a hand to his head and slumped in his chair.

Nedurian elbowed him, murmuring, 'Congratulations!'

The mage pinched his brow, his expression pained. 'Gods please deliver me.'

Surly's narrowed gaze now shifted to Choss. 'You are the commander of our military then,' she announced.

With his long history of working with the woman, burly Choss merely waved a raised finger. 'No. Not me. I'm no commander.' He pointed to Dassem. 'The lads and lasses will follow this one, though.'

The swordsman, pale for a Dal Hon, shook his head. 'No. I am a swordsman. Not a general. I do not have the training.'

Her voice tight with impatience, Surly observed, 'No one here has the training or the experience.'

Into the following silence Urko leaned forward and said, 'I nominate Cartheron.'

Cartheron Crust, Nedurian knew, was currently at sea, coordinating the raiding.

Surly pursed her lips, considering.

'I second the proposal,' Tocaras quickly put in.

Surly nodded, and banged her glass to the table. 'Done. Cartheron is military commander.'

'And his title?' Urko asked, rubbing his hands together. 'Lord High Commander of All Armies?'

Tocaras threw his hands out. 'What armies?'

Urko appeared affronted. 'Well – mine's the Seventh.'

Surly pinched her brows again. 'You can't call your command the Seventh Army, Urko. We only have one.'

The huge fellow leaned back, crossing his thick arms. 'Seven is my lucky number – so my command is the Seventh.'

Surly exchanged a significant look with Choss and Tocaras then waved her acceptance. 'Fine. As you like.'

It occurred to Nedurian that Cartheron wasn't here – and only Cartheron had any influence over his gigantic brother.

Surly looked to the veteran Dujek. 'You have a command,' she told him.

Dujek rubbed a hand over his thinning hair then pointed to Jack next to him. 'This one has the officer training . . .'

Surly shook her head. 'Cartheron has expressed his confidence in you. So, for now you're in command.'

Dujek nodded. 'My thanks . . . ah, what do I call you, if I may ask?'

The woman appeared genuinely surprised by the question. She waved it aside. 'I prefer to work behind the scenes.'

'She's in charge of intelligence,' Tocaras put in. 'In command of the – what do they call themselves again?'

'The Claws,' Surly supplied, in a subdued voice.

'Right. The Claws.'

'So,' Urko pressed. 'Is there a title there?'

Surly eyed him for a long time without saying anything, until the big fellow cleared his throat and shrugged. 'Just asking. But what about Cartheron? Could we make him, like, the Munificent and Splendid Lord High Inspector General? Because he'd really want that, I'm sure.'

Leaning forward, Nedurian dared to offer, tentatively, 'In the Talian hegemony, the title would have been Sword of the Emperor.'

Surly studied him, and he felt himself shrinking under her evaluating gaze. 'How go things with the battle mages?' she asked.

Nedurian coughed to clear his throat. 'Well. We now

have as many middling talents, hedge-wizards, wind-callers and such as we want to assign to the ranks.' He didn't supply that this only happened after Agayla gave her tacit approval to his recruiting efforts.

'Infallible Highest Lord of All High?' Urko suggested.

Surly's hard gaze swivelled back to the giant Crust brother. 'We have Claws,' she said meditatively. 'Why not Fists? Fists for commanders rather than Swords. That would make Cartheron High Fist.'

Urko rubbed a paw across his chin, thinking, then he shrugged. 'Not nearly as embarrassing as I'd hoped, but it'll do.'

'And the sea-lord?' Choss asked.

'I will ask Admiral Nok,' Surly said. 'I believe he will accept.'

Nedurian blew out a breath. Admiral Nok! Last great Napan sea commander. The man had scuttled his vessel in defiance of Tarel's taking the throne and been in hiding all this time. Through her corps of messengers and intelligence agents – these Claws – Surly must be in communication with him.

The lean woman nodded at that, as if in conclusion. 'That about covers it, I believe. Unless anyone has any other issues to raise?' No one spoke. 'Very good. Then this meeting is adjourned. I suggest we all have work to do.' And she pushed back her chair, rising.

Everyone rose with her, bowing.

The Napans went their separate ways, but Dujek, together with his young aide Jack, lingered behind with Tayschrenn and Nedurian. The Kartoolian mage eyed Nedurian speculatively, then said, 'You are a veteran of the military – are you as appalled by all this as I expect you must be?'

Nedurian blew out a breath, surprised by such frankness. In truth, he had been shocked by the chaos and disorganization. But in another way he was reassured, as he saw no blind dumb blowhard aristocrat striving to take control of things, as had been a problem in the later Talian hegemony. Surly was obviously brutally efficient, while Kellanved's partner, this assassin Dancer, also struck him as no fool.

'Everyone has to start somewhere,' he offered diplomatically.

The High Mage's answering smile was one of amusement – guarded amusement. 'Indeed.'

'And what about you?' Dujek asked Nedurian. 'No command?'

He waved a hand, demurring. 'I've had my fill of that, thank you. I'll help get things rolling, then I'll take a position in some regiment or company.'

'In my command, I hope,' Dujek said, slapping his shoulder.

They exited the hall, Nedurian heading for Rampart Way, and the long walk down into town. He reflected that all this concern about military command would have been funny if it weren't so pressing and dire – as Malaz Island had no military to speak of.

Oh, there were fighting men and women aplenty; an entire isle of them. But an army? No, that was something else entirely, as he knew full well, having seen the most organized and regimented example of recent times close up.

His duty, then, was to do everything he could to help these fledgling soldiers have a fair chance on the field.

Footsteps behind brought him up short and he turned to see the Dal Hon swordsman Dassem. He nodded a greeting, which the wiry youth returned sombrely, as was his manner.

For a time they walked together in silence. Nedurian enjoyed the cool wind and the view over the harbour. Most vessels, he noted, were still out on raids. Then he looked at the swordsman. 'Tayschrenn asked me if I was dismayed after what we witnessed in there. What of you? Any second thoughts?'

The youth shrugged his enviably wide shoulders. 'Hood directed my footsteps here. That is enough for me. As for the personal foibles or inadequacies of any of these people, all that is irrelevant. I am reminded of a story I heard of a duellist in Unta who was considered very boring and dull in his style. He possessed no flair or inspiration – no, how do you say, panache. Everyone mocked him and looked down upon him for it. Yet in bout after bout he emerged victorious. He simply ground down his opponents.'

Nedurian nodded expectantly. 'And so . . . ?'

Dassem waved a hand. 'And so, what appears as a weakness may in fact prove a strength. No one can know until contact with one's opponent is made.'

Nedurian allowed himself a half-smile, and continued down the stone steps. 'Well . . . to my mind a good dose of preparation wouldn't hurt.'

'Our thinking,' murmured Dassem, 'runs on similar lines, I believe.'

Nedurian scratched the scar down his cheek; it always itched in the cold. 'Oh?'

The dark youth eyed him sidelong. 'Tell me of the famous Talian military. What in your opinion worked, and what did not?'

* * *

121

The crossing to the Isle of the Blessed was a boggy stretch of tidal mudflats exposed a few hours a day at each low tide. Heboric waited patiently for the tide to go out, along with a shabby gathering of sick and crippled who sat wrapped in their tattered remnants of clothes on the sands. Some rocked themselves in silent misery, others jabbered insanely to no one. For a time the more hale of them had pawed at Heboric, begging for food or coin, but seeing how the man merely brushed aside their reaching hands, all diseased and rotting, some flowing with pus, the beggars turned away in disgust – no coin could be cadged from this one, even if he bore the mark of a priest of Fener.

Once the waters of the bay became low enough, the day's gathering of penitents pushed out into the waves. The passage was difficult; some became trapped in the heavy clinging mud. These, the most infirm, called out to their fellows for aid but the passing file, all struggling through the muck, ignored them.

Save for Heboric, who slogged over to the nearest and heaved him free. The man promptly pulled a rusted blade from his clay-smeared rags, demanding, 'All your coin, fool!'

Heboric gestured down his naked torso to his sodden loincloth. 'I wear only this wrap, friend – but you are free to search it if you wish.'

The hunched pilgrim flinched from him and floundered away, snarling, 'What are you? Some kind of freak?'

Heboric watched him go, amusement crooking his mouth.

'The sick are ever selfish,' another voice called from farther away, and Heboric turned. A slim hooded form, wrapped in tattered lengths of dirty rags, stood in the waves some distance off.

'Not all,' Heboric answered.

This one tilted his, or her, head in acquiescence. 'True. But none of those will you find on the Isle of the Blessed.'

Heboric glanced to the island rising just a few leagues distant. The other struggled onwards to join him. 'And what of you?' he asked the stranger.

'I am as selfish as any other,' the figure answered, closer now, and from her voice Heboric knew her for a woman. 'Those,' she added, 'who claim not to be selfish are usually lying.'

Heboric nodded his agreement. 'True. Those who find it necessary to make the *claim*.'

'And you?' the woman rejoined.

Grinning his frog-like lopsided grin, Heboric gestured to his naked form. 'As you see, I have spent a lifetime acquiring enormous wealth.'

She looked him up and down. 'Well, I see that you are at least rich in faith. What errand brings a priest of Fener to Poliel's house?'

Heboric lost his grin and slogged onward, his pace slow to accommodate the woman at his side. 'This plague. It is unlike our sister of sickness. Its touch seems . . . different. I would ask about that, and other things.'

'And you expect answers?'

He shook his head, chuckling. 'Do I look that much a fool? No, I can only ask. That is all we mortals can do – make the effort. Try. The rest is in the hands of the gods.' He extended a hand to her. 'And you?'

She lifted her rag-wrapped shoulders. 'The truth is the island is my home. It is one of the few places I am welcome.'

Heboric nodded at that. Where else might the afflicted go? 'Yet you would leave it?'

'I am not yet ready to let go of the world.'

'I am told none leave the Isle of the Blessed.'

The woman cocked her wrapped head. Only her eyes peered through, brown and large, and Heboric found them very attractive eyes indeed. 'Well,' she allowed, 'that is at least poetic.'

He smiled. 'Yet isn't it dangerous for you? I mean . . .' Heboric realized he was treading into uncomfortable ground. 'That is, some people would fear you as a carrier . . .'

She nodded. 'Some do throw rocks and garbage to drive me away. Some have attacked me with staffs and rods.' She shrugged again, conveying equanimity. 'But they are not the worst. The worst are those who ask how much for sex.'

Heboric coughed into a fist, quite taken aback. 'Sex? Really? I mean . . . not that you are no longer . . . that is . . .'

She rescued him from his floundering, saying, 'It is believed in some circles that sex with an afflicted will make the partner immune.'

Heboric nodded his understanding. 'Ah . . . I see. But that is absurd.'

'Yes. Just like the other belief that sex with a virgin will cure various illnesses, or make the partner younger.'

'*That* I've heard of,' Heboric commented, shaking his head.

They had reached the island and climbed a shore of black gravel. Here stood ramshackle huts of sea-wrack and hides. A few small cookfires smouldered about. The inhabitants of the huts scrambled away as they approached, limping, some crawling on no more than stumps. Heboric wondered if they were fleeing in shame.

'Why do they hide?' he asked his companion.

'They are frightened of you,' she answered. 'You are obviously strong and healthy. They fear you are here to

124

take from them what little they have.' She gestured ahead with a hand that may have been wrapped in dirty linen but was quite obviously nothing more than a knot of bone. 'This way to the house of Poliel.'

They climbed a path of beaten dirt. Crude shrines and altars lined the way, no more than piled stones draped in ragged scarves or covered in wax from countless candles. One larger shrine, tall and humped, like a hood, was obviously dedicated to the god of death. Heboric gestured to it, surprised. 'Hood?'

'The Grey One is no stranger to this isle,' she said, passing on.

They came to a narrow gorge between two tall cliffs pocketed by caves. Again the inhabitants scurried away before them, all bent and limping, some on crude crutches of sticks. It was as if, Heboric mused, he carried the plague or some such thing.

'This is not the reception I was expecting,' he told the woman.

'We are not yet at the house. Come.' She urged him onwards.

Uneasy, but unable to pin down his suspicions, he followed, warily. The path led to a wide valley, cultivated with fields. Workers, perhaps the more healthy of the isle's inhabitants, could be seen hoeing and scraping the stony soil. Beyond rose a structure of dressed bluish native stone – the Temple of Poliel, goddess of pestilence and illness.

The woman calmly walked on and Heboric was beginning to suspect that he had fallen in with one of the priestesses of the house. 'I will be welcome?' he asked. 'I do not wish to trespass.'

'All visitors to this isle are welcome. You may make your petition before the altar.'

He bowed to the woman. 'Thank you. You have some authority here, I take it?'

The woman paused as if surprised. Her liquid brown eyes regarded him with humour. 'Some.' She urged him on with the hand that was no more than a stump.

The entry to the Temple of Poliel possessed no door; it stood as an open archway of stone. Shabby ragged figures lined each wall, every one of them hardly more than bundles of sticks. Outstretched arms ending in bone or rotting pus-filmed flesh beseeched Heboric. He could not help but cringe from them as he and his escort passed up the hall between.

Another, inner archway opened on to a broad central courtyard paved in stone. Across its expanse rose the central sanctum, tall and domed, the dwelling of Poliel herself. The woman paused in the archway, gesturing ahead. 'Here the children of Poliel once congregated, having sworn pilgrimage to her presence. Now it stands empty, awaiting the devoted.'

Sighing, she turned to continue on and Heboric followed. 'Passage to the isle is difficult,' he suggested.

'No more so now than before.'

Again, a third entranceway stood as an open undoored arch. A pillared hall, thick with hanging layers of incense, lay before them. Here, at least, sat a crowd of worshippers. And within the enclosed space, despite the cloying scented incense, the rank stink of rotting flesh and voided fluids was enough to make Heboric pause and determinedly force down the rising gorge of his stomach.

The woman at his side, however, walked forward without pause. She stepped over huddled shapes, either dead or near to it; Heboric could not tell as he followed her. They approached the altar and its shape both fascinated and repelled him, for it was carved in a human form, slightly larger than life, reclining, yet contorted in agony – presumably the agony of a deathly illness.

He turned to ask what next of the presumed priestess, but she walked on, climbed the dais, settled herself languidly upon the starvation-hollowed stomach of the humanoid altar, set chin on stump, and silently regarded him. Amusement now played openly upon her large brown eyes.

Quite chagrined, Heboric fell to one knee, then, thinking better of that, went even further to lie flat upon his stomach, offering full obeisance despite the sticky layer of dried blood and other bodily evacuations upon the stones.

'And what,' asked the goddess, 'can Poliel do for Heboric, chosen of Fener?'

He slowly rose, but kept his gaze downcast. 'O goddess, I believe I have been quite frank. You know what I wish.'

'Indeed you have been quite frank. And so too shall I be. You are correct in surmising that this most recent affliction shares no origins with me.'

'Then . . . who? If I may ask.'

'Another.'

'Another,' he repeated. 'I . . . see. Why? I mean, who would dare?'

'Why? A demonstration, no doubt.'

'A demonstration. I see. To what end – if I dare ask.'

'To what end? Why, power, of course.'

'Power. And your answer to this?'

'I am . . . considering.'

A wave of dizziness took Heboric then, and he pressed a hand to his brow, finding it hot and sweaty. He suddenly felt quite poorly. 'Apologies, m'lady,' he stammered, 'but I feel . . . unwell.'

The goddess eased out of the throne and came down to him. 'You have been too long in my presence.' She brushed one rotted remnant of a hand across his forehead and pain lanced him there. He weaved upon his feet, hardly able to stand.

'You have been marked for a great fate, Heboric,' she murmured. 'And I admit I was curious to meet you. The next step in that fate may be found in Li Heng. Try to remember that, Heboric. Heng. For if you recall anything else of this audience, you will dismiss it as a fever dream.

'Now,' she breathed, 'you must go.' She touched the tip of one diseased finger to his forehead and an explosion of agony blasted him into darkness.

He awoke lying in the wash of waves. He pushed himself up on one arm and promptly vomited up the thin contents of his knotted stomach. Groaning and wiping his mouth, he peered about, groggy.

He was on the mainland shore of the shallow crossing to the Isle of the Blessed. He must have passed out when some sort of sickness took him. He pressed a hand to his fever-hot brow. What a fool he'd been, thinking of attempting that pestilential isle! Who knew what contagion or disease surrounded it? Obviously, something of its fetid air had already infected him before he'd even managed the crossing.

A timely lesson, he decided. His arrogance may yet be the undoing of him.

The hermit ascetics in the hills south of Li Heng – that was where he should go. They had dedicated their lives to religious study. If he were to find any answers, it would be there – not here on this island of the wretched. Merely being ill didn't make you holy!

He strove to rise to his feet, paused, then clutched his

stomach as his bowels exploded in a hot wet gush. He sank back into the frigid water, whimpering.

* * *

Orjin Samarr was at his usual post on the south catwalk peering gloomily over the pointed logs of the fire-treated palisade wall when a messenger came scrambling up the ladder, followed by his escort, Terath.

The squat hill-man touched his brow, bowing his head. 'M'lord, forward scouts have them sighted. Their van is entering the pass.'

Orjin rubbed his unshaven cheeks. 'About bloody time.' He squinted up to the high slopes. 'Four days? Who in Hood's name is in charge over there?' He nodded to the messenger. 'That's captain, by the way. My regards to Prevost Jeral. Remember – the baggage train! Hit the train.'

The hill-man touched his brow once more. 'Yes, captain, m'lord,' then he scrambled off.

Orjin eyed Terath dubiously. 'What are they up to?'

The Untan duellist drew off her helmet and ran a hand through her brush-cut sweaty hair. Orjin thought her very handsome but for her habitual expression of sour disapproval of everything before her. 'Taking their time,' she judged.

'Damned foolish decision.'

'In your view,' she answered; she was second in command, officer-trained, and saw it as her duty to test her commander's views. 'They think these forces beaten already. Why rush?'

He shrugged. 'Gives the enemy time to organize.'

'You don't understand, Orjin. They don't consider the Purge military a real threat.'

He regarded the south once more. 'Well,' he mused, 'I'm not of Purge.'

'That's for sure. You're from some rotten little fishing village, right?'

'I wouldn't even call it a village.' He gestured her to her post. 'Looks like a dusk attack. Get everyone ready.'

The Untan duellist saluted smartly, hand to chest. 'Aye aye.' Watching her go, Orjin wondered once again what might have taken her from Unta; clearly she missed the city, her friends and family. Her silences and obvious discomfort when talk among Orjin's troop came to love interests – who was currently chasing or pining for whom – made him suspect that an unhappy romance was involved in her quitting the city.

It certainly wouldn't be the first time a bad love affair had driven someone to run away and join the military, mercenary company or not.

As for himself, well, it was hard growing up in a hamlet you could throw a fish across. Especially for anyone with a dollop of wanderlust. It hadn't taken him long to sail across to the mainland and dive into the only thing he was ever good at – fighting.

Jeral's hill-folk were accurate in their estimate; soon after they disappeared the first of the Quon Talian mounted scouts appeared, investigating the valley. Orjin made no secret about his occupation of the Two-River Fort. His troops on the walls watched the Quon Talians ride by on their way further down-valley.

Next came the foremost elements of the force's van: light cavalry followed by loose parties of skirmishers and light infantry.

The infantry surrounded the fort, just outside

bowshot, and squatted down to wait. Orjin knew what they were waiting for – orders from higher up.

He saw the main force long before he heard it; three dark columns appeared high in the pass to come crawling down – the famed Talian medium and heavy infantry. Cavalry flanked the columns, kicking up clouds of thin snow that rose like banners in the winds.

Orjin's worried gaze climbed to the bare rocky slopes overlooking the valley but saw no sign of anyone; nor was there any alarm or excursion from the invading force betraying detection of Jeral's troops.

He did a quick calculation of numbers and came up with close to thirty thousand. His brows rose: damn, they meant it this time. Troops enough to quell and control Purge. This was no quick punitive excursion. It looked as though the Quon Talians were coming to stay.

No wonder it had taken four days to pull together.

Still – not the way *he'd* have done it.

While Orjin and his troops watched from the palisades, more and more Quon Talians settled in to surround them. As the medium infantry arrived, the lights quit to continue on down the valley.

All this took most of the day. And still not one bow had been shot in anger; the investiture was handled in a very professional manner. Eventually, very late in the afternoon, a mounted delegation of ten approached the closed front gates. Here Orjin met them on the wall, together with Terath and Arkady – the Wickan scowling ferociously, his hands tight on the antler grips of the curved long-knives sheathed across his chest.

Terath noticed Arkady's fierce expression and murmured to him, 'I see you have your war-face on.'

He answered from the side of his mouth, 'There's a damned lot of them.'

Once the ten were close enough, one of their number called out: 'Hail, Fort Two-River!'

'Hail, invaders,' Orjin answered.

The spokesman was a lean older fellow, in a mail coat set with larger plates of iron at his chest and upper and lower arms. He undid the strap of his helmet and pushed it up his head until it sat high above his brow, then he started pulling at the fingers of his leather gloves. 'To whom am I speaking?' he called.

'Someone who asks that you pack up your dog and pony act and go.'

That got a small smile. The fellow leaned forward from the cantle of his high saddle, gloves dangling in one hand. 'Come, come. Don't be coy. You are obviously no Purge or Nom officer. Who are you?'

'Who in Hood's name are you?' Orjin called back.

The fellow nodded. 'Fair enough. I am Commander Renquill of the Quon Talian Legion. And you?'

'Orjin Samarr, in the queen of Purge's service.'

The fellow ducked his head once more. 'Ah. I have heard of you.' He gestured about with his gloves, and, leaning forward even further, asked, 'What in Burn's mercy do you think you are doing here?'

'I'm about to kick a lot of pissant Talians off Purge territory.'

Renquill peered about at his infantry circumvallating the fort. 'I'm told you can't have more than a few hundred in there,' he called.

Orjin's long grey hair blew about and he pulled a hand through it to drag it back. 'More than enough to beat you arselickers.'

Again the thin smile. 'I see your game.' He sighed. 'Very well. You've made your point. How much do you want? How much to go away?'

At that question, Terath, at Orjin's side, snarled and jerked forward as if about to jump the wall, a hand going to one of her swords.

'You lot packed up and headed back south would do it,' he answered.

Renquill shook his head in regret. 'Foolish.' He turned to the officer next to him. 'Keep them in there until the only thing left to eat is each other.' The officer bowed his acceptance. Renquill pulled his gloves back on, calling up, 'I'd like to stay and have you put down like the dog that you are, but I can't have you holding us up, now can I?'

The party turned and cantered away.

Orjin yelled after them: 'Who's the damned dog slinking off now, hey!' But the commander merely waved negligently over his shoulder, apparently big enough to ignore Orjin's proddings. He muttered to Terath, 'Well, that didn't work. I guess we'll have to see what Jeral can cook up.'

'If she's still out there,' she commented darkly.

'She's still sending messengers. They're even sweeping together broken elements of the Purge army up there.'

As the hours passed, the Quon Talian main force continued its march northwards, filing by the fort. Orjin's lieutenant, Arkady, made a circuit of the walls and reported back, 'I make it some seven hundred surrounding us.' He glowered, his long moustaches fairly bristling. 'That's a damned insult.'

Orjin raised a placating hand. 'It's all right. They don't know who they're dealing with – yet.'

All they could do now was wait. For him this was the hardest part of any engagement. Where he had control he was at ease; where he had no control he was unbearable. And so he stood the wall as the hours passed, thinking, reviewing his choices. What more could he have done? Every twelve hours he'd sent messengers northward to the Purge commanders, informing them of his preparations – and the enemy's deployment. Now, he had only to wait. Would they respond and send a contending force? Or had they already pulled back to Purage, reconciled to a siege? For Orjin, these unknowns were more uncomfortable than a dose of the clap.

Though he burned to know what was going on high in the pass, he kept a northward post, watching the Quon Talian forces marching onward; it wouldn't do for the Talians to wonder why everyone in the fort was eyeing the south with such anticipation.

Towards sundown word came from Terath that the baggage train was now descending the pass. He clenched the logs before him, rocking, forcing himself to remain. Now came the gamble. Would Jeral take this opportunity to hit the invader? That at least was his reading of her. She'd struck him as a fighter, not a runner.

After an agonizing wait in which he absolutely decided that she'd betrayed him, then flipped to grant her more time, then changed his mind again a dozen times over, gasps of awe – and a good deal of relief – sounded from his troops scanning the south. He turned, squinting into the purpling distance. Everyone was shouting now, and pointing high to the pass far above, even the surrounding Talian forces.

It all unfurled in breathtaking silence at first. Boiling clouds of snow descending not one but both slopes of the pass simultaneously, closing in on the ant-like file of the army baggage train like the twin arms of a vengeful god. Orjin was staggered by the scale of it; he'd expected a few falling rocks and logs, not this complete sweeping of the high slopes. It occurred to him that the witches and shamans of the hill-folk must have thrown their weight behind it.

Then the thunder of the avalanches hit his chest, momentarily drowning out the appalled cries of the surrounding Talians and the cheers of his troops. Terath appeared at his side, flushed and panting from running across the enclosure. 'What now?' she bellowed.

A massive storm of snow now utterly obscured the pass. The Quon Talian train – all the supplies, the support, the wagons with their teams of oxen, horses and donkeys gathered for the coming campaign – must have been obliterated. The catwalk of the log palisade juddered and shook beneath him; the very wall rocked as in an earthquake.

He peered round at the halted ranks of the invaders, the thousands upon thousands of backward-staring infantry, no doubt enraged by the attack, and nodded to his lieutenant.

'This is a far greater blow than I'd hoped for. I'm thinking we're about to be overrun. Time to head for the hills.'

She jerked a nod and ran to spread the order. Orjin waved his troops off the north wall and pointed to the east. They'd scale over and make a run to join Jeral.

Opposition was determined but thin. Orjin's command broke through the encirclement and charged on. The Quon Talians were slow to react; they seemed completely stunned by the scale of the catastrophe. By the time mounted skirmishers were sent after them they'd reached a wooded slope and then it was too late. From there on they loped upwards, always searching out higher ground. When it became too dangerous to continue climbing in the dark Orjin ordered a halt.

They hid among tall boulders, their breath pluming in

the cold night air. The most canny veterans among them always carried travelling blankets and these they wrapped about their shoulders, keeping watch through the night.

No pursuit appeared chasing after them; no files of torch-carrying infantry poking among the rocks. The lights they could see bobbed up and down the pass: this commander fellow, Renquill, was rightly concentrating on searching through the wreckage choking the pass, salvaging what troops and equipment he could.

Orjin leaned up against a great granite boulder, unlit kaolin pipe between his teeth, his hair blowing about his face. He watched the torches and lanterns moving like tiny fireflies.

Yune came to his side. He nodded to the high slopes. 'The pass is well nigh unusable now. If we cross over we'll be stuck on the wrong side for the winter.'

'A small force could make it back.'

The Dal Hon elder pursed his wrinkled lips. 'Perhaps.'

'And there's always the coast.'

The shaman gave a snort. 'Too many days.' Orjin nodded his agreement.

'What are you planning?' Arkady asked, his dark gaze narrowing suspiciously.

Orjin studied his pipe. 'We'll see on the morrow.'

The Wickan bared his teeth in a savage grin to show that, knowing his commander, whatever it might be it would no doubt involve a fight.

With the dawn a pink light came crawling down the westward slopes and Orjin awoke where he sat leaning up against a rock. A rime of frost glittered on his vambraces and gauntlets and he groaned, straightening his arms and legs. He rubbed and thumped his chest to warm up.

Once everyone was kicked awake they headed up-slope once more. They kept to the thinning woods, seeking what cover they could. Orjin was worried about Quon Talian archers, but no sudden salvo came rattling down among them from the sky.

The valley wall steepened and the pine gave way to brush, lichen, and tufts of sharp grasses. They scrambled up on all fours now, seeking the crest of the wall. The wind was much stronger here, cutting through Orjin's cloak, his cuirass of laminated iron bands, and even the quilted and padded hauberk of layered linen and cotton wadding beneath. He shuddered at the biting cold, so high and exposed. From this elevation the Talian troops still digging among the avalanche now appeared to be the ants.

A light flashed in the corner of his vision and he peered higher. There, among the uppermost teeth of the ridge-line, a light blinked – sunlight reflected to them. Terath now pointed, and he nodded. Hill-folk scouts arrived shortly thereafter and guided them to Jeral's position high above.

Here, amid bare granite and a howling wind, they met. Orjin gave the Nom aristocrat a hug. 'Well done.'

She shrugged. 'It was your plan.'

He pulled his long wind-whipped hair from his face. 'How many have you cobbled together?'

She gave a mischievous grin. 'Near four thousand sur-vivors of the battle have come to us.' He grunted, impressed; more than he'd dared hope for. 'Now we hit them from above, don't we,' she said, her eager grin widening.

He shook his head. 'No.'

The grin faltered and she frowned, confused. 'No? Why ever not? They're in disorder, disheartened. They may even break.'

He continued shaking his head. 'No. We may win that one battle. Maybe even the next. But there're too many. We can't beat that army.'

The frown became a scowl of disapproval. 'I'm not scurrying back to Purage.'

It was Orjin's turn to grin, chidingly. 'You were planning to four days ago.'

She almost blushed, looking away. 'That was ... before.'

He raised a hand, waving aside his remark. 'Don't worry. We won't be withdrawing.'

'Then what?'

In answer, he peered down the long broad slopes of the south side of the pass to the misted green farmlands, fields, and hills below that led onward to Quon Talian lands. 'They've invaded Purge territory, prevost, so I intend to return the favour. We will march south, and burn and loot and destroy until their barons and burghers howl for the return of their army to drive us out.' He shifted his gaze to her. 'What say you, Prevost Jeral?'

The Purge officer's eyes had grown huge. 'Invade Quon Talian lands with only four thousand?'

Orjin nodded. 'We'll keep moving, burning everything before us until they squeal for Renquill to come chase us down.'

The woman's mischievous grin slowly climbed anew and she took hold of her thick braids, one in each hand. 'I'm with you, Captain Samarr.'

Chapter 7

AFTER SIX DAYS OF CONTINUOUS MARCHING – pursuing the shifting forces of Gris and its diminishing allies – the army of the Bloorian League reached a halt. Gregar was beyond caring by this point. He knew they'd doubled back upon themselves at least twice while the opposing knights and nobles jostled and manoeuvred for an advantageous field position. He was so foot-sore and tired all he wanted to do was sleep.

This morning he had his wish, as no order to break camp rousted them before the dawn. Later, however, a Yellows trooper stuck his head into their tent and announced, 'This looks like it.'

'I don't give a shit,' Gregar groaned from his heaped straw and ratty blankets.

'Now you're getting it,' Leah called from across the tent.

The drums to muster came soon after. Before pushing aside the flap of the tent Gregar made certain of the rag wraps at his feet, legs, and hands against the cold. Haraj appeared then, dragging himself from his blanket; the skeletally lean fellow looked even worse for wear than he.

'This ain't the life for you,' Gregar told him.

Haraj nodded dejectedly. 'Maybe we'll see them today,' he croaked, coughing.

'Who?'

'What do you mean, who? The Crimson Guard, of course.'

Gregar pulled the lad outside with him. 'Let's try to get something to eat.' As they walked, he whispered, fierce, 'No more talk about the Guard, okay? Everyone would laugh.'

'You still want to join though, right?'

Gregar winced, and peered round to make certain no one was within hearing. 'Look – it was a dream, okay? Just a dream. Now it's time to grow up. You should go, though. This isn't for you.'

The skinny youth shivered and coughed anew. 'They'll take you, I'm sure.'

Gregar shook his head ruefully. 'Thanks, but things like that just don't happen.'

They joined a line, and when they reached the front a portion of hard bread was thrust at them. They returned to their squad's tent, gnawing on the rations. Haraj had been eyeing him, and now he said, 'I don't think I'll make it on my own.'

Gregar sighed. *He's right about that.* 'Fine. You got me out of Gris – I'll get you to them.'

'Thanks.'

Leah was waiting outside the tent, glaring. 'Where have you two been? Get your gear. Marching orders.'

Haraj sagged. 'Not more marching.'

Leah snapped up a spear. 'Marching to battle this time. Let's go.'

Gregar's regiment was formally the Second Yellows; he and Haraj were assigned to the Fourth Company, Seventh Lights. While Baron Ordren of Yellows formally commanded, the noble considered such duties to be beneath him as they would take him away from his beloved cavalry, so direct command fell to a veteran soldier, a commoner, Captain Rialla of Bloor. Sergeant Teigan ran the Fourth Company, and the colours Gregar carried were those of the Fourth.

Once a column was formed, Teigan handed Gregar the tall pike with its limp yellow banner secured just behind its iron dagger-like head. Then the sergeant marched them to their field position, which proved to be a hillock in a broad meadow between two steeper forested hills. He had the company spread in lines four deep to block any path across the clearing.

Down-slope before them lay the agreed upon field of battle proper – a wide stretch of pasture and meadow with a meagre stream winding between. Only a few small copses and a couple of wretched crofters' thatched hovels looked to impede the nobles' charges. Early morning mist pooled in the lowlands and lay like banners across fields. Regiments raised by other Bloorian nobles, such as those of Larent and Netor, marched in column to their positions. The early slanting morning light flashed from spearheads and helmets, while the nobles trotted their mounts to marshalling grounds. Gregar had to admit they were a pretty lot in their mail coats and leggings, and long flowing tabards. Far away, close to a distant treeline, the Grisian forces arranged themselves into lines and massed cavalry as well.

On the left flank a swift column of cavalry caught his eye. Long pennants of a dark red flowed above them as they charged to a new position, and from those rippling banners flashed silver as well – the colours of the Crimson Guard.

Too far off, and moving too fast anyway.

In the Fourth's lines, Gregar was standing front and

141

centre with his pike and he considered their position far too exposed. When Teigan paced by, inspecting the lines, he called to the sergeant, 'Shouldn't we form square?'

The sergeant swung round, his thick black brows rising. 'Oho – got us a regular military scientist amongst us.' He halted, hands on hips, just in front of Gregar. 'Graduated from the officer academy, did you? Years of soldiering experience, have you?' Several in the lines sniggered at the suggestion.

Gregar just gave him a look. He motioned to the lines. 'What are we supposed to be doing here? Watching?'

'Our orders are to deny this particular staging area to the enemy and cover our betters should they rally here.' He looked Gregar up and down. 'Is that acceptable or would you like more honey on that?'

'So what do we do if the Grisians try to take the hill?'

Teigan motioned to the pike's top. 'You poke them with that pointy end until they fall down.'

Several in the lines nearby laughed. Gregar gave them all a sneering smile. *Very funny.*

Teigan moved on, saying, 'Just stand your ground and they'll veer off – trust me.'

Gregar watched him go, glowering, teeth clenched against what he'd like to say.

'Doesn't matter anyway,' Leah murmured from behind. 'We're just a sideshow. The nobles'll decide things among themselves. They're not gonna risk wounding their warhorses. Them beasts are worth way more than us.'

'I thought you said the knights enjoyed riding us down.'

'Ah. Well, only when they've got nothing better to do.'

Gregar turned to her; she looked too unhappy to be mocking. *Wonderful.*

Though possessing something of a privileged position from which to watch the proceedings, Gregar didn't have the training or experience to really know what he was seeing. Massed cavalry of mailed knights and petty nobles shifted about, perhaps seeking some sort of advantage. Lightly armoured skirmishers from both sides flowed about the field, harassing one another. At one point a column of archers came hurrying through the Fourth's lines on their way to a new position. Green cloth strips tied to their arms or round their necks identified them as Bloorians. They were a poor and scruffy lot indeed, in ragged shirts and pants – some were even barefoot.

In his outfit at least everyone had some sort of footgear, be it plain sandals, like his and Haraj's. Thinking about it though, and peering round, Gregar had to admit that few possessed even one item of armour; most wore quilted cloth jackets stuffed with straw. A few, such as Leah, wore a soft leather hauberk, plain, or sewn with bronze rings. So he supposed those poor Bloorian archers were only a touch scruffier than they.

A distant rumbling of hooves announced two larger masses of mounted knights and nobles closing upon each other. These two misshapen groups milled about one another in a moving savage scrum. This free-for-all scrimmage then overran a nearby regiment of infantry and the poor sods who failed to scatter like geese went down beneath the horses' hooves. Gregar was beginning to comprehend Leah's dire warnings.

This mounted boiling melee roiled on randomly across the field, leaving behind in the churned mud fallen and trampled bodies. Infantry from both sides harried its edges, and each other.

Watching the maces and axes rising and falling freely,

143

the mounts crashing into one another, Gregar allowed that at least these nobles knew their one and only trade – fighting.

Hooves crashing the ground behind their position brought Gregar and everyone round. A small group of knights was bearing down upon them from the rear. The Fourth scrambled to reverse, spears and pikes clattered into one another, a few panicked soldiers even tripped and fell. Teigan was bellowing non-stop, taking troopers by their shoulders and yanking them into position.

As the cavalry closed, the sergeant threw up his hands and ordered, 'Make way! Make way for our lords!' The Yellows troopers hesitantly parted and the ten knights reined in. 'Guard the perimeter!' Teigan then bellowed, and he took hold of the jesses of one mount, soothing the horse. 'How goes the day, Lord Gareth?' he asked.

This knight had seen fighting. His mount was steaming with sweat and was dappled in blood. His jupon was torn to rags about his mail coat; it might have once been a bright festive orange. The flanged mace hanging at his side was wet with blood and gore, even what looked like a tuft of human hair. He drew off his helmet and set it on the saddle's pommel. He was an older fellow, his long sweat-matted hair shot with grey, his beard tied off in two long braided rat-tails. 'The day goes well – so far. Damned thirsty work, sergeant. Have you any drink among you?'

'Drink!' Teigan barked. 'Drink for Lord Gareth!' A water skin was handed up to the fellow, who took a long pull then tossed it back to Teigan.

All this time the other knights constantly eyed the surroundings, their war-axes, picks and maces readied in their mailed hands. Gregar realized that these knights were a bodyguard, or the personal household troop of this Lord Gareth.

'May Togg and Fanderay watch over you today, m'lord,' Teigan said, releasing the mount.

Gareth put his open-faced helmet back on, chuckling. 'And Fener too, hey?' He heeled his mount and took off down the hillside, his troop chasing behind.

Leaning on his pike, Gregar turned to Leah. 'Who in Burn's name was that?'

The woman was staring after the lord, a strange expression on her face. 'That? That was King Gareth of Vor. One of the three kings of the Bloorian League.'

'Didn't see any fancy bird plumes on his helmet.'

The young corporal almost blushed. 'No. Not him. He's one of the real warhorses. Him'n'the king of Rath, they go way back. Hret of Bloor is young, but he's the third. Some say there's a fourth as well – of the Crimson Guard.'

'The Guard?' Haraj asked, from Gregar's side. 'Really?'

Leah looked surprised. 'Of course. Duke Courian of the Avorean line. They were kings of the north of these lands, long ago.'

'Quiet in the ranks!' Teigan bellowed. 'Form line, dammit!'

Gregar returned his attention to the field; he alternately blew on his hands to warm them and stamped his feet. Far across the churned field the scrum of mounted combatants still surged about, parting sometimes as one portion pursued the other. Wounded knights wandered out, or sagged on aimless mounts, while fresh ones charged in from far quarters. To Gregar it looked like little more than a glorified bar-brawl of chaos and blind flailing about.

Eventually, numbers told as the far smaller contingent of the Grisians and their allied city states gave ground, then broke off entirely, separating into individual groups and withdrawing. Gregar's Fourth sent up a great cheer at that but quickly choked it off as one of the troops, some twenty knights, came storming up the gentle slope directly for them.

'Contain them!' Teigan yelled. 'Don't let them through!'

Gregar didn't know how a thin line of Lights could possibly throw back a determined charge, but levelled his pike in any case.

The knights charged straight for the Fourth. Gregar firmed up his grip on the pike and sent a prayer to Fener. But at the last instant the cavalry veered aside, knocking spearheads aslant as they passed along the line. Then, near the centre – and Gregar – they yanked their mounts inward, stamping and kicking into the ranks to break the line and flailing to either side with their axes and war-picks. The Yellows infantry, completely unarmoured, flinched like an animal from these assailants.

Gregar, however, charged in. He took a horse in the neck with his pike. It threw its head in agony, ripping the weapon from his grip. Its rider kicked free of the falling animal, rolling, then drawing a longsword. Gregar met the knight with drawn twinned fighting sticks.

He parried a flurry of blows, giving ground, then struck, numbing an arm and backhanding the man across his neck, bringing him down. A mounted knight attempted to trample him but he shifted aside, giving the woman a solid blow to her kidney and unhorsing her in passing.

The Yellows infantry surged in around him then and he saw Haraj in the middle of the churning chaos, dodging and weaving, as yet unarmed. He wanted to take the

146

fellow by the neck and shake some sense into him, but even as he watched the lad flicked out a hand and did something to a passing knight and the man flew off his mount, his saddle having somehow become completely uncinched.

Another knight attempted to push past Gregar but he took hold of the man's arm as he threw an awkward mace swing and yanked him from his horse. As he fell, however, the knight returned the favour and gripped Gregar's arm to drag him in a tumbling roll. The knight rose first and drew a killing dagger, a misericord, which he raised over Gregar's chest.

Something impacted the man's head with a meaty crack and he slumped. Gregar pushed the heavy dead-weight aside to see Sergeant Teigan standing over him, a war-hammer in each hand.

'Raise the company colours, soldier,' Teigan told him.

Lying flat, almost in a daze, Gregar saluted. 'Aye, aye, sergeant.'

He found the pike and raised the bloodied colours to wave it back and forth. The surviving Fourth, having pushed back the charge, set up a great cheer, shaking their spears and taunting the remaining Grisians, who were quitting the field.

Teigan moved from trooper to trooper, alternately cuffing and squeezing shoulders, congratulating every single man and woman.

Leah came limping up to Gregar – she'd taken a blow to her left arm and cradled it as she offered him a rueful grin. 'Well done. Our best showing yet. I think you took down three all by yourself.'

He just shrugged. 'Bastards got my blood up.'

Haraj appeared then, nodding to Gregar, who looked the lad up and down – he hadn't been touched in all that chaotic confusion of kicking warhorses and swinging weapons. 'There's not a mark on you, man,' he observed, almost resentfully.

'No one can hit me,' the lad answered, and he offered a weak smile as if in apology.

Gregar gaped at him. 'Did you say no one can hit you?'

The skinny youth nodded. 'That's right.'

'*Ever?*'

'Not if I don't want them to.'

Gregar took a fist-hold of the lad's shirt. 'Do you mean that all this time I was worried sick that you were gonna be—' Cutting himself off, he pushed the youth away. 'I don't fucking believe it. Burn take it, you're safer out here than me!'

Leah looked between them both. 'I don't understand. What does he mean, Gregar?'

He waved a hand at Haraj. 'He means he's a mage.'

The woman's eyes grew huge. 'A mage?' She studied Haraj. 'In truth?'

The lad shrugged, embarrassed. 'In a very narrow sort of way . . . yes.'

'Baron Ordren will have to be told,' she said. 'He may want to hire you into his household.'

Gregar raised a hand for silence. 'Please, this is just between us. Haraj here, well, he – he wants to . . .' He looked to the bright noon sky. 'Gods, how do I say this?'

'I want to join the Crimson Guard,' Haraj said, rescuing Gregar from his dilemma.

Leah's mouth opened in stunned amazement and she blew out a long breath. 'Hunh. Just what I used to imagine doing – long ago. But if you are a mage, then they should take you. They take all mages. At least, that's what I've heard.'

Haraj nodded eagerly. 'Exactly.'

Gregar looked to the sky again, then squinted across the field. 'We're too far away.'

'Far from who?' came a loud bark from Sergeant Teigan and Gregar jumped; they had failed to keep a careful watch.

'Far from victory . . . as yet,' Leah offered.

The sergeant gave the first open belly-laugh Gregar had heard from him, cuffing Leah. 'Soon!' he guffawed. 'Soon, lass.' He eyed Gregar. 'And as for you! Well done, lad. Well done. There's a promotion in the offing, I'm sure. I knew the moment I laid eyes on you. There's a fighter, I'm sure, I said to myself. That's why I gave you the colours!'

Exhausted and in a sudden cold sweat now, Gregar could only shake his head in disbelief. 'Of course, sergeant.'

That evening Gris and its allies relinquished the field and the Bloorian League was one step closer to cutting off another allied barony from Gris. The Crimson Guard also decamped, shadowing the movements of the Grisian forces.

As to chasing after the Guard, Gregar realized it was a forlorn hope. Best to wait until the campaign threw them together once again, then he could deliver Haraj. Until such time, he had to admit the soldier's life was becoming far less bothersome – or he was adapting to it. The Fourth was even enjoying something of a reputation for its repulse of that cavalry charge, and Sergeant Teigan was glad to take full credit for the performance.

* * *

On board his flagship, the *Insufferable*, off the Itko Kanese coast at night, Cartheron Crust sat in Mock's old quarters and in the light of a swinging lamp read the reports from the captains sent by their fastest and lightest message-boats.

None of the missives, even the slimmest, was encouraging. Shipping had fallen to its lowest point in years. The towns and forts of the coast had shifted to a war footing. Garrisons had been bolstered, harbour defences mended. Suddenly Itko Kan was ready for a build-up in attacks. Meanwhile, the many cities of the Bloor–Grisian coast were already at war, and prepared to repulse any questionable vessel that approached.

He set down the sheaf of pages and reached for his wine. Surly was not going to like this. They were expending too many resources for too little gain. He would have to give the recall. He tossed back the drink and shrugged. Well, it was winter anyway, not the traditional raiding season.

The last page, a larger piece of finer parchment, he kept in hand and read again, shaking his head. Apparently, in his absence, he'd been put in charge of all the military; promoted to some damned fool made-up rank of High Fist.

He toasted the page. *I can blame my blasted brother for this, I'm sure.*

Shouted alarms from the deck brought him to his feet and he charged for the door, snapping up a hanging sheathed falchion. The night was particularly dark, overcast and threatening a bone-chilling rain. Even as he peered round, searching the surrounding waters, he realized the cause of the panic as strangely contrary and warm gusts of wind blustered about him.

'Stand back!' he yelled to the sailors, gesturing them away from the mid-deck.

What looked like shifting tatters of night, or shadows,

flitted about the deck, thickening to an obscuring dark. Sailors raised hands in warding signs against evil, while some muttered prayers. Two ran below-decks. Cartheron readied his sword – though he suspected who it was, he couldn't be certain *what* might emerge here.

A strong gust of dry gritty air buffeted him, stinging his eyes, and then the darkness faded away to reveal two men, one lean, the other short and apparently aged, and Cartheron stepped up, sheathing his sword. 'Welcome aboard, m'lords.'

The lean one, Dancer, greeted him, saying, 'Cartheron.' The little old fellow walked past him without even an acknowledgement and disappeared into the cabin. Cartheron sent a questioning glance to Dancer, who shook his head. 'Make for Malaz, captain,' he said.

'Aye aye.' He searched for and found his mate, Algar. 'Relay the order.' The mate hurried off.

The wiry knife-fighter had gone to the side and was looking out over the rolling waters. Cartheron noted the dust and dirt on his clothes and gear – all signs of hard travel. He cleared his throat. 'If I may . . . why here? Why not go straight there?'

The young man nodded. 'Too many eyes on the island now. Best we arrive without announcing it.'

'Ah. Well, Surly will be relieved.'

'Will she?' the fellow murmured, as if to himself.

Cartheron frowned for a moment. 'Of course. Your pact – ah, that is, the plan.'

Dancer's gaze moved to the cabin door, and pinched in worry. 'Yes. The plan. We should be able to go ahead with that now.'

Cartheron crossed his arms against the cold, nodding again. 'Good, good. And you and your, ah, partner? How did that go, if I may ask?'

The still quite youthful-looking lad ran a hand through his thick, night-black hair – dislodging dust – and shook his head. 'It was a dead end.'

* * *

Malle of Gris sat in one of the twin thrones of Gris her parents had commissioned the day she and her twin brother were born. Her brother Malkir's throne had remained empty since he died the previous year in a hunting accident outside Li Heng. A death Malle blamed on his hired escort, the Crimson Guard, who should have died to a man and a woman protecting him.

Her official title remained something of a question as her mother, the queen, lived still, sickly and bedridden. 'Princess Regent' was one suggestion, or 'Duchess', as many of the eastern city states were regarded as duchies. However, the only title she allowed was 'Malle of Gris' as, she argued, this should be good enough for anyone.

This evening she sat among representatives of Gris's dwindling allies. Present were lords, knights, or siblings of the rulers of the far eastern duchies, principates, and baronies: Haljhen, Nita, Balstro, Jurda, Habal, and Baran. They all sat at board in the huge stone hall, eating and talking in low voices, until Malle raised a hand for silence. 'Lords and ladies . . . as you know, we have suffered a setback. Jurda is now isolated and besieged. What course of action do you suggest?'

An older, bearded knight, Lord Fense, uncle of the ruler of Jurda, Duke Rethor, climbed to his feet. He bowed. 'Malle of Gris . . . my nephew and lord, Rethor, sends assurances that he will hold against the damned Bloorians for as long as it takes – all he asks is that a relief force be assembled.'

All present banged the table and shouted their support for Duke Rethor. Malle raised her hand for silence once more. She was not surprised; hundreds of years of feuds, raids and attacks lay behind a mutual hatred between the Bloor and the Jurdan ruling families. 'My compliments to the Duke. Please assure him that every effort will be made to push back the Bloorians.'

Lord Fense inclined his greying head and sat.

'Anything else?' Malle asked of the table.

A woman as young as Malle herself cleared her throat and rose; Lady Amtal, daughter of the Countess of Haljhen. Slight and pale, affecting a mousy demeanour, she was, as Malle knew, in truth a skilled sorceress, and a rumoured agent of the Queen of Dreams herself. She curtsied to Malle. 'Gris,' she began, 'I mean no disrespect, but duty demands I place my mother's words before you – and I beg you take no offence.'

Malle nodded. 'Go on. We are at council here and all may speak.' She did, however, reach out to the armrest of her brother's throne, as she used to reach out to his arm.

Lady Amtal curtsied again. 'My mother counsels that we consider negotiation. Our position yet remains one of relative strength, but who knows what the future may hold?'

Malle squeezed the armrest. *Negotiate while we still can.* She took a calming breath. Such counsel anticipated defeat. *Which I refuse to accept.* 'Thank your mother the countess for her wisdom, Lady Amtal. All options remain open, of course.'

Lady Amtal curtsied once more and sat. No one else rose. Malle nodded to them. 'Very good. We assemble a force, then, and push back to relieve Jurda.'

All present banged cups and fists to the table – even

the slight Lady Amtal tapped a hand. Malle ordered another round of refreshments be served.

Usually, such meals ended with an evening of entertainment from singers, jugglers, and other such mummers. Malle of Gris, however, kept a very sombre table, and so one by one the gathered nobles and knights-at-arms bowed and took their leave.

Once the last had left – a thoroughly soused knight of Baran half dragged along by his two hirelings – Malle regarded the broad chamber, empty but for servants cleaning up, and cleared her throat. She spoke into the darkened hall. 'What say you, Ap-Athlan?'

From the shadows along one wall a slim, aged man in leathers stepped forward. He bowed to Malle and, walking past a table, helped himself to a few leavings of grapes. 'Our list of allies grows shorter by the month,' he observed, and tossed the grapes into his mouth one by one.

'And?' she asked, a touch wearily, chin in hand.

'We need more. More allies, more troops. More of everything, frankly.'

'And?'

'Since we have impressed and recruited all we can, I suggest hiring.'

Malle scowled her disapproval. 'You know what I think of mercenaries.'

'Skinner and his troop are close by . . .'

The scowl became a grimace of distaste. 'Collecting Wickan scalps for Duke Baran. You do know why he's called *Skinner*?'

The sorcerer shrugged his indifference. 'Fear is a potent weapon, Malle.'

Malle looked at the empty throne next to her, and sighed. 'I know this. But it can fuel hate,' her narrowed gaze slid over to the mage, 'which is *far* stronger.'

Ap-Athlan daintily cleared his throat and stroked the small grey goatee at his chin. 'Indeed. Perhaps so.'

She waved him off. 'That is all for the night.'

Bowing stiffly from the waist, he left, still tossing grapes into his mouth.

Alone but for the servants, Malle sat in thought upon her throne. One by one they finished their tasks and slipped away until one last servitor – a skinny, sleepy-eyed youth – came and sat at her feet.

After peering down at him with something like affection, she asked, 'You watched and listened as I taught you?' The lad nodded. 'And who do you think?'

'Ranel of Nita,' the youth said, with a yawn.

'Really? Not Amtal of Haljhen?'

The youth shook his head. 'No. You wouldn't speak openly of negotiation if you were considering betrayal.'

Malle nodded. 'Very good. Why that brat Ranel?'

The youth closed his bruised eyes, tilted his head in remembrance. 'He sat sullen all through the meal. Rolled his eyes when anyone spoke – thinks he's smarter than everyone. That's the type to try something stupid, thinking it's smart.'

Malle nodded again. 'Very good. Keep an eye on him, yes? And if he acts . . . I give you permission to respond.'

The youth peered up, slyly. 'Show me your trick.'

Malle waved a hand. 'Not tonight, little one.'

'Pleeeease?'

Malle sighed, pushed herself from the throne and walked to the centre of the hall. 'See the far pillar timber nearest the door?' The youth nodded. Malle eyed it for a time, then turned her back upon it. She let her arms fall loose at her sides, took one steadying breath. Spinning, she threw one arm up, aiming for the pillar, and a small blade hammered home in the meat of the thick wood.

The youth jumped to his feet, applauding.

Smiling only very slightly, Malle walked over and yanked the slim blade free.

'It never works for me,' the lad complained.

'More practice, as I showed you,' Malle told him. She tapped the blade to her palm, studying it. 'One day,' she murmured, perhaps only to herself, 'I'll get close enough to Courian D'Avore to put this in his one remaining eye.'

Chapter 8

WHAT FEW HORSES ORJIN SAMARR'S RAG-TAG force possessed they gave over to the scouts and messengers. And so Orjin paced alongside everyone else, close to the arrow-point of the wide, cross-country chevron that was his marching order. His soldiers raided and burned as they went. Their orders were to herd the farmers and peasants towards the twin cities of Quon and Tali, where their clamouring and hungry mouths would eventually force the recall of the expeditionary army that now invested Purage in the north.

Orjin's force ate whatever they could scavenge from the countryside, and as it was winter pickings were slim; his own lads and lasses were feeling the pinch of hard times just as badly as the farmers they were rousting from cottages and hamlets. Yet he insisted no one was to be slain, save where any resistance emerged.

For the first week of raiding he kept relatively close to the coast, despite advice from Prevost Jeral and Terath that they strike straight for the walls of Tali and break through, if possible. Burning Tali would definitely bring Commander Renquill's prissy arse running – as Terath had phrased it.

But Orjin had something else in mind, a longer game.

157

However, it would have to wait, as he faced Terath and Prevost Jeral in an emptied and raided cottage to decide what to do about the first firm opposition to take the field against them.

Jeral pointed to the crude vellum map of north Quon Tali province. 'They will meet us at this crossing,' she said. 'Good roads in all directions – roads put in by the Talians specifically to move troops, by the way.'

'We could go round,' Terath put in, a hand at her scarred chin.

'Do you want them to dog us for ever?' Jeral answered, a touch sharply.

'Numbers?' Orjin asked, breaking up the exchange. These two lieutenants, he noted, seemed to get on each other's nerves. Too much alike, he figured.

'Some fifteen hundred,' Jeral supplied. 'We're not absolutely certain. They have a strong skirmishing screen.'

'Damned few to march out to challenge . . .' Terath mused.

Jeral nodded, and rubbed a hand through her matted hair – she'd undone her braids to accommodate the helmet. 'There's more. Scouts report a core in the force. An infantry square all in black tabards.'

Orjin and Terath shared a glance. Black tabards – the uniform of the Talian Iron Legion.

'Size?' Orjin asked.

Jeral blew out a breath. 'No more than a hundred.'

Again too few, Orjin reflected. Why come out to face them? Better to husband the force in the defence of Tali. But then, since when were the Talians the type to sit back and wait for the enemy?

Orjin's own force currently numbered close to four thousand. 'Over-confidence?' he pondered aloud.

Terath shrugged. 'Who knows? We can't let ourselves

get bogged down in an exchange. We should ignore them and strike straight for Tali and gut it while we can.'

Orjin shook his head. 'No, we can't leave them behind us.' He looked to Terath. 'You're right. Their goal might very well be to slow us down, buy time for Tali, so we have to do this quickly. We meet them tomorrow head on and sweep our wings around them in an encirclement.'

Jeral picked up her helmet, gave a quick, fierce nod. 'I'll inform the flank officers.'

Once the Nom officer had left, Terath turned to Orjin. 'Their goal may be to break this army, Orjin. Scatter it. Remember, they succeeded not too long ago.'

'Those Purge nobles could ride away from their mistakes – I can't.' And he laughed, heading for the door.

'Cold comfort,' Terath grumbled, following.

His Wickan lieutenant, Arkady, waited outside with the hetman of the hill-folk, a squat and lean fellow, Petel, who appeared as tough as a hewn stump. This fellow nodded to him. 'We are far from our families,' he began, 'and it is winter – not the time we choose to be away.'

Orjin nodded. 'You are free to return, of course. Thank you for your aid. We are grateful you are with us.'

Petel snorted his scorn. 'The noble Quon lords treat us like dirt.'

'You have our gratitude, and I wish I had gifts to give . . .'

The hetman waved that aside. 'We have the weapons and goods we've collected.' He flashed a grin. 'It was a good raid.' He motioned to a number of his people. 'For you.' One hill-woman came forward with a great shaggy cloak in her arms which she extended to Orjin. He would have sworn it was a bear-cloak, but for its amazing colour: a dirty white.

'This comes from a great beast of the ice fields of the far north. It is yours – to match your own pelt.'

Orjin self-consciously pushed back his own shaggy, prematurely grey hair and laughed. 'I understand. My thanks.' He motioned to the south. 'Tomorrow we fight. I hope you will stay for that. We could use you.'

Petel grinned savagely. 'Oh, yes. Every raid needs at least one good fight that the young bloods can boast about.'

Orjin answered the grin. 'Excellent. My thanks.'

The hetman bowed and walked off. Arkady gave a nod and went with him. Terath leaned closer, murmuring, 'We need them.'

Orjin nodded. 'Yes. But they've done enough, and this isn't really their fight.'

'You're too quick to let people have their way. You should demand more.'

He was watching the hill-folk settling in around the fires, teasing one another and laughing, and he answered, distracted, 'The things I want from people are the very things you can't demand.'

The woman eyed him, her gaze questing. 'And what if they don't give those things voluntarily?'

He lifted his shoulders, still watching the hill-folk. 'That's just how it is sometimes.'

She pursed her lips, saying nothing, her gaze falling.

He frowned then, noticing the silence, and glanced to her. 'What is it?'

Her mouth hardened. 'Nothing.'

'Well,' he offered, 'you and I should try to get some sleep.'

She nodded, letting out a long breath. 'Yes. I suppose so.'

The morning dawned cold and crisp. Orjin's breath plumed in the air as he exited the cottage and paused there, setting a booted foot on to a rock to adjust the cloth wrappings he wore up his legs against the cold, and tighten the bronze greave over the top. He lowered the set of his sword-belt round his long mail coat, and, a touch self-consciously, adjusted the new bear-fur cloak at his shoulders, affixed by a large round clasp over his left breast. He then crossed to a fire to warm his hands. The Dal Hon shaman Yune was there in his ratty cloak, which made him look like a shabby crow. The shaman gave him a hard eye, then nodded. 'Suits you.'

Orjin sent him a questioning look. 'Anything?'

The fellow shook his head. 'Nothing important.' Orjin grunted his satisfaction. Yune extended a steaming glass. 'Tea?'

'Thanks.' Prevost Jeral walked up, fully caparisoned, helmet lowered and strapped. Orjin asked, 'Our friends still with us?'

She nodded. 'Waiting for us.'

'They must think they can break us.'

'They have reason.'

Orjin scanned the south. 'Not this time. I will lead the attack.'

The Purge officer actually stiffened. 'Is that wise?'

'It's necessary. No one will retreat so long as I'm fighting.'

'And if you should fall?'

Orjin raised a brow at that, but laughed and clapped her on the shoulder. 'Then avenge me!'

Prevost Jeral wasn't assured, but she did note how all the troops nearby smiled in response to Orjin's loud and confident laugh. *He knows what he is doing, this one.*

We just have to keep him alive, then.

'Set the horns to call order, prevost,' he told her, and started walking.

*

161

The Talians had chosen their ground as well as they could, given the flat domesticated countryside of fields and orchards. They occupied a crossroads – the stout Talian military roads being built up above the surrounding fields. Concentric circles of shieldwalls faced Orjin and his troops as they closed in.

He drew his longsword, its grip manufactured with enough extension for a hand and a half. He eschewed a shield, blocking instead with the sword, when necessary.

The Quon Talian infantry stood their ground. Their bronze shield-edges scraped as they adjusted their footing. Somewhere within that rough circle waited its core – men and women in the black tabard of the Iron Legion. Personally, Orjin was not all that impressed; he didn't think this new corps would in any way be as formidable or hard-bitten as the old imperial force.

He picked up his pace as he closed, sword rising. He now kicked through the stiff brittle stalks of a harvested field, barley or rye. A war-shout was growing deep within his chest, both to intimidate his opponents, and to stoke his own fighting rage.

To his right, Orhan loosed his own shattering war-bellow; he had set aside his tall poleaxe for a mace in each hand, while on Orjin's left Arkady had out two long-knives for thrusting in the chest-to-chest brawl that was to come.

They struck with a bone-jarring crash and all planning or consciousness of the larger engagement fled Orjin's mind as he gave himself over to the animal ferocity of killing. Enemy faces screamed at him over shields, some eyes slit, others wide. Teeth were bared in grimaces of rage, or of agony.

Through it all he swung and bashed, exultant at the very fact of still being alive, until the troops to either side of him rebounded suddenly as if from a stone barrier; they faced now a solid wall of blackened rectangular shields emblazoned with a simple circle, or crown, of silver. Above the shields cool eyes regarded them, the gaze of those long inured to battle.

This pause allowed Orjin to raise his head and study the battle, and he saw that despite his hopes of allowing an opening to the rear of the enemy for them to retreat or break, his troops had washed round the much smaller force completely. He raised a fist for a halt, and Orhan lent his war-bellow to the order, ringing out, 'Cease!'

The two forces eyed one another across the short gap of a few paces, one a tiny dot of black surrounded by thousands. Breathing heavily, Orjin cleaned his blade, sheathed it, and approached. A fellow in a black tabard over a long mail coat slipped out of the shieldwall to meet him.

Calm now, Orjin could see that every face belonged to a lined and seamed veteran. Some were clean-shaven, others carried grey beards braided in the decades-old style. All were calm, some even smiling.

The legionnaire who met him was a compact fellow no taller than Orjin's shoulder; his thin hair was brush-cut to a grey stubble, his face sun- and wind-darkened to a deep umber brown, and his eyes, like those of Orjin, a bright glacial blue. His tabard was threadbare, yet clean and much mended – stored reverently for decades, no doubt.

Orjin inclined his head to the veteran. 'You've made your point, oldster. There's no need to continue. You may quit the field with pride.'

'It is you who should quit the field, lad. Go back north, or we will break you.'

'No. Not this time, I think. Stand down, please.'

The oldster shook his head. 'No. There is no standing down. You don't understand.'

Orjin raised his face to the sun and wind, let out a long breath. 'Yes. I do understand. Once more you've answered the call. Once more you've set down your shovels and hoes and you feel the weight of armour at your shoulders, the heft of your weapon at your hip. But most important – once more you stand together as in the old days, shoulder to shoulder.'

The veteran had started nodding as Orjin spoke, and now he eyed him narrowly. 'You do understand. Then you know what must be done?'

Orjin gave one slow nod of assent. 'Yes – though I wish it were not so.'

The oldster saluted him and slipped back into the ranks of the shieldwall.

Orjin returned to his troops. Orhan sent him a questioning look he would not meet. He peered down the curved line of massed troops, right and left, then raised his sword, held it poised, then dropped it forward.

His force charged bellowing their war-cries, converging to meet the eerily silent black-clad veterans. Orjin, however, did not advance. He watched and waited, sword ready if necessary. The Iron Legionnaires fought efficiently, silently, and they held out for far longer than he could have imagined. Yet outnumbered so vastly they eventually fell, first one by one, then more swiftly as the shieldwall crumbled, until finally the last few fought back to back to fall amid their brothers and sisters. None threw down their weapons or yielded. They perished to a man and a woman.

With victory came great whoops and cheers from Orjin's force, and they hugged and clapped one another, but Orjin did not join in. He slammed his weapon home and headed off to a nearby cobblestone hut.

Prevost Jeral came jogging up to him, saluted. 'Congratulations, commander.'

Orjin raised his face to the clean wind once more. 'Think you so?'

The officer seemed to understand his tone; she lost her smile. 'The troops needed this. They'll pull together now.'

He nodded. 'Yes. That is true at least.'

'I'll start the burial detail,' she said, and headed off.

'Captain!' he called after her, and she turned. 'Leave them be. Do not disturb them.'

'Really, sir? But don't you think – that is, it would be disrespectful not to give them the proper rites.'

'I am giving them their proper rites, captain. Leave them to lie together, shoulder to shoulder. It's what they marched out here for.'

The Nom officer tilted her head at this, a touch confused, but bowed. 'As you order, sir.'

That evening the troops celebrated their victory over the storied Iron Legionnaires. Out came long-hidden flasks and wine skins, and campfires roared high through the night.

Orjin sat staring into his fire before the hut he'd taken as the field command. With him sat Yune and Terath. He held his tea-glass in his fingertips, idly swirling the dregs and watching the firelight glint from the glass.

Prevost Jeral approached from the darkness in the long and loose sweat-stained shirtings and leg-wraps she wore beneath her armour. A bloodied field dressing was bound about one arm. She nodded to Orjin. 'We march for Tali, then?' Still eyeing the dregs of his tea, he shook his head. She frowned, glanced to Yune and Terath, perhaps for guidance, but neither spoke. 'Then what? Care to inform your staff?'

Orjin crooked a grin at her impatience with his reticence, which was well deserved. He finished his tea and sucked his teeth. 'What do you think will happen when we show up outside Tali's walls?'

Jeral shrugged. 'They'll tell us to go bugger ourselves.'

'And if we invest the city – don't you think there's a chance they may not even send messengers requesting Renquill's return?'

The Nom officer nodded at that. 'Yes. Those old generals are proud and stubborn.'

'And that Renquill might even refuse to abandon the siege?'

She snorted a laugh. 'If he thinks he can win it – especially so.'

Orjin was nodding. 'But what if we threatened Quon instead?'

Jeral crouched before the fire. She adjusted the bindings at her upper arm, wincing. Terath poured her a glass of tea, which she accepted with a nod. 'But there's nothing there. No armoury, no garrison. It's not a military target.'

'But the Quon merchants *will* demand Renquill's return, won't they?'

'They will squeal like cornered pigs.'

'Yes. And while Renquill can refuse his own generals without any political consequences . . . what of Quon?'

The prevost sipped her tea, nodding. 'He dare not – cannot – refuse them. The alliance.'

'The old saying,' Terath put in: 'Quon pays so that Tali can fight.'

Jeral looked to the old Dal Hon mage. 'What do you think?'

Yune smoothed his wispy grey moustaches. 'I think fate is like water – you cannot push it uphill. Therefore it behoves one to find the easiest – that is, the most likely – path downhill and hope to ride it.'

Jeral frowned at the old shaman, clearly trying to find her way through his comment. Terath threw a pebble across the fire at him. 'And how long did you spend on that one?'

He opened his hands. 'What? You didn't like it?'

'That's one of your stupidest ever!'

Yune appealed to Orjin. 'I thought it had a good balance.' Orjin laughed.

Terath motioned to Jeral's arm. 'Let me take a look at that.' She took Jeral into the hut.

Later, when Jeral had reappeared and bowed her departure, Orjin pushed open the door and entered. He found Terath washing blood from her hands in a ceramic basin.

He worked to keep his face straight as he asked, 'How did it go?'

The tall Untan dried her hands and threw down the cloth. 'All she did was ask me about you.'

They marched double-time for Quon, which occupied the shore-side slopes of the gentle hills the twin city states were founded upon: Quon, expansive and rambling, consisting of extensive family estates, large warehouse district, and several market squares; Tali, inland, confined and walled, consisting of towers and enclosed baileys and yards for layered defence.

Orjin requested that all those among his force who had worked as labourers for the Quon trading families report to him on its walls and streets. After that meeting, he decided to head to the waterfront district, where the walls were described as 'more gesture than barrier'.

Two days later, without encountering significant opposition – the Quon Talians clearly not thinking such an expedition even possible, let alone feasible – they came within sight of the north walls of the broad waterfront harbour and warehouse district.

The 'gesture' part of the description immediately became clear to Orjin. Walls there had been, formidable and thick, from the old days when the Talians besieged Quon every few years. Now, however, entire sections had been taken apart, stone by stone, no doubt ending up in the buildings of some impressive new family estate.

At Orjin's side, Prevost Jeral, reviewing the jagged remnants of the north wall, snorted her disgust. 'That's a damned disgrace,' she announced.

'With the alliance, it came to seem irrelevant,' Terath, on Orjin's other side, supplied.

'Hiring mercenaries only gets you so far,' Jeral muttered. Orjin looked at her and cocked a brow. She cleared her throat. 'Present company excepted.'

Workers had been scrambling over the scavenged missing sections, hastily mounting wooden barricades and piling rubble. They abandoned their efforts when Orjin's broad-fronted chevron approached. A thin line of what must have been conscripted city watch and private estate guards remained at the wall – these put up very little resistance to Orjin and his heavies.

Once he'd stepped down on to a cobbled street, Orjin ordered three columns to spread out and occupy the warehouse district. Here he stood on the main way, amid abandoned wagons and carts of cloth and fine leather hides, salt slabs and boxes of spices – a sampling of all the goods of this, the richest western port of the continent. Orjin planted his sandalled feet, crossed his arms, and waited.

Later that day a delegation approached down the broad avenue. It consisted of three canopied palanquins, each carried by bearers and preceded by what must be elite personal bodyguards. Impressive guardsmen, Orjin thought: Dal Hon giants and armoured northern Bloorian knights – but not soldiers, these. He knew the least of the hill-folk scouts had been far tougher than any of these pampered house guards.

He raised a hand for a halt. 'Close enough! Leave the bearers and guards behind and approach on foot!'

'*What?*' an old woman squawked from within one palanquin. 'Leave our attendants behind? Approach on foot?'

Orjin sighed. 'That's what I said.'

The palanquin rocked in evident agitation. 'This is unprecedented! Uncivilized!'

'Yes it is.' At his side, Terath, he noted, was openly smirking.

'Inevitable,' a deep voice rumbled from the middle palanquin, and it sagged alarmingly as a thick leg in bright silk pantaloons emerged, a dainty silk-slippered foot feeling about for the cobbles.

'Very well!' the ancient crone-voice answered, sniffily. The palanquin's gauzy pastel-hued cloth parted, emitting a gout of smoke, and to Orjin's surprise out stepped a petite, even dwarf-like young woman, a long-stemmed pipe clamped firmly in her mouth.

The thick leg belonged to a correspondingly large barrel-shaped fellow in rich silks; out of the third palanquin stepped a tall and bearded oldster in unadorned dark robes. The odd trio approached together, the fat one wincing each time a slippered foot touched the stone cobbles.

The tiny young woman drew herself up as tall as she

could, raising her chin. 'We are the elected representatives of the great trading houses of Quon,' she announced in her smoke-roughened voice. She motioned to the huge fellow, 'Imogan,' the thin old one in simple dark robes, 'Carlat,' and finally herself, 'Pearl. So,' she continued, not even waiting for Orjin to introduce himself, 'now we must discuss your price.'

Even though Orjin had been fully expecting this, he couldn't help stiffening at what, to him, was a terrible insult. Terath actually growled her seething rage. He shook his head, looking to the sky. 'You people . . . just because you can be bought doesn't mean others can.'

'Everyone has a price,' Pearl sneered, and she blew out a great plume of smoke.

Orjin was glad his arms were crossed as it stopped him from immediately going for his sword. 'You people need a lesson that there are more important things than coin – and I think I'll demonstrate it.' He looked to Terath. 'Burn the warehouse district.'

The Untan duellist smiled hugely. 'Immediately.' And she turned on a heel and jogged off.

The fat merchant, Imogan, raised a hand. 'A moment, please. Perhaps we may negotiate . . .'

'We were negotiating,' Orjin answered. 'Your approach was to insult me. Negotiation failed.'

Pearl snatched the pipe from her mouth and jabbed it at him. 'You cannot do this.'

'I am. I suggest you gather your labourers and guards to contain the fire so that your estates aren't consumed.'

'But artwork,' the tiny girl spluttered. 'Fine leathers from Seven Cities. Spices. Silks! You barbarian!'

'Fisherman, actually.'

Now her tiny eyes slit almost shut. 'We, the representatives of the trading houses of Quon, will see you crucified for this. Your motley gang will line the road from Quon to Purage!' She raised her chin as if in a coup. 'Long ago we demanded the return of Talian forces. Even as we speak they are probably on the way!' She jammed the pipe back into her mouth, sneering her triumph. 'You will all be dead within the month.'

Orjin inclined his head to her. 'We shall see. But for now, I suggest you throw every man and woman you have into a bucket brigade.' He motioned to the guards. 'Even that lot, though their pretty livery will get all sooty.'

Pearl opened her mouth to reply but the third of the trio, who had been studying Orjin all this time, hand at chin, forestalled her. 'You planned all along to relieve Purage, and in case word has not yet reached you I can tell you that you have succeeded. But at a price. So far you have been the cat, but from today onward you are the mouse.'

The woman turned a glare upon the tall and rail-thin oldster. 'Now the great prognosticator of Quon speaks? Now? When it's too damned late? What use is that? Faugh!' She turned on her foot and waved the other two to follow.

Orjin watched them go. Nothing of what transpired had come as a surprise to him, save that last comment. The old fellow had the right of it. From now onward he would be the prey. He just hoped to prove a fox rather than a mouse.

Later, he met with a large portion of his troops in a broad square surrounded by the Quon merchant warehouses. Atop a loading dock, in his thick grey bearskin cloak, he raised his hands for their attention. 'Take all the food you can carry!' he shouted. 'Load any mules and carts!

Prepare for a damned long march! Then,' and he waved to the warehouses, 'burn everything behind you!'

A great roaring cheer answered that, and a chant of a word from some quarters. He climbed down to Terath and Prevost Jeral. 'What's that they're saying?' he asked Jeral.

She smiled in answer. 'They like you, so you've earned a name. Sort of a title.'

'What is it?'

'Greymane.'

He laughed, and pulled a hand through his long greying hair. 'Well . . . better than Greybeard, I suppose.'

* * *

Heboric walked the main trader road of Itko Kan that ran as a spine along the thin north–south conglomeration of united city states. It lay far from the coast, as a precaution against the ever-present threat of pirate raids from Malaz and Nap. Also, as an inland route, it served as an unofficial border with Kan's warlike neighbour, Dal Hon.

It was winter, and thus cold and wet. At places the road was nothing more than a mud track of pools and glutinous ruts. Protected only by sandals as he slogged through the muck, his feet were sodden, caked in mud, and frozen all day. He was in no particular hurry, and so he chose a leisurely progress from one wayside inn or horse-post to the next. Each evening, by the fire of one such establishment, he would warm his feet and wait to be served whatever fare his obvious calling as priest might garner from the innkeeper. Sometimes it was a full hot meal; other times he was offered leavings no better than those meant for dogs.

So did he make his way north, aiming, roughly, for the great city state of Li Heng.

Fellow travellers came and went: mounted messengers, merchant caravans, local farmers and craftsmen and women. He passed the time with a few, but most took in his boar tattoos and moved on, as the Great Boar was, among many things, one of the gods of war.

Outside Traly he came upon a richly caparisoned wagon – the conveyance of some noblewoman – with an armed escort of ten men-at-arms. The rear wheels were stuck in the mud up to the axle and half the guards were down in the muck pushing while the noblewoman within berated them.

Shaking his head, Heboric clambered down into the ruts to help. With his aid, and the driver whipping the four horses, the wagon lurched free.

The guards nodded their wary thanks and took up their arms. Heboric tried to shake the mud from his legs.

'You will attend me, priest!' came a command from the covered wagon.

Heboric raised a questioning brow to the guard captain, who nodded him closer. 'Yes, O noble-born?' he asked.

'Walk with me. I would have your prayers – gods know I have need of them!' The wagon rocked onward and Heboric kept pace. 'Where do you travel?' she demanded.

'To the Valley of Hermits, east of Li Heng.'

'Excellent! Our path is similar. I myself am for the new sanctuary of Burn to pray for the welfare of my family. Are you intent upon becoming an ascetic yourself?'

He shook his head. 'No. I would ask questions of them.'

'Ah, you are on a quest for knowledge.'

'Something like that.'

'Well, join your earnest entreaties to mine. I am so very worried by the fecklessness of this new generation. They know only to spend money like water and have no concern for the future.'

Heboric crooked a smile – having heard that very complaint from his own elders.

'Tell me,' the ancient demanded, 'have you seen the Holy Enclosure of Fener at Vor?'

'Indeed I have, mother.'

'Tell me of it.'

For the remainder of the day Heboric described the situation of the enclosure, its location and layout. The old Kanian aristocrat then questioned him thoroughly as to its rites and rituals; it seemed she was a dedicated student of all the gods' practices and obeisances. Her guards, he noted, appeared quite relieved to have a new target for her ceaseless interrogation.

Three days' travel passed in this manner, the Kanian elder, Lady Warin – who, it turned out, was a distant relation of the Kan and Chulalorn line – demanding an account of every scrap of eldritch worship or rite that Heboric had ever come across – which was extensive, as he considered himself something of a historian of the field.

On the fourth day the slow slogging progress of the heavy wagon was interrupted by three mounted figures blocking the road. Lady Warin's guards immediately drew their weapons, their captain calling, 'What is the meaning of this?'

The central figure kneed her mount forward. 'It is what it looks like,' she answered, rather lazily. 'The lady will hand over all her coin and jewellery.'

Heboric eyed the bandit woman. She wore a ragged

cloak, yes, but beneath he believed he saw the glint of blackened mail. And *three* horses? Rich bandits indeed. 'Captain,' he called, 'have her shrug off that rag she's wearing.'

The captain waved the three away with a shake of his sword. 'Choose your targets with more care, fools. This is Lady Warin, an elder of the Kan line!'

'I know she is,' the bandit leader answered, as lazily as before, and Heboric gripped the wagon's side. *No!* 'Fire!'

A fusillade of crossbow bolts came flying from the woods and Lady Warin's guards all grunted, taken by multiple shots. Heboric himself crumpled, a leg kicked out from under him by the impact of a bolt.

He lay in the mud, panting, while the jangling of harnesses announced the approach of the three mounts. Through the roaring in his ears he heard the old woman say, with great disparagement, 'So . . . are we to return to the old dynastic wars?'

The bandit woman dismounted. Heboric noted from under the wagon that her boots were tall and of fine leather. 'They never ended,' the woman answered, and the wagon rocked as she climbed inside. Reaching up, snarling with the effort, Heboric pulled himself upright.

'Curse all of you to Hood's darkest pits!' Lady Warin hissed, then gasped.

Heboric stood, panting, and examined his leg – the bolt had passed straight through the meat of his thigh.

'This one's still alive,' a new voice observed from nearby. Heboric looked up, blinking. More of the so-called bandits now surrounded the wagon, crossbows resting in their arms. Boots squelched in the mud as the bandit woman leapt down from the wagon. She'd thrown off her old cloak and was using a piece of torn rich cloth to clean her blade. Her armour was plain and functional; ex-military, Heboric thought.

She looked him up and down. 'Sorry, priest. But there are to be no witnesses to this bandit attack.'

He did not bother pointing out the obvious truth that this was no bandit attack. Instead, he drew a snarling breath and grated through his pain, 'Do not make me call the Boar.'

The woman raised a brow, nodding. 'I've heard the stories, of course. The Boar-wildness. Never seen it myself. I think of it as apocryphal.'

Through clenched teeth, Heboric ground out, 'Do not force me. It is very painful.'

Brow still raised, the officer asked, 'For you?'

'For everyone involved.'

Sighing, she turned to her troop. 'Well? What are you waiting for? Reload.'

Damning the woman for forcing this on him, Heboric called inwardly upon the Great Boar, the roaring god of war's wildness, petitioning: *Ride my flesh!* And charged.

When Heboric awoke, it was night, and he lay half in a small creek. Groaning, he turned over to wash the thick sticky layer of drying blood and gore from himself in the icy cold water. He spat out something that might have been a piece of human flesh and washed his mouth, gagging. Then he passed out once more.

With the warmth of the sun, he rose and staggered about until he saw the raised bed of the road and returned to it once more, heading north. Of the Lady Warin's wagon or party, he found nothing. He must have run or wandered far from that location. At the first farmer's thatched hut he limped over and banged on the door until it opened and hands took him to heave him on to a straw pallet. Here he sank into a deep sleep of near death, as the Boar cares not for the demands he places upon the flesh he rides.

Chapter 9

A FULL-COMMAND GATHERING WAS SLATED FOR the very night the *Insufferable* docked in Malaz City harbour. Surly, Cartheron, Tayschrenn and Dassem all called for the meeting to be held in Mock's Hold, but Kellanved would not budge: his office was to be the place.

Luckily, Smiley's was now unoccupied, as Surly's burgeoning agency had long since outgrown its limited quarters and had moved its operations to an undisclosed location among the warehouses along the waterfront, so Dancer had to unlock the doors to the bar and light the lamps along the walls in the abandoned common room. Kellanved walked up the stairs as if nothing had changed. Sighing, Dancer picked up a lamp and followed.

He found the mage slumped behind his desk, chin in both fists, staring at nothing. The fellow had barely said two words since leaving the field of flints, and Dancer was becoming rather worried. 'So it didn't pan out,' he offered as he lit three more lamps. 'Not everything's going to work out. Look at Heng.'

'Yes,' the mage murmured, his eyes slit. 'I haven't finished with Heng.'

'Let's not get ahead of ourselves, shall we? What's the plan?'

'The plan?' Kellanved echoed, distracted. 'Plan for what?'

'The plan for Nap,' Dancer answered, rather tersely. 'The topic of the night.'

'Ah.' The mage shrugged dismissively. 'As before, I suppose. It doesn't matter.'

Dancer studied him for a time: chin in fists and elbows on the desk, he looked like a sulking child. Yet Dancer knew this was much worse – the mood was one of those black pools of melancholia that could swallow a man. It was strange; the fellow could be so driven at times, yet one setback and he was utterly dejected. Bickering, however, would only make things worse, so he clenched his teeth and nodded. 'Very well. As before then. You haven't eaten in ages – are you hungry?'

Kellanved shook his head and let go a deep sigh.

Dancer pushed from the wall. 'Well I am. I'm going to see if Surly's left us anything here.'

The mage merely waved him off.

The kitchens, unfortunately, had been emptied. Dancer emerged to find the Dal Hon swordsman in the common room. 'Dassem!'

The swordsman opened his mouth to answer, but paused, frowning his uncertainty. 'Just what,' he asked, 'do I call you?'

'Dancer will do.'

'No title?'

'Gods no.' Dancer invited him up the stairs. 'And what have you been busy with?'

'Training the troops. Your marines.'

'Marines?'

The lad pushed open the door to the offices. 'Yes. They all fight at sea, and can double as sailors, and vice versa. Therefore, marines.' He bowed to Kellanved. 'Magister.'

The mage did not answer; he was playing with something on his desk.

'Training in what style?' Dancer asked.

'Shortsword, shield and spear.'

Dancer was surprised. 'Like the old legion?'

'Exactly.'

'But cavalry dominates the field from Quon to Gris. Infantry is an afterthought.'

'These days, yes. But that's not how it used to be. A well organized and disciplined infantry can repulse a horse charge. Cavalry used to have a very minor role in war.'

'War,' Dancer echoed, with some distaste. And yet, he supposed, that was what this was about, after all.

Tayschrenn entered, then peered about looking rather perplexed. Dancer realized that the only chair in the room was the one under Kellanved's bum.

Well, perhaps it would help shorten the meeting.

Surly and Cartheron entered, with nods all round. The Napans, the Kartoolian mage and Dassem all looked to Kellanved, but the wizened mock-old mage didn't raise his head from the object he was turning on the desk.

After a few uncomfortable moments Dancer cleared his throat and addressed Surly. 'We are secure here?' She nodded. He looked at Tayschrenn. 'Any active Warren magics?' The mage shook his head. 'Very well. Cartheron, when can we move against Nap?'

The fellow looked to the ceiling and scratched his unshaven jaw. 'Dawn of the third day from now.'

'How many ships?' Dassem asked.

Their High Fist blew out a breath. 'Some forty. All we can scrape together.'

The swordsman eyed Surly. 'And is that a credible threat?'

Her habitual stern expression soured even more. 'Not really. It's not enough.'

Arms crossed, his back against a wall, Tayschrenn leaned forward. 'Are you saying they will see through it?'

'They will wonder why we would be so . . . hasty, and foolish . . .'

Dancer looked at Kellanved. *Ah. I see.* He cleared his throat once more. 'So, Kellanved . . .'

The mage rubbed his eyes and let out a long-suffering sigh. 'Yes, yes. They will see a foolish inexperienced ruler throwing away his forces in an ill-considered attack. Very well.' He waved his hands as if to shoo them from the room. 'Go on – go ahead.'

Surly crossed her arms. 'There is still the matter of who goes.'

Kellanved's beady eyes slit almost closed. 'Meaning . . . ?'

She pointed a finger. '*You're* going.'

He slumped back in his chair, appalled. 'Really? I'll have you know I have important matters to pursue. Research into forbidden secrets. Lost artefacts. Mysterious . . . things.'

'If you have him you do not need me,' Tayschrenn told Surly.

Kellanved had returned to toying with something on his desk. 'You'll keep all those Ruse mages off my back,' he said.

To this, the Kartoolian renegade arched an ironic brow that said, *Oh, is that all?*

Surly studied everyone, then nodded to herself as if reaching some sort of conclusion. 'We're *all* going.'

Tayschrenn huffed; Dassem nodded his agreement.

Dancer realized that, yes, they all should go. Why leave your strongest pieces off the board? He inclined his head in assent to Surly. 'Very well. It's agreed. We leave at dawn in three days.' He brushed his hands together. 'I don't know about all of you but I'm famished. Where can we get something to eat?'

The crew bowed to Kellanved, who made further shooing gestures, and left with Dancer. On the stairs Surly beckoned him aside, obviously wanting a word. He didn't blame her.

In the empty and cold kitchen she turned on him, arms crossed. 'Our dread mage. He seems out of sorts.'

Dancer nodded, rubbing his forehead. 'Yes. Our search didn't work out, and it was a blow to him. He seemed so utterly certain of it.'

One narrow brow rose and a single finger tapped a biceps. 'Well, he had better be prepared to perform. Uncertainty regarding his . . . capabilities . . . is one reason we have time.'

'Time?'

'Before an attack. Perhaps from Dal Hon, or Itko Kan. While we are relatively weak.'

'Ah. I see.' He hadn't considered that. But then, in his defence, he'd been busy . . . babysitting. 'I'll bring him round,' he assured her.

She gave a slow, serious nod. 'You'd better. For all our sakes.'

He motioned to the doors. 'You are coming with us?'

'No. Not . . . that is, I have work to do.'

'Very well. Another time.'

She smiled, but it appeared forced. 'Yes. Another time.'

Bowing, he left to join Cartheron, Dassem, and Tayschrenn waiting in the street. Surrounding these three, at a discreet distance, stood a rather large contingent of Malazan soldiers. Dancer motioned to them. 'Who are these?'

Tayschrenn, hands clasped behind his back, tilted his head to Dassem. 'His bodyguard.'

Dancer quirked a disbelieving smile. If anyone did not need guarding, it was the swordsman.

'Self-appointed,' Dassem supplied, by way of explanation.

Tayschrenn continued, 'I, unfortunately, have to prepare,' and he bowed to take his leave.

Dancer looked to Cartheron. 'So, where should we go?'

Cartheron motioned him onward. 'Anywhere my brother's not cooking.'

* * *

Nedurian leaned up against the side of the *Insufferable* as the crew raised the sails and the vessel gained headway out of Malaz harbour. At this point – rather belatedly – he decided that he was of two minds regarding the expedition.

He wanted it to succeed, of course, and end the pointless waste and loss of life of the feud between Nap and Malaz; but on the other hand it was reckless, and to his mind pretty damned foolish, and could lead to the loss of even more lives. Lives of lads and lasses he'd had a hand in training, whom he'd become rather fond of, and perhaps couldn't bear to see thrown into the meat-grinder of yet another leader's overweening ambition or selfish greed.

As he had seen all too often before.

So he had told himself he didn't care, and eventually, over the years, he'd even come to believe it. But that was then. Now, he left the gambits of king-making to others; he would content himself with what was important – looking after his lads and lasses.

He walked the deck, which was crowded with

lounging marines, eyeing each squad in turn. When he came to the First Army, Seventh Company, Eleventh Squad, he stopped and set his hands on his hips before one marine in particular. This lad sat hunched beneath a mule's load of equipment: two shovels, a pickaxe, tent pieces, rolled canvas and blankets, an iron cooking pot, an infantryman's shield, two shortswords, and a spare helmet strapped to his straining belt.

Nedurian gestured to the shop's worth of gear. 'What is all this?'

The lad saluted with a fist to his chest. 'Proper equipage, cap'n.'

'Is that so? Proper equipage for an entire regiment, maybe. Why're you carrying all this?'

'Me squaddies said I had to on account of me being the designated siegeworker'n'saboteur'n'such.'

'Said that, did they?' Nedurian spotted them nearby, pretending to be uninterested but eyeing him sidelong. He waved them over. 'Spread this gear out. You know the rule: share the load.' Grumbling, they plucked pieces of gear from the lad and divided it among them. Nedurian watched the process, then frowned, uncertain. 'Where's your mage?'

'That one?' said a Malazan girl, sniffing. 'Too good for us, she is. Won't dirty her fine sandals with trash like us.'

Nedurian rubbed the scar at his cheek; he knew the one. 'Where is she?' They all glanced up at the shrouds. He sighed, crossed to the ratlines, and climbed.

He found her sitting up against the mizzen mast, legs straight out and crossed atop a spar. He took hold of the spar and swayed there in the netting far above the deck. From her papers he knew her name to be Hyacynth, but he suspected that she must be mortified by it as she was known only as Hy. 'Going to hide up here all day?'

'I'm not hiding,' she corrected. 'I happen to be in plain view.'

'Okay – run as far as you can?'

'I didn't run,' the pale, delicately featured redhead corrected again. 'I climbed.'

Nedurian blew out a breath. 'Look, child, I know this isn't some fine salon in Quon, but you signed up for this, and this is how it is.'

She rolled her eyes to the sky. 'What is that supposed to mean?'

'It means that yes, they're crude and lewd and ignorant and use rough language and just want to drink and screw, but what do you expect? Half are fresh off the farm or the fishing boat. You'll just have to put up with it for now.'

Hy crossed her arms over her thin chest. 'Why for now? What could possibly change?'

'Action, child. Once you all see action, everything will change. Trust me. I've seen it a thousand times.'

She bit at a gnawed thumbnail. 'You're obviously an educated man, captain. How could you bear to serve with such . . . such . . .'

'Peasants?' he offered.

'Gauche rubes,' she supplied.

'Because some of them proved to be among the best people I've ever known. Now, c'mon down and stop pouting.'

'I'm not pouting,' she corrected yet again.

He popped his head back up to say, 'Yes you are,' and climbed down.

At the stern deck he joined the fleet's admiral, Choss, who alone among Surly's Napans would not be accompanying the landing party. The burly veteran raider gave him a nod.

'So, an attack on Dariyal's harbour defences – defences that have never been breached.'

'That's the size of it,' Choss affirmed, distracted, as he eyed the progress of the ragtag flotilla spreading out from Malaz.

'After the failed assault we pull back to form a block-ade.' The admiral nodded. 'Will they respond?'

'Oh, they'll probably come chasing out right after us.'

'And that's good?'

The fellow murmured orders to a flagwoman, then returned his attention to Nedurian. 'Good and bad. We might be overrun, but at least everyone will be watching the harbour.'

'Ah. And Surly?'

'On board the *Twisted*, with the mage and Dancer.'

'Will she head in with them?'

'She keeps threatening to. So I wouldn't be surprised. Now,' and he gestured with a wide hand to the surrounding vessels, 'I have to send some messages.'

Nedurian bowed, withdrawing. 'Of course.'

Despite all his decades of campaigning, Nedurian had never before been in a proper naval engagement. Oh, he'd seen river crossings and lakeside assaults aplenty, but no ship-to-ship action. So he leaned on the side and eyed the preparations with the appreciative eye of an interested, if inexperienced, fighting man.

The trip would take nearly the full day. He watched the vessels using the time to order themselves. Fat and heavy modified merchant caravels lumbered to the front. These, he knew, from sitting in on briefings, had been adapted to look like the troop-carriers they would be in any normal port assault. In this case, however, they were not. They were hollow canards, meant to lead the way and attract the heaviest barrages from the formidable harbour mangonels, catapults, and scorpions.

Behind these would slip in the majority of the Malazan galleys. Swift and low, the troops they carried actually working the oars, they would strike while the caravels took the punishment – at least that was the plan.

The rest of the fleet, including the *Insufferable*, would follow.

Caught up in the atmosphere of the preparation, Nedurian had to remind himself that all this was actually merely a diversion, meant to keep attention focused on the water, and away from the palace.

It occurred to him that should these Malazans subdue Nap, they would effectively rule the seas and the entire coastline surrounding Quon Tali – a continent where none of the cities or states had invested in a navy of any significance. Why bother when you had potentially hostile neighbours on all sides? And hence his own lack of naval experience even after so many years.

So, he wondered, did this mage Kellanved *know* all this when he selected Malaz as a base from which to launch his ambitions? Or had he merely chosen to make the most of the available strengths of wherever he found himself? It was a debate that could go back and forth for ever, he supposed. Scholars might grind their quills down to nubs over it all – but only if they succeeded this day.

When afternoon came, he went from man to man and woman to woman, examining their gear, pulling on straps, and setting aside heavy equipment they wouldn't be needing, such as the shovels and other siegeworking and saboteur gear. Their job would be to repel boarders. And there would be a lot of them, as the Napan fleet outnumbered them well over three to one.

Later, as the afternoon waned, a call went up from the

high shrouds and everyone, Nedurian included, looked to the west. After a few moments he caught a glimpse: the bonfire atop the great lighthouse at the end of the Dariyal harbour mole. Defensive lookout during the day, and light to guide Napan mariners by night.

There was certainly no turning back now, for if they could see the lighthouse, then the Napan lookouts could see them.

*

It was a statement of where the Napan Isles' power and interest lay that the traditional palace of the kings stood next to Dariyal's harbour. Tarel hated the damp draughty place, and planned to move to the upland estate district of the capital once he'd settled things with his sister, which looked to be soon.

He and his inner circle of advisers – those who had backed him early on and now held high political appointments from him, and were profiting mightily from said positions – all waited, laughing a touch nervously and loudly, in one of the guardrooms overlooking the harbour while a steady stream of messengers came and went.

'Fewer than fifty ships, you say?' Tarel demanded of one naval officer messenger.

This officer bowed. 'So say the lookouts.'

Tarel turned to High Admiral Karesh, frankly incredulous. 'So few? Could this be a trick?'

The admiral shook his head. 'No, my lord. Our spies on Malaz reported such numbers. This is all their complement, thrown in together against us. This usurper mage is a fool,' he added, and chuckled in a self-satisfied way that irritated Tarel.

'My sister is no fool,' he snapped.

Admiral Karesh bowed, hands fluttering. 'Of course,

m'lord. But what choice does she have? She has thrown in her lot with these criminals and murderers.'

Tarel nodded to himself while peering through an arrow slit to the waters beyond the harbour. Yes, criminals and murderers. A dark mage and an assassin who – and he could not help but rub his neck – reportedly had already killed one king . . . 'I do not see them,' he complained.

'Soon, m'lord. Then, as agreed, we allow them to push into the harbour. There they will not find us unprepared and surprised. Every vessel is already manned and crammed with soldiers. We will overwhelm them.' He finished, confidently, 'Not one Malazan ship will escape.'

Tarel eyed the corpulent fellow uneasily. He did not like such confidence – to him it bespoke stupidity. 'My sister will be on board one of those vessels. It is *her* I do not want to escape.'

Admiral Karesh bowed again. 'Of course, m'lord.'

Tarel found the eye of a waiting messenger. 'A hundred gold Untan crowns to whoever brings me the head of the traitor Lady Sureth.'

The messenger bowed and darted from the chamber.

Admiral Karesh pursed his thick lips in disapproval. 'Unnecessary, m'lord.'

'It should help the fighting spirit, I imagine,' Tarel opined, eyeing the open waters anew. He clenched and unclenched his hands and found them damp. What had he forgotten? Had he forgotten anything? Those impetuous lawless Malazans would be encircled and eliminated – along with his sister who sought refuge with them. Malaz would then be his for the plucking, and Nap would once again rule the southern seas.

All under his rule. He might go down in history as among the greatest of her kings and queens.

And as for this dread dark mage who had taken the island in his fist. Well, he had his check in place for that contingency as well.

What more could one do? One placed the pieces on the board as best one might and prayed. It was all in the hands of the gods now, and he must await with everyone else the turning of the throw.

Chapter 10

As if having lost her nerve for the coming fight, the *Twisted* peeled away from the flotilla at the last possible moment. She swept west, skirting along the base of the salt-stained stones of a towering seawall. Dancer watched from the side while the skeleton crew of volunteer sailors dashed from line to line, adjusting their running.

'They'll let us go,' opined the veteran sailor on the wheel, Brendan. He'd been promoted to captain of the vessel but somehow couldn't part from his usual station. 'One less ship to fight.'

Dancer nodded his distracted agreement. Getting to shore somewhere, somehow, and relatively undetected, was the puzzle that occupied him. But – his gaze strayed to the shut cabin door – it wasn't his responsibility. That lay elsewhere.

Surly's Napans watched from the side as well, Surly herself among them. How they had howled when she climbed aboard! But what could they do? Throw her off? She'd played her hand well; demurring and quietly agreeing to Cartheron's advice to hold back, all the while fully intending to come along anyway.

The main body of the force was some thirty Malazan

fighters, hand-picked and led by Dassem, and including their early recruit Dujek and his shadow, Jack.

The last of the party was the Kartoolian mage. Tayschrenn stood with Dancer, which said a lot, as it implied he was comfortable with neither the Napans nor the Malazans, and apparently preferred to stand with a notorious assassin instead.

They now hugged Dariyal's built-up city shore, the Napans scanning it eagerly for something. It was nearing dusk, the sun lowering towards the western horizon, more or less behind them – a deliberate choice of timing in the assault as it put the sun in the defender's eyes.

Despite keeping a close eye on the shore Dancer was startled when a long low vessel came darting out between two piers and aimed straight for them, churning the waters with double-banks of oars.

''Ware!' he shouted. 'Ready to repulse!'

The Napans crowded the side. Surly stood behind, arms crossed, a strange sort of secret smile on her lips. The vessel came aside quickly, blue banners fluttering. It was a swift bireme, some sort of shore picket. Urko actually threw down a rope ladder then, and Dancer opened his mouth to object, but Surly raised a hand, asking for a moment.

A single Napan climbed aboard, one of the largest Dancer had seen to date, almost as wide as Urko, but much heavier about the middle. This man opened his arms and the Napans, Cartheron, Urko and Tocaras, all exchanged slapping hugs with him. Then he approached Surly and took her hand, bowing from the waist.

'Amaron,' Surly greeted him.

'You are all under arrest,' Amaron announced with a wink. 'I'm afraid I must escort you to the palace.'

*

Everything went well, at first. Nedurian watched from the *Insufferable* as the empty caravels bulled ahead into the harbour, taking a pounding from the mole defences. But no flame attacks, he noted, thinking that the Napans must be worried about their own vessels.

Yet he could not see most of the harbour piers and docks from where the *Insufferable* was laid up, sails lowered, waiting while the troop-carrying oared galleys and longboats charged in ahead.

After a time, Choss ordered minimal canvas, and the *Insufferable* leaned in, heading for the harbour mouth. Uneasy, Nedurian headed to the stern deck.

'Won't we be unable to manoeuvre in there?' he asked the admiral.

'Oh yes,' Choss agreed, cheerily enough. He turned aside to give orders to a flagwoman.

Nedurian raised a brow. 'Speaking as an ignorant landsman – perhaps we shouldn't enter, then.'

'Have to. Under orders to give a good show.'

'I understand that. But we might end up being captured.'

The admiral rubbed a hand over the kinky black beard he was growing. 'Just might.'

'So that's the plan? Lose?'

Choss offered up a disturbingly merry smile. 'Surly made some refinements on the plan. The idea is to lose the battle to win the war.'

'*Now* you tell me this?'

The admiral slapped him on the back. 'Don't worry yourself. That doesn't mean we can't put up a good fight.'

Nedurian returned to his troops, shaking his head. *These Napans are crazy.*

The full Malazan fleet was now crowding the harbour entrance and it immediately became obvious to Nedurian that he was right – there was no way to manoeuvre in the confines of the sheltered bay behind the mole.

Moreover, the Napan ships at their piers were now coming to meet them en masse. In no way had they been caught unawares or unprepared by the Malazan strike. Any sane commander, facing this, would order the retreat. Choss, however, raised the flags for attack.

Nedurian understood a desperate gamble, but this seemed unnecessarily callous. How many good men and women had to die to feed a diversion? It was frankly distasteful, and he stormed back up to the stern deck.

'Crews are going to die for this!' he shouted to Choss. 'A fighting withdrawal at the least!'

The blue-hued commander was in the midst of belting on a set of matching long-knives. Instead of being insulted, he gave Nedurian a nod of understanding. 'All captains have been given leave to decide for themselves how long to fight, or to withdraw at will.'

'Withdraw at will . . .' Nedurian echoed, eyeing the two fleets now coursing towards each other. Three of the gigantic lumbering Malazan caravels had caught fire at last and were now bearing down upon the Napans as fireships of their own creation. 'Generations of enmity and you think any one of them would dare be the first to withdraw?'

Choss gave him a wink. 'For a Talian you catch on fast.' He pointed to a flagwoman, who signalled furiously, then slapped Nedurian on the shoulder again. 'Don't worry. Surly doesn't waste resources. I'll order the general retreat long before that.' He motioned Nedurian to mid-deck. 'Your concern does you credit. But, if you don't mind, I'm rather busy right now . . .'

The old soldier in Nedurian reflexively saluted. 'Of

course, admiral.' He returned to his troops, yelling, 'Prepare to repel boarders!'

The marines lined the sides, shields raised.

As he watched the limited jostling among the vessels that was the only manoeuvre possible, it slowly became evident to Nedurian that Choss's flag-waving and communiqués had established a loose arc, or Malazan defence, just inside the harbour mouth – he was prudently not about to allow his retreat to be cut off.

That at least was something of a relief. Now it was up to them to hold out and wait – for a time. It occurred to him then, rather belatedly, that as the flagship the *Insufferable* would be the last to withdraw.

He pulled a hand down his face and rubbed the scar that bisected his cheek. Things just kept getting better and better.

*

While the landing party climbed down the side of the *Twisted* to the waiting bireme, the *Blue Star*, Dancer bade farewell to the sailors who would take their vessel offshore to await the dawn, and the outcome of their gamble. He then knocked and entered the single stateroom to fetch Kellanved.

He found the fellow at the desk, hastily dropping something into his pocket. Irritated, he asked, 'What *is* that thing you keep fiddling with?'

The short mage brushed past him, walking stick in hand. 'Nothing.'

Jaws clenched, Dancer followed.

On deck, Kellanved frowned down at the launch. He cocked an eye to Dancer. 'This wasn't the plan.'

Dancer nodded. 'Apparently Surly's made some refinements.'

Yet instead of being angered, or insulted, the mock-ancient mage lifted his brows in appreciation. 'Of course. The little details.' He motioned to the launch, inviting Dancer onward.

On board the *Blue Star*, Urko, Cartheron, Tocaras and Surly changed into Napan guard uniforms, while Dassem and his troop, Tayschrenn, Dancer and Kellanved would play the part of captured Malazan invaders. Dassem handed over his weapon to his Napan 'captors' first, and the rest of the troop followed suit. Dancer surrendered his two visible weapons – the rest he kept.

Docking at a pier, they filed up the gangway under the watch of Amaron's picked crew, and were then marched to the palace.

Walking the empty narrow city streets, Dancer noticed that Kellanved had his hand in his pocket again, and lost his temper. 'What *is* that?'

The mage yanked his hand free. 'Nothing. Nothing at all.'

'No. What is it? Show me.'

The grey-haired ancient waved a dismissal. 'It's nothing, really.'

'No. Now,' Dancer hissed furiously.

'Quiet, prisoners!' Amaron barked from the front.

Dancer glared his impatience as they walked along. At first Kellanved looked away as if admiring the architecture, but he kept glancing back, guiltily, Dancer thought, until finally, quite sheepishly, he dipped his hand into his pocket and withdrew a dark object.

Dancer couldn't believe he was looking at the flint spear-point. 'I knew it!' he yelled, and reached for it. Kellanved covered it in both hands.

They tussled until strong arms – Urko's – pulled Dancer away, and he found himself staring at a very worried-looking Cartheron. 'Prisoners will remain *quiet*,' the Napan hissed.

Dancer nodded his cooperation and Cartheron appeared relieved. Urko released Dancer's arms and he returned to being marched along. All the while he glared at his partner, who was whistling soundlessly, seemingly engrossed in the shop-fronts.

After crossing a section of the city waterfront they passed through guard checkpoints at tunnels through doubled, many-feet-thick walls, and entered the grounds of the palace proper. Palace, however, was something of a misnomer, as the immense stone fortress served first as harbour stronghold, garrison and arsenal, and only last as residence for the Napan rulers.

Dancer didn't like this marching into the lion's den, but Surly appeared to have sympathizers all over the city. She and Amaron seemed to have planned this quite carefully.

Once admitted to what Dancer presumed was the main keep, Amaron's people quickly subdued the guards. Amaron turned to Surly. 'We'll hold the doors. The rest is up to you.' Surly gave a cool nod in answer. Everyone's weapons were returned. Dassem had Kellanved and Tayschrenn in the middle of his picked Malazans while he led the way with the Napans. Dancer drifted to the rear with Dujek and Jack.

They started through the immense hulking building. Everyone they came across either ran or had to be subdued – few had been killed so far, only knocked unconscious or tied and left aside. They were, after all, soon to be Surly's people.

To Dancer's experienced eye everything was going too smoothly. Still, it just might be a testament to this Amaron fellow, and the degree of Surly's secret support among the Napans. Yet, glancing back to empty halls, he could not shake the feeling that there was more to this play than had been revealed so far. At one point he caught Tayschrenn's eye and sent a silent query. The mage shook his head in a negative – he'd detected nothing strange so far.

Now that they had reached the higher floors of the rambling fortress, the dull roar of the battle beyond reached them. The assault on the harbour continued, at least for now.

At the fore, Urko and Cartheron eventually reached tall double doors, plated in gold, and bearing scenes of past naval glories of the island. These they pushed open to reveal a long reception hall, apparently empty. Dancer looked to the arched ceiling – also gilt – and shook his head. A godsdamned set-up, for certain. He set Dujek, Jack, and four other Malazans at the doors while everyone else advanced.

Doors opening ahead confirmed Dancer's suspicions. Palace guards filed in, followed by a slight younger fellow, richly dressed in velvet trousers, silk shirt, and brocaded jacket. His Napan bluish hue was flushed very dark with emotion.

Dassem ordered his troop to surround Surly. Footsteps from the rear brought Dancer's attention there and he glimpsed more soldiers approaching up the hall. Dujek sent him a questioning look. 'Bar the doors,' Dancer ordered, then slipped forward up to Kellanved's side.

'We don't have to do this,' Surly was saying to the young fellow.

'You know we do,' he answered. 'And you are losing.' He laughed then, rather nervously. 'You think I don't have *my* allies? Well, I do. And they warned me. Your wretched little handful of ships is being overrun as we speak – what a waste!'

'I did not come alone.'

The fellow, King Tarel, Dancer assumed, daubed a cloth to his sweaty face. 'Oh, yes.' He laughed again, a touch strained. 'The fearsome dark mage, ruler of Malaz – *him*, I assume?'

Kellanved stepped forward, shaking his head as if disappointed. 'This confrontation is very ill-advised. You really should capitulate.'

'First things first. There is someone here who would very much like to meet you.'

Kellanved made a show of peering round, 'Oh?'

But the near-glee in Tarel's voice put Dancer's nerves on alert and he clenched his weapons at his back. Black opaque tendrils gathered at one edge of the room, and coalesced to a pool out of which stepped a woman in black, her hair a long, full mane of iron grey that fell all down her back. Tayschrenn, at Dancer's side, hissed a breath of recognition.

'Who is it?' Dancer whispered.

'I know her by reputation. The Witch Jadeen. A near Ascendant, some say.'

Dancer mouthed a curse: this Tarel had prepared well.

The witch pointed to Kellanved and crooked the black-nailed finger in a 'come-hither' motion. 'You have poked your nose up too high, little one. Time for a true match of powers.' Tayschrenn stepped up to Kellanved's side, and the woman sneered. 'What is this? Hiding behind lackeys?'

Kellanved urged Tayschrenn back, but his other hand, Dancer noted, was in his pocket, worrying that ridiculous stone. 'This is my responsibility,' he told Tayschrenn. The Kartoolian mage adjusted the clip of his long black hair, musing aloud, 'Jadeen, they say you have walked the lands of Quon Tali for centuries. Plumbed many mysteries of the Warrens . . .'

The witch showed her teeth. 'I will whisper all that into your ears . . . after I have removed them from your head.' And she threw down a hand and both she and Kellanved disappeared in bursts of darkness and a rush of dry air.

Dancer clenched Tayschrenn's arm in a fierce grip. '*Follow them!*'

'I – I will try,' he stammered, and, inclining his head to Surly as if in apology, he gestured and the chamber disappeared round Dancer.

*

Nedurian had long ago exhausted himself using his Warren to protect the *Insufferable* and the men and women of her crew. Now he merely fought with sword and shield, defending the deck against a constant rush of boarders as vessel after Napan vessel stormed alongside.

It was clear that they were losing by attrition and that there was nothing to be done about it. He stepped back, untangling himself from the melee, and went to find Choss.

The Napan admiral had seen fighting himself, his shirt hacked and bloodied. He was busy directing communication between the Malazan ships – those not yet taken, nor withdrawn from the harbour. 'We must go!' Nedurian shouted to him.

In answer, Choss gestured to the harbour mouth. 'They got past us!'

Nedurian peered into the gathering dark of the evening. It looked as though a few vessels, Napans, had sneaked past to choke the narrow harbour mouth, and were probably lashing themselves together there. He mouthed a curse to Mael. Now what was to be done? Ram them? There was not enough wind here.

A release of enormous power rocked him then. Of the Rashan Warren, his own, and from the direction of the palace. He stood blinking, staring in wonderment. Familiar too. The witch he had duelled with so long ago, who had defeated every mage in Quon Tali who dared face her. Himself included.

He nodded. Only one thing would bring her here. A challenger. She'd come for Kellanved, gods help him.

Nedurian pulled a hand down his face again, thinking, *Well, nothing to be done.* They had their own problems here. And even as he returned his attention to the vessels surrounding the *Insufferable* and the many lines and grapnels clutching at her, a dense salvo of coordinated bowfire flew up skyward from all around to arc directly for the Malazan flagship.

He watched all this in a heartbeat and cursed that there was nothing he could do about it.

A wind suddenly buffeted him, nearly knocking him to the deck. The rigging snapped and lashed, the spars creaked and groaned overhead, and the countless arrows curved, gyring all together as in a funnel-cloud to hammer down on to the nearest Napan ship holding them back.

All eyes on board the *Insufferable* turned to a pale, red-headed girl at mid-deck, arms raised, her clothes whipping in an unseen wind. She lowered her arms, glaring all about. 'Well?' she demanded. 'What are you all staring at? Let's get out of here!'

'Full canvas!' Choss bellowed from the stern deck.

Sailors scrambled into the rigging and fierce winds bellied the sails as they fell. The *Insufferable* lurched round in a tight arc, dragging the smaller Napan vessels with her. The marines hacked at the grapnels and hooked lines until they all flew free.

'Strike between vessels,' Choss ordered his steersman as they rounded towards the harbour mouth. The few remaining uncaptured Malazan ships did their best to angle in behind the *Insufferable* as she stormed past.

Hy had her arms raised once more, hands twisting as she sculpted the winds, and the deck actually tilted towards the bows as the *Insufferable* rocked anew. Nedurian smiled to see Hy's squad covering her back now with raised shields as she worked.

'Ramming speed,' Nedurian mouthed to himself, and he hooked an arm round a stanchion, bracing himself for impact.

The gigantic flagship struck the roped barrier like a mountain of timber. The stout hemp lines stretched, creaking, straining, and finally snapped, first singly, then in multiple numbers, until the *Insufferable* lurched through and free.

The crew sent up a great cheer, but Choss was not smiling; he was peering back at their wake and Nedurian was straining to see as well. Slowly, in stops and starts, the Malazan fleet emerged and Nedurian let go a long-held breath. The *Insufferable* had done enough to break the blockade and it appeared that the Napans were letting them flee – tails between their legs, presumably.

Inevitably, however, there had been losses, despite Kellanved's and Surly's intent of a mere diversion. The question was, would they prove too heavy? And if so, it occurred to Nedurian that it might not be healthy for Choss, as a Napan and one of Surly's crew, to return to Malaz. Return to what? Censure? Arrest?

It all depended, he supposed, on what was happening in that great bulk of stone that was Dariyal's harbour keep.

*

When the Witch Jadeen plucked Kellanved from their midst, and Dancer followed shortly thereafter with the mage Tayschrenn – presumably in pursuit – Cartheron almost let his arms fall. *Typical! Bloody typical!* They hit a tight spot and the mad mage disappeared once more.

Surly, as usual, collected herself more quickly than anyone. 'What now?' she demanded of her brother, as if nothing had happened.

Tarel just laughed. 'Now? What happens now? You die!' He waved the palace guards forward. 'Kill them all!'

Surly threw up her arms, calling out loudly: 'No need! No need for Napan to kill Napan. Or for any more to die. That is exactly what I had wished to avoid. I will surrender – but with one condition.'

Tarel's face wrinkled in sour disbelief. 'Condition? You are in no position to make demands. I have beaten you. And now you die.'

A commanding officer with Tarel leaned in and whispered something to him. Cartheron thought the officer was looking towards the Malazans – to Dassem in particular – and it occurred to him that the Dal Hon swordsman might very well be able to fight his way out of this singlehanded, and that a lot of Napan soldiery would die in the process. The king rolled his eyes to the ceiling and huffed.

'Oh, very well,' he allowed. 'What is it?'

'Grant safe passage to the Malazans,' Surly said. 'They aren't really involved in this. This is a Napan affair.'

Tarel waved a hand. 'Very well. Escort these Malazans

to a captured vessel and send them off. They'll no doubt be killed by the mob when they return, anyway.'

Surly turned to Dassem. 'Keep order. Handle a transition of leadership if necessary.'

The swordsman bowed. 'I will help keep order, for a time. Until we see what we shall see.'

Surly nodded her understanding.

Yes, Cartheron thought, *until we see if Kellanved will ever return*. He caught Dujek's eye and saluted him.

The burly fighter shoved his sword home. 'We'll stay, dammit!' he growled.

Surly shook her head and motioned for him to remove his sword-belt. He eyed the surrounding guards for a time, then gave a reluctant nod and complied. All the other Malazans followed suit, even Dassem.

Palace guards escorted the Malazan contingent out. Tarel eyed the four remaining Napans. 'Drop your weapons as well,' he commanded.

Cartheron, Urko and Tocaras did so – Surly was unarmed.

Tarel motioned to his guards, 'Throw them into separate cells to await their execution.' He took one step nearer to Surly, and it seemed to Cartheron that this was as close as the man dared get to his sister. 'And you,' he said, pointing to her, 'I know your tricks. You will be under constant observation, and if you escape your followers here will all be killed immediately. Is that clear?'

She crossed her arms, almost sighing. 'Yes, Tarel.'

*

Dancer found himself on damp ground in the middle of thick jungle at night. Tayschrenn was with him and he released the mage's arm. 'Where are we?' he whispered.

The mage peered round. 'South Itko Kan, I presume. Jadeen's territory.'

'Are they near?'

Tayschrenn motioned to one side. Dancer edged forward, pushing through wet fronds to a clearing where, beneath hanging rain-clouds, Jadeen stood over a prostrate Kellanved. Dancer decided that he probably had no chance of actually stealing up on the woman, and so he chose to walk up openly. He glanced behind to see Tayschrenn following, hands clasped at his back.

As they closed, the witch shot them a glance, then urged them forward with one lazy beckoning gesture of a black-nailed hand.

Kellanved, Dancer saw, lay enmeshed in ropes of writhing night.

'You followed,' she observed, and she peered past Dancer to Tayschrenn. 'You have some skill – and power. Do you too challenge?'

Dancer eyed the Kartoolian sidelong. Tayschrenn remained impassive, droplets of rain now darkening his long straight black hair, which was pulled back and tied by a silver clip. He lifted and dropped his thin shoulders, seemingly indifferent. 'If he falls I shall be paramount.'

The witch bared her teeth again, in evident approval, and regarded the prostrate Kellanved. 'There. You hear that? The law of might. Those who are weak fall. So should it be. So it has always been.' She crooked a finger at him. 'Should've kept your head down for a hundred years or so, little man. Perhaps then you would've been a challenge to me. But you chose to reach too high too soon.'

'A trade then,' Kellanved gasped, struggling.

The witch snorted her scorn. 'So now you beg. This

has been no fun at all. Trade? What could you possibly trade?'

'Incomparable power.'

Jadeen peered round and opened her hands as if in wonder. 'Power? You possess none.'

Kellanved glanced down his side. 'In my pocket. A key to the greatest power on all the earth.'

Fat rain droplets struck Dancer's shoulders as he eased his hands behind his back and took hold of the grips of his slimmest throwing daggers. He wasn't going to just stand by—

Slightly behind, Tayschrenn reached out and gently set a hand on his elbow; he glanced back and the mage edged his head in the faintest of negatives. Dancer clenched his teeth, but relaxed his grip. *Very well – for the moment.*

Jadeen had been eyeing Kellanved in disgust. 'Please. No pathetic tricks.'

'No trick. Here. In my pocket.'

'Very well.' She gestured to Tayschrenn. 'You, mage. Remove the thing and toss it this way.'

Tayschrenn bowed, and approached. The twisting night-black ropes of Rashan parted to allow him access to the pocket. He withdrew what looked like a stone tool of some sort, which he gently tossed to Jadeen's feet. She urged the mage back again with a wave.

The witch peered down for a time, studying it, then threw her head back, her hair tossing, and barked a harsh scornful laugh. Her reaction reminded Dancer uncomfortably of the Seti shaman's when *he* saw the spear-point as well.

'So,' she said, 'you too have found a stone compass to the fields of flint. This is your power, is it?' She shook her head, amused. 'An ancient puzzle, yes. But false. No power lies at what so many wrongly call the Graveyard of the Army of Bone.'

Dancer heard Tayschrenn's breath leaving him in a long hissed exhalation and he glanced to the man to see open amazement upon his features.

'But it points . . .' Kellanved began.

She smirked, smiling still, but it was not a pleasant expression. 'Yes, it points. Come then. Let me show you what your life is worth. Nothing.'

The witch gestured again and the two disappeared in smears of thickening darkness.

Dancer snatched the mage's arm again. 'Follow them!'

Tayschrenn was shaking his head. 'The Army of Bone. Dancer . . . is that where you've . . .' He actually tried to pull away. 'No one should meddle there. An Elder horror. To disturb them . . . you do not know the legends . . .'

Dancer squeezed the arm. 'There's nothing there. I've seen it. Now go!'

The Kartoolian mage had visibly paled. He swallowed. 'Well . . . for now. But you have no idea . . .'

'Go!'

Tayschrenn threw a hand down and their surroundings shifted once again.

It was night still, but the sky was clear, the air much colder. Dancer and Tayschrenn stood upon a familiar hillside, a valley before them. Dancer motioned ahead. 'This way.'

It did not take long to find the witch. She was pacing about, picking up objects and letting them fall, brushing her hands together, speaking to someone as yet unseen. Closer, Dancer spotted Kellanved on the ground, still wrapped in tendrils of Rashan.

The witch nodded to Dancer as he approached. 'You

are persistent.' She tilted her head, examining him. 'You possess no talent, yet you have strong instincts. Are you the one who slew Chulalorn?'

Dancer saw no reason to dissemble, and he nodded.

The witch snorted again, and turned to Kellanved. 'I warned him! He, too, over-reached. And look how he ended up.' She opened her arms to encompass their surroundings. 'Behold the Graveyard of Bone – so called. I, too, pursued this mystery for a while.' She peered round, as if in remembrance. 'But that was a long time ago. This puzzle has consumed entire lifetimes of study. Driven mages insane.'

She prodded Kellanved with a toe. 'Like your Meanas. A cute trick, mastering it. But not enough.'

Tayschrenn came up to stand next to Dancer, and for the first time the mage appeared worried.

'Yet they all point . . .' Kellanved objected.

Jadeen nodded impatiently. 'Yes, yes. They point. But where, yes?'

The little mage attempted to shrug within his bonds. 'Well, here.'

The witch was shaking her head and grinning anew, obviously enjoying toying with him. 'No. It is here, but not *here*. The Army of Bone was of the Imass, yes? You knew this?'

Kellanved nodded. 'I have read such research.'

'And,' continued Jadeen, 'they were an Elder people. They possessed their own source of power – what we call Warrens, but they named Holds. Yes?'

Kellanved was nodding eagerly. 'Yes!'

'Theirs was named Tellann.'

Kellanved's face fell, his shoulders slumped. 'And it is closed to us.'

Jadeen nodded, and stooped to pick up a small

arrowhead that she then flicked away. 'Yes. Tellann is inaccessible to us. No human can reach it.'

'Yet these items – their Tellann-infused tools and weapons – can,' Kellanved mused.

Jadeen shrugged. 'What of it? That is no help to me or you.'

'I was just thinking,' Kellanved said, letting his head fall back as if he were studying the night sky, 'that they touch Tellann at all times, anywhere. So why . . .'

Dancer was startled by Tayschrenn's hand now suddenly gripping his arm.

Jadeen turned upon the little mage, her eyes widening. 'A physical access point! Here!'

Kellanved nodded. 'Also known as a gate.'

She paced, muttering to herself. She stooped again to snatch up a flint tool and tapped it with her nails. 'But gone now, over the aeons,' she murmured. 'Somehow.'

'Destroyed,' Kellanved affirmed. 'However—' He clamped his mouth shut.

Jadeen marched to him and set a foot upon his neck. '*What?* However what? Speak, damn you! Or I shall flay you alive!'

Dancer reached behind his back once more, but Tayschrenn squeezed anew and Dancer sent him a glare. The mage edged his head in a negative. Dancer gritted his teeth, seething.

'Well,' Kellanved gasped. 'It just occurs to me that where there was *one* gate . . .'

Jadeen lifted her foot, letting go a hissed breath. 'Yes . . . there may be another. Somewhere. One just need find it . . .' Then she froze, as if struck by a stunning thought, and turned a gaze full of wonder upon Kellanved, whose own mouth opened in understanding.

'*No!*' he breathed. 'Damn you.'

The witch threw back her head and laughed anew. She squeezed the flint tool in her hand and saluted Kellanved. 'You have bought your life, little man. My thanks. Live and howl to see me command the Army of Bone!' She waved a hand and darkest night took her.

The moment after the witch disappeared Kellanved leapt from the ground, his walking stick already in hand. 'We must hurry,' he told Dancer, who stared, stunned.

'But you were . . .'

'I replaced her bonds with mine some time ago. I had reached a dead end here. I hoped she possessed pieces I needed.'

'But you gave her all she needed!' Tayschrenn accused him. He pointed to where she had disappeared. 'That witch must not succeed. *No one* should succeed in this!'

'Then why did you stop me?' Dancer demanded.

Tayschrenn waved a hand in dismissal. 'Your blades would not have struck home and we'd all be dead now.'

Kellanved nodded his agreement. 'Yes. She is far too experienced and wary, that one. We are lucky to be alive, frankly. I had to give her more than I wished – but it couldn't be helped.' He tapped his fingertips together. 'Now, if you don't mind, we really must be going.'

'But Surly!' Tayschrenn objected. 'What of the Napans? We must return at once.'

Kellanved waved Tayschrenn off. 'Go ahead. See to it.'

'They could all be facing execution at this moment.'

The little mage rolled his eyes. 'Oh, please. Surly has her agents, the Claws, all over that island. If anyone is in danger of having their throat cut, it's that king.' He urged the Kartoolian off. 'Now go on. You have your own resources, do you not? Salvage things – if Surly hasn't already.'

'But I—' Tayschrenn stopped himself; he was alone.

That little mage seemed to be able to slip away instantly, or pretend to, in any case. Furious, he turned his face to the night sky, taking a deep breath. *Calm yourself. Calm. Anger solves nothing. It is an impediment.* 'Salvage things', he says? *How am I to—* He lowered his head, shaking it.

Very well. But if he returns and complains about any step I have taken – that will be it! We will be finished. I will not have him critique my choices.

Chapter 11

TAYSCHRENN RETURNED TO THE ISLE OF NAP. Here, in Dariyal, he sought out a certain inn that catered to foreigners. Entering, he spotted the renegade mage at table and sat down opposite him. When the burly, muscular fellow glanced up and saw him there he nearly choked on his wine. 'Hairlock,' Tayschrenn greeted him.

'Tayschrenn,' the fellow grunted, recovering, and leaning back. 'What in the name of the Enchantress are you doing here?'

'Why didn't you warn us? You were supposed to warn us.'

The mage shrugged his thick, meaty shoulders. 'Look – when I found out it was too late. And I wasn't about to go up against Jadeen. That wasn't the agreement.'

Tayschrenn tapped his fingers to the scarred table. 'And Calot?'

The fellow shrugged his rounded shoulders once more. 'Same for him, I suppose.'

'And where is he?'

Hairlock gulped his wine; Tayschrenn noticed he was sweating now. 'Best bordello in town, no doubt. Why? It's over. Our agreements are null and void.'

'No they aren't.'

The mage, who was either naturally dark-hued or deeply tanned a rich nut brown, cocked one hairless brow. 'Bullshit. You're kiddin' me. That little ancient . . .'

Tayschrenn gave a slow serious nod.

'Really?' Hairlock shook his head. 'Thin. Too thin.'

'Then consider me his representative and honour our agreement.'

'You?' The squat mage snorted. He returned his attention to his meal of boiled pork and parsnips, shoved a forkful into his mouth, and chewed. Swallowing, he took up his wine and sipped, eyeing Tayschrenn over the rim. 'Whatcha gonna do?' he asked, grinning lopsidedly.

Tayschrenn crossed his arms. 'Enforce it.'

The mage grunted, finished his wine. He tapped the glass. 'Proprietor! More wine!' Then he leaned forward, lowering his voice. 'Really? Right here? In front of everyone?'

Tayschrenn made a show of raising his eyes to the timber ceiling above, as if to say, *Must you bore me so?* 'If necessary,' he sighed.

A serving girl refilled Hairlock's glass. He swirled the wine, eyeing Tayschrenn speculatively, then shrugged. 'So . . . he's alive, you say?'

'Last I saw, yes.'

'He actually finished Jadeen?'

'No. They're both chasing something else.' Tayschrenn's gaze drifted aside, and he added distractedly, 'Something I hope neither discovers.'

The bald mage frowned momentarily at this, then gulped his wine. 'Well, if he is, then yeah, I'm in – for a while.'

'Fine.'

'What's the plan?'

Tayschrenn uncrossed his arms. 'We finish what we came here for.'

They found Calot in the best room of the bordello, but as he was not alone they retreated immediately and waited in the salon. Hairlock gulped more wine and Tayschrenn sampled a Kanese fruit liqueur. Calot soon descended, adjusting his shirt and pushing back his hair.

'Yes?' he asked, his cherubic face rather bemused, while he perused the choice of wines.

'Our agreement still stands,' Tayschrenn said bluntly.

Calot raised one brow. 'I'd heard Jadeen ate our benefactor.'

'Not so. Apparently,' Hairlock growled.

Calot's brow remained raised. 'Indeed. When shall we know?'

'When we know – which will be when we're done.'

Calot, looking like a young boy, smiled winningly. 'Excellent.' He raised a finger. 'Question. Do we still get paid? Because I have debts. Rather a lot, I'm afraid.'

Tayschrenn sighed. 'Yes. I'm sure you'll get paid.'

Calot raised a glass to that.

Outside, Calot, a skinny youth, bundled himself in a thick fur coat while Hairlock, seemingly indifferent to the weather, remained in his leather vest. Tayschrenn wore the same plain dark robes he'd picked up in Malaz, and he asked, 'Surly?'

'The dungeons beneath the palace,' Calot supplied.

'Do you know the way?'

'Yes.'

'Then let's go.'

'That's it?' Hairlock grumbled as they walked the evening streets of Dariyal. 'That's your plan? Go get her?'

'She's probably not even there any more,' Tayschrenn

sighed. 'But it's a place to start.' He eyed the rising dark silhouette of the palace, thought of the many guards within, and glanced to his two companions. 'Neither of you know any Mockra or Rashan, do you?'

Hairlock cracked his large knuckles. 'Not my forte.'

Calot shook his head. 'Sorry.'

Tayschrenn was beginning to reconsider his haste. This could get very loud and very destructive very quickly. Fortunately, a figure stepped out of the dark ahead and he relaxed, recognizing her from among Surly's guards – one of her Claws.

This woman inclined her head to him. 'She said you might show up.'

'And where is she?'

The woman invited them to follow her. 'This way.'

The Claw led them to a side entrance – one curiously unguarded – and up narrow stone staircases and back servants' ways to the main reception halls of the palace proper. All were dark and empty, save one doorway where firelight flickered. The Claw pushed open the door and moved to one side, guarding. Within stood Cartheron, Urko and Tocaras.

Tayschrenn frowned his appreciation. Well, well. Everything seemed to be in hand. And why not? Why should he have doubted Surly? He turned to his two companions. 'Wait here and stand guard.'

Hairlock peered inside and rolled his eyes. 'The Inner Circle. I get it.' He jabbed at Tayschrenn's chest, 'Just make sure we get paid for tonight's work.'

'Yes,' Tayschrenn hissed in answer. 'You will get paid.' And he pulled the door shut behind him. Within, he asked, 'Where is she?'

Cartheron glanced to the tall arched stone ceiling far above. 'Dealing with Tarel.'

Tayschrenn couldn't keep a frown of disapproval from his face. 'She's not going to . . .'

'She's offering him one more chance,' Urko explained, scowling his disapproval.

'And Kellanved? Dancer?' Cartheron asked. 'What happened?'

'Still alive last I saw. We shall see what happens.' He peered round, spotted a comfortable-looking chair, and sat. 'So I suppose we wait.'

Urko grunted his impatience and paced the room.

*

Despite having specifically chosen a windowless room with one barred and locked door, Tarel slept poorly. He kept thinking he'd heard the door open, and had to glance at it, checking it in the light of his single candle, again and again. It was the spectre of his sister, of course. Haunting him.

But he'd beaten her. Finally. After so many years. And soon she would be a ghost, in a very real headless sense. The thought calmed him, and he lay back once more.

Then he stiffened, unable even to breathe. In the chair, in the shadows, had someone been . . . ?

Very slowly, he raised his head to peer over. Indeed, someone was now occupying the one chair. His sister. Sureth.

His breath left him in an explosive gasp – almost a cry.

'I gave you every chance,' she said, sounding her old disappointed self.

'I beat you,' he whispered back. 'Beat you.'

She shook her head. 'This was inevitable. I'm sorry.'

He managed to swallow. 'And if I were to call for the guards?'

'They are my guards.'

'Damn you! Damn you, damn you! I *won*!'

She raised a hand, as she always did to silence his tirades. 'You have one choice.'

'And what is that choice? Death?'

'Abdication. Relinquish your authority to the Council of Elders. Retire to the family villa on Rueth Isle.'

'Relinquish authority to *you*, you mean!'

She shook her head once more. 'No. The Council. They can have it. I'm interested in . . . other things.'

He waved a finger at her. 'No, no, no. It's a trick. A trick! You'll take it.'

She surged from the chair. 'I have no need for tricks, do I?'

Tarel pulled the covers higher. 'You're threatening me. Your own brother! Why can't I rule?'

Now she rubbed her forehead, sighing. 'Just abdicate. In the morning. I will have the Council summoned.'

He was thinking ahead now. He could abdicate – for the moment. But on Rueth he could plan anew. Regroup. Try again. Yes! A better plan. 'Very well,' he said. 'I will do as you ask. Devolve power to the Council.'

'Very good,' she answered, and headed to the door. Unbarring it, she paused, and turned back to him. 'By the way. Remember that half the people you will contact to plot with, and half your guards, and half the servants at the villa . . . will all, secretly, be working for me. You'll just never know which half.' She shut the door behind her.

Tarel pressed his face into his pillow and screamed.

*

When Surly entered the hall, Tayschrenn thought that for the very first time he detected emotion upon her features. And strangely enough, she appeared almost sad, or regretful. Cartheron spoke then, asking, 'Tarel?' and the mask snapped back into place and she straightened.

'Retiring to his villa.' The Napans all nodded at this, perhaps secretly relieved. 'The Council will rule,' she added, and Urko's great bushy brows rose in surprise. 'We have bigger concerns,' she finished, looking at Tayschrenn. 'Kellanved and Dancer?'

'Both still alive, as far as I know.'

She frowned, a touch perplexed. 'And Jadeen?'

He rose and went to a sideboard and examined the decanted wines, selected a deep red, and poured himself a glass. Turning, he leaned back against the table and sipped the wine – rather disappointing. 'It's very complicated,' he began. 'They chanced upon a mystery, she and Kellanved, and now they are both off pursuing it.' He rubbed his forehead, grimacing. 'Frankly, I hope neither succeeds.'

'Yet another mystery,' Surly echoed with a tired sigh. 'Very well . . . we proceed as usual.'

'And that is?' Cartheron asked.

'We refurbish the fleets and pick our targets.'

'What of the Council?' Tocaras asked.

'The Council will do what I tell them to.'

Cartheron and Urko exchanged looks; Cartheron cleared his throat. 'So . . . we wait for the announcement tomorrow.'

'Yes.'

Tayschrenn set down his wine. 'I will inform Malaz.'

Surly nodded to him. 'Thank you.'

Bowing, Tayschrenn took his leave. Without, he waved Hairlock and Calot to him. 'Your employment still stands – for the time being. Now we must look to the mainland.'

Hairlock crooked a sideways eager smile.

*   *   *

It was beginning to look to all involved, Gregar included, that the siege of Jurda was shaping into the engagement to end this, the latest of a long line of Bloor–Gris wars. Even if 'siege' really wasn't the proper term for what the Bloorian League allies were currently up to. 'Camping' was more the word Gregar would apply to the ring of bivouacs surrounding Castle Jurda. All contingents of the League ran their own troops; the Yellows, the Vorian, the Rath, each pursuing its own plans for the siege – the result being complete chaos and confusion.

And all the while the surrounded Jurdan forces kept watch from their layered battlements, no doubt rather bemused, if not downright amused.

The Fourth Company of the Second Yellows, with Gregar and Haraj, had laid claim to an abandoned outbuilding, half roofless, but built of a sturdy cobblestone – which was fortunate as the ruin lay just within the longest bowshot range of Jurda's outermost cantonments. Here they cooked common meals and bedded down, if not actively besieging, then at least contributing to the circumvallation.

Gregar tended to stand his watch from the building's ruined loft, exposed to bowshot, but confident that the defenders, mindful of wasting arrows and bolts, wouldn't bother with a single target. This day had been overcast and cold, with a few snow flurries, and he was thankful for the roaring cookfires below and looking forward to warming himself at one later that evening.

He eyed the imposing grey, cliff-like bulk of Castle Jurda and frankly didn't think much of the League's chances. This ancestral home had withstood determined sieges from both sides of the interminable Bloor–Gris wars. It contained an entire town within its layered curtain walls, and its outlying cantonments alone stood as large as some of the independent fortress-keeps brazen enough to field forces against it.

A voice called from the timber stairs and he turned. Haraj was gesturing him over. 'What is it?' he called.

'Over here!' the lad urged, waving.

Sighing, he came to the stairs where Haraj crouched behind cover. 'What is it?'

'It's the—' the skinny fellow cast a wary eye to the rearing castle walls.

'Don't worry. They won't fire.'

'But we're exposed here.'

'They won't bother.'

The lad hunched, regardless. 'Have you heard the news?'

'What news?'

'The Guard – they're here! Arrived yesterday.'

Gregar leaned more of his weight on the rain-slick haft of his spear and looked across to the snow-obscured grey walls. 'What of it?'

'What of it? Now's our chance! We should head over.'

'Your chance, you mean.'

Haraj coughed into a fist, wincing. 'Well, won't you come with me? Aren't you even curious?'

For a time Gregar tapped the butt of the haft to the ruined, fire-blackened timbers beneath his feet. 'Fine. I'll have a look.'

Haraj raised a fist. 'Fantastic! Let's go.'

Below, their new sergeant, Leah – Teigan having been promoted to master-sergeant – met them at the broad doorless entry. 'Where are you two going?'

'Word is the Guard's here,' Gregar explained, and was surprised when the woman stiffened, as if shocked.

'But I thought you'd—' she began, only to clamp her lips shut. Then she stepped in front of them. 'You're not relieved, soldier.'

There was a question as to whether Leah could pull rank on Gregar, as among all the promotions he'd been made colour-sergeant. So he simply motioned to the roof. 'My watch is almost over, and you know Haraj here . . . well, you know.'

'Yeah, Haraj, I know,' she answered, her gaze narrowing. 'Well . . . all right.' And she stepped aside.

Gregar was a little mystified by her attitude, but gave her a half-salute, and pushed by. 'You'd think she'd be curious too,' he told Haraj, who shrugged.

They traced the broad circle of the envelopment, passing encampments, corrals, and tent towns of camp-followers. A few crofters' huts had been taken over as quarters for the various nobles, but most preferred to erect their large field tents. One such collection displayed the bright orange pennants of the Vorian king, Gareth.

Leaving behind the last of the outlying pickets of the Vor camp, they passed beyond the curve of a Jurdan cantonment that commanded a rise to the north of the keep that contained the main entrance. In the fields and small copses beyond rose the carmine tents of the Crimson Guard bivouac.

Other off-duty soldiers were also passing, curious like them to take in the sight of the legendary company. Haraj, however, did not keep to a respectful distance and instead walked right up to two of the Guard who watched this side of the camp. Gregar followed, reluctant, but still curious.

The pickets on the path, a man and a woman, were

221

accoutred similarly, in mail hauberks, with belted leather trousers and tall crimson-dyed boots. Both were helmetless, for the moment. The woman, very heavy-set, cocked an eye their way in greeting. Gregar, however, wasn't set at ease – he knew that it was common practice among the company for all to pull regular duties no matter their experience or rank, and so he knew that he could be facing a legendary champion, even Petra.

'I want to join!' Haraj announced, and Gregar groaned inwardly, resisting the urge to press a hand to his brow.

The two pickets shared a glance that could only be described as jaded. 'Is that so?' the woman drawled. She looked the skinny, spotty, gangly lad up and down. 'You a fearsome champion of some sort?'

Haraj blushed, hunching self-consciously. 'No . . . I'm a talent. A mage.'

The two shared another glance, this time a doubtful one. 'That so?' the man said. 'Why don't you show me something. Prove it.'

'All right,' Haraj answered, and he extended a hand to the woman, who promptly smacked it aside, scowling. Haraj threw both hands up. 'Just a demonstration.'

The woman eased her stance, though remained wary. 'A demonstration,' she repeated, a hard edge to her voice. 'Fine.'

The lad slowly reached out and somehow the woman's weapon-belt promptly fell to her feet. The two guards, as well as Haraj and Gregar, remained in shocked silence until the male mercenary sent up a loud laugh. 'That lad's gotten into your pants faster than anyone I've ever seen, Petra.'

Fener's tusks! This *was* Petra, one of the most fearsome of the Guard!

The woman's lips compressed into a tight white line

and she reached out to grasp Haraj. 'C'm'ere, you little shit. I'll show you a trick . . .' But somehow he evaded her hand, twisting side to side. Snarling, she sent a backhanded cuff his way, and missed. Finally, her face reddening, she reached down for one of the maces at her feet.

The guardsman stepped out in front of her. 'Whoa there, lass. Who's on duty now for this?'

'Red,' Petra growled, adjusting her belt.

'Then why don't you get him so we can sort this out?'

The woman sent Haraj a dark look, but nodded. 'Fine. We'll sort this out all right.' She stomped off.

The fellow turned to them, shaking his head. 'Lookin' to have your face caved in there, lad?'

'But you asked for a demonstration . . .'

The guard raised a hand for silence. 'Just show some judgement, will you?' He looked at Gregar. 'And what about you?'

Gregar motioned to Haraj. 'Tryin' to keep him alive.'

The guard grunted his understanding. 'Looks like you've had your work cut out for you.'

After a short time Petra returned with a slim, unimpressive-looking fellow in loose, faded red trousers and shirtings, who despite his name did not have red hair, but instead a scruffy dark beard and equally scruffy dark curly hair. 'This the one?' he asked Petra.

'That's the one.'

Red looked Haraj up and down. 'Yeah. He's a talent all right.'

'Dammit,' Petra grunted beneath her breath.

Haraj raised a hand to the newcomer. 'A word, if I may?'

'Watch your trousers, Red,' Petra warned. Haraj and the Guard mage spoke briefly, Red eyeing Gregar a few times before he nodded and waved Gregar over. 'Let's go talk to the boss.'

223

Gregar pointed to himself. 'Me?'

'Yeah – you can come along.'

Hunh. Well, what d'ya know? I'm gonna get a first-hand look at the Guard. He followed, very curious now – if not a touch envious of his friend.

Red led them into the sprawling encampment, past tents and horses being fed and brushed. The men and women of the Guard lounged about, most in the quilted and padded long shirts worn beneath armour that some named aketons, or haubergeons. Gregar struggled to put names to faces; two fellows sitting together looked quite similar and so he imagined they might be the famed Brothers Black, the Lesser and the Greater. A broad-shouldered woman sitting and having her hair curry-combed for lice might be Urdael of the two swords.

They headed for the largest of the tents, Courian's command quarters, Gregar assumed, and passed its pickets. Within, a large central bonfire blazed while tables all around held more of the Guard. Everyone's attention, however, was upon two figures close to the bonfire, a man and a woman, who appeared to be engaged in some sort of slow, ritualized duel. Each held a stave, and they circled one another in an awkward-looking upright and painfully slow gait. The reason for this soon became apparent as Gregar made out that each held an apple balanced atop their head, and each was attempting to knock the other's off.

Bets flew thick and fast across the tent, together with crusts of bread tossed at the duellists, all amid a huge uproar of laughter and cat-calls. Red stopped here and crossed his arms to watch.

The woman sent a great sweep at the head of her opponent which fell just short, perhaps even brushing his nose. A great cheer went up at that. Both apples wobbled, but did not fall. The fellow eased one step to his left and sent an answering sweep, but was well adrift. Experienced stick fighter that he was, Gregar instantly saw that the man was deliberately holding his grip short, and had a good hand's breadth of reach yet.

The woman shifted forward, her boots dragging over the dry bare earth; the man appeared to yield more ground, but it was a feint, and the woman came on.

Even as Gregar saw her mistake, the man swung, knocking her apple flying in a spray of pulp. An enormous roar went up, half of triumph, half of displeasure. A great giant of a man was banging a tankard to his table and yelling, 'Too eager, Lark! Too eager by far!'

By his great shaggy greying mane and beard and his one good eye, the other a blind white orb, Gregar knew this was Courian D'Avore, commander of the Crimson Guard. On his left sat a dark Dal Hon native, in oiled leathers, who Gregar imagined might be one of their most famous fighting mages, Cal-Brinn; while on the commander's right sat a lean youth with a very sharp hawk-like gaze that he took to be Courian's son K'azz, whom some named the Red Prince.

Red took the opportunity between amusements to lean towards Courian and speak to him. The Guard general cocked his head, listening, then nodded and gruffly waved Haraj forward. 'So, you wish to join, do you?'

'Ah, yes sir. If you please.'

Courian snorted. 'Please me or don't! I'm no damned spoiled noble to care either way!' He tore at a haunch of meat and chewed, glowering. 'You're a mage, I understand?'

'Yes.'

The great shaggy giant of a man looked the pale and pole-thin Haraj up and down and obviously didn't think much of what he saw. 'You'd better be, son. What can you do?'

'No one can hit me,' Haraj answered, and Gregar looked to the tent ceiling, suppressing a wince.

The mercenary general's thick bushy brows rose and he peered about, greatly amused. 'Now that's quite the boast – given present company. But, ah,' and he picked up another piece of rare meat, studied it, and popped it into his mouth, 'we'll be happy to give it a go.'

Now Gregar did wince.

Courian raised a paw to the fellow who'd just finished the staff fight. 'You first, Cole.' And he leaned back, his grin widening, to announce, 'Fifty gold Untan crowns to land a hit on our boastful friend here!'

The wagering erupted in a roar. Cole immediately swung at Haraj only to stagger forward as the staff passed through nothing but empty air.

The tent fairly exploded with renewed betting. Half the Guard cheered Haraj on while the other half baited Cole mercilessly.

'Have you forgotten how to fight, man!' Courian yelled.

Lark offered, 'Sure you're holding the right end of that stick?'

Cole smiled tolerantly and waved to the crowd; he made a pantomime show of taking careful aim at Haraj, who wisely now retreated behind a main support pole.

This time Cole thrust straight out, and though Gregar would've sworn he should have hit Haraj a solid blow to the stomach, once more he stumbled forward, impacting nothing, and the skinny youth slid aside.

Most of the assembled Guard cheered Haraj now. Thrown bits of bread and gnawed bones came pelting at Cole, who lost his smile and focused on stalking Haraj round the central hearth. After three more determined swings, each striking nothing, Gregar saw the lad, K'azz, lean over to murmur to his father, and the commander, until then laughing at the guardsman's troubles, frowned, leaned back and waved an end.

'Good enough!' he ordered, and Cole stood down. 'So you're hard to hit – that will come in handy when you're married, lad, but you do understand that we're a fighting company.'

Haraj nodded. 'Oh, yes, sir. I'm also rather good at getting in and out of places . . . if you know what I mean.'

Courian frowned, not particularly impressed, but he did glance over to the Dal Hon at his side. 'What say you, Cal-Brinn? Do we have a use for such things, you think?'

'I believe that we do, sir.'

Courian scratched his unkempt beard. 'Very well. It appears we *do* have a use for you after all.'

'And possibly his friend there,' Cal-Brinn added.

Gregar stared, quite stunned. Courian now studied him, narrowing his one good eye. 'This one? And what about you? What is it you do? Perhaps you can make flowers bloom? Or goats dance?'

Struggling to find his voice, Gregar stammered, 'Ah, no, sir. I'm just a fighter.'

Courian made a show of glancing round the gathering. 'Well, thank Burn for that! Now we're getting somewhere. For a moment there I thought I was starting up a travelling carnival.'

'And he's a mage,' Cal-Brinn supplied.

Gregar shook his head. 'No. You're mistaken. I'm no mage.'

The mercenary commander turned his good eye first to one then the other, glowering even further. 'Well? Which is it, dammit to Togg!'

The Dal Hon mage replied calmly, 'I was informed I

would need to look hard for it, but it is clear now.' He addressed Gregar. 'You didn't even know yourself, but it is true.'

Gregar simply stared, completely uncomprehending. *A talent? Really? All this time?* He shot a glare to a grinning and nodding Haraj.

Courian waved such concerns aside. 'Yes, yes. But you say you can fight?'

Coming back to himself, Gregar hurriedly nodded. 'Yes, sir.'

The general cracked his knuckles, visibly relieved. 'Good. Then—' He stopped as a tall guardsman at one end of the main table stood, seeming to unfold so lean was he. 'Yes, Surat?'

'He and I will have a bout.'

Courian's brows crowded together. 'Really? I hardly think it worth your effort.'

'Nevertheless.'

'Very well.' The commander offered Gregar a sympathetic shrug. 'Sorry, lad.'

His spirits falling, Gregar watched the man's easy, fluid grace as he rounded the table and thought, *So this is Surat. New champion of the Guard*, having beaten the last – Oberl.

It looked as though his demonstration was going to be a rather short one.

Cole extended his staff to Gregar while Lark threw Surat hers, and, belatedly, Gregar assumed a ready stance. This close, he realized he'd seen this man before – the day they'd encountered the Guard and Haraj had made a less than inspiring impression.

Reading the recognition in his eyes, Surat nodded. 'Yes. We've met before. Something about joining was mentioned. I see you are determined. I have also heard of a feat of arms by a trooper of Yellows who unhorsed three knights.'

Gregar nodded. 'Yes, that was me.'

'And so we must meet in challenge.'

Gregar nearly gaped. 'I'm sorry . . . why?'

The tall fellow smiled, almost affectionately. 'Because one of those horsemen was a certain Lusmarr of Habal, who on more than one occasion claimed to be my equal.'

Ah. And I bested him.

Surat eased his stave up into a formal crossbody ready stance, hands high, tip low to the right. Gregar matched it. In the next instant he was blocking a nonstop flurry of blows that drove him all the way across the open centre of the tent to the entrance. In the very last few paces he managed to circle round. He continued to back, not even glancing behind – it was only as he passed them that he saw the men and women of the Guard who'd jumped up to pull chairs and benches from his path. He struck a table and edged along it, still only barely managing to deflect or block the blur of strikes, unable to muster a counter, let alone turn to the offence.

Then it ended, suddenly, and he stood panting, staff still raised, but another now pressed hard against his neck. He lowered his, sagging.

Clapping sounded then from the main table: Courian, applauding, and the rest of the Guard joining in. 'Well done!' the commander shouted. 'Well done!'

'I lost,' Gregar exclaimed.

Surat gave him another smile, this one wry. 'You lasted longer than any I've faced all season.' He approached the main table, stave held respectfully behind his back, vertical. He inclined his head to Courian. 'I judge this candidate skilled – perhaps even gifted.'

The commander slapped a hand to the table. 'Excellent!' He turned to Cal-Brinn. 'We have quarters for them, yes?'

Cal-Brinn nodded, smiling. 'I believe we can pull something together.'

Gregar peered about, confused. 'Quarters? Now?'

'Of course,' Courian answered, returning to his meal. 'You'll have no need for your old gear now. The Guard will supply all.'

'But there's going to be a battle ...'

Courian raised a huge tankard, downed nearly all. 'Well, I should damned well hope so! If Gris comes to Jurda's aid there should be.'

'Then ... I'm sorry ... but I can't leave my company.'

Courian had turned to speak to another of the Guard and said, distractedly, 'Hey? What's that?'

Gregar took a steadying breath. 'I have to return to my company.'

The commander pushed aside the guardswoman he'd been speaking to. 'What's that?'

'I'm sorry, but—'

'You're refusing?'

'I can't leave my company before a battle.'

'And which company is that?'

'Yellows.'

Courian snorted and waved his dismissal. 'Don't worry, son. There's no glory to be had with that sad lot.'

'They've never disgraced the field,' his son K'azz observed.

'But what honours have they won?' Courian demanded. 'None!'

Surprised by how much Courian's scorn stung, Gregar straightened, saying, 'Nevertheless. Yes.'

Courian's flushed face darkened even more. 'Do you

230

have any idea of the honour that has just been granted you?' He waved to the entrance. 'Every day knights and fighting men and women come petitioning, waving damned testimonials, citing stupidly tenuous family connections, you name it!' He shook a blunt finger at Gregar. 'And now you have the gall to say no thank you?'

K'azz raised a hand to Courian's arm, but was angrily shaken off. 'Who in Hood's bony arse do you think you are?' He turned his furious glare on Haraj now. 'And what about you? Too good for us as well, I suppose?'

Haraj practically withered under the man's thunderous glower. He wrung his hands together, glanced between Gregar and the mercenary commander. 'Well,' he managed, barely audible, 'I think maybe I should stay with my friend – if you know what I mean . . .'

Courian surged to his feet, sending his chair crashing. K'azz rose as well, a hand on his father's shoulder that he pushed away, roaring, 'Give me that stave, Cole!' He fought to edge past his son. 'I'll show these two how we treat impudent dogs in the Guard!'

'Please, Father,' K'azz murmured, his voice low, 'don't . . .'

'I'll . . .' the man roared, 'I'll . . .' Then he clenched his left arm, grimacing, and it appeared to Gregar as if K'azz was now supporting the man rather than trying to restrain him.

Surat moved to stand before Gregar, and, glancing back, shot a significant look to the entrance. Gregar reached out, grasped Haraj's shirt by the neck, and began backing away.

'Out of my way, damn you dogs!' was the last bellow he heard from Courian as the heavy canvas flap closed behind them. He dragged Haraj onward by his shirt and didn't stop until they were well clear of the encampment.

When they neared the Fourth's bivouac Gregar cleared

his throat and glanced at Haraj. 'Sorry about that,' he said, gesturing back to the Guard camp.

'Sorry?'

'I mean, so much for joining. I know how much it meant to you, an' I went and messed it up.'

Haraj waved it aside. 'It's all right. I have a place.' He shrugged. 'That's all I wanted, really. A place – like a home.'

Gregar kicked at the ground. 'Well, sorry just the same.' He eyed the boy sidelong. 'So, a mage? Really?'

'Oh yes. For certain.'

'Really.' He shook his head, still disbelieving. 'But how could that be? I mean, I've never . . . you know . . .'

Haraj shrugged as they walked along. 'Just the same. It's there. You just have to have the training to know how to bring it out.'

'You?'

'Sorry. I don't know much about training. Maybe I can try, though.'

They were nearing their camp and Gregar glanced about, sighing. 'Yeah. Well, as if we have time for that anyway.'

When they entered the barn Leah jumped to her feet, looking very surprised. 'You're back!'

Gregar offered a resigned shrug, 'Yeah. It – ah, it didn't work out.'

'Good.' She tossed him a spear. 'Because I'd have lost a lot of faith in the Guard if they'd taken either of *you*.'

Chapter 12

THE RANGE THAT BEGAN AT THE COAST TO RUN eastward of Quon Talian lands was rugged, but unfortunately very small as mountains went, and Orjin Samarr was beginning to think he and his troop had hiked over every square league of it. They had survived to date by keeping to the roughest, most uneven ground available to better keep the Talian cavalry at bay, a strategy that could only work for so long, as they were running out of ground, and steadily being forced eastward.

The Quon Talian commander, Renquill, had indeed been recalled from his assault upon Purage, and had since dedicated himself to chasing down Orjin Samarr and his 'band of outlaws', as Quon would have it. So far Orjin had managed to stay ahead of his pursuers, all the while waiting for word from Purage command. For surely they would dispatch a relief force; after all, he'd ended the siege and drawn the invading force out of Purge.

This evening he made the rounds of his forces huddled at shared fires – wood at least was plentiful, and Renquill knew they were up here anyway. No, the real limiting factor was food. The isolated hill tribes had been grateful enough to offer what they could, but they

233

did not have the resources to feed both themselves and another four thousand hungry men and women. And nor would Orjin expect them to.

He paced the bivouac, showing his undaunted face, clapping shoulders and making small talk. Out here, among the men and women, he was now 'Greymane', their leader and champion. Finished, he returned to the fire that was his unofficial camp headquarters, where among his old command he was still plain old Orjin. Here, however, smiles were even fewer. Young Prevost Jeral was showing the longest face; she was taking the silence from Purage personally.

It was Terath who finally broached the subject none other would say out loud when late into the night she announced to all: 'We're running out of mountains.'

No one disputed this, or everyone was too tired to argue.

'Indeed,' rumbled Orhan, 'the beaters are so close I hear them night and day.'

'Renquill must be ahead, waiting for us,' said Orjin – stating the obvious to invite comment.

Prevost offered a sour nod. Gone now were her long braids; she'd had her hair hacked short as there was no way to care for it. 'He's a prissy officious bastard, but he knows his stuff.'

'Could we make a dash for Cullis?' Terath asked, though she did not appear hopeful.

Orjin shook his head. 'They have no reason to take us in. Quon's named us outlaws, remember?'

That at least raised a few chuckles.

'In the jungle Horn,' Yune murmured, hunched in his multicoloured rags, 'we use lines of beaters also.' He poked his staff at the fire. 'But sometimes the hunted deer turns out to be a jungle cat. Many beaters are lost this way.'

Orjin peered at the fire-lit faces arrayed round the camp – none appeared to oppose the intent behind Yune's comment, and so he nodded. 'Very well. It's decided. We'll wait till the last moment then turn upon the line, try to break through westward.' He looked to Jeral. 'Perhaps then we'll have word from Purage, yes?'

But Prevost Jeral would not raise her eyes.

Word spread through Orjin's command that night and eager faces met him the next day; it seemed everyone was tired of running and looked forward to a fight. Their hill tribe guides led them eastward, and all had been briefed to keep an eye out for the best place to turn back. Towards noon word came of a wide gorge, one of the last before the easternmost slopes, and Orjin gave the order to pass through, although he, Orhan and Terath held back, since they would lead the charge.

Once the last of his troops had filed through, Orjin passed the word to halt and everyone sought cover to wait. The shadows in the narrow gorge lengthened. Thirst plagued Orjin – they were also nearly out of water – and he picked up a pebble to hold in his mouth. Some two hours later – measured by the movement of the shadows – the beaters arrived: a column of Quon Talian regulars following their trail.

Orjin offered a nod to Orhan across the way, who answered with a grin and unlimbered a huge hammer he'd taken from a Talian camp. Orjin drew his two-handed sword. He knew they'd be spotted at any moment, so he stepped out, howled his war-cry, and charged.

Momentum, of course, was all. He had to keep charging forward, shouldering men and women out of his way, not bothering with any finishing blows – those that followed would take care of that.

So Orjin cleared the trail, always pushing westward, hammering more than cleanly striking, counting on shock and surprise to help him. Eventually, however, a spear between his feet tripped him up and Orhan stepped over to take the lead, sweeping his weapon left and right. Terath pulled him to his feet and shortly thereafter they burst through the column and were outside the noose, and Orjin stepped aside, panting, waving everyone forward.

Terath stopped with him, and she offered a salute. 'Well done . . . Greymane.'

Orjin gave her a face. 'Thanks a lot.'

Troops cheered as well, and shouted '*Greymane!*' as they passed.

Orjin straightened, raising a hand, and nodding to all.

'They will tell stories of this,' Terath said. 'How you bulled aside an entire Talian column.'

'Easy to do when you have a giant on your arse.'

Terath shook a negative. 'You led, Orjin. You led.'

He turned away. 'Another week of short rations and none of us will have the strength for this.'

Terath nodded. 'We'll see what Purage says. Perhaps a relieving force.'

'Yes.' Orjin agreed, for form's sake, exhausted, leaning on his two-handed sword. But still – why the long silence?

They marched west, guided by hill tribesmen and women through the remotest and most precarious paths Orjin had ever seen; some no more than cliff trails that he thought would challenge any damned mountain goat. But they were surrounded now, with Quon Talian troops on all sides. Privately, Orjin thought they had another ten days at most.

It was three days later that Prevost Jeral joined them at the campfire and proffered a cylinder of horn, sealed in wax. 'Word from Purage, by way of the hill tribes.'

Orjin took it, vaguely troubled by the woman's lowered gaze – he had thought she would be far more pleased. He walked off a way, breaking the seal and reading the unfurled scroll.

It was a long time before he re-joined the group around the campfire.

Terath raised her eager gaze. 'What word?'

Orjin tapped the rolled scroll in his hands, took a heavy breath. 'We are ordered to surrender to the Talians.'

Terath gaped. '*What*? After all this? That's outrageous.'

Orjin was nodding. 'I agree. The order is ridiculous. But it is signed by the Council of Nobles *and* the queen.' He looked at Jeral, who still would not meet his eye. 'It seems we are being forced to make a choice.'

'Choice?' Orhan asked, his brows furrowed.

'We are being thrown to the wolves,' Yune supplied.

Orjin didn't disagree. 'Follow orders or become outlaw in truth.'

'The bastards!' Terath seethed.

Prevost Jeral surged to her feet. 'A word, commander. If you would.'

Orjin nodded – he'd been expecting this – and invited her aside. Off a distance, he turned to her, expectant.

The prevost was rubbing her hands down her thighs. After a long silence, she said, 'Two cylinders arrived from Purage. Orders for you. And orders for me.'

He nodded, unsurprised.

She looked skyward, drew a hard breath. 'I am ordered – that is, if you refuse to obey your orders – I am

237

ordered to arrest you and hand you over to the Quon Talians as a criminal.' She crossed her arms, hugging herself. 'A cessation of hostilities has been negotiated. The price is your head.'

Orjin turned away. It was just as he'd suspected. Facing away into the night, so very impressed by their damned tenacity, he said, 'Hood take those Quon merchants. They meant every word they said, didn't they?'

'I'm so very sorry . . .'

He raised a placating hand. 'It's all right. I understand.' Turning, he faced the woman, and regarded her for some time before saying, slowly, 'The choice isn't ours, then. It's yours.' He cocked a brow. 'What will you do . . . prevost?'

In one fluid motion the woman drew her sword and dropped to one knee before him, blade proffered in both hands. 'I say damn them to Hood's deepest abyss.'

Orjin took hold of her shoulders and raised her up. 'You realize you will be declared outlaw as well?'

She shrugged. 'I can't return without you. I'll be arrested. Perhaps we should break out across Seti lands after all.' She offered a fey laugh. 'There're plenty of wars in the east.'

He shook his head. 'We'll settle this here. One way or another.' He beckoned her back to the campfire. 'We'll just have to find a way out of this knot, hey?'

The furious debating at the fire died down as they returned. Orhan, Terath and Yune peered up, expectant, and Orjin eyed each in turn, then sighed. 'We run. Prevost Jeral here wishes to stay with us and I say yes.' He glanced to her, considering. 'However, perhaps you should offer the choice to your troops: stay or try to break through to the north, re-join Purge forces.'

She nodded. 'I'll speak to them.'

'Welcome, Jeral,' Terath said. 'But the problem remains – run where? There's nowhere to run *to*.'

Orjin waved the objection aside. 'We'll just have to stay alive long enough to find an answer to that.'

Terath was obviously not satisfied but chose not to argue any further. Orhan slapped his leg and laughed. 'We will lead them on such a chase, hey?'

Orjin laughed as well and passing soldiers smiled to one another, their mood brightening. Jeral smiled also; the gift of leadership – this man had it. She leaned to him, saying, 'I will speak to my sergeants,' and he nodded her off.

Orhan rose, quite stiffly. 'I will rest for the morrow.'

Terath stood, appeared about to say more, but reconsidered, shaking her head, and marched off into the dark.

Orjin lowered himself to the ground before the fire. The Dal Hon shaman, Yune, regarded him steadily from across the flames. Orjin cocked a brow. 'Yes?'

The elder sighed and poked anew at the fire. 'I will work to locate our beaters as before, but now they are all about. I won't be able to see them all.'

'Thanks for the warning. Do your best.' The old shaman nodded, a touch glumly, and returned to studying the fire. Orjin reflected that their state was indeed dire if this tough old campaigner was showing his concern. 'We'll get out of this – don't you worry.' The Dal Hon didn't answer, and Orjin rose to limp to his bedding.

* * *

A young girl ran across the grassed savanna of northern Dal Hon at night. The bright moon lit the landscape in a silver monochrome. She wore a simple slave's shift and her long dark hair coursed behind her. She gasped and stumbled, nearly spent, peered back with wild wide eyes, then pushed onward once again.

Eventually, staggering and panting, she halted. Tears smeared her dirty cheeks and she sobbed, gesturing into the empty night. The air ahead seemed to brighten as a light like that of the moon began to shimmer there.

A snarled 'No!' sounded from the night and the girl yelped, jumping. The brightening snapped away.

The thick grasses wavered all round her, lashing and writhing, and a knot of them twisted about her legs, yanking her from her feet.

The tall swaths of grasses parted, revealing a handsome Dal Hon woman, her thick black hair bunched in woven braids. Bright silk ribbons held gold coins, shells and precious stones tied among the braids; vest and trousers were of untanned hide. She thrust an arm forward and the grasses shifted to lash the girl's hands behind her back.

Crouching, the woman set to starting a fire. 'Who sent you?' she asked as she worked.

'I don't know what you mean,' the girl gasped. 'I . . . I am just a slave.'

The woman barked a laugh. 'A slave who is a talent of Thyr? Unlikely.' Once a small fire of grass was alight, she rose and disappeared into the dark. Alone, the girl let her head fall back, and cursed under her breath.

A short time later the woman returned, a load of dead branches in her arms. These she set down next to the diminishing fire. 'Regardless,' she suddenly began again, 'whoever it was is cruel and thoughtless – sending a child to spy among the tribes. Think about that.'

'I am just a—'

Snarling again, the woman snapped a hand and the

grasses lashed themselves across the girl's mouth. 'I am not interested in your lies,' the woman ground out. 'I want only the truth. And the fire will reveal it – if only in your cracked and whitened bones.'

Once the fire became high enough the woman dragged the girl towards it until her bare feet touched its edge. The girl struggled, but the thick grasses roped her from her neck to her ankles. 'Who sent you!' the woman yelled and gestured again, pushing the soles of her captive's feet up against the embers.

The girl screamed behind the gag of twisted grass and passed out.

When she came to, blinking, she saw the woman sitting cross-legged in the flickering light of the fire, a set of thin slats, or cards, arrayed on the ground before her. Seeing her awake, the woman indicated the cards. 'Not what I was expecting. I assumed the Queen of Life would be high – involved. But she is in the far left arcade, detached.' She tapped the deck of remaining cards to her lips. 'You do not work for the Enchantress.'

'I don't work . . . for anyone,' the girl murmured. 'I'm just . . . a slave . . .'

The woman sighed and shook her head. She rose, took hold of the girl again, and thrust her feet into the fire once more. '*Who do you work for?*' she shouted.

The girl screamed anew until her voice cracked and then she mewled, pleading wordlessly, sobbing, until unconsciousness took her again.

When she awoke the second time she found the woman, a Dal Hon witch, seated again, the wooden slats arrayed before her anew. The woman picked up a card and held it up to her. 'This one keeps emerging. Over and over again, with each reading. Do you know which one it is?'

The girl just shook her head, her hair matted to her face and head with sweat and dirt.

'The new one,' the witch told her. 'This meddler. Shadow – or Shadow House, as some would have it.' She regarded the girl narrowly. 'What is Shadow to you?'

The girl looked to the night sky, tears running from the corners of her eyes. 'He pays,' she finally stammered, her voice a thin whisper. 'Pays for information.'

'What kind of information?'

'Anything. Everything.'

The witch stood over the girl. 'Such as? What have you found? Anything?'

But the girl continued to look up, a smile slowly growing on her lips.

The woman spun, scanning the starry sky. 'Someone is coming.' She eyed the girl. 'How could anyone have found you so quickly?'

The girl just smiled, and with a growl the woman gestured again, and the twisted grass ropes tightened round the girl's neck. She gagged, thrashing, her face darkening.

The fire burst into a gyre of rising embers and flaming branches that flew, swirling, to engulf the woman, who roared her rage, ducking, and covering her face.

When the searing heat had passed she bashed her hands over her hair and leathers to put out any fires, then glared about. She stood in a widening circle of scorched ground, the grasses burning in a ring around her – alone. She pressed her fists to her chin and screamed her rage.

*

Two figures lay smoking in a landscape of sand and rock under a dull pewter sky. One, a lad, rose and shook the other, a girl.

'Janelle!' the lad called. 'Speak to me.'

'You took your time, Janul,' she whispered, smiling. 'Where were you?'

'The west. I know a healer. Come.'

She looked down to the blackened oozing meat that used to be her feet. 'I cannot walk.'

'I will carry you.' He picked her up in his arms. 'It is not far. As these things go.'

When she did not answer he peered down to see that she'd passed out. He hurried onward.

After walking across the dusty landscape for a time, the lad Janul made a gesture and with a burst of dry dusty air he emerged into darkness and a rainstorm. He squinted into the lashing rain. Nearby, waves struck the coast in a strong slow beat. He walked on until a weak yellow light grew ahead. It resolved into a lantern under the eaves of a rude hut of greyed slats and thatch. He pushed open the door.

The hut was empty but for a wizened elder seated in a chair next to a small fire. Candles of all lengths burned everywhere, giving the single-roomed dwelling a golden light. The ancient tilted her head, blinking, 'Who comes to old Rose's poor home?'

Janul saw by her frosted opaque eyes that she was blind.

'My sister is wounded,' he said, and laid her upon the bed of bundled straw.

'Ah,' Rose said. 'Your sister, you say? There is a price for healing in this hut – and I do not mean coin.'

He waved his curt assent, then realized his mistake and said, 'Yes, yes.'

The old woman pushed herself from her chair and approached, a hand extended. 'Well, let us see . . .' Janul guided her to Janelle. The ancient hissed when her hands found the girl. She tsked. 'So young, yet her life's flame gutters. She hasn't enough strength left to pay the price.'

'I have.'

Rose laughed, a harsh mocking cackle. 'It's not so easy as that, boy!'

'For us it is,' and he guided the woman's other hand to his face. She felt at both, Janelle's and his, and her breath hissed from her in wonder. 'Twins! Bonds forged in the womb.' She nodded, 'Aye, it may work.' She pinched his chin. 'Know you the price, then?'

'Yes.'

'I shall take of your life's candle. Both of your years shall diminish while mine shall lengthen. You are agreed?'

He looked down at his twin, her face such an eerie echo of his own. 'Aye. Agreed.'

Rose waved a crooked hand to the bed. 'Lay you down next to your sister, then. I must prepare.'

He gently edged Janelle over and placed an arm under her head and closed his eyes.

Janelle awoke in a cramped bed in a cramped hut full of evil-smelling, choking smoke. Waving a hand before her, coughing from the harsh sooty fumes, she found the door and staggered out.

Then she stopped and stared at her bare unmarred feet.

What had happened?

Her ears were roaring and somewhere distant it sounded as if someone was calling her name. She raised her gaze to peer uncomprehendingly at a rocky coastline and a horizon of iron-grey water. A figure rose from a boulder near the surf and climbed the shore. As he neared she recognized him and could not believe her eyes. Grinning so familiarly, he took her shoulders.

'Good to see you.'

She raised her hands to his face, brushed her fingertips there. 'It really is you – I thought I'd dreamed you.'

'Yes, it's me.'

Her gaze sharpened. 'What happened?'

'I brought you to a healer.'

She studied his face, so like her own – wider and blunter than she'd have wished. 'We have no coin, brother.'

He lifted his chin to the hut behind them. 'She's a wax-witch.'

Janelle sagged a little. 'So, I paid with my life's years.'

He shrugged. 'We both did, sister.'

She clenched his hands now, tightly. 'Both? Oh, Janul . . .'

'You don't think I'd let a few years come between us, do you?'

She now touched her own face, expecting to feel wrinkles and dry ancient flesh. 'What will happen? How will it happen?'

'The witch, Rose, said we will just age more quickly.' He directed her to a nearby rock and invited her to sit. 'I don't imagine I'll be living too long, in any case.'

She chuckled at that. 'Nor I.'

They sat side by side in silence for a time, until the crunch of footsteps behind made them turn. A woman approached, in skirts, a knitted shawl about her shoulders. Janelle thought her just past middle age.

'Rose?' Janul asked, wonder in his voice. 'You are . . . that is, you can see.'

She nodded. 'Aye. I bloom brighter for a time. But that

too shall pass, as all years do. You two are young; you do not understand as yet.'

'Nor do we want to,' Janul said.

The witch smiled knowingly. 'In time you will. Then you will clutch at your years as all do.'

'Not I,' Janelle said.

The witch, Rose, drew a blackened pipe from her bosom. 'Ever foolish are the young – perhaps that's what makes them young.'

'Any more fireside wisdom?' Janul asked.

The woman was scraping the pipe bowl. 'Do not think me simple, little ones.' She gestured to them with the pipe. 'You two are children of Shadow. Your master is set upon overturning every applecart he can reach. I do not approve of his methods, but I understand his motives – how else is he to make room for himself, hey?'

The twins eyed one another uncertainly.

Rose waved a dismissal. 'Faugh. Do not worry. Your secrets are safe with me. I am just a simple wax-witch. Push and pull go the fates.' She walked off, repeating in a singsong voice, 'Push and pull.'

The twins waited until she was out of earshot, then Janul asked, 'What did you learn?'

Janelle nodded, and whispered, 'The tribes bicker as always, but they are close to moving against Itko Kan. All it may take is a push.'

At that last word Janul frowned and glanced at the witch, who walked the shore now, hands at her back, puffing on the pipe. 'Very good,' he murmured, distracted.

'And the west?' Janelle asked.

'I am with a troop of soldiers.'

Janelle waved him from that. 'Head to Dal Hon – I'm known now. You'll have to take over.'

But her twin shook his head. 'No. I see possibilities. I should remain. You stay here in Kan. Keep an eye on things.'

Janelle nodded. 'Thank you, brother. But ... what possibilities?' She took his hand.

'These troops have been outlawed and are on the run, hunted by both Purge and Quon Talian armies with nowhere to turn.'

'So?'

He shrugged, but a grin climbed his lips. 'Well – they're only a few days from the coast.'

Her eyes widened as she saw it, and she squeezed his hand before releasing it. 'Yes. Go. I will try to make the arrangements, but I have not heard from the Magister of late.'

'He is travelling beyond reach.'

Janelle gave a curt nod, accepting this. 'Ah. Then I will contact one of our sisters working among the Claws.'

Janul seconded the nod. 'Accepted. You will be all right?'

She waved him off. 'Yes. Go. You may be missed.'

He rose, still reluctant, but she gave him a hug. 'Thank you, brother.'

He nodded. 'Very well. Until later.'

'Yes.'

* * *

Ullara rode her two-wheeled cart northward across the rolling central Seti Plains. The sickly mule her father had given her – the least of his stock – flourished under her care. Free to eat as much wild grass as he liked, he filled out; his coat thickened and became glossy.

She had never been outside Li Heng proper, but she'd

heard that northward lay the trading outpost of Ifaran, and beyond that would lie the barrier of the Brittlewash that ran down to meet the Idryn at Ipras. She understood that the headwaters of the Brittlewash could be found somewhere in the immense tracts of the Forest Fenn. And beyond that, everyone claimed, rose the vast mountains of the Great Fenn Range – which few, if any, had ever actually seen, let alone visited.

The Fenn Range was her goal, unrealistic though it might be – especially for a young blind girl all alone. Though she was not alone, not really. Her helpers and guardians hovered close, sometimes even perching upon the much-scarred wood of the cart, while the chief of her companions soared high above, taller than a man, able to bring down an adult bhederin: one of the giant eagles of the Fenn Range, whom she had given the name Prince. And her aim was to return him to his home.

She did not have to hunt, as her providers were many. Each day they came, depositing their offerings of the wild's abundance: mice, voles, ferrets, mink, hares, badgers, and once Prince even dropped an entire rust-hued deer.

After that near disaster she trained them to bring her only the long-eared hares, which she preferred.

When evening came she would merely reach out to the mule, whom she'd named Bright, to halt, then climb down and unharness him to let him roam free. She could not see herself, but even when she did have eyes she'd always 'borrowed' the vision of her birds to see far and wide. Now she maintained these connections day and night and found that she could *see* far better now than with her old eyes. In fact, she could see better at night than during the day, and would even have travelled through the dark but for poor Bright.

248

She was also not alone on the wilds of the Seti plains. Fellow travellers skirted her, warily giving her distance, as did hunters and other such wanderers. Honest travellers, however, were not the only ones on the plains. Exiles, outcasts and other such criminals also haunted its hills. Early on, one such gang had chanced upon her trail. A young woman alone – they thought they'd found easy prey.

The moment the party closed upon the cart her companions tore their faces off and ate their viscera. She left their bodies where they lay as a warning to others. Word, she imagined, was spreading of the crazy woman, or whatever they were calling her, travelling northwards.

The only time she was truly alone was each evening when she made a modest fire and set her meal to cook on a stick. Her companions did not like the fire. During these times her vision occasionally failed her.

It was during one such evening, by the fire, west of the trading post of New Seti, that she had her first true visitors. Thanks to all her night-hunting companions, her night vision was sharp, and so she watched them approach: a band of Seti who dismounted at a respectful distance while one of their number closed upon her small fire. She recalled the strongest of her night hunters and waited.

Her visitor proved to be an old Seti woman wrapped in a thick shawl covered in feathers. The woman paused a short distance off and called, 'May I share the warmth of your fire?'

'Come.'

Sighing, the woman eased herself down close to the weak flames and extended her hands to the heat, such as it was. 'My thanks. Hospitality is rare among you outsiders.'

'What of your band who wait in the night?'

'Band?' the woman echoed, chuckling. She waved a dismissive hand. 'Just my honour guard. I am Tolth, daughter of Amal, shaman of my clan – the Eagle Clan.'

'Ullara, daughter of Renalt.'

The old woman inclined her head in acceptance of this, all the while eyeing her carefully, and it did seem to Ullara that the woman's gaze was sharp and piercing – like that of a bird of prey. 'You are out riding at night?' Ullara asked.

Tolth smiled. 'No. Word has spread among us Seti of the bird-woman.'

'Bird-woman?'

'That is what you have been named.'

'Ah.'

'And I am here to offer you a place among us. Among the Eagle Clan. It would be a place of honour, you can be certain of that.'

This was not what Ullara had been expecting at all and she let out a breath, quite overwhelmed. It took her a while to find the words to respond. 'I . . . well, my thanks. But I must . . . that is, I feel called to the north. I don't know why – I just feel it.'

The old woman was obviously disappointed, but she nodded knowingly. 'I understand. A journey of the spirit and the flesh.' Grunting with the effort, she pushed herself to her feet. 'Very well. But the offer stands. Once you are finished in the north and wish to move on . . . think of us.'

'I will. My thanks.'

The woman paused, raising a hand. 'Permission to leave a few of my young bloods as escort?'

Ullara was not comfortable with the idea. 'I don't – that is, there is no need.'

'They would consider it an honour. And there are river crossings ahead. You may need the help.'

She considered this, and relented. 'Very well, my thanks. But they must keep their distance.'

The old woman chuckled once more. 'Oh, they will. Of that you can be sure.' She inclined her head. 'Travel well. And I hope we shall meet again.'

'Fare well.'

So she acquired her own honour guard, of a sort. And they did keep their distance, either at the shaman's orders, or their own discretion. Only when the cart became stuck did they approach, as the ground became rougher the further she journeyed north.

Weeks after this, close to the northern boundary of Seti lands, Ullara had one last visitor.

He came at dusk, walking openly, and she saw him long before her escort. Once they caught sight of him the warriors of the Eagle Clan came rushing in, pale, bows readied.

Their leader stood before her. 'The man-beast approaches,' he managed, his voice hoarse. 'We will defend you, of course, as we swore. But ready yourself, as there is little anyone can do against him.'

She raised a hand to him. 'Stand aside, Orren – it is Orren, isn't it?'

'Yes. But—'

'Stand aside,' she repeated. 'I order it.'

'But—'

'Stand aside! I will meet him.'

Amazed, perhaps even awed, the Seti warrior bowed to one knee before her. 'As you order.' He waved off the ten men and women of his troop, and they withdrew.

A short time later the tall shape of the upright man-beast, Ryllandaras, the White Jackal – whom some named the Curse of Quon – approached. Frankly terrified, yet determined to hold to her instinct not to run, she stared up at the great giant. All wire and muscle he appeared, his shaggy pale pelt crossed with scars, his eyes slit and glowing like hot amber. His blunt muzzle swung to left and right as he surveyed the surroundings; then he spoke, roughly, more like a measured cough. 'And where is your guard?'

'I sent them away.'

He crossed his thick, white-pelted arms. 'Why would you do such a foolish thing?'

She replied, 'Because I am in no danger,' and was quite proud of the lack of quaver in her voice.

'Really? You are in no danger? And why is that?'

She swallowed to steady her voice once again, and managed, clearly, 'Because I know what a hunting animal looks like. And you are not hunting.'

The black lips drew back – revealing even more of his huge teeth – in what she thought might be an attempt at a smile. 'You are correct. If I were hunting, you'd be dead.'

She saw no reason to dispute this. 'To what, then, do I owe the honour of this visit?'

'Honour?' Ryllandaras grunted. 'Few would name a visit from me an honour. But you are correct again. I have come to have a look at you.'

Her heart felt as if it were throwing itself against her chest – rather like a trapped bird. 'Really? Whatever for?'

'To see for myself. I have sensed it . . . but could not believe it. It has been a very long time.'

'A long time since . . . what?'

The creature tilted his head, examining her. 'Since anyone has touched upon the Beast Hold.'

252

'The what?'

The monster grunted. 'Instinctive, then. Perhaps as it should be. The Beast Hold is all about . . . instinct.'

Gathering her courage, Ullara dared, 'I heard a rumour that the Five had captured you in Heng.'

Ryllandaras's lips twitched as if in scorn. 'Captured, hey? Well, haven't you heard – I'm everywhere across the plains.' And the creature seemed almost to wink one amber eye. It peered about as if searching the surroundings. 'In any case, I have lingered long enough. I offer you your due.'

And to Ullara's amazement, and terror, the man-beast inclined his head to her, as if in salute, then quick as thought bounded away. She sat stunned until her escort reappeared, and the first thing they did was bow on one knee to her.

A half-moon later they had reached so high into the foothills of the Fenn Range that the cart was of no more use. Her escort packed her remaining supplies on to Bright's back.

'You are bound to continue, then?' Orren asked.

She took hold of Bright's lead. 'Yes.'

The youth – perhaps no older than she – eyed the heights dubiously. 'There are things up in these lands that would care nothing for your . . . friends.'

'Monsters, you mean?' she asked, half-teasing.

He set his jaws. 'You know what I mean.'

'All the same.'

He sighed, eyed the distant snowy peaks once more. 'Perhaps we should . . .'

'No. Return to Tolth. Tell her what you have seen.' The youth's jaws worked. 'I have my escort,' she offered.

He sighed again, his hands clenching. 'Very well. It is not for me to interfere.'

'Fare well, then. And my thanks.' Leaning forward and up, she kissed him on the cheek. The lad blushed a very livid red. His troop burst into laughter, quietening only when he glared.

She raised a hand to them all. 'Fare thee well, children of the plains!'

Turning, she pulled on Bright's lead, and started climbing. Her companions soared above, circling higher and higher, eager, it seemed, to feel the fierce winds of the heights.

Chapter 13

DANCER FOLLOWED KELLANVED THROUGH Shadow. The geography of this particular region was one of dry washes, steep canyons, and twisting erosional gullies that cut through multicoloured layers of compressed sands and gravels. They were rushing, but the quickest the seemingly aged mage could manage was a frustratingly slow shuffle. His patience with his partner near exhausted, Dancer asked again, 'Is it there?'

'I believe so,' Kellanved answered, though his tone said he wasn't certain.

They were searching for a gate – a permanent constructed archway, or portal, call it what you will, that allowed access to other Realms, other places. They had come across a few such ancient constructs during their explorations of Shadow, and Kellanved was leading them towards the nearest he could recall.

As they hurried, or rather limped, along, Dancer asked, 'So, carrying one of these items while passing through one of these active arches – this should take us to the Imass Warren . . . or Realm?'

'Not usually, I think,' the mage puffed in answer, winded despite merely scurrying along. 'I'll have to have my Warren up and working on it. It must be deliberate . . . I think.'

So, not a sure thing. It sounded to Dancer a bit like trying to pick a lock. Then the last thing he wanted to hear echoed through the surrounding canyonlands – the deep hunting bay of the Hounds. He and Kellanved froze and exchanged glances. His was one of narrowed questioning, Kellanved's of surprised alarm, quickly veiled.

'I thought you had these things in hand,' Dancer accused him.

Kellanved was tapping his fingertips together. 'Ah, of course! Certainly . . . I believe so.'

Dancer snarled at the man's prevarication and drew his heaviest parrying gauches. He urged Kellanved onward. 'Keep going.'

They shuffled on, Dancer with a hand at Kellanved's back, pushing him forward, all the while glancing about. He spotted the beasts soon enough; they had them surrounded. Two on sand ridges ahead, the other two blocking either end of the gully they traversed. Growling his frustration, he halted, put his back to Kellanved. 'What do you think?' he demanded over his shoulder. 'Have they come for us?'

'I don't *think* so.'

'Wonderful.'

The beasts let out one last howl that shook stones from the steep eroding canyon walls, then came on. One was the larger, dirty-white female – possibly the matron of the pack – the others were the lean brown one, the tawny one, and the muscular black one, so dark as to be a shiny blue.

The black hound approached, its muzzle lowered, head close to the ground, eyes blazing differing colours: a hot amber and a bright cerulean blue. Closer now, Dancer made out the fresh splashing of blood upon it, gaping cuts at shoulders and head, and patches of torn fur.

The others halted a good few paces distant and seemed content to just glare, their great broad chests working, their black lips drawn back.

Crouched, weapons raised, Dancer glanced from one to the other, uncertain. Then, silently, without a sound, they turned as one and bounded off. Dancer eased up from his ready stance. He turned to Kellanved, his gaze narrow. 'Did you do something?'

The mage lowered his gaze and fiddled with his walking stick. 'Well, I may have let them know about Jadeen, and—'

'You sicked them on *Jadeen*!'

The mock-elderly Dal Hon winced, his greying brows crimping. 'Not exactly – well, sort of. Kind of. I guess. Yes.'

'You should not have done that.'

'Why ever not?'

'You saw them! I'm sure they came here to let you know they were not happy.' Dancer kicked at the dry dusty ground. 'Do that again and you might lose them.'

Kellanved looked to the iron-grey sky. 'Well, what ever else are they *for* then, pray tell?'

'Pick an easier target! Let them taste some blood – that was the deal, yes?'

Kellanved huffed. 'I do not need help with easier targets, thank you very much.'

'Whatever. You know what I mean. Throw them a bone.'

The little mage shot Dancer a glance. His mouth quivered. Dancer suppressed a snort, and they both broke out laughing. Kellanved poked Dancer with his walking stick. 'That was a good one. I liked that one.'

Continuing onward, Kellanved led the way to a seemingly unremarkable heap of stones amid a desolation of wind-blasted ruins. 'The nearest remnant of a gate that I know of,' he announced.

'Very good. Let's go.'

The mage raised a hand for a pause. 'In time, in time. Just a moment.' He withdrew the stone fragment and held it up close to his eyes, squinting at it. While Dancer watched, the fellow spat upon the flint piece, rubbed it, squinted again through one eye, turned it this way and that.

Finally, his patience worn away, Dancer asked, 'What in the Enchantress's name are you doing?'

Kellanved peered up, distractedly. 'Hmm? Tricky magical things beyond your ken – now be quiet.'

The mage continued to fuss over the object. He rubbed it between the palms of his hands, blew on it, muttered over it, seemed even to whisper to it. Dancer was about to walk off to sit down when all about them dust began to rise from the ground. It swirled upwards and coalesced towards the remnants of the 'gate', forming a sort of gyre.

'A pressure differential,' Kellanved observed. 'We're getting somewhere.'

Ever careful, Dancer drew two blades. He noted now that the dust was indeed disappearing over the footprint of the gate; it appeared to be falling into nothingness.

'Try it,' Kellanved invited.

Dancer pointed to himself. 'Oh? I'm supposed to go first, am I?'

'Do your part.'

'My part?' he grumbled. 'I don't think much of my part.' Then something came to him. 'I don't have the spear-pointy thing.'

Kellanved mouthed a curse, his shoulders falling. 'Fine! Very well. Together then.'

Dancer and the mage stepped on to the stone flags of the ruin's threshold. The next instant Dancer gasped as if stabbed; he hugged himself, his breath pluming, teeth chattering, and saw they now stood amid blowing snow on a dark snow-covered landscape below thick black and grey clouds.

The little mage groaned into the savage wind. 'Ye gods! I shall die!'

Dancer pointed behind: domed hide tents shuddered in the wind, their bases secured by rings of heavy stones. He steered a stiff and shivering Kellanved towards the nearest, pushed aside the heavy hide flap and shoved the mage in before him, then fell in himself.

It was dark within, and stank of rotten fish and animal fat – but it was exquisitely warm, and Dancer just lay panting, grateful, clenching his numb fingers.

As his eyes adjusted to the dark he made out the faces of three elders staring at them in open wonder round a small central hearth. One spoke, an old man, his wide, blunt face lined and seamed. Dancer did not understand the language.

His vision improved and he saw that the three wore crude hides, painted and sewn with beads and bones. Their hair was grey and long and hung in greased tangled lengths; he wondered if this was the source of the sour animal fat stink.

The eldest spoke again. Kellanved roused himself and sat up. He gestured, grasped Dancer's shoulder, and asked the trio, 'Do you understand me?'

The oldster grunted his assent. 'You are not spirits?'

'No,' Kellanved answered. 'We are men.'

'You are strange men.'

Kellanved nodded. 'Well . . . I suppose we are. Now, where are we?'

'Our village is named the Place of the Booming Ice,' said another, an old woman – or so Dancer thought. The three appeared quite identical.

Kellanved shot Dancer a look. 'How very helpful.'

'What do you want here?' the woman asked.

'We seek a throne, a seat, a place of authority – do you know of what I speak?'

The three eyed one another, uncertain. One said, 'We will take you to our eldest.' They rose, and Dancer was startled by how squat they were; squat but wide. They searched about the hut and produced hide blankets that they offered to him and Kellanved. Then the eldest pushed aside the flap and exited. Dancer and Kellanved followed, wrapped in their blankets.

Their guide led them into the driving snow. Through the blowing whiteness a huge looming bulk took shape. Because of the darkness Dancer couldn't be certain of the scale, but it appeared gigantic. They entered an opening, broad and low, like a cave mouth, except that the stone was worked smooth and dressed.

They walked a tunnel, of sorts; very broad, with slim descending steps cut into the solid rock of the floor. Snow and dirty wet straw littered the channel. Light glowed ahead – the flickering amber of firelight. The tunnel ended at a large chamber, one so huge that Dancer had no idea of its dimensions, as the walls and ceiling were hidden in darkness. A meagre fire lay ahead; their guide headed for it.

Something of the proportions of this structure, whatever it was, troubled Dancer. It didn't seem built to a human scale, but for something far larger. Noises rebounded, echoing from the distant unseen walls: the tap of Kellanved's walking stick, the crackling of the fire, and the booming of distant surf.

At the fire sat a single, tiny figure. A young girl wrapped in a crude hide similar to their own. Tiny she might have been, but her features were not gracile: her brow was much too thick, her cheeks too wide, and her nose far too large. Their guide bowed to the girl, and Dancer was quite startled when the fellow greeted her as 'Grandmother'.

The girl peered up at them with sharp brown eyes that soon flicked aside, dismissing their guide, who bowed again and withdrew.

'And you are?' Kellanved asked.

'Jahl 'Parth,' the girl piped. 'Bonereader to the tribe.'

'Ah,' Kellanved observed. 'We are—'

'I know who you are,' the girl interjected. 'And I know why you are here.'

'Indeed . . .' Kellanved mused, sharing a troubled look with Dancer.

'And where is here?' Dancer asked.

The girl opened her arms, the wrap falling away to reveal that despite the terrible cold she wore only a hide vest, leaving her thin arms bare. She eyed Kellanved, and her lips quirked, almost mischievously. 'Where are we, mage?'

Kellanved made a show of studying the silver hound's head of his walking stick. Eyes downcast, he answered, 'Well . . . broadly speaking, we are in the Warren, or Hold, of Tellann. Perhaps in the past – or in a moment held from the past.'

The child offered the mage a lofty, arched look of acknowledgement that only an ancient could summon. 'Well done,' she granted.

'That old fellow called you grandmother,' Dancer said, eyeing her now more carefully.

Jahl shrugged. 'That is because I am his grandmother – many times removed.'

261

Dancer shot Kellanved a questioning look that the mage declined to acknowledge. Instead, he said, 'You carry your years well, Jahl 'Parth.'

She smiled. 'Your humour is welcome – you know I do not speak of the flesh.' The Dal Hon inclined his head, and Dancer was struck by their dissimilar similarities: he a false ancient, and she a false youth. 'At my birth the elders identified me as Jahl 'Parth returned,' the girl continued. 'Ancestor to many here.'

Kellanved rocked now on his heels, back and forth, and Dancer recognized that he was done with the pleasantries. 'Well . . . greetings, Jahl. We are here—'

'As I said – I know why you are here,' the girl cut in once again, but far more sharply this time. 'And I asked you where we were.' Her thick lips hardened, drawing down. 'So far you have declined to answer.'

Kellanved tapped the silver hound's head to his lips, looking away to the surrounding darkness, almost pained. 'Ah . . .'

Dancer managed to catch his eye and mouthed: *Time – we must go.*

The mage raised a hand, but not peremptorily, rather a begging for indulgence. 'Well,' he began, drawing out the word, 'if I were to guess . . . an immense structure, strange larger-than-human dimensions . . . arcane mechanisms hinted at in the dark recesses . . . I would have to offer the guess of a Mountain that Walks.'

Dancer could not help but snort a laugh. 'Children's tales. Mountains that walk? Just stories.'

Jahl turned her narrowed gaze on him. 'And were not structures that flew similar stories to you?'

Dancer coughed into a fist. He rubbed his neck, almost wincing. 'But an entire *mountain*?'

The ancient – a true ancient – returned her piercing

eyes to Kellanved, and Dancer followed the gaze to see the mage nodding. 'And who built them?' she asked, almost accusingly.

Kellanved cleared his throat, clearly uncomfortable. 'The K'Chain Che'Malle,' he murmured, half under his breath, as if afraid to say the name aloud.

Jahl 'Parth nodded now, her gaze softening, as if some sort of test, or threshold, had been passed. 'You are not entirely ignorant, I see. Good. Indeed, the K'Chain. This was one of their cities, their bases. My tribe was tasked with destroying it. It was our bloodline's only purpose. Eventually, over the span of twenty genera-tions, we succeeded. It was a war to the death between them and us.'

'You being the Imass,' Kellanved observed.

Jahl nodded. 'Indeed. And in the full knowledge of such a history – which is but one chapter in a library of wars beyond your comprehension – you would still dare meddle in this? Is your lust for power that blind?'

For his part, Dancer *was* beginning to reconsider. He remembered Tayschrenn's own appalled reaction once he understood their goal. Kellanved, he noted, was now shaking his head.

'I do not seek power,' the mage said. 'I seek know-ledge.'

Jahl also shook her head, almost in disappointment. 'Do not pretend that knowledge is neutral. It can be dangerous.'

'And ignorance isn't?'

Dancer cocked a brow – that almost sounded like a good point.

Jahl lowered her gaze, as if considering, then raised her head, chin out-thrust. 'I know where the throne lies,' she announced. 'But I choose not to tell you.' She tilted her head speculatively, eyeing Kellanved. 'What will you do now, seeker?'

The mage blew out a breath, tapped his walking stick on the stone floor. 'Oh, blunder about searching for it. Be a terrible pest. Knock things over. Cause all sorts of problems and upset and generally make things worse than they need be as I meddle everywhere in everything. And everyone will blame you for it all.'

The grandmother who looked like a girl threw back her head and barked a laugh. 'In other words, be an ass until you have your way.' She shook her head anew, almost in wonder. 'Very well.' She rose, but stiffly, as an ancient, groaning and rubbing her legs. Seeing them eyeing her, she shrugged, 'Memories. This way.' She led them back to the entrance.

Outside, they once more pushed through the howling winds. The girl wore nothing more than a leather vest and tattered hide skirts tied about her emaciated waist by a belt of woven cord. Dancer offered her his hide wrap. She blinked, surprised by the gesture, appeared about to say something, but reconsidered, lowering her gaze. Frowning, she continued walking.

Eventually they came to a coastline of bare black rock, wet with spray from a frigid-looking iron-grey sea. By this time Dancer's face, hands and feet were numb and he hugged himself beneath his hide wrap, shivering uncontrollably. The girl gestured across the water to the darker jutting spur of a small island. 'There. On that hilltop rests the throne. Once we could walk to it. But over the centuries the waters have risen. Soon it will lie beyond the reach of all, submerged.'

Kellanved's greying brows climbed very high indeed. 'Oh dear. Just how do we get to it?'

Jahl 'Parth shrugged. 'That is not my concern.'

'Can't you just do your Shadow thing?' Dancer suggested. 'Walk us out?'

The mage grimaced a negative. 'This is Tellann we are in now.'

Jahl 'Parth moved to go, but paused, and turned back. She took a breath. 'You do not seem the usual sort who come here seeking the throne. Take my advice: do not go. None who have gone have ever come back.'

Kellanved bowed to her. 'My thanks. But it looks as though we shan't be going in any case.'

Dancer saw the girl's gaze flick down to the shore; then she turned away to disappear amid the fat swirling flakes of blowing snow.

'I don't know about you,' Dancer stuttered to Kellanved, 'but I'm not going to last much longer.'

'Agreed,' the mage sighed. 'Thwarted once again.'

'Perhaps not,' Dancer offered. Wincing, he opened his thick hide wrap to clamber down among the wet black rocks where the waves washed and sprayed. A short time later he called Kellanved down to him.

When the mage arrived, using his walking stick to help him balance on the slick icy rocks, Dancer motioned to what he'd found: a small boat of wood and hides. Kellanved sniffed.

'I am not going out in that.'

Dancer dropped his extended arm. 'Fine. Back to Nap.'

Kellanved looked at the thick clouds above them and flapped a hand. 'Oh, very well. If I must.'

Dancer struggled to push the boat into the water. 'Looks as if we have to.'

Within, he found two hand-carved paddles. He motioned Kellanved to the bow, and the spindly mage crouched down awkwardly. Dancer pushed off and crouched at the stern, paddling. 'Use the other paddle,' he told Kellanved.

The mage waved his hands. 'I don't know how.'

Dancer snarled curses under his breath and dug into the waves with even more power. Fortunately, they were not too high, though the water was so frigid the spray seemed to burn when it touched him. His hands became frozen blocks on the wood of the paddle. 'They're not making this easy,' he grumbled.

'We're closing,' Kellanved announced.

Dancer nodded, concentrating on powering them forward. The hide boat was taking on water and his legs were numb from resting in the icy wash.

A dark cliff-wall of wet rock emerged from the blowing snow. He peered right and left, searching for a place to land. 'Which way?' he mumbled, his lips and face frozen.

Kellanved pointed the walking stick right and he turned the boat that way. They rounded what appeared to be a tall headland, which descended to a bare rocky slope. The boat was now sluggish with water and Dancer drove it straight in to land. They struck submerged rocks and Kellanved was pitched forward into the waves; Dancer leapt for the shore.

He bruised himself on the rocks and turned to search for Kellanved. He saw the mage floating face down in the surf and staggered through waist-high icy water to reach him. Grasping the fellow's sodden jacket, he dragged him like a wet rat out of the waves and laid him on the bare, scraped-smooth stone slope, then sat and hugged himself, shivering savagely, and felt the pull of a dreamy exhaustion.

Yet he knew that to fall unconscious now would mean death, and so he shook Kellanved, yelling, 'We have to keep going!' Or something like that, as his lips were completely numb.

The mage's walking stick emerged to point, shaking, up the slope. Dancer squinted and just made out a darker shadow ahead – a cave mouth in the rising cliff face?

He took hold of a squelching Kellanved once more and half dragged, half pushed him upward. They fell into the cave and Dancer blinked, frowning, as he felt something smothering him. It took a moment for him to recognize warmth; with that realization he could fight off unconsciousness no longer and he allowed himself to slip down into oblivion.

He awoke with a start and peered about; it was still the pewter grey of a snowstorm without, and he couldn't tell if it was night or day. Kellanved still lay asleep amid a litter of dry branches and leaves. Dancer flexed his fingers – he was warm. The heat seemed to be coming from the very rock of the walls and the floor beneath them. He threw off his hide wrap and was amused to see actual steam rise from his sodden sleeves.

He shook Kellanved. 'Well, at least we won't freeze to death.'

The seeming ancient peered up blearily, grumbled, 'Cold comfort, that.'

Dancer ran a hand through his short hair, then rose and began searching the cave. 'It leads to a tunnel,' he announced. 'Damned dark.'

The mage appeared, a dry torch in hand. 'Try this.'

Dancer gaped at the thing. 'You weren't *carrying* that, were you?'

'No. I was lying on it.'

'Oh.' He crouched down, gathered together a bunch of the dry twigs and leaves, pulled out the tiny flint and steel he always carried, and set to work.

In a short time he had the torch lit and he rose,

adjusted his weapon-baldrics and belts, and offered Kellanved a nod. The mage tapped his walking stick to his shoulder and pursed his lips, answering the nod; then they started down the tunnel.

The passage was very rough; they clambered over uneven jutting rocks and ducked through narrow throats of stone. Along the way Dancer noticed that the natural walls had been widened here and there to allow easy passage, but the gouging and scraping was not smooth. It was as if a harder stone had been used rather than a metal tool.

After quite a long time Dancer saw a weak flickering glow ahead: more torch-light, in fact. Wary, he drew his best throwing blade and switched the torch he carried to his off hand. He went first, crouched, blade held behind his back.

The tunnel opened on to a wider natural chamber, or cavern. Multiple torches lit it, their sooty smoke rising to a distant ceiling hidden in darkness. Kellanved slipped in beside him and the dark-skinned mage's breath caught.

For there, across the cavern, against a wall of natural stone, sat an object that could only be the throne of the Army of Bone. It was assembled from gigantic antlers and tusks of bygone beasts; leather straps wove the pieces together, forming a seat of sorts. Natural precious stones glinted upon it, as did shells and beads, and rotting animal furs lay heaped about, some obviously taken from huge animals of legend, such as the cave bear, or the great-toothed cat.

But what probably drew the gasped breath from Kellanved was the Witch Jadeen sitting upon it.

The hungry smile on the woman's lips drew them even further from her teeth, and she raised a hand, beckoning them closer. 'I knew you'd turn up quite soon,' she said. 'And so I prepared the place. Come here.' She pointed to her other arm, the sleeve of her robes torn and blood dried black upon her hand. Her eyes narrowed upon Kellanved. 'I have a bone to pick with you, little Shadow-mage.'

Dancer looked to his partner and their eyes met, and for the first time it seemed to him that Kellanved had been caught at a complete loss as to what to do.

Chapter 14

BARON RANEL OF NITA PUSHED OPEN A SIDE DOOR to the stables of Castle Gris and peered round the darkened hall. Horses snorted in their stalls, while a single lantern set on a stool provided the only light. He shut the door behind him and called, 'Stabler! Where are you, man? Stablemaster!'

A great-bellied older fellow came stumbling out from the rear, pulling on his jacket. 'Yes, m'lord? You called?'

'Yes, dammit. That horse-dealer out of Unta – is she still here?'

The stablemaster blinked, still somewhat bleary, then nodded. 'Oh, yes, sir. I believe so.'

Ranel glared, expectantly. 'Well? Go get her, dammit!'

The stablemaster flinched, ducking. 'Of course, m'lord. I'll send one of the lads right away.' He rushed to the rear.

Alone, Ranel tapped his hands nervously on his thighs and peered about the stables. He lifted a tankard and sniffed, only to make a disgusted face and set it aside. He then approached the nearest stall; the horse within reared, nickering, and he flinched away.

A short time later there came a knock from the rear and the stablemaster emerged accompanied by a slim woman, her long dark hair slightly dishevelled, who was adjusting a long quilted wrap about herself. She bowed to Ranel. 'You called, m'lord?'

'Yes. I've been thinking about that offer you made – the roan mare. I must say I am most interested now.'

The woman bowed again. 'Excellent. M'lord is wise to consider the offer.' Her gaze shifted edgewise to the stablemaster next to her, and Ranel started as if realizing something. He dug at a pocket to pull out a few coins, which he extended to the stabler.

'Here you are, my man – for your trouble.'

The stablemaster touched his brow, bowing. 'Many thanks, m'lord.' He withdrew, bowing again as he did so.

'The offer—' Ranel began, but stopped speaking as the woman raised a hand for silence, her gaze fixed on the rear where the stabler had disappeared. A door shut there and she lowered the hand.

'The offer remains as stated,' she said.

Ranel waved a hand. 'Yes, yes. I just want assurances.'

The woman had yet to withdraw her hard gaze from the rear. 'There are no assurances in our business,' she said, adding, 'Horse trading, of course.'

Ranel laughed, a touch nervously. 'Of course, yes. Horse trading.'

'You are leaving for Jurda?' the woman asked.

Ranel sighed his frustration. 'Yes. All forces. On the morrow.'

She nodded. 'We will finalize the deal there, then.'

The nobleman eyed her, frowning. 'How will I—'

'We will be in touch,' the woman said.

'Ah. Of course. Yes. Until then.'

The horse-dealer bowed once more, backing away. 'Until then. May you profit greatly from this wise choice.'

Ranel waved her off. 'Yes, yes.' He returned to tapping

his thighs nervously, and once the woman had disappeared he ran to the side door, yanked it open and fled.

The stable remained quiet for a time until straw came filtering down from the loft above and a youth straightened to brush the husks from his shoulders and hair. After a large yawn, he descended rather recklessly from the loft, using slim handholds, and plopped down to the dirt. Here, hands on hips, he regarded the closed double stable doors. Turning his back to them, he straightened, took a deep breath, then quickly knelt to pull a blade from a boot, and in that same swift motion threw it over his shoulder at the doors.

The slim throwing dagger struck home in the wood with a solid blow; the youth turned and nodded his satisfaction. He crossed to pull it free, muttering, 'Well, that's *something*, anyway.' He pushed the blade home in his boot, then peeped out of the side door and slid out into the darkness of the Gris bailey.

In a slow circuitous walk, the lad avoided posted torches and lanterns to approach a train of wagons being loaded with supplies and materiel. Here he studied them, one after another, until coming to one bearing great bags and straw baskets of arrows and crossbow bolts.

A sly smile crept up his lips and he reached in to take one particular crossbow bolt which he then tucked into his shirt. Stooping, he slipped away towards the main keep.

Taking servants' halls and entries the lad made his way higher and higher. With each floor the passageways became more narrow, the traffic less, until guards he met at barred doors waved him onwards.

The last door, guarded by two youths quite similar to him, opened to allow him entry to a lit bedchamber. Here, Malle of Gris sat in her bed, reading. Peering up, she waved the youth to her. He clambered up on to the piled furs and blankets at the foot of the bed.

'Well?' Malle asked.

He nodded. 'It will be at Jurda.'

She tapped the book in the palm of her hand, her gaze becoming distant. 'Yes. It would have to be, wouldn't it?' Her gaze sharpened, turned upon the youth. 'You will follow. Finish things there.'

He nodded, and then a mischievous grin twitched his lips.

She eyed him sidelong. 'What is it?'

From his shirt he withdrew the crossbow quarrel, extended it to her. She took it and ran her fingers through its fletching – the blue and yellow of Nita – and a similar smile crept across her lips. Handing back the quarrel, she ruffled the youth's hair. 'You were always my favourite, Possom.'

Grinning contentedly, the youth snuggled down amid the heaped blankets and closed his eyes while Malle returned to her book.

* * *

Recruitment and training was now Nedurian's preoccupation. Cadre mages had to be assigned and integrated into squads. The marine army style of engagement had to be differentiated from the traditional ship's crew free-for-all fighting they all knew. Dassem was at the fore of this, transforming Mock's Hold from a pirate admiral's personal manor into a military training facility, and Nedurian was grateful; things got done when the Dal Hon swordsman spoke, and everything proceeded so much more smoothly than if he were out there trying to convince everyone himself.

This day he was surprised to glance over to find Tay-schrenn with him at the crenellated wall overlooking the Hold's main yard cum training ground. Their 'High Mage' stood with crossed arms, his long face registering a sort of peevish confusion as he watched the swordwork routines.

Nedurian cast him a questioning look. 'You are troubled, High Mage?'

The man's brows wrinkled in distaste. 'Not that title, please.' He pointed to the ranks of trainees, recruits and veterans all mixed together at Nedurian's suggestion. 'The cadre mages training in their units, I understand. But sword- and shieldwork for mages? Really? Isn't that a waste of their time?'

Nedurian gave a curt nod in appreciation of the question. 'Some will probably always feel that way no matter what. It took some convincing from me'n'Dassem to bring them into line. Nothing heavier than shortsword for them, of course. But the same basic training for everyone. Builds unit cohesion, helps our cadre mages understand what their cohorts have to go through. And they'll have to defend themselves sometimes.' The High Mage grunted his acceptance of the point, though his face still registered his distaste for it.

'Cohesion?' he asked next, dubious. 'Really?'

'Oh, yes. Once they've seen action together and fought side by side, it'll happen. I've seen it again and again.'

The Kartoolian mage eyed him sidelong. 'The old Talian formation.'

Nedurian nodded once more. Then, since he had the man here, he asked, 'Any word?'

There was no need to say more; both knew he was asking after their erstwhile leaders. The High Mage let out a frustrated sigh. 'Still missing, but alive, I hope. At least, Jadeen hasn't reappeared either.'

'They are hiding from her, you think?'

A wintry smile came and went from the severe Kartoolian. 'Yes, I imagine that is what most people are thinking, hmm?'

'But no?'

The High Mage waved a negative. 'No. They came upon a clue to an ancient legend, and they are now chasing that.'

Nedurian raised a brow at that. *Really?* 'What legend, may I ask?'

Tayschrenn glanced about, perhaps checking that they were alone. Visibly reluctant to say anything, and hesitating for a time, he finally murmured, apparently against his better judgement, 'The Army of Dust and Bone.'

At first Nedurian could say nothing – he must've gaped, stunned. '*The Army*—' he began, almost shouting, then choked himself off. 'You're joking. That's impossible.'

'I do not joke,' the High Mage huffed, offended.

Nedurian reflected that yes, this was true. So far the Kartoolian struck him as one of the most humourless, stiff, and even obtuse people he'd ever met. Some used much stronger language than that, such as arrogant, haughty, and pompous, but he did not see the preoccupation with hierarchy or the lust for prestige or status those terms suggested – rather, it seemed to him as if the fellow simply did not know how to get along with people, or couldn't be bothered to try.

So, the Army of Dust and Bone . . . Nedurian shook his head, awed. Outrageous. Who in their right mind would dare meddle in that terrifying mystery? Everything he'd ever heard or read about those ancient legends warned everyone to stay away. The Elders were powerful and dreadful – it was a blessing their days were over. Only a fool, or an insane, power-craving . . .

He shook his head once again, this time in exasperation. *Ah . . .*

After a moment he cleared his throat, and leaned his forearms on the crenellations before them. 'Well, from all I've heard about that I'm guessing we won't be hearing from either of them ever again.'

Tayschrenn nodded his assent. 'That is the most likely outcome.'

Footsteps announced the approach of a guard, who bowed. 'Mages, your presence is requested by the commander.'

Commander – Nedurian understood that here on Malaz that could only mean a naval commander, so, Choss, not Dassem. The Dal Hon swordsman was usually referred to as the Sword, in any case.

As he and Tayschrenn, following the guard, reached the second floor of the keep, Nedurian immediately sensed that something was amiss: the tension and heightened awareness of the guards virtually screamed the fact. 'What happened?' he demanded of their guide, who gestured them ahead to a meeting chamber.

Within, they found Choss seated, his shirt hanging in tatters, a guard dressing his torso in fresh cloth. Blood gleamed wet down the old sailor's trousers. A thrown rug covered what could only be a body on the floor.

Choss raised his chin to the corpse. 'What do you two make of her?'

Nedurian pulled away the rug. It was a woman, probably in her twenties, muscular – hard-trained. Black-haired, her skin was paling now, but carried a swarthy olive hue such as characterized the inhabitants of the west coast. 'I don't recognize her,' he said.

'An outsider, then?' Choss asked.

'Possibly,' Tayschrenn answered. 'I do not recognize her either.' The High Mage crouched to examine the body more closely. He ran his hands down her back, her arms, squeezed her hands. 'City bred,' he announced. 'No typical development associated with rural farm work. Hands soft except for weapon-calluses.'

Choss grunted, then winced, his wide shoulders bunching in pain. 'The mainland, then.'

'Most likely.'

'Where?'

Nedurian and Tayschrenn shared a weighing glance. 'Not Dal Hon,' Nedurian supplied.

Tayschrenn gave his curt agreement. 'They wouldn't trust an outsider. And Bloor and Gris are too preoccupied,' he added.

'As are the far west city states.'

'Yes.'

'Itko Kan,' Nedurian judged.

Tayschrenn seconded that with a nod. 'Someone is already attempting to break up our alliance.'

Choss frowned, uncertain. He lifted a decanter of wine, but Nedurian stepped up and pushed it back down to the table. 'No. Thins the blood.' He glanced to one of the guards. 'Bring boiling soup to the commander.'

The burly Napan pulled a face. 'Soup? Am I a child to be fed hot soup? What's next? Milk?'

'Listen to the veteran,' Tayschrenn said. 'I'm sure he's cared for more wounded than he wishes to remember.'

A touch surprised by the support, Nedurian offered the High Mage a nod of gratitude, which the Kartoolian missed entirely, his gaze unfocused as he pursued his own thoughts and speculations.

Choss, meanwhile, was considering what had caused him to pick up the wine. 'Break up the alliance?' He looked to Nedurian, who sat back, thinking.

'Our High Mage has leapt to the end conclusion. Consider it.' He gestured to Choss. 'The one Napan commander here on Malaz. Perhaps the calculation was that Surly would retaliate, or one of the Malazan captains would take the opportunity to wrest control of the island from her – that is, from Kellanved. A new admiral, and back to the old rivalry.'

Choss pulled a hand down his beard, grunted a sort of grudging understanding. 'Maybe.'

A guard set a bowl of broth before the commander, who wrinkled up his mouth.

'Eat it,' Nedurian told him. 'Denul training supports my opinion here.'

The muscular Napan grimaced, but hunched forward, and raised the bowl to his lips.

'I have contacted Calot in Dariyal,' Tayschrenn announced. 'He will inform Surly.' He cocked his head, thinking. 'This also raises a broader issue . . .'

'Which is?' Choss asked.

'Communication. How to stay in touch across distance.'

'A problem throughout all history,' Nedurian answered. 'We have the mage cadre . . .'

'Indeed. However, not all possess the capability.' He stroked his long chin, thinking. 'Perhaps we could manufacture items for communication. Certain crystals' natural resonance would work well for this . . .'

'Whatever they might be, they would have to be portable,' Choss put in.

Tayschrenn nodded absently, already lost in thought. 'I will work with Nightchill on this. If I can find her. Gods know where she spends her days.' He inclined his head to Choss. 'I leave you in good hands, then,' he said, and walked out, hands clasped at his back.

Choss watched him go, then turned a raised brow on Nedurian, saying, 'Now that is one odd bird.'

Nedurian couldn't help but crook a small smile. 'We're lucky to have him. He's extraordinarily powerful, just doesn't know how to mine it yet. Sort of like a natural archer who hasn't yet learned how to draw a bow properly.'

'Breathing,' Choss said. 'I'm told it's all in the breathing.'

Nedurian sat at the table and took up the wine, sipping it while Choss watched, his lips tight. 'I've heard that too,' he said.

* * *

Iko was reviewing the latest candidates for the guard when news reached her via her own paid palace informants of some sort of incident involving the young king. Bowing out quickly, she set off across the sprawling grounds for the Kan family residences; the location surprised her, though she had noticed that lately the Kan family had been working to increase their influence, considerable though it already was.

As she hurried, she could not help but reflect upon the disappointing quality of this year's crop of candidates. Years ago none would have even been considered. Was this a sign of their society's falling dedication to tradition and plain hard work? Or was it a sign that she was now officially one of the veterans, despite her tender years? Yes, tender, she reaffirmed to herself, dammit!

The Kan family guards and retainers at the compound doors hesitated as she approached, but seeing her determined not to slow her pace one whit, they reluctantly opened the doors at the last moment. Within, a long, richly decorated hall led to an equally gilded main reception chamber and here she found the young king before the seat of the honorary head of the extended Kan noble family, the ancient dowager, Lady Serenna.

Between two Kan guards stood one of the king's tutors, the youngest of them, a brilliant scholar of history, logic and calligraphy, Bahn Throol. The fellow was pale and sweaty, obviously ill at ease.

Iko pushed through to the fore of the gathered crowd of functionaries, petty bureaucrats and Kan family hangers-on. Catching sight of her, Lady Serenna glowered her distaste, then glanced away, dismissing her. She returned her attention to the scholar. 'Touching the king's person without his permission is a serious charge,' she announced, her voice high and thin. She addressed the young King Chulalorn the Fourth. 'You said he did so, yes?'

From the youth's flushed face and hunched shoulders Iko could tell he was fairly withering in embarrassment. He nodded his lowered head.

Lady Serenna rapped her camphorwood fan against the armrest of her chair. 'Speak up! Remember, you are the king!'

The child raised his chin, said hoarsely, 'Yes.'

'I was merely adjusting the grip of his stylus—' the scholar Throol began, only to be cut off by another rap of the dowager's fan.

'Quiet! You will speak only when invited to do so!'

Scholar Throol wisely ducked his head.

'And you struck him for his impudence?'

The young king nodded.

Shocked, Iko pushed aside the last functionary blocking her way and strode forward. 'You struck one of your tutors?' she demanded.

The youth spun, his face brightening. 'Shimmer!'

Lady Serenna repeatedly rapped her fan against her armrest. 'Quiet – remember your place, Chulalorn!' She turned a slit gaze upon Iko. 'This does not involve you, Sword-Dancer. This is a family matter only.'

Since Iko did not owe any allegiance or debt of patronage to the Kan family, she ignored the dowager and instead addressed Chulalorn the Fourth. 'You must *never* strike an unarmed man or woman, yes, my king?'

The lad nodded morosely. 'Yes, Shimmer.'

'And you must respect those with wisdom and learning – yes, my king?'

'Yes, Shimmer. I'm sorry.'

'Do not apologize to me, my king. Apologize to Scholar Throol.'

A choked breath from Lady Serenna brought the lad's attention to the dowager. 'A king,' the old woman fairly snarled, 'does *not* apologize.'

Iko crossed her arms, eyed the ancient; she offered a nod of agreement. 'Perhaps not. However, an honourable man does,' and she turned her gaze to Chulalorn, waiting.

The lad glanced between her and the dowager, swallowed, and lowered his head. He turned to the scholar, murmured, 'My apologies, Scholar Throol.'

The tutor paled even further, a hand at his throat. 'Really – there is no need – my king is most gracious . . .'

'*Leave us!*' Lady Serenna hissed. She waved the fan to encompass the entire chamber. 'Leave us! You will now leave us! *All of you!*'

In a rather undignified scramble the chamber cleared until only the Kan guards, Lady Serenna, Iko and the young king remained. Scholar Throol had been marched out by two of the guards.

The Dowager Lady Serenna sat glowering down at Iko. Finally, she turned her dark gaze upon Chulalorn. 'Does a king command?' she demanded.

The lad nodded. 'Yes.'

'Is he commanded by his underlings?'

Chulalorn blinked, uncertain, shot a sidelong glance to Iko, but nodded once more. 'No.'

Lady Serenna appeared to relax; she turned her disapproving gaze upon Iko. 'Sword-Dancer,' she announced, 'you failed in your duty to protect my nephew, King Chulalorn the Third. Such incompetence has long troubled me greatly, and makes me doubt your ability to fulfil your duties.'

Iko let her arms fall, suddenly shaken. 'You have no authority—'

'This is true,' Lady Serenna agreed. 'However,' and she pointed the fan to Chulalorn, 'the king does.'

The boy stared, obviously confused.

'Chulalorn,' Lady Serenna explained, 'your personal guards serve at your pleasure. You may choose to dismiss them at will.'

Her ward glanced between them, frowning, until understanding came and his mouth fell open. 'But . . .'

'Be a *king*,' Lady Serenna demanded.

Tears welled from the young lad's eyes and he twisted his fingers together. His pleading gaze begged Iko for guidance, any sort of help, and seeing him tortured like this broke her heart.

She quickly knelt to one knee, saying, 'I beg permission to withdraw my service, my lord.'

He nodded, quite beyond words. His voice was barely audible as he whispered a cracked 'Accepted'.

Rising, Iko bowed to the lad one last time then turned on her heel without a single glance to the dowager. She would not give the old lizard the satisfaction.

The doors to the Kan compound closed behind her and she looked up at the sky, blinking back her tears. *Stupidly done, Iko*, she told herself. *So stupidly done.*

Dismissed, she no longer had any claim to quarters in the palace, and so she packed what few personal belongings she owned. Her fine mail suit and the whipsword she had to leave behind, as they were possessions of the crown.

Packing, she turned and saw the regent, Mosolan, watching, arms crossed. She offered him a nod that he answered with a long slow regretful shake of his head.

'I could hire you into the palace guard,' he suggested.

'No. I couldn't bear to stand there . . .' She shook her head.

'I'm sorry,' he said. 'But they've long been jealous of your relationship with the king. I should've warned you, I suppose, but,' and he shrugged, 'it never seemed the right time.' He let out a long sigh. 'They couldn't allow an outsider that much influence . . . they just couldn't.'

She noted that he was merciful enough not to add: *And you walked right into it.*

'What will you do?'

She shrugged, closed up her single bag. 'I don't know. Join the army, maybe.'

'You? In the regulars? I don't think so.'

'Whatever. I don't know.'

He pushed away from the jamb, appearing troubled. 'Listen. Stay in touch. I could use someone on the outside – you never know.'

She knew he was trying to be helpful, but she was just angry. Angry at damned palace politics, at the pathetic dance of influence and favour that she thought she'd been above all this time. But mostly she was just damned furious at herself.

She dipped her head in acceptance. 'Yes, thank you. It's just . . . I'm not sure. We'll see.'

He extended his arm and they clasped wrists, as veterans, and she headed out across the gardens towards the main front doors to the palace grounds. Along the way she glimpsed a few Sword-Dancers, those off duty, watching from a distance. But none approached, and she knew why.

Dismissal. Shameful dismissal.

Better to die in service than endure such. She reached the tall and ponderous iron-bound doors, one of which the guards pushed open a crack for her.

Without, she paused in what seemed a brighter, and harsher, light. The door thumped shut behind her. The bustle, noise and clatter of the city of Itko Kan assaulted her senses and she winced, blinking, shading her eyes.

She realized that for the first time in her life she had no duties, no calling. No . . . purpose. Nor did she have anywhere to go. A slim purse of coin was all she now had to her name. She strode forward into the traffic of the city and let it take her where it would.

* * *

Three days after the disastrous attempt to join the Crimson Guard, Gregar was off duty, playing troughs with his squad-mates, when Leah came and set a hand on his shoulder.

'Visitors for you,' she murmured, rather subdued.

A quip died on his lips as he saw that their new sergeant appeared quite serious; she also waved Haraj up. 'You too.' She motioned them to follow.

'Who is it?' Gregar asked.

She gave them a strange evaluative look. 'You'll see.'

Gregar shrugged, unconcerned. Anything to break the boredom of this waiting was welcome. All pretence of actively besieging Jurda had long been abandoned, and their presence had lapsed into plain dull garrison duty. Meanwhile, more and more forces gathered; every would-be princeling, duke, petty baron and man-at-arms east of Cawn seemed to want a share of the glory to come – allies and enemies of both Gris and Bloor. And both had more than enough of each.

Beyond the Yellows encampment stood two men wrapped in long crimson cloaks against a cold drizzle. Gregar and Haraj exchanged looks of wonder, for here were the unmistakable figures of young K'azz D'Avore and the mage Cal-Brinn, of the Crimson Guard.

The Red Prince bowed to Leah. 'My thanks.' The girl curtly lowered her head and turned away, probably, Gregar thought, to hide a blush. 'Thank you for seeing me,' K'azz continued, to him and Haraj.

'Why wouldn't we?' Gregar asked, bemused.

The young fellow – perhaps Gregar's own age, he realized – appeared apologetic. 'Well, my father was not very complimentary.'

Gregar just shrugged. 'He was right . . . we wasted your time.'

K'azz and Cal-Brinn shook a negative. 'No,' said K'azz, 'it was sprung on you and that was not proper. You must forgive my father – he believes every man and woman who has ever picked up a sword wishes to join the Guard.'

Haraj rubbed the back of his neck, almost wincing. 'He's probably right.'

Gregar peered about, at the passing soldiers – keeping a respectful distance, but always staring, as the bright red cloaks could mean only one thing. 'So . . . what can we do for you?'

K'azz nodded, growing serious. 'As I said, I've come to apologize on behalf of the Guard. I – we,' and he gestured to Cal-Brinn, 'want you to know that in declining to abandon your comrades before battle you displayed the very qualities we want the Guard to stand for. Loyalty. Comradeship. Honour.' The young man shrugged, almost sheepishly. 'Rather than being angered or insulted we should have saluted you. At least, that is how I and many others feel. So, the invitation stands. Who knows, perhaps in the future you may wish to seek us out.'

'And your father?' Gregar asked.

'He will grumble about it,' murmured Cal-Brinn, 'but Surat would be in favour.'

Gregar let out a long breath, quite surprised and quite unsure what to say. 'Well . . . my thanks . . .'

'You will not think poorly of us, then?' K'azz asked.

Gregar fought a laugh at the thought of *his* opinion mattering to anyone. He waved a hand. 'Gods, no. Not at all.'

The young man smiled winningly and saluted with a fist to his chest. 'Very good. Perhaps we shall see you again.'

Gregar gave an awkward half-bow. 'Ah, yes. Perhaps.'

The two Crimson guardsmen walked off and all heads at nearby cookfires turned to follow them. Gregar and Haraj exchanged looks of bewilderment. Gregar scratched his head. 'What do you make of that?'

'I think he meant it. I think he really admired that you

chose to stay with your troop – even though you're sure to be trampled like an idiot for your trouble.'

Gregar threw a swing at the lad. 'I'll just hold you ahead of me. Wouldn't that work?'

'I'm obliged to say no, it wouldn't.'

Back at their camp a worried-looking Leah met them, tapping a hand to her newly issued shortsword. 'What was that about?'

Gregar and Haraj shared another look, uncertain what to say. Gregar shrugged. 'Just that we can try again, maybe. In the future.'

The sergeant visibly relaxed. 'Good.'

'Good?'

She flinched, sneering. 'A'course! Good for the company! They expect to see you holding the colours. What else could I mean?'

Gregar rubbed his chin, a touch puzzled by her reaction. 'Sure . . . whatever.'

'Damned right!' she growled. 'Anyway, word's going round. Tomorrow or the next we withdraw from the siege and march east, to the marshalling grounds.'

'We're gonna be there for the fight, hey?' Haraj said.

The young woman's mouth turned down. '*Everyone* is gonna be there. Shaping into a godsdamned bloodbath.'

Chapter 15

WITHOUT PAUSING TO THINK OR BREATHE, Dancer whipped a blade at the Witch Jadeen. The throwing knife swerved aside before touching her, somehow deflected, and Jadeen raised a shocked brow.

'You *are* fast,' she acknowledged. 'That would've reached me had I not already prepared.'

For his part, Kellanved peered about the apparently otherwise empty natural cavern. He shook his head in disappointment. 'So . . . just an old chair, after all.'

The smug, one-sided smile remained on the witch's lips. 'No. Far more than that. Unfortunately for you.' She extended her arms out as if beckoning. 'Arise.'

The plentiful dust and debris lying about the rough cavern floor stirred at the witch's call. The small hairs on Dancer's neck stirred in atavistic dread as shapes began to coalesce from the gathering motes and swirls. Like their namesake, the Army of Dust and Bone, from dust came bone, and five individuals emerged – not skeletal, but each a desiccated, or mummified, corpse. Flesh still clung as a layered tannic-hued veneer over bone. Four wore bulky headdresses of animal skulls and hides, the fifth plain half-rotted leathers; a long heavy blade at his side was clearly worked from one immense shard of brown flint. Dark eye-pits regarded Dancer, empty yet somehow animate with intelligence and awareness.

And despite his lifetime of training, of fighting and self-discipline, Dancer found himself frozen in fascination and dismay at the sight. The manifestation of stories and legends of terror before him now – what could he possibly do? Then the moment passed, and he snapped back into his heightened readiness. They were flesh, dried and hardened perhaps, but flesh all the same. Not ghosts or apparitions beyond the touch of his blades – or so he reassured himself.

'Behold,' Jadeen announced, 'the army of the ancient T'lan Imass.'

One of the individuals spoke – a breathless guttural utterance, somehow conveyed perhaps through the magic of its very existence. The words, however, remained unintelligible to Dancer. Puzzlement must have shown on his face, as the same individual waved a hand of dried ligament, bone, and leathery flesh, and spoke again. 'Well come, traveller,' he announced. 'We are the Logros T'lan Imass, tasked with the guardianship of the throne. I am Tem Benasto, Bonecaster.' Gesturing to each, Tem introduced 'Ulpan Nodosha, Tenag Ilbaie, Ay Estos, and Onos T'oolan'.

The Bonecaster wore upon his head the skull of an extraordinarily large hunting cat, placed so that his face stared out of the opened jaws, while his hide cape, or wrap, where the hair still clung, bore a tawny hue, suggestive of a lion. Ulpan Nodosha wore the headdress of a gigantic bear, likewise staring out of the gaping jaws, the remaining thick fur brown and black. Tenag Ilbaie, however, bore the largest headdress – what appeared to be a woolly elephant skull, or stylized representation thereof. Ay Estos wore a far more slim and lean wolf's headdress, the remaining fur of his – or her – hide wrap a dirty grey and white. The last, Onos T'oolan, wore no headdress at all and was all the more horrific for it, his skull half bare of flesh, nose gone, perhaps shorn away, eye-sockets empty, the dried flesh of his lips and cheeks drawn back from stained grinning teeth.

Jadeen waved impatiently. 'Yes, yes. No need for the full explanation. Onos, step forward.'

He did so, bowing to Jadeen upon the throne.

'As your first official act in my command – I order you to slay these two.'

The creature's dried hand creaked as he took hold of the leather-wrapped grip of his flint sword. Dancer drew twinned heavy parrying gauches and pushed Kellanved behind him. Though he frankly thought it hopeless, he still wondered how to slay an apparent undead. The usual killing techniques certainly wouldn't apply . . . perhaps dismemberment was the only practical answer. A tall order with his daggers.

Onos hunched slightly, drawing the blade from the belt of twisted leather at his waist. That same motion continued, blindingly fast, as the blade arced behind in one blink of an eye to pass through Jadeen's neck.

Dancer stared, stunned; even Jadeen appeared shocked, her eyes blinking rapidly. Dancer was certain the blade must have passed just before her throat until the witch's head began to slide, wetly, forward on her neck to topple down her front in a jet of blood. Shortly thereafter, her body tumbled forward from the throne.

Dancer and Kellanved stepped backwards from the spreading tide of blood.

Onos calmly thrust his flint blade home in his belt once more. 'This one,' the Imass grated, 'has been found unworthy.'

Dancer swallowed, his mouth dry. He shared a glance with Kellanved, who appeared to have paled. 'I . . . see,' Dancer managed. 'Then that about does it for us . . .' He glanced back, searching for the way they had entered, but the tunnel was gone. They appeared to be trapped within the cavern.

'If you could—' he began, but Kellanved stepped forward – rather daintily around the pool of fresh blood – and motioned to the throne.

'So . . . it is unoccupied now?' he asked.

Dancer hissed: 'You're not really considering—'

'Yes,' Tem answered, breathlessly and emotionlessly. 'It is unoccupied.'

Dancer lunged forward, nearly slipping on the blood, to take Kellanved's arm. 'Don't. Isn't it obvious? *No one*'s been found worthy. Not in all these ages.'

The wizened Dal Hon mage eased his arm free. 'That is entirely possible, yes.'

'So?'

Kellanved raised his walking stick and tapped its hound's head to his temple. 'I have a plan.'

Dancer had to roll his eyes. 'Please, this is not the time or place for one of your tricks.' He pointed to Jadeen's staring head. 'You'll end up like that!'

'On the contrary,' the little mage huffed, 'this is entirely the time and place for such things. Where ever else would one need do so?'

Dancer shook his head, pleading. 'Please. Don't do this. Let's just go . . .'

The mage fluttered a hand to where the tunnel once lay. 'It may be that leaving is no longer an option. Therefore . . .'

Dancer let out a long hard breath. If they could not go, then fine. What other choice had they? Still, he couldn't help but see in his mind's eye all the other countless hopefuls before them driven to the same conclusion – and all failing, one after the other.

He stepped away, nodding.

Kellanved moved, and the five Imass watched, silent and immobile, as he turned and eased his bum down on the leather cradle of the throne's seat.

Dancer and he waited, peering at the Imass, all silent and watchful. Then, as one, they half bowed to Kellanved, who raised his brows to Dancer. 'So,' he murmured, 'am I . . . worthy?'

Onos T'oolan appeared to look him up and down. 'We are . . . considering . . . your occupancy.'

'And when will I know?'

'You will know,' T'oolan answered.

Kellanved rubbed his neck, wincing. 'Ah. Yes. Of course.'

The one named Tem bowed to Kellanved. 'Your orders?'

The mage flinched, fluttering his hands. 'No orders! No, none at all.' He appeared to shoo them away with his fingers. 'Do what you must . . .'

The dry flesh of Tem's neck creaked as he inclined his head. 'Very good. We shall go, then, to search out our brothers and sisters.'

Kellanved brightened. 'Yes! Excellent. Do so.' One by one the hoary shapes dissolved into dust until only Onos remained. 'You, Tool,' Kellanved called.

'T'oolan,' the Imass corrected him.

Kellanved waved that aside. 'How shall I, you know . . . contact you?'

'You call us,' the Imass answered, sloughing away into dust.

Kellanved drummed his fingers on the antler armrests of the throne, squirming now, edging back and forth. 'Damned uncomfortable seat,' the Dal Hon grumbled.

He rose, rubbing his behind, and Dancer had to shake his head.

'How did you know?'

Kellanved blinked up at him. 'How did I know what?'

He pointed to the decapitated corpse and Kellanved nodded. 'Ah. Well, you see, did you not notice how she was fine until she ordered them to do something? And that order was to slay *us*?'

'So?'

'So – it is in the legends and stories, my friend. The Imass are sworn to war against their enemy, the Jaghut. And we are not Jaghut. There you go.' He paused then, thinking, tapping his fingertips together. 'That, or just the fact that she gave an order. It may be that just because you occupy the throne doesn't mean you can give orders. Perhaps you are more a chief than a king – you sit at their permission.' He threw his hands in the air. 'Or one of those two. I'm not sure which.'

'And on that you bet your life,' Dancer muttered, shaking his head once again.

Kellanved shrugged. 'Well, 'tis done. Ah!' He pointed his walking stick. 'The tunnel.'

Dancer glanced behind: indeed, the way by which they had entered was open again. Kellanved extended an arm, inviting him to lead on.

Outside, in the howling contrary winds, the mage paused for a time, peering out at the long stretch of the headland where it extended straight out to the choppy iron-grey sea, which itself stretched on to the cloud-choked horizon.

'Such a feature could be called a "reach",' the mage mused aloud. He squinted to Dancer. 'And such a portentous and important place ought to have an equally portentous and weighty name – do you not think so?'

Dancer eyed him, suspicious. 'What do you . . . No. You can't . . . you didn't!'

The mage gave a distorted twitch that might have been an attempt at a wink. ''Tis done, my friend.'

Dancer pressed a hand to his brow. 'Gods, no.' He half turned away. 'Let's just get back to Malaz. They must be certain we're dead by now.'

The mage tilted his head, then his brows rose in surprise. 'I can reach Shadow now! Perhaps because our trial is over . . .'

'I think you're still on probation,' Dancer muttered.

This drew a vexed look from Kellanved. 'Faith, my friend.' He gestured and shadows gathered about them in the manner now familiar to Dancer. They thickened, blotting out his vision as always before. He felt himself being shifted in the alien, cold fashion of Shadow. Yet at the last instant a new and unfamiliar greyness seemed to inject itself into the swirl of shade and he felt a sharp sideways yank that tore a shout of pain from him as if he were being ripped in two. He blacked out.

Noise of soft surf, and a soothing warmth, woke him. Groaning, he sat up, blinking and holding his head. It ached like murder – far worse than any hangover or blow he'd ever endured. He peered round, wincing at the bright sunlight. He was on another shore, but one as different from the earlier one as was possible. The soft warm sand of a beach lay beneath him, and turquoise wavelets lapped gently. Inland, a wall of rich verdant foliage stood solid, seemingly impenetrable.

And no Kellanved. Panicked, he rose – which was a mistake as he was assaulted by a wave of pain and nausea and almost fell. He was standing, hands pressed to his head, fighting the dizziness, when Kellanved spoke.

'Ah! *There* you are.'

He peered up, blinking, to see the man off a distance, upon a dune, apparently none the worse, and he gritted his teeth. 'What happened?' he ground out.

The little fellow came gingerly down the sand slope. 'We were intercepted in mid-shift,' he explained. 'Not an easy accomplishment, I must add.'

'Intercepted?'

The mage nodded. 'Yes.' He pointed his walking stick. 'By whoever it is in a tent just down the shore here.'

Dancer was still cradling his head. 'I don't like him already.'

'Now, now. Let's see what he has to say.'

Dancer tried straightening and shuddered; he realized he actually felt physically ill and he looked to Kellanved. 'Why do I feel so sick?'

The mage nodded. 'Ah. It affects you strongly, does it? I suppose it must, you not being a talent so having no way to shield yourself.'

Dancer gritted his teeth anew. 'What does, damn you!'

'Chaos itself. Our host here appears able to draw upon it more directly than anyone ought.'

'Chaos? Am I going to get sick?'

Kellanved eyed him closely. 'It *should* be temporary.'

'How very helpful.' He tried a few tentative steps, pointed ahead. 'Let's get this over with as quickly as possible, then.'

A short way round the shore of what looked to be a very small island lay a sprawling tent of canvas and hides, its many ridge-poles poking up like mismatched ribs. Oddly, given the heat, smoke rose from almost every gap, tear and hole.

Dancer and Kellanved eyed one another, uncertain,

then made their way up to it and the mage used his walking stick to edge aside a flap.

Within, it was unnaturally gloomy, given the bright sunshine outside – hazy with hanging smoke, and uncomfortably hot as braziers of shimmering coals stood here and there about the interior. A hunched and broad shape, draped in rags, appeared to rise across the murkiness.

'You made it – excellent,' called a strong voice.

'Your invitation was rather ... abrupt,' Kellanved answered.

The hunched figure, his head almost hidden so low was it, like an old bent ancient, nodded. 'Apologies. Given my, ah, *state* I cannot venture beyond my sanctuary here. And so I must reach out to those I wish to address.'

Kellanved waved the hanging layers of smoke from his face. 'You wish to talk, then?'

'Yes.' A rag-wrapped lumpy hand rose to point. 'I have had my eye upon you for some time, my tricky friend. I think we are much alike, you and I.'

The mock-elderly mage peered at the deformed figure. 'Oh? I fail to see it.'

'Dominion!' their host answered, an edge to his voice. 'You and I! We both seek power and dominion. With you as my worldly representative and I the well-spring of your power – we would be unstoppable!'

Kellanved paced aside to study a nearby standing iron brazier. He poked his walking stick at the coals. 'I appear to be doing just fine,' he mused.

The figure chuckled. 'Do not try to fool either of us. You think yourself accomplished. But you also know there are powers out there that could snuff you like a candle. I could shield you from them.'

'Thank you, but I do not think I need shielding.'

Dancer caught the mage's eye and glanced to the entrance.

The figure shambled closer, raised a knotted rag-wrapped fist. 'You little upstart! You have no idea what you meddle with. Like a child you foolishly grab at flames – and you will be burned.'

'How do you propose—' Kellanved began, and turned quickly. As he did so his walking stick struck the brazier, which fell, its coals scattering against the tent in a rain of embers. 'Oh dear,' he murmured.

'*You fool!*' their host snarled. 'What have you done?'

The sun-dried canvas burst afire.

'Apologies.' Kellanved thrust a handful of nearby furs on to it, which themselves immediately roared into flame.

The bent rag-wrapped figure waved his arms in a panic, backing away. 'You *idiot*! You utter complete imbecile!' He pointed at Kellanved. 'I will cast you so far afield for this you shall never be seen again!'

As the fire spread Dancer took the mage's arm and yanked him away. He pushed through the thickening smoke, dragging Kellanved after him.

A wail sounded, and glancing back Dancer thought he saw a squat, flaming figure flailing amid the conflagration.

They emerged into the sunlight and Dancer kept going, a roaring bonfire growing behind them. Coughing, wiping his eyes, he finally relinquished his grip on Kellanved and leaned, hands on knees, gasping for breath.

The wrinkled mage turned to the rising black smoke. 'Oh dear. That didn't go so well.'

A circle of coursing and roiling energies rose about them like a gyre and Kellanved let out a hissed breath. 'Ah . . . this might be . . . difficult . . .'

Dancer turned on him. 'Difficult? What do you mean? Like *really* difficult?'

Kellanved grimaced. 'Yes. Like *really*—'

Then the wall of moiling greyness closed upon them and Dancer felt himself torn sideways once more, only this time with such cruel savageness that he blacked out immediately.

* * *

More out of boredom than anything else, Sister of Cold Nights agreed to help Tayschrenn with his project of creating devices for the projection of communication. She knew that she should trust K'rul's assurances that this was the right place and the right time to further her own long-term plans, but personally she did not see it and was frankly rather disheartened.

Oh, certainly the woman Surly was an excellent administrator and leader, and she saw great potential in her, while the Dal Hon mage had forged remarkable mastery of Meanas, and his ... arrangement ... with the ancient hounds showed true cunning. Still, her goals ran far deeper than the establishment of mere mundane telluric rule.

She wondered whether there really was anything here for her at all.

As for this Kartoolian mage; certainly he was powerful, and his grasp of Warren fundamentals was impressive. Still, he was so young, and had so much to learn. His initial instinct of using certain crystals as foci was, she felt, correct; however, she worried that the mage was not giving sufficient attention to the considerable forces involved in such channelling.

They were in his quarters in Mock's Hold, examining

the remnants of the Kartoolian's latest efforts. She raised one fragment of the shattered gemstone to her eye, then glanced at the frustrated mage. 'Why so small?' she asked.

'To fit in the hilts of daggers.' He rubbed his face, clearly exhausted. 'Or something of that sort. Portable, concealable, unobtrusive.'

'I see. Well, I am sorry, but you are going to have to go with something larger. A globe. At least fist-sized, I should think. Otherwise the forces are too concentrated.'

The mage tapped his fingers to his lips. 'It would be very difficult to procure such items.'

'The crystals need not be precious. Quartz should suffice.'

He eyed her, raising a brow. 'You appear very well versed in such research.'

She waved negligently. 'Oh, over the years one—'

She halted, blinking, and pushed herself from the table so hard books tumbled to the floor.

'Are you all right?' Tayschrenn asked, though she hardly heard him over the roaring in her ears.

Waves of power had just washed over her; it was as if an enormous bell had just been struck far off beneath the earth and she felt, more than heard, the reverberations.

And they spoke of one source and one source alone, though she could not believe it.

'Tellann?'

'What was that?' Tayschrenn asked. 'Tell . . .'

She hadn't realized she'd spoken aloud. *Tellann! Impossible!*

'Are you—'

But she was at the door and descending the circular stone staircase. The mage shouted something after her, but she shifted in mid-stride and was gone.

*

She stood at the bottom of a deep ravine of bare rocky cliffs, their faces pockmarked by cave openings. The light was dim here, as it was late afternoon and the ravine lay in shadows. She clambered up to the nearest cave.

Within, she found four bearded hermit ascetics, naked but for soiled loincloths, seated on dirty reed mats. Were she a normal person the stink of excrement, urine, and long unwashed bodies would have caused her to gag; instead, she surveyed the men then pointed to the opening.

'Out! All of you! Get out. Take your damned mats and go squat elsewhere.'

The four blinked up at her, uncomprehending, and she realized that they probably weren't even certain she was really there before them.

She sighed, then raised her hands into the air and announced: 'Get thee hence! Spirits are stirring and they demand private communion! Dare not witness their glory!'

All four drew sudden breaths and bowed to her, two so vehemently that they bashed their heads on the bare rocky ground. They hurriedly gathered up their mats and shambled out.

'You!' she called to the last to leave. 'Bring firewood.'

He bowed again.

Alone, Sister of Cold Nights surveyed the dark filthy cave and shook her head; why K'rul favoured such desolate, out of the way locales was beyond her. She raised her chin, shouting, 'K'rul! Come to me, damn you! You know why!'

Perhaps as a measure of the gravity of the question – or the heat of her anger – she only had to wait that night, the following full day, and part of the next night. During her vigil the firewood kept being delivered, and she noticed a growing crowd of the valley's ascetics, hermits and pilgrims gathering outside the entrance like some sort of gawking audience.

She paced the entire time before the fire, clasping and reclasping her hands at her back as she worried about that sudden renewed presence she'd sensed; everything had been quiet since, after all, and that was quite unlike *them*.

She turned in her pacing and there he was, hunched cross-legged before the meagre fire, in a dirty hooded cloak. Sister of Cold Nights nearly pounced on him. 'There you are! Did you foresee this? Did you?'

The hooded head nodded. 'Yes, Sister—'

'Tellann awoken?'

'Yes, Sister. I—'

'The very worst eventuality I would wish?'

K'rul raised his hands imploringly. 'Please, Sister. Hear me out . . .'

Sister of Cold Nights crossed her arms, jerking a nod. She suppressed her rage, but so great was its power that she saw the flame of the fire jump, while the ground beneath her feet shuddered. Loose rocks fell from the uneven ceiling and a great gust of dust and sand burst from the cavern mouth.

She heard the gathered crowd's distant murmur of awe.

'Sister,' K'rul began, 'be assured we are in accord. We agree that the only way forward is to leave behind these ancient vendettas and crusades. And I know the Jaghut in particular concern you, though they remain indifferent to your efforts.' He shook his head in wonder. 'They are a . . . difficult . . . kind. In any case, ask yourself: how can a conflict end if one of the contestants remains hidden?'

'It was *peace*!'

K'rul shook a negative once more. 'It was but an interregnum.'

Arms crossed, she scowled down at him. 'This is a catastrophe for *all* kind. A return to the ancient conflicts.' She jabbed a finger. 'Do not fool yourself! The K'Chain and the Forkrul are sure to take note of this!'

'Such is the hope. Now none dare remain indifferent. Change is difficult and a risk – but it is the only way forward. Yes?'

'There will be blood.'

'Yes. It is necessary. All fates are in question now – mine included.'

Sister of Cold Nights lifted a sceptical brow. 'Even you, brother? I find that difficult to believe.'

'Look to yourself, sister.'

She dropped her arms with a sigh, returned to pacing. 'I committed myself to this ages ago, brother.'

After a long silence, empty but for the crackle of flames, K'rul spoke, his voice soft. 'Your path will be hard.'

'I am ready.'

'Then we are done.'

A curt nod from her. 'Indeed. And there is much to do.'

'Fare thee well, sister.'

'And you, brother.' She gestured and disappeared in a swirl of dust.

K'rul began to fade away as well. As he did so, he murmured, 'May it be worth it . . . for you, and me.'

It was another day and night before any of the valley ascetics dared edge into the cave. Finding it empty, the four original occupants eyed one another in wonder, then fell to their knees in prayer.

* * *

Silk was at the crenellations of Heng's west wall; not on duty, merely taking the air, thinking, as was his habit of late. By order of the Protectress all travel restrictions and curfews had been lifted, and so now traffic was thick beneath him on the Great Trader Road westward to Quon and Tali, as was the river traffic as well. Normally, he would be lingering in the Inner Round, at one of the trendy eateries or courtyards, mingling with the daughters – and mothers – of the richer merchant houses and what passed for local Hengan aristocracy, such as it was.

But his thoughts kept returning to Shalmanat. And lately his usual amusements and dalliances had lost their fascination. Become rote. Even dreary.

While she remained cloistered, refusing all company. Even his. He let out a long breath and brushed dust from the sleeve of his white silk shirt. What was one to do?

'Greetings, mage!' came a great bellow from behind, and Silk turned to peer down to the street below. There stood two of his mage compatriots, the great shaggy giant Koroll, and the mage of Telas, Smokey.

'What is it?' he sighed. 'Magical pilfering from the market stalls again?'

The giant rumbled a laugh. 'Nay. I am come to give you my farewells.'

Silk started from the wall. '*What?* A moment.' He hurried to the nearest stairs.

He found them waiting at the bottom and peered up at Koroll, confused. 'You are given an errand?'

'No, no.' The huge fellow was wearing his usual shapeless hanging rags and tatters, his tall stave in hand. 'No errand. Travel. I am called away to the north. To my people.'

Now Silk was even more confused. He'd never

considered Koroll's people. Who would they be? The Thelomen? 'Your people are in the north?' The *north*? A thought struck him. 'Wait! You are of the *Fenn*?'

Koroll waved a great paw. 'Just an ancient word for giant. Or monster. Not ours, by the way. One of yours. Humans'.'

'Ah.' Silk was relieved – all sorts of dire and dark rumours and legends surrounded that name. 'You have spoken with Shalmanat?'

The giant's wide expressive mouth drew down and he nodded sombrely. 'Yes. I have taken my leave. It is unfortunate, but unavoidable. I must go.'

'Now? You are going now?'

'Yes. Ho and I have spoken at length and Mara and I have said our farewells. And now I shall pass on my thoughts to you two,' and he nodded to Smokey. 'I am no reader of the Deck of Dragons, or any such, but I have been troubled of late. This is another reason why I hearken to this call. And so I warn you as I have Ho, Mara and Shalmanat – something is coming. I do not know what, but it troubles me greatly.'

Silk was reminded of Liss's words months ago. 'You sound just like Liss,' he said, half jokingly.

'Then listen to her too, my friend.'

'And you have no idea?' Smokey asked, stroking his goatee. 'If it is a danger, then stay and help.'

The alien, fading tattoos that crossed the giant's face writhed as he grimaced. 'I am sorry. It is just a new smell in the wind; a strange new bite to the cold air. Ancient, but somehow familiar.' He shook his wild mane of dirty hair, and bits of chaff and straw came dusting down. Then he chuckled, his old self, and cuffed huge hands to Silk and Smokey's shoulders. 'So! Keep a weather eye out, my friends! And good luck to you!' He turned and shambled off up the main way, parting the heavy traffic of carts and wagons like a lumbering man-o'-war.

Silk and Smokey stood silent, watching the giant go, then the mage of Telas let out a long breath and pulled on his goatee once more. 'Excellent. Some sort of trouble might be on the way and now we're shorthanded.'

'We'll have to recruit.'

Smokey snorted. 'Can't imagine anyone good enough. I, after all, am the famous mage of Telas, while you . . .' he paused to look Silk up and down, 'I never could figure out what it was you did.'

Silk offered a smile. 'I make us look good.'

'Hunh. That's what I do just by showing up.'

Silk extended an arm. 'I suggest a drink while we hash that out.' He pointed to Smokey's leather shoes. 'I mean, really? Tradesmen's footwear.'

'Better than those silk slippers.'

Silk raised a foot. It was indeed in a silk slipper. He wiggled it back and forth, sighing. 'It's all the fashion these days, my friend. You should stay informed.'

'How can you even walk in those?'

'That's the whole point. They declare that their wearer is above such pedestrian concerns.'

Smokey shook his head, but he quirked a rueful smile. 'Why you hang around sponging off those rich arseholes is beyond me.'

Silk shrugged his shoulders. 'Well . . . there's little to be gained from sponging off the poor.'

Chapter 16

IN DARIYAL, CARTHERON WATCHED WHILE EVENTS unfurled as Surly predicted, or perhaps enforced: Tarel ceded power to the Napan Council of Elders and Nobles and retired to the family's private island, while the Council – suitably chastened – heeded most suggestions from Surly herself, who remained hidden from pretty much everyone else.

Since generations of bloody rivalry could not simply be brushed aside, the navies were not officially merged, remaining independent and separated into two task forces.

For the marines, however, Cartheron deliberately pushed for no distinctions whatsoever. Despite this, or because of it, recruitment and training was proceeding with remarkable success. Privately, Cartheron was under no illusions, as everyone was eager to serve the man who had no formal rank, but was known simply as the Sword.

This evening Cartheron sat in the Anvil, a waterfront inn – though, in truth, almost all taverns and drinking houses in Dariyal were waterfront. It had become something of an unofficial rendezvous for the officer corps – if it could be called such.

His brother was with him, back from raiding. In fact,

almost all vessels were in harbour as pickings were particularly thin this season. Fighting almost everywhere on the continent had merchants going to ground.

He sipped his watered beer and reflected that this raised the salient point so plaguing the conferences with Surly: what next?

Also at the table this evening were Dujek and his second in command, Jack, like Urko back from raiding, and the cadre mage Hairlock, who, though not pleasant company, apparently loved to talk and drink and so showed up uninvited all the time.

Urko nudged his brother, gestured round the table and observed, 'We're the only Napans left.'

Cartheron grunted his agreement. 'We're getting thin on the ground these days.'

'Where is Tocaras, anyway?'

'Mainland. He proposed some kind of mission to Surly and went.'

Urko nodded. 'Hunh. Never was comfortable at sea. Born on the mainland, right?'

'Yeah. His family's related – but we're all related here, hey? Damned small island. Anyway, a trade delegation, I believe. He's half Napan.'

Urko peered down at his tankard. 'That's the Old Crew, then. An' Choss is in Malaz.'

His brother, he knew, could sometimes slip into melancholy, and so to change the subject Cartheron looked to Hairlock. 'What of our glorious leader?'

The mage stroked his wide jowls and nodded solemnly. He peered right and left then leaned forward, lowering his voice conspiratorially. 'Been poking round. All indications are he's still alive. Don't know just where he is, though.' The squat and sun-darkened mage raised a blunt finger. 'But, here's the kicker.' He paused to glance about again and Cartheron realized that here was a fellow who loved to be 'in the know', dispensing juicy bits of gossip; he'd have to warn Surly and Tayschrenn about that. 'Jadeen had a whole organization in south Itko Kan, right? Found out it's now in complete disarray. Word is, she's dead.'

Despite his disapproval of Hairlock's smugness and gossiping, Cartheron was impressed. The Witch Jadeen, dead? Could the little runt really have . . . He shook his head.

'I didn't think he had it in him,' Urko announced, and thumped the table. Cartheron winced.

'Perhaps it was Dancer,' Jack murmured, keeping his voice low.

Urko jabbed a blunt finger to the young officer. '*That* I'd believe.'

'That's enough about that,' Cartheron warned, and he sipped his beer.

Hairlock just grinned and tapped a finger to the side of his nose.

Dujek cleared his throat and leaned to Cartheron. 'Got a request, if you don't mind.'

'What is it?'

Dujek gestured to Jack. 'The lad here has a far better head than most for runnin' things, so has pretty much been doin' all the work without the rank. So, I request he formally has command.'

Cartheron studied the young officer, who in fact was no younger than many of them – he just had kept his youthful looks for longer. He was even trying to grow a beard, perhaps to compensate. He nodded. 'I'll draw the papers up tomorrow. Congratulations, Jack. You're now command rank.'

'Drinks!' Urko called out.

A young servitor came to the table and Cartheron asked, 'What would you like to celebrate, Jack?'

'Whisky.'

Cartheron raised a brow. 'Well, well. Whisky, Jack?' Then he slapped a hand to the table. 'That's it. *Whiskyjack* – the cunning bird. There you go.'

Urko's forehead furrowed. 'What?'

Cartheron pointed to the thin ropy fellow. 'His name. Whiskyjack.'

The lad actually looked embarrassed. 'I don't know about this . . .'

But Dujek was nodding. 'I like it. It has – whadyacallit – *panache*.'

Cartheron ordered the round, then spotted a slim dark figure slipping into the tavern and frowned. One of Surly's dark birds, her Claws. This one, a young woman, approached the table and bowed, murmuring, 'Your presence is requested.' She looked to Hairlock as well. 'And you, mage.'

Hairlock appeared surprised. 'We're ready?'

The young woman slipped away without answering. When the round arrived Cartheron drank his swiftly, saluted the lad in his new command – and name – then rose. Hairlock accompanied him.

They crossed the waterfront to the ancient pile of stone that was the harbour garrison, armoury, and informal palace of Dariyal.

'You'll like this,' Hairlock chuckled. 'If it's what I think it is.'

They passed through numerous guarded entryways and doors, and were directed towards a small side room, a private meeting chamber. Two of Surly's Claws guarded this door, and when they opened it Cartheron saw Surly at a table flanked by two more Claw bodyguards, the boyish-looking cadre mage Calot, and their 'High Mage' Tayschrenn.

The table held some sort of glowing object, not unlike a lantern, except that the pale light was constant, not flickering.

'Hairlock,' Tayschrenn called, 'if you would please . . .'

Grunting, the burly mage went to the table and raised his hands to the globe.

'Been working on this for a while,' the High Mage explained to Cartheron. 'This is our first trial.' He raised a questioning brow to Surly, who nodded her assent.

'Ap-Athlan,' Tayschrenn called to the table. 'I would speak with you.'

Everyone waited in silence. Cartheron couldn't help cocking a sceptical eye to Surly; her attention, however, was steady upon the single bluish light in the darkened room.

Something flickered in the glow, a blurry shape, and a voice whispered faintly, wavering in and out, 'Who would speak?'

'I am Tayschrenn. I speak for the ruler of Malaz and the Napan Isles.'

A long silence followed this, until the weak voice answered, 'Very well. Speak.'

'I wish to propose an agreement to our mutual benefit.'

Silence again, until a whispered, 'I see . . . I shall take your request to my mistress.'

'Agreed. We shall speak again – one day hence.'

'Agreed.'

A collective gasp of relief burst from the mages as the glow snapped out, plunging the room into darkness. Light blossomed from a lantern Surly now held, its sliding panel raised. Cartheron saw other shielded lanterns and opened them as well. The light revealed the three mages clinging to the table like shipwreck survivors. Their faces gleamed with sweat and they were gasping for breath.

'One day?' Calot complained to Tayschrenn, when he could speak. 'You're optimistic.'

* * *

Orjin cleaned his nicked and gouged two-handed blade as best he could, then eased himself down on a rock to rest. He was exhausted, famished to his core, and hadn't had a proper drink since a mouthful of muddy rainwater someone had kept too long in a goatskin gerber.

At least the numerous bruises and cuts up and down his body weren't serious enough to slow him down – yet. He was lucky in that. Many were down one good arm, or had leg wounds that meant they were barely able to keep up when the troop was on the move.

He gathered up a handful of dirt and rubbed his hands together to scrape off the dried blood.

Soon. It would have to be soon now. The decision he'd been putting off.

If it wasn't already too late.

One by one the other principals of the troop came limping up to sit with him at his fire in the traditional dusk gathering. Not that there was anything to discuss these days. They were surrounded, and the ground was disappearing beneath their feet. At some point ahead – not so far off at all – things would settle into an informal siege, with Renquill starving them out.

At least, that's what *he'd* do.

He nodded to Orhan, Terath, Yune and Prevost Jeral as they either sat or squatted down, inviting any ideas.

This night the Wickan Arkady was with them too, back in camp between his contacts with the hill tribes.

Orjin looked from one haggard and drawn face to another, Terath and Jeral with eyes downcast as if unable, or unwilling, to meet his gaze, and decided then that now would be the time. He drew breath to speak, just as Prevost Jeral raised her hand. He lifted a brow. 'Yes?'

She extended a sealed scroll. 'Another message from Renquill.'

Orjin took it, commenting, 'Downright chatty, our pursuer.' This raised a few half-smiles.

He broke the seals and read the message, then tossed the vellum roll into the fire. 'As expected – my head for the lives of the troop.'

'As I said before,' Terath cut in, '*he* may mean it, but we cannot trust Quon and Tali. They want everyone's head.'

Orjin pulled a hand down his face, as if he could draw the exhaustion from his spirit and flesh; how hard it was to concentrate when just standing was an effort! 'An exchange *could* be arranged,' he mused. 'Perhaps right at the Seti border. You could all make a run for it there.'

'No more talk of that,' Jeral growled.

'But that pretty much is my proposal,' Orjin explained. 'We break out to the north, then east along the Purge border – that may slow Renquill down – then part into small companies and spread out. Some of us will make it.' He didn't say that if it came to it he would offer himself as a diversion to allow as many as possible to get away.

Orhan and Terath were shaking their heads. 'Not good enough,' Terath answered. 'It's all or none.'

'There's nothing else.' Orjin eyed everyone in turn. 'Unless anyone else has a better idea?'

Heads turned as the group looked at one another; but no one spoke.

Orjin nodded. 'Very well then. Tomorrow at dawn. We strike north, then dash east.'

Terath threw a handful of gravel into the fire, saying, exasperated, 'But Renquill will be expecting just such a move.'

He held out his arms in an open shrug. 'What choice do we have?'

At this point Yune raised a skeleton-thin hand. It shook with a terrible palsy, and Orjin knew the ancient had been driving himself harder than any of them, keeping tabs on as many of their pursuers as he could. He nodded for him to speak. 'Yes?'

The elder cleared his throat. '*We* may have nothing to say, but there is one present who is very eager to speak indeed. And has been for some time, though he has held himself back as he is afraid of how he will be received.'

Everyone was puzzled. 'Who, and why?' Terath demanded.

'Well,' said Yune, 'you see . . . he is a spy.'

Both Terath and Jeral surged to their feet, hands going to weapons. '*What?*' Jeral snarled, glaring about at the surrounding encampment.

Orjin gestured for them to sit; he wasn't surprised. Many states kept hired informants and even infiltrators in their neighbours' armies – or should, if they were smart enough. 'And he or she is eager to come forward now? Has a proposal?'

Yune shrugged. 'Let us hear from him.'

Orjin nodded his compliance and the Dal Hon elder crooked a hand to the night.

A short, sturdy figure rose from one of the nearest campfires and approached, hesitantly. It proved to be a youth, in simple rags, not even armed. Orjin raked his memory, but couldn't recall seeing the lad before. He eyed him narrowly. 'And you are . . . ?'

The lad gave an uneasy shrug. 'Names can change, yes?'

Terath pointed a finger. 'I know you! You claimed to be a runaway from a Quon estate.'

The youth nodded. 'That much is true.'

Orjin waved for silence. 'Never mind. Who do you speak for?'

'An interested third party.'

Orjin was unimpressed. 'Interested in what? Watching us get run down?'

The youth flushed, showing some measure of inexperience, but nodded to Orjin. 'You said you had no options . . . I am empowered to offer one.'

Orjin rubbed his jaw, still a touch puzzled. 'I believe my tactical evaluation to be pretty damned accurate.'

The young lad flushed anew. 'It is. The picture changes, however, when you consider that while the party I speak for might not possess an army, it does possess a great number of ships.'

Everyone save Yune and Orjin jumped to their feet, all speaking at once.

'How many ships?' Terath demanded.

'How soon?' Arkady asked.

'And from *where*?' Jeral growled.

Orjin raised his hands for silence. 'Quiet!' He looked round. 'Our friend here might not be the only spy in our camp.'

They sat once more, Jeral grudgingly. She extended a finger to the newcomer but spoke to Orjin. 'I don't like it. This one may be an infiltrator from Renquill sent to lure us to the coast with some cock and bull story of ships. At the coast we could be cornered and slaughtered.'

'Yune?' Orjin asked, a questioning brow raised.

'Our friend is telling the truth when he says he speaks for a distant party.'

'Who?' Terath demanded.

The old shaman almost winced as he confessed, 'The ruler of Malaz and the Napan Isles.'

Orjin's hope soured; he'd heard the rumours regarding the powers there. Some sort of sorcerer who could summon demons, and his right hand a murderer who everyone believed had slain King Chulalorn the Third.

In the silence following Yune's admission, the giant Orhan murmured, 'Perhaps we cannot be so choosy.'

Orjin nodded. Orhan was right. If there was any chance at all to save his people he had to take it. 'How soon can the ships get here?' he asked the lad.

'Three to four days.'

He rubbed his stubbled cheeks, thinking. So they just had to last another four days or so, and make it to the coast. He looked at Arkady, who was being his usual silent self. 'Speak to our hill-folk guides, yes?'

The Wickan padded off.

Orjin regarded the agent. 'Looks as though we have a deal. But if the ships don't arrive – you die with us.'

The fellow nodded. 'I will send word.' Bowing, he departed.

A short while later Arkady returned with two of their guides in tow. Orjin couldn't quite read their impassive and set faces as they joined the group round the fire, but to him they appeared troubled.

Arkady blew out a breath. 'The west is where they're thickest. The most forts. The most patrols. And the mountains peter out. We lose our cover.'

Terath was frowning. 'But the ravine choking the coastal road where this whole campaign started . . .'

Orjin looked to their guides. 'Uh-huh. What of that?'

The two eyed one another, clearly reluctant. Finally, one cleared his throat, murmuring, 'Yes. Hidden River.'

'And?'

'They say there is a way,' Arkady put in. 'But there's a problem.'

Orjin gestured, inviting them to speak. 'Please. What is it?'

Clearly uncomfortable, one shifted, uneasy, then began, 'It is a series of caves, and a river that goes underground. It comes out at a cove between cliffs on the shore. Our elders speak of it, but our people have not travelled its full route in generations.'

'Why not?'

The young fellow made a sign against evil. 'It is . . . guarded.'

Jeral made to rise, as if this was all a waste of time, but Orjin bade her sit. 'Guarded? By what?'

'Generations ago the earth shook. It was the goddess's anger. After that the river's route changed, and something barred the way.'

'Something? You don't know what it is?'

Once more the two exchanged uneasy glances. The one speaking finally confessed, reluctantly, 'A dragon.'

Jeral openly rolled her eyes; Orjin did feel his brows rise in scepticism, but he nodded, accepting the information. 'I see. Well . . . will you guide us there regardless? You need not go all the way. Just point us there.'

They grasped at leather pouches strung round their necks; amulets, or charms perhaps. 'We are not cowards,' the speaker said. 'We will show you the way. That is land we once walked. You lowlanders may think it is yours, but it is still ours.'

'And perhaps this, ah, dragon, has left,' Terath suggested.

The two eyed her, dubious, and the spokesman nodded solemnly, clearly not believing it for a moment. 'Perhaps this is so.'

* * *

Ullara had to leave her loyal companion Bright behind when the way became too steep. She stuffed her few remaining sacks and skins of supplies into a pack that went on to her back, threw two thick horse blankets, rolled and tied, over her shoulder, took up a tall sturdy staff cut from a branch, and felt her way onward.

It was slow going. Her guides were leaving her alone for longer and longer periods. A fall now would be deadly – any serious enough injury would be deadly. Sometimes she had to feel her way with her hands, or tapping the stick, or sliding her feet about.

At least thirst was no problem, as she was high enough now to find snow clinging in shadows and cracks; she would gather up a handful and melt it in her mouth. As for food, she'd actually been eating far better than she had in Heng – meat almost every day. So hunger wasn't a problem either, as yet.

And the bare rocky slopes of the Fenn Range were remarkably uninhabited. She hadn't met another human being since taking leave of her Seti guides. Rugged wild sheep and mountain goats were her companions now.

But she wasn't completely safe. Once she was startled by what sounded like a sudden fight nearby: hissing and squalling and the crashing of huge flapping wings. She was then given an intimate glimpse of a bloodied dead mountain cat, clutched in Prince's talons as he proceeded to eat it.

She was not too shaken; she knew that she'd have been dead a hundred times over were he not watching over her.

No, her greatest worry was that she was forced to follow what could only be described as a thin trail, deeper into the range. A trail meant her kind – the kind she least wished to meet. She hoped it was a hunting trail, or supply route, the sort of path travelled only once or twice a year.

So she was not entirely surprised when she followed a curve in the steep path – it zigzagged upwards day after day – and the vision taken from a nearby soaring raven revealed an upright human figure where the way levelled ahead, awaiting her. She paused to collect herself, then continued onwards.

She closed within hailing distance then paused again, mostly because her vision had slipped away with the haphazard twists and turns of the raven. From what she had glimpsed, it was a man wrapped in a dark cloak that snapped around him in the fierce winds. Gathering her resolve, she brought to mind the story she'd decided upon, straightened her back, and called out bravely, 'Greetings! I am merely passing through as a pilgrim. I ask for no charity – I only ask to be left alone.'

'Greetings!' the man answered over the winds, his accent sounding as if he were from the south, the Itko Kanese coast, perhaps. 'You are fortunate to have found us. We are, I believe, the only people between here and the empty ice wastes of the north.'

'And may I ask who you are?'

A rather long silence followed this request. Then the

man called back, his voice revealing amusement, 'I thought you knew. But perhaps that's vanity on my part.' She heard him advancing. 'I thought the red cloak would be known – but no matter. We are of the Crimson Guard. Welcome to our last redoubt and refuge, the Red Fort.'

Ullara was quite stunned. She'd heard the minstrel tales and songs of the famed Guard, of course; their champions and their battles. And of the hidden Red Fort, though most thought it didn't actually exist.

Closer, she heard his breath catch as he made out the holes where her eyes once had been. 'By the Seven!' he exclaimed. 'How did you manage this?'

'I am not without help,' she answered.

'You are not alone, then?'

'I have talents.'

Silence, then a spoken, 'Ah! I see – that is ... I mean ...'

She waved a rag-wrapped hand. 'No matter. I did not come this way to seek you out. I travel north and do not mean to intrude.'

'*Intrude?*' the fellow echoed, shocked. 'I insist you join us! We can't have you wandering around these wastes.'

Ullara frowned at that; she did not like the way it sounded. 'I am not wandering,' she answered, a touch testily.

A laugh from the man, and this troubled her as well: it was too dismissive. But then, she'd heard so many such laughs from men. 'Well, be that as it may,' this one said. 'Please, let us feed you and offer you a warm bed for the night ... I'm sure it has been a long time since you've slept in the warmth.'

This was true, and the offer did sound tempting. She felt now the bone-weariness that she'd grown used to all these weeks. She sighed. 'Very well. Thank you for the offer.'

'Thank you. This way – that is, how . . . ?'

She gestured forward. 'You lead. I'll follow.'

'Ah . . . of course. Very good.'

Her vision returned as they neared the fort. Ravens, it seemed, liked its crenellations. It was quite large for its isolated location, or so it seemed to her. Tall stone walls looked to meld into natural rock cliffs. A square inner stone tower filled most of the enclosed space. From what she could see it appeared that very few cloaked men and women walked its grounds or paced its walls.

The mercenary guided her through the open timber doors, faced in iron, and along an enclosed tunnel to the grounds. When they entered the tower and the heavy door closed she immediately lost her vision. The relative heat of the building – the greatest heat she'd felt in months – struck her like a heavy blanket and she suddenly felt her exhaustion.

'I am Seth,' the guardsman introduced himself. 'I command this installation.'

'Oh!' She was startled that such a high officer would be out patrolling the paths, but then she'd heard such things of the Guard's strange organization – or lack thereof. 'Ullara.'

'This way.'

Blind, she did not move. She cleared her throat. 'I'm sorry, but within doors without my helpers I cannot see.'

'Ah. Sorry.'

A hand, large and rough, took hers but she pulled free. 'Let me hold your arm, please.'

'Yes, of course.' He guided her hand to his forearm and she followed his lead up a long hall. After a few more turns and doors they came to an even warmer

320

room; a fireplace crackled here and chairs scraped as a number of people rose.

'Our guest,' said Seth. 'Ullara.'

'Greetings,' a number of men and women answered.

She bowed her head. 'Thank you.'

Seth guided her forward to a chair. She sat and now found herself so close to the fireplace that she imagined if she reached out she'd burn herself. A table was scraped across the stone flags until she felt it in front of her. 'Soup is on the way,' Seth said. 'And bread. And watered wine.'

'You needn't go to all this trouble . . .'

'Nonsense. When we had word of your approach we couldn't believe it. I myself had to meet you – so you see, our encounter was no chance.'

'Word?' she asked, suddenly feeling troubled once more.

'Yes, our—Ah, here he is.'

Someone sat at the table opposite her. She could not see him, but she felt him immediately. A powerful aura. A mage.

'So . . . Ullara is it?' a new voice asked.

'Yes. And you are?'

'Gwynn. My name is Gwynn.'

'You saw me, did you?'

'Felt you, more than saw. Yes.'

A fragrant bowl of something arrived before her. She gingerly felt for it.

'Careful,' Gwynn said. 'It is hot.'

'My thanks.' She found and sipped from the bowl. Some sort of vegetable and drippings soup.

A yawn overtook her then and she almost dropped the bowl.

'Finish and I will show you to a bed.'

She nodded her thanks, sipped more of the oh-so-good hot soup.

Later, she almost fell asleep in her chair, but the mage, who seemed to have the manners of a youngish man, guided her hand to his arm and led her through more halls and rooms to a small-sounding chamber containing a low straw pallet.

'There are blankets,' Gwynn said.

'Yes.' She'd felt them.

'I will shut the door, but only for your privacy, I assure you.'

She frowned anew, slightly puzzled. 'Thank you – of course.'

'Yes. Of course.' Yet he'd paused there, as if meaning to say something else. She was so warm and drowsy, however, that the bed pulled at her and she thumped down on to the straw.

She barely heard the door rattle shut.

Seth convinced her to stay two more days. During this time they fed her constantly, had her clothes mended by the servants who did the cooking and cleaning, and even gave her new warmer wraps, and a thick woollen cloak – one *not* crimson, they assured her.

She began to learn her way around the keep. At times she would be startled by flashes of vision – of mountainsides, the fort's exterior – and she knew then that she'd chanced upon a window.

On the third day she sat at dinner with Gwynn, as was typical.

He told her of his youth and upbringing, which was as different from her own as could be imagined, and fascinated her. Of rich privilege in Unta. Of tutors and schools. Of great prospects all thrown away by youthful foolishness. Of exile and much wandering – the young man had even visited the near mythological Seven Cities.

While she had never before been out of Heng.

After dinner he guided her back to her room, as was their routine. 'Well,' she said, at the door, 'I will continue on my journey tomorrow.'

A long silence followed, and she tilted her head enquiringly.

'About that,' Gwynn began, slowly. 'I am so very sorry, but Seth will not allow you to leave.'

At first she laughed. 'Gwynn! That's absurd. You can't keep me prisoner here.' He did not answer; she imagined him knitting his fingers in front of him. 'I am not one of your company – I am a free woman. I can go when I choose!'

'I'm sorry—' he began.

'Where is the commander? Where is Seth? I demand to speak to him!'

She imagined him shaking his head. 'Speaking with him will make no difference. It is decided. You will stay.'

'You will not keep me prisoner,' she answered, and was surprised by the power in her voice.

'In three months' time our relief will arrive. A mule train out of New Seti. They will come by a much more circuitous route than the one you found. We will then escort you back to the lowlands. You can go anywhere you choose after that.'

'Let me go,' she fairly snarled. 'I *must* go.'

'Oddly enough we are in agreement in this, you and I. I argued against keeping you back. It seems to me that your arrival here was nothing short of a miracle. That it was almost as if you were being guided, or watched over – and that therefore we ought not interfere. Seth, however, believes that sending you on your way would be the equivalent of murder by negligence. And that we cannot do. Therefore, you must stay.'

She gaped, utterly at a loss. *Imprisoned!* How *dare* they! Yet there was nothing she could do. She bit her lip – *mustn't cry*! 'Leave me,' she managed, all in a gasp.

'Of course,' he murmured, and the door groaned shut. This time she heard it lock.

Chapter 17

I T WAS NIGHT, AND DAMNED COLD. HOW THE BLASTING furnace heat of the day could be whipped away so quickly was a mystery to Dancer. The dark bowl of the sky was clear and glowing with stars. That at least was some consolation; he'd been given rudimentary training in how to tell direction by the stars and so he knew that at least they weren't walking in circles.

He paused to catch his breath – something he found himself having to do more and more often – and adjusted the woven rope across his chest. The rope drew a tossed-together sledge of two branches as runners supporting broken lashed boughs as crosspieces. Upon this lay Kellanved.

It had been four days, or rather nights, of travel since their banishment by whoever – or whatever – that entity had been. He'd recovered first, while Kellanved was still having trouble. It seemed the entity had attacked him with particular vehemence – Dancer couldn't imagine why.

He'd awoken to find himself in a blasted wasteland of a desert. So alien did it appear he'd at first thought them cast into some other Realm, or some nether reach of the Paths of Hood himself. But that night the stars came out and he knew they were still in the world – and if he was reading the sky correctly, far to the south of Quon Tali.

A flat featureless plain of wind-blown dust, crusted salt pans, and outcroppings of barren crumbling rock lay in every direction. Here and there bits of broken and rusted metal poked out like wreckage. To his eye the fragments had the look of the mechanisms they'd encountered in the flying structures they had seen before.

By day the sun seared the ground like a forge – waves of heat shimmered like will-o'-the-wisps – while by night the winds snatched all heat away and left one shuddering.

Dancer had opted to travel by night. By day he levered up the ramshackle sledge as cover against the sun and they lay in its shade. By night he dragged it as far as he could before falling exhausted.

Faced with the choice of four directions he'd chosen east, and crossed his fingers that this land lay mostly north–south. Since then there had been four nights of endless trudging, with only the stars as evidence that he was making any headway at all.

A groan from behind brought him up short. He let the rope fall and turned to peer down at Kellanved. He'd have knelt to inspect him, but he suspected that if he knelt just then he'd not be able to straighten again.

He swallowed – or attempted to – to wet his throat, and croaked, 'Back with us?'

The mage nodded, wincing, then raised his hands to his head with the tentativeness of someone expecting to find a wet mess. He felt at it gingerly, groaning anew. 'The touch of whoever that was is particularly virulent.'

'Where are we?' Dancer asked.

Kellanved opened his eyes and peered about owlishly. 'Haven't the faintest.' His head fell back down.

Dancer looked to the sky. 'Not helpful.'

A quavering hand rose to wave. 'I'll work on it.'

'Fine!' He picked up the rope and returned to hauling.

When the first glimmerings of golden light brightened ahead, Dancer dropped the rope and started digging with his knives to create a trench for them to hide in from the sun's blasting heat. This finished, he returned to stand over Kellanved. 'Can you get up?'

''Fraid not.'

Dancer grunted, took hold of the fellow's clothes at the shoulders, dragged him into the trench, and started working on levering up the sledge as a shading lean-to. That done, he lay down himself and, despite his ferocious gnawing hunger, immediately fell asleep.

The sun's glaring light in his eyes stabbed him awake. Kellanved lay with an arm over his face. Dancer roused himself to shift the sledge to the opposite side of the trench then lay down once more, his face turned to the salty, ashen earth.

A nudge woke him; it was dusk. A purple light was gathering in the east. He staggered off and undid the front of his trousers but found he couldn't urinate. In fact, he couldn't remember the last time he'd relieved himself. Seemed the need had passed.

He returned to the trench, blinked down at Kellanved. 'Can you stand?'

The mage twiddled his fingers at his chest. 'Sorry. Can't seem to feel my legs . . .' And he laughed, a touch nervously.

Dancer merely grunted once more, readied the sledge, and dragged Kellanved back up on to it. Stooping, and fighting a wave of dizziness, he picked up the rope, tucked it under his armpits, and leaned forward until the damned contraption started moving. He kept it moving by leaning as far forward as he could.

While Dancer walked the endless leagues of the white salt pans, Kellanved started talking. Or babbling – depending upon how generous Dancer felt at any particular moment.

'I do believe I have narrowed it down to one viable candidate for our location,' he was saying. 'Have you heard of Korel?'

Dancer managed a hoarse 'No'.

'No? Really? Well . . . how about the land of Fist?'

It took Dancer a while to say, 'Yeah. Heard of that in stories. The Stormwall.'

'Indeed. Korel is another name for the region. It lies south of Quon Tali.'

Dancer grunted to show he was still listening.

'And south of this subcontinent lies yet another land – one I have only seen depicted on maps – named Stratem. Have you heard of that?'

'No.'

'Really? Your geographical education has been shockingly neglected, I must say.'

Dancer rolled his eyes.

'In any case, even farther south than Stratem lies a long peninsula with no name. I myself have only come across one account of it. A traveller who passed its shores. No one has ever actually dared walk it.'

'And?' Dancer asked, as he knew the mage was aching to impart his knowledge.

'Ah. It is described as a great flat monotonous wasteland of salt pans and blasted rocks where nothing can live as the soil is too poisoned.'

'Sounds familiar.'

'The legend I came across is of one of the most savage

battles waged between the Elders. A clash of the K'Chain Che'Malle and the ones known as the Forkrul. So ferocious was the exchange that the very land was laid to waste, poisoned and seared to glass. Even the Warrens here are wrenched and tattered – like slashed cloth. I can attest to that. So, it is very possible that we were cast into the middle of that very wasteland to die.'

Dancer grunted again. 'And?'

'And? What do you mean, and? I proffer an amazing piece of deduction and that is the best you can do?'

'In other words, this doesn't help us at all.'

'Well . . . if you *must* put it that way . . .'

Dancer just shook his head.

They endured another day of glaring heat. That night, with twilight coming on, Kellanved staggered to his feet. 'I will try to walk,' he told Dancer, who was so doubtful he pulled the sledge along in any case. And it was fortunate that he did so, for later that night he glanced back to see no sign of the mage. He had to backtrack a good distance to find the fellow lying face down in the dry crusted dirt.

He levered him back on to the sledge and turned round.

A short while later he too found himself face down in the dirt. Blinking, he pushed himself up, leaned forward, and plodded onwards. After the third time he came to in the dirt he lost track of where he was or what was going on. It all became rather dreamlike – or nightmarish. In this strange swirling nightscape he had to keep walking. He wasn't really certain why, he just had to. And so he did, onwards again and again. Even, it seemed to him, crawling on all fours in the end.

Then he lay down – or thought he did – just for a short rest, as he was so very drained.

*

Moisture tickling his lips teased Dancer. He cracked one eye open a slit. He was inside some sort of crude dwelling. Water touched his lips with a sweet ecstasy that made him flinch and he blacked out again.

Some time later he woke once more. This time he blinked, rousing himself, trying to sit up. Then he flinched again, for facing him was a monster.

All in black it was – some sort of black-hued plated armour, complete with gauntlets and helmet. But it was holding out a seashell containing a few sips of water and this Dancer gingerly took, nodding. He drank it.

The monster sat back, echoed the nod.

Peering round, he could see no sign of Kellanved. Alarmed, he rose – or tried to – and would have fallen but for the creature taking his weight. He motioned that he wished to go outside, and the thing nodded again and walked him out of the enclosure.

They were at the coast. White sands sloped down to turquoise waters.

'My friend,' he asked hoarsely. 'Where is he?'

But the creature just shook its armoured head.

Just up from the strand more of the black-armoured things were busy working on what could only be described as a large raft. Dancer spotted another rickety dwelling and pointed. His nursemaid nodded again and walked him over to it.

Within, he found Kellanved and another of the creatures, apparently talking.

The mage looked up, beaming. 'Ah! With us at last. Excellent!'

'What's going on? Who – what – are these?'

'These are our benefactors. Saviours. One of them spotted us and brought us here. All due to you, my friend.

330

Apparently you nearly crawled right into the sea. Anyway, they are stranded here, just as we are.'

'And . . . what . . . are they?'

The mage's grey brows rose in incredulity. 'You have not heard of the legendary Moranth?'

Dancer felt his shoulders falling. 'No. I have not heard of the legendary Moranth.'

Kellanved lifted a single brow in disapproval. 'Well, they are a people of the continent of Genabackis. You *have* heard of that, I should hope.'

At the word Genabackis the two Moranth nodded.

Dancer gave his companion a thin smile. 'Yes, thank you, I have heard of Genabackis.'

'Very good. Now, as far as I can make out, our friends were exiled, or fled, from their homeland and ended up here. Struck the coast and have been stranded ever since. Sailing not one of their skills, apparently.'

Dancer eyed the armoured monsters. 'Just what is it they do, then?'

An eager smile came to Kellanved. 'Oh, they are soldiers, my friend. Bred from birth.'

Dancer grunted, impressed despite himself. 'Well, thank them and let's get going.'

The mage tapped his fingertips together, and Dancer knew there was a problem. 'Well . . .' Kellanved began, 'that's the thing. Remember I said that the Warrens were all torn apart and pretty much inaccessible across these lands?'

Dancer frowned. Actually, he didn't. 'What of it?'

'Well . . . they are. And so we're stuck here. Unless, of course, our friends here,' and he gestured to their hosts, 'find it within their generosity to grant us a place on the fine craft they are currently constructing.'

Now Dancer scowled his disgust. 'I saw it. That raft is a sad piece of trash.'

Kellanved raised a hand for silence. He turned to the Moranth he'd been speaking to. 'As I said, Tull, I can send you home if you would just take us far enough from land.'

'No room,' the monster answered, startling Dancer.

Kellanved opened his hands. 'Yes. I understand. But if you *make* room I will send you back to Genabackis.'

'You lie for room,' Tull replied.

Kellanved pressed a hand to his head in exasperation. 'Have you no mages among you? None of that – caste – who deal with the unseen? Who do things you cannot?'

Tull nodded his armoured head. 'Ah. You speak of Silvers. Priests and sages. You are priest?'

Kellanved continued to rub his brow. 'Something like that. Now – once I am far enough from the coast I assure you I will be able to send all of you to Genabackis. Really. I promise.'

Tull lumbered to his feet. 'I will speak to our commander.'

'Thank you,' Kellanved answered.

Both the Moranth left the enclosure, which was nothing more than a hut of driftwood, and Dancer looked at his companion. 'We could build our own raft.'

'I believe we'll get farther with all of them paddling.'

Now Dancer shook his head. 'I mean it. We're better off on our own.'

'Maybe not necessarily. I sense opportunity here. I really can send them along to Genabackis. Well,' and he rubbed his chin, 'as close as I can manage, anyway.'

Their two Moranth companions returned with a third. Dancer could tell who was who by differences in the armour plates enclosing them. This new one's armour was very scarred and bent, as if he'd seen a lot of battle. He knelt on his haunches before Kellanved, and, alarming Dancer, reached out to take a handhold of the mage's short kinky hair in an armoured, gauntleted hand.

'We make room,' this one said – the commander. 'But if you lie we cut off arm and cook then eat before you. Then next arm. Then leg. You understand?'

Kellanved swallowed, and nodded in an exaggerated manner. 'Yes. I understand. Very good. Thank you. Yes.'

The commander released his handhold and rose. 'Agreed, then.'

Kellanved raised a hand. 'Ah – how soon do we go?'

'Soon,' this one said.

'And your name? You are . . . ?'

The Moranth commander paused, peering down at the mage. 'My name? If changed to your language? Would be Twist.'

Over the following days, as Dancer regained his strength, he got to know the Moranth assigned to nursemaiding him. Food, thankfully, was plentiful. As far as he understood it, no pots or such had survived the Moranth shipwreck, but they found natural pits in the rocks along the shoreline that they filled with fresh sweetwater from small creeks, dropped hot stones in, and boiled caught seafood, which they cracked open with rocks.

He and his companion walked the shore working on a shared vocabulary. Each spoke of his own homeland, as best he could. His nurse's name, as far as Dancer could make out, was Balak.

'We are soldiers,' Balak explained. 'We only. We Black, and the Red. Silvers are our priests and sages and . . . ah, how you say . . . orderers?'

'Managers? Bureaucrats? Governors?'

'Ah, yes. Governors. And wise males and females. Golds are our rulers. Always. For ages uncounted. Always the Gold caste. And we always following orders. Fighting. But with no say in why. So, some of our higher commanders, Twist among them, began to question such things. Began to . . . how you say . . . push back?'

'Resist? Agitate?'

'Ah yes, resist. And for this they are caught, tried, and exiled.'

'I am sorry.'

Balak shrugged his armoured shoulders. 'It was the risk we took.' He motioned to the camp. 'Your friend . . . he is, how you say, a mage? Can he really take us home?'

Dancer nodded. 'Yes. Or as close as he can.'

Balak shook his helmeted head, obviously rather doubtful. 'Such things are of the lowlanders who are our enemies. In the cities of Pale and Darujhistan. It is difficult for us to trust such things.'

'He will try.'

Balak resumed pacing the shore. 'Let us hope so.'

Within the week the raft was ready – or as ready as it ever would be. Remaining supplies were loaded aboard and it was pushed out into the surf. The Moranth piled on. Space was made for Dancer and Kellanved right at the very edge, where their feet dangled in the water. The last of the Moranth were tied to the raft by twisted ropes wound round their chests.

Paddles no more than carved branches and planks churned the water. The overburdened craft broached the surf like a waddling, drunken sailor. Dancer got off and helped by kicking with his feet. After more than a few attempts they pushed past the breakers at last and out to open sea.

A touch worried about sharks, Dancer levered himself out of the water and brought his legs up to his chest. Water splashed as those at opposite edges heaved away with their makeshift paddles. They worked on through the night.

The sun blasting down woke Dancer, and reminded him uncomfortably of his trial in the wasteland. A new shift of the Moranth roused themselves and set to paddling once more. They were heading east, trying to get as far from shore as possible – perhaps as Kellanved advised. Dancer shot a significant glance to the mage, who shook his head in answer.

At the end of the first full day Twist came pushing through the jammed bodies. 'Now?' he demanded.

Kellanved shook his head. 'Not yet.'

'Tomorrow then,' the Moranth said, sounding final.

'Possibly . . .'

'Tomorrow.'

Dancer gave Kellanved a glance. He leaned closer, murmuring, 'Perhaps just *us* if need be . . .'

'Well,' the mage answered, 'I'm not going to simply sit there while he cuts my arm off.'

Thirst began to assault Dancer on the second day. He thought he'd seen the last of that agony. It could turn into his march across the desert all over again, and he was not looking forward to it. He couldn't help casting worried glances to his partner, who sat with his eyes firmly shut, concentrating – or so Dancer hoped.

At dusk Twist returned to them. 'Now?' he demanded.

Kellanved shook his head. 'Not *quite* yet . . . Best to wait one more—'

The Moranth to either side of Dancer grasped his arms and held firm, pulling. Woven ropes were wound about him and yanked taut. Twist pointed to him. 'We know who is danger now. Not you,' he said, 'this one,' meaning Kellanved. He drew a honed curved blade that he held to Kellanved's shoulder. 'Dawn.'

The mage raised a brow. 'You can't force these things,' he observed, remarkably composed.

'No,' answered Twist. 'But you can do your magic with only one arm.'

Kellanved now raised both brows. 'Well . . . I suppose you *do* have a point.'

Twist rapped his blade to Kellanved's forehead and edged away. Dancer sat tied up next to him. He couldn't help but murmur, 'You're quite certain . . .'

The mage sighed. 'Do you want to appear in solid rock?'

'You're just going to have to.'

'If he would just give me four days. *Four* days would be perfect.'

'Was that the left or the right?'

'Oh, shut up.'

It was not quite dawn when Twist returned. Dancer had barely slept throughout the night. The Moranth commander took hold of Kellanved's left arm and yanked it taut. 'I believe you lie,' he said. 'You lied for room on raft. Now you serve us. One must die so that many may live. We honour your sacrifice.'

'You know,' said Kellanved, 'this is my favourite time of day. The half-light of dawn. When shadows are so very thick. Are you certain you wish to go through with this?'

'No tricks,' Twist snarled. 'You take us. Now.'

'Where do you think we are now?' And Kellanved shot a significant glance to the waters.

Dancer glanced out. There was no horizon. All was

dark surrounding them; it was as if the raft rocked in a bowl of night.

Twist straightened away from the mage. 'What is this? What trickery?'

The raft had begun to spin, slowly gaining in speed. The waters too, gyred, churning as if in a tornado. 'One should be careful what one asks for,' Kellanved called to Twist over the roar of the surging waves. 'One might receive it.'

Dancer's arms were tied to his torso, but his hands were free and he grasped the slats and logs beneath him with all his might as the spinning increased to a dizzying speed. In fact, it was quite alarming now, even to him. 'That's quite enough!' he yelled to Kellanved.

The mage too was grasping the timbers. 'Things are beyond my control now! We are falling and I don't know how far!'

Several Moranth went flying off the raft, and the spinning reminded Dancer of a child's top. The gyre of water now rose all about them in walls of whirling darkness. 'What's—' he began, and then something punched up from below, knocking the breath from him, and the logs burst apart.

He came to lying amid tall grass, and, given what he'd endured recently, that was actually a comfort. He let his head fall back for a moment just to luxuriate in green growing things. Then, steeling himself, he rose. All about, Black Moranth were likewise rising from a broad meadow that bordered a rocky shoreline. They stood peering about, utterly dumbfounded.

Dancer went searching for his partner.

He found him sitting inland, a long blade of grass in his mouth. The mage gave him a nod. 'Well, that went far better than I feared. It was too rushed, and there was interference from the mainland, but still ... ach, you saw how it went.'

Dancer gave an offhand shrug. 'Not too shabby.'

Kellanved glanced past him and he turned; Twist was approaching. The Black Moranth commander walked straight up then knelt to one knee before the mage, helmeted head bowed. 'We are yours.'

Kellanved waved that aside. 'Continue your struggle for your people, commander. And keep an eye out. I may call upon you in the future.'

Twist bowed once more. 'So it shall be.' Rising, he walked off, gesturing his officers to him.

Dancer looked to Kellanved. 'And us?'

The mage pressed his fingers to his brow and massaged it. 'Tomorrow. Please.'

At that admission Dancer allowed his shoulders to ease. It surprised him to feel the level of tension he'd been carrying there all this time. He let out a long breath, and raised his eyes to an unfamiliar southern horizon where mountains rose to the clouds. He nodded to himself. Good. Tomorrow. It had been far too long already.

* * *

Cartheron was with the quartermaster of the main warehouse complex in Dariyal going over the books. Dull, and not the stuff of any bard's tales of war, but essential just the same. There was an old saying he knew: amateurs talk battle, generals talk logistics.

He hadn't thought much about it before, but now his life was all timber, nails, cloth and damned disgusting salted pork. The largest problem consuming him – and

Napan command – these days was the old and tired one of corruption.

Unavoidable, of course; human nature being as it is. He was under no illusions. But still, there were limits. Outright fraud, for example – that could not be tolerated.

He gestured his disgust to the open books. 'All this timber. Where is it? I've looked. I don't see it.'

The quartermaster laughed uneasily and peered round at the staff of bookkeepers Cartheron had working in the office. 'Well, sir, it hasn't been delivered yet, I imagine.'

Cartheron eyed the fat fellow. 'You imagine? You don't know?'

He opened his hands. 'Well, sir, I do not oversee *every* transaction. I'm sure you understand.'

Cartheron glanced to the guards he'd brought with him and nodded. 'Oh, I understand.' He opened another fat book to a pre-chosen page and gestured to it. 'What about this series of transactions? Pay, uniforms, food and weapons for twenty-seven troops in the Seventh Company of the Eighteenth Regiment?'

The quartermaster-general blinked his heavy-lidded eyes and laughed anew. 'Yes? The Eighteenth . . . ?'

'The Eighteenth marines. Seventh Company.'

The quartermaster peered about now as if aggrieved, his face darkening. 'And what of it?'

'Their weapons, their uniforms, their supplies, food, pay . . . all backdated four months. All vouchered by a certain . . .' Cartheron squinted at the page, 'a certain "Quartermaster Sergeant Nellat".' He eyed the sweating man. 'Tell me, general . . . who is this Sergeant Nellat? He's not on any other book that I can find.'

The man laughed again. 'I'm sure this is just some

clerical error. A mere oversight. That is all. Nothing for someone of your rank, High Fist, to concern yourself with . . .'

Cartheron nodded. 'Yes – you're right, of course. It is nothing.' He closed the heavy books, one by one. 'Because unfortunately, what concerns me is that someone will order the Seventh to hold a position, or support another troop, only to find, belatedly, after the battle is lost . . . that there is no Seventh.'

The man was nodding now, vigorously. 'Yes, that would be unfortunate. And I promise you that I shall certainly get to the bottom of this!'

Cartheron nodded to the guards. 'Let's try.' They opened the door and two more guards escorted in a soldier, his face an ashen grey. 'I could not find a Quartermaster Sergeant Nellat, but I did find a Sergeant Tallen. Your son-in-law, I understand.'

The man glowered now, his mouth hardening. 'You have no proof.'

Cartheron waved for the guards to take them away. 'That's for the military court to decide. You've wasted enough of my time.'

The bookkeeping staff now started to examine the next set of books and Cartheron peered round, wishing for a drink, as his throat was dry from all this dust. Unfortunately, there was not a drop in sight. He sighed. An easy and egregious case, that one. There were far more sly swindlers out there, but their trials, and the confiscation of their entire estates, would serve as a very public warning to others, and perhaps give them pause for reflection.

The door slammed open then and he turned, startled. One of Surly's Claws stood in the doorway, breathing

340

heavily, his eyes wide. 'Come!' was all the man blurted before he was gone again.

Cartheron nearly dropped the sheets of personnel he was examining. He'd never before seen one of her people agitated like that – in fact, he'd never seen them agitated at all. His first thought was, *Gods! Someone's finally gotten through to Surly.* But if so, they'd hide the fact, wouldn't they?

He nodded to the staff of bookkeepers. 'Carry on,' he said, and hurried out of the door.

The palace, just across the harbour, proved to be an overturned anthill of activity. No one he spoke to quite knew why – just that there was a confusion of contrary orders and shifting duties flying about. As he climbed the stairs Napan guards waved him onwards and upwards until he was within the private living quarters set up for the rulers – quarters Surly never used. Now, however, the place was swarming with servants and staff, all bustling about, dusting and cleaning, some with armloads of bedding, others bringing up platters of food and carafes of wine and liqueurs.

Cartheron stood scratching his brow, quite bemused. At least, he reflected, it doesn't look as though anyone's been murdered.

Then, as the door to the inner private bedroom swung open, he caught a glimpse of the rake-thin form of Dancer, looking very much the worse for wear, leaning up against a wall, arms crossed. He went to him and they clasped wrists. 'Dancer! It's good to see you again. Is . . .'

The assassin nodded and glanced across the room. Behind a crowd of servants sat a huge copper tub full of sudsy water, and above the mass of foam protruded the shrivelled and wrinkled chest and head of their wizened leader, Kellanved. The man was raising his arms and directing servants with long-handled brushes to his back.

Also present, pacing back and forth, was Surly, her arms likewise crossed, looking rather vexed.

'Where—' Cartheron began, but Dancer shook his head.

'I don't want to talk about it.'

Wherever they had been, or whatever they had done, it must have been terrifying, as the man before him appeared to have aged years. His face was blistered and peeling from exposure, his shirt and trousers hung torn and soiled beyond recognition, and his boots were split and cracked. And slim to begin with, he had lost so much weight he was now no more than rope wrapped round a pole.

'And Jadeen?' Cartheron had to ask.

'She proved unworthy,' Kellanved supplied from the bath.

Cartheron crooked a questioning brow to Dancer, who waved the comment aside. 'Never mind.'

'Please do continue,' Kellanved invited Surly.

She clenched her lips tight, but continued, 'Forces out of Malaz are committed to the east, while a Napan task force is preparing to leave as soon as possible for the west.'

Kellanved nodded. 'I see. And does this constitute all our forces?'

'Virtually yes, excepting those held back for defence, of course.'

Kellanved nodded again, held out an arm for brushing. 'Well, I happen to have a target in mind on the mainland and we must attack immediately!'

Cartheron and Surly exchanged alarmed glances; even Dancer frowned his confusion. 'What target?' he asked.

342

The mage, falsely aged and Dal Hon dark, his chest hair grey, stood from the bath and Surly looked away. Servants wrapped a towel round his waist. 'I intend to attack Cawn!' he announced.

Cartheron felt his brows crimp almost painfully. 'Cawn has no military,' he muttered, bewildered.

'Cawn is not a strategic target,' Surly confirmed, dismissively.

'None the less,' Kellanved huffed.

Dancer, arms still crossed, tilted his head and enquired, 'You'd have us pull forces away just to beat up a pack of merchants?'

The mock-ancient's eyes slit almost closed and his wrinkled features took on a sly look. 'I didn't say that.'

'Then what?'

The servants were dressing him now, pulling on a new brushed-cotton shirt. He thrust a finger into the air. 'I shall loose the Hounds upon Cawn.'

Cartheron gaped openly, and only barely stopped himself from blurting aloud, *What?*

Dancer started from the wall, obviously quite alarmed. 'You can't do that,' he said.

The mage's tiny eyes darted right and left. 'Actually, I'm pretty certain I can.'

'I believe he means you don't want to do that,' Surly supplied. 'It would be a slaughter. They're all civilians. Families. Women and children.'

Kellanved flapped his hands. 'Well, then, *warn* them. Yes, send a warning! They have incurred my displeasure and now must suffer the consequences, blah, blah, such and such.'

Dancer raised a sceptical brow. 'And just how have they *incurred* your displeasure?'

The mage threw his hands into the air. 'I don't know!

Make something up.' He raised a finger. 'Wait! I know. Shadow. Two nights hence Shadow will visit them. There, that's it.' He brushed his hands together. 'After that, our main force will land there. Cawn shall be our foothold. After the Hounds there will be no fight left in them. Oh, and also, I want an official historian. Find one.'

Cartheron and Surly shared a puzzled glance. 'An official historian?' Cartheron repeated, just to be certain that was what he had heard. 'Okay. We can get on to that.'

'Very good.' Kellanved pulled on new shoes, took a moment to admire them, then headed for the door. 'Let's have a look about the place, Dancer. We didn't have the chance last time.'

The lean knifesman was good enough to offer Surly an apologetic shrug, then a servant handed him a set of new clothes, trousers and shirts, as he headed for the door. Cartheron went to Surly where she stood shaking her head, perhaps in disbelief.

'You forget,' he said. 'You start thinking he's just a harmless oldster – then he goes and does something like this.' He, too, shook his head. 'What are we going to do?'

Surly raised a hand for silence. 'We can allow him his little pet project, so long as it doesn't interfere with prior commitments. We can send a small contingent to Cawn. No one gives a damn about Cawn.'

Cartheron would have objected, but he saw that she was struggling to salvage the situation as best she could so he said nothing. He watched, instead, while her lips drew down so very far.

Chapter 18

I‌T ALL STARTED WITH SOMEONE SHOVING A SUM chalked on a slate piece in front of her. Iko threw it aside to shatter on the floor. It appeared again and she blinked; she thought she'd gotten rid of the damned thing. She threw it away again and took another drink to celebrate.

Someone was now tapping her on the shoulder; she ignored the pesky irritation. The tapping became an ill-mannered resolute jabbing. She grabbed the hand and twisted and was rewarded by the snapping of bones.

She was allowed to drink in peace for some time after that.

Then some fellow appeared sitting opposite her. She blinked at him and decided to ignore him, hoping he'd just up and disappear as quickly as he'd appeared. Unfortunately, the fellow did not go away. In fact, he had the temerity to speak to her.

'We were wondering,' he said – or she thought he was saying, 'when you would be good enough to cover the bill?'

She waved the impertinent fellow away and refused to look at him. That should serve him right. However, when she next sneaked a glance, he was still there.

'I'm sorry,' he said, 'you appear to be a cultured

woman. But I must let you know that if you do not pay you will be removed from the premises.'

She laughed, and even slapped the table. '*That* I would like to see you try.'

He looked up past her and that was his mistake. She lurched to her feet, elbow rising, to smack meatily into someone's nose. A hand grasped her shoulder from behind and she turned under it, raising a knee into the fellow's groin.

Both bravos were stunned, staggering backwards, but she could not press the advantage as her sudden movements now drove her stomach to come surging up into her mouth and she clasped a hand to the table, vomiting painfully.

She clutched the table as if drowning, groaning and gasping. Then, straightening, she realized she was in some sort of shipboard bar as everything tilted one way then the other. She pointed to a group at a nearby table, four of them gaping up at her, and shouted, 'Stop all this damned moving!'

They all promptly scrambled away.

She turned, blinking anew, and squinting. A huge number of bravos now faced her though their number kept changing. She waved at them too. 'Stop all this damned changing!'

Someone grasped her arm from behind. She slammed her free palm into that person's nose, and turned in time to find someone else charging her; she planted her foot into his stomach. Two grabbed each arm. She kicked each in turn in the head.

Then she had to pause to hold her own head. It was throbbing as if a knife had penetrated it. And everything kept wobbling from side to side – why wouldn't it just stop?

Someone took her in a bear-hug. She threw her head back, smacking into his or her nose with a crunch. A kick to her leg brought her down to her knees. She grabbed her assailant's crotch and pulled him down with her.

A blow to her head darkened her vision momentarily. She leaned down to her hands and lashed out with one leg, taking that attacker in the stomach. Another blow to the head and she grasped that foe's shirt to pull herself up, taking him in a headlock and driving his head into a timber post.

She spun to face any others, but that was a mistake as the inn would not stop spinning and spinning, faster and faster, and she blinked, her vision darkening, until the floor hit her face and that was all she knew.

She awoke in a bed. A bed that stank of sweat and puke – unless that was her – in a room decorated garishly with hanging silken wraps and paintings of nudes. Rather like, well, a bordello. Her head ached abominably and her mouth tasted vile.

A carafe of water sat next to the bed, along with a glass. She sat up, gingerly, and gulped down a glassful of water. Her clothes were dirty and sticky with sweat, and her knuckles were crusted in blood. She felt her head – her hair too was matted in blood, over the lumps.

She staggered to the door, opened it, found a narrow hall lined by numerous similar doors.

She was now certain that, yes, she was in fact within a bordello.

A door opened across the hall and she was surprised to find herself facing not a woman but a slim young male, his eyes heavily shadowed, his lips painted. Caught in mid-yawn the fellow nearly choked, staring. 'Burn's mercy, lass, but you're a mess!' he exclaimed.

'Thank you so very much. How the fuck do I get out of here?'

He pointed up the hall. She went, thinking, well, they must cater to everyone here.

She found stairs that led down to a sort of salon, or parlour, call it what you would. Here the girls and boys were gathered, relaxing, clearly off duty. All conversation stopped and everyone stared.

'I'm leaving,' she announced. 'Where's the door?' Several pointed. 'Thank you.' She headed that way and found another hall leading to a sturdy exterior door.

'You owe me!' came a harridan's screech. Iko paused, her hand inches from the latch. 'Or shall I call the authorities?' She turned. A bent ancient, as garishly made up as the premises, faced her.

'I have no coin to pay you,' she said.

The old woman gestured impatiently. 'I know. I had you searched.'

'So?'

She crooked a bent finger. 'Come. Let us talk business.'

She was led through a series of narrow, private staircases to what proved to be a verdant roof garden. Here Iko shielded her eyes, blinking; it had been some time since she'd been outside. The ancient picked up a jug and began watering large, oddly shaped flowers of a sort Iko had never seen before. 'Very rare, these,' the old woman told her. 'I sell them for a good price – not unlike those downstairs.' She gestured to chairs round a low table. 'Sit.'

Iko did not move. 'Why?'

'Because you have nowhere else to go.'

She crossed her arms. 'And how is it you know so much about me?'

The ancient sighed, set down the jug and crossed to sit

in one of the chairs. She picked up a long-stemmed pipe from the table and began the rather laborious process of preparing d'bayang powder for smoking. Doing so, she gestured to a pot. 'Tea.'

Iko dropped her arms and sat. She poured herself a cup and sipped – quite good. An expensive cut. 'I'll not serve in your whorehouse,' she said.

The woman gasped on a lungful of smoke. 'Gods no! I should think not! That would not end well for the client, I imagine.' She shook her head. 'No. Not that.' She relit the pipe with a long sliver of wood from a brazier on the table. 'You may call me Wen. I am quite old and have seen many people come and go. I know your type. You are from the military – an officer perhaps. But now you are out, discharged or otherwise. Some scandal no doubt.'

Iko drew breath to object but the woman waved for silence. 'I care not. All that matters is that you have talents. Gods, you can fight, girl! Those are the talents I want.'

She curled her lip. 'Bloodsports.'

A shake of the head. 'Goddess, no. A waste, that. No, keeping the peace. Sometimes there is trouble and I need someone who can quietly, and efficiently, restore order.'

'I'm sure you have all sorts of bravos and arm-twisters available.'

Now Wen curled her lip. 'Thugs. Dullards. Brutes. They can handle the usual riff-raff. No, in this establishment I specialize in sophisticated and exotic . . . wares. And, my dear, that description fits you so very beautifully.'

'And if I refuse?'

Wen's painted lips drew down round the tortoiseshell mouthpiece. 'There is still the matter of all that coin, because I own the inn you nearly wrecked.'

Iko nodded, finished the tea. This roof garden was

atop a relatively tall building, and she saw it afforded a view of the royal palace compound's curving rooftops, less than a handful of leagues distant across the city centre. She nodded once again. 'I have two conditions.'

A raised brow, plucked and painted. 'Oh?'

'That I be allowed access here in my free time. And that I wear a veil – or a mask.'

The old madam exhaled a lungful of smoke. She studied Iko, her narrowed eyes taking on the dreamy sleepiness of the d'bayang stupor. 'A mask, I think, my dear. *Very* exotic.'

*

Iko was given a mask; a small one, which covered half her face. Wen also dressed her in a rather plain costume of a simple tunic and trousers and insisted she go barefoot when on duty. Why this particular get-up she had no idea, but Mistress Wen seemed to think it a very funny joke. Iko merely shrugged and played along; it certainly helped her anonymity, for no one would ever recognize the former Sword-Dancer in this costume. And nothing ever came of it except when members of a foreign trade delegation from some distant land visited. These people nearly jumped out of their skin when they saw her.

And her instincts concerning her anonymity were correct: twice already she'd come face to face with high officials from the palace who she was certain could have identified her. As for the vices and habits of off-duty bureaucrats and officers of the capital – she was quite shocked.

By day she walked the streets of Itko Kan, sans mask, of course. She had used to esteem her native nation as the most civilized people on the continent of Quon Tali, but now, seeing the poor being kicked aside in the streets, the contempt of the privileged for the oppressed, and the constant naked pursuit of the god of greasy gold, she wondered. Her compatriots were beginning to strike her as a rather hard-hearted and cruel lot.

As for the 'exotics' who populated Wen's establishment, she'd treated them with her own contempt at first. But now she was beginning to pity them. Some were foolish, shallow creatures, to be sure. And indeed some were as truly venal and selfish as venal selfish people everywhere. To her mind, however, most were simply victims. Victims of a callous human marketplace. A marketplace that had set her value, as well.

It was, as they say, a job.

Her solace was climbing the narrow staircase at dawn, at the end of her duties, to spend her free hours gazing at the tiled rooftops of the palace compound and wondering what a young lad was up to, how he was doing . . . and who, if anyone, truly had *his* best interests at heart.

* * *

When Heboric set out for the Valley of Hermits east of Heng, famed as a place of quiet retreat and meditation, he'd assumed it would be relatively uninhabited and, well, serene. Instead, he came upon the noise and crowds of some sort of religious festival.

Campfires and makeshift lean-tos and yurts crowded the valley floor. Celebrants of Burn chanted in a large circle round one bonfire, while crowds sat at others listening to multiple speakers exhort and preach. Banners and flags hung in the weak wind. It reminded him of the fete of Gedderone's Return, but without the public orgies.

'Brother!' a celebrant welcomed him. 'You are come

in propitious times! A miracle! A Kynie has come to us! Witnessed by many.'

Heboric frowned. A Kynie was a legendary messenger of the gods, usually one of fury and fire. And usually *not* a welcome omen. His informant, in filthy robes, with wild dirty hair and rather wild-eyed, took him by the arm and pulled him along. 'Brothers and sisters!' he called to the crowd. 'Look! Fener is with us!'

Heads turned and a great cheer went up. The crowd closed round him, men and women reaching out to touch the tattoos – this, at least, was familiar to Heboric. During the holy days of Fener it was quite common for strangers to reach out to the Gift of the Boar.

He was drawn along towards the front of the main press, cries of 'Fener!' rising all about. At the head of the crowd, in front of one particular cave opening crowded with candles, garlands and offerings, sat four aged men, all alike in dirty loincloths and tangled ropy hair. One of these straightened, waving him forward. 'Come!' he invited. 'Grace us with the Boar's wisdom.'

Quite bemused, Heboric found himself urged along to sit with the four. He nodded a greeting. 'I understand you have been blessed with a visitation . . .'

The four ascetics nodded vigorously, calls and shouts to the gods echoing from the crowd. 'A Kynie has come to us,' one of them pronounced. 'Never in my lifetime did I expect to be so blessed.'

'Fire and rage accompanied her,' another put in.

'The ground shook with her wrath,' said a third.

'It is a warning,' said the fourth.

'A warning of what?' Heboric asked.

'False gods!' a woman shouted from the crowd.

The first of the four raised a hand to silence her. 'We cannot be certain—'

'It is no coincidence that the Kynie should appear here – not two days' journey from Heng!' the woman continued regardless.

'And what is in Heng?' Heboric asked.

The woman rose, pointing west. 'A false goddess is suborning the people! This *Protectress* would pose as goddess of Heng! Not to mention the many new cults seducing worshippers.'

The first of the four now raised both hands for calm. 'Some have lost their way and turned to her, this is true. But she herself has made no claims.' He turned to Heboric. 'What says Fener on this?'

Heboric pulled a hand down his face – a religious debate was the last thing he'd been expecting to have thrust upon him here in the valley. Fortunately, however, he was no stranger to such discussions. 'Curiously, I too have been troubled of late,' he began, and the four nodded sagely. 'Disquiet among the pantheon worries me. Troubling rumours of unrest among the devoted of D'rek, on Kartool. A certain tension in the still airs of the Temple of Poliel. All this suggests to me that we are entering a time of trial, a time of instability.'

The four bowed their heads. 'It is an exhortation, then,' said the second.

'To greater faith.'

'To greater devotion.'

'To an end to backsliding!' added the woman from the crowd.

The first raised his arms, calling, 'Thank you all! That is enough for today. I ask that we turn to quiet prayer, devotion and contemplation now. Bless all of you.'

Heads bowed. The ascetic drew Heboric aside. 'Your presence here is an unlooked-for blessing as well, brother. I am Sessin. Thank you for answering the call.'

353

'Actually, I was on my way here regardless. I knew nothing of this.'

Sessin raised his eyes to the sky. 'The gods work in mysterious ways. You will be of great help.'

Heboric rubbed the back of his neck. 'Well, in truth, I, too, am a seeker.'

Sessin gave another knowing nod. 'Of course, brother. We are all seekers in our own way.'

Heboric resisted the urge to roll his eyes. 'Yes, well, imagine that. No, I came because of the unease I spoke of. Do you not sense it as well?'

Sessin nodded vigorously. 'Yes indeed, brother. Sister Hav is not so far from the truth in this.'

'Sister Hav? The one in the crowd?'

'Yes. Once a high priestess of Burn. Anathematized for her, ah, enthusiastic practices.'

'Enthusiastic?'

'Yes. She instituted tests of purity of faith to weed out the inconstant. The holding of red-hot rods, for example. The branding of the unfaithful.'

Heboric shuddered. 'I see. And she was in Heng?'

'Yes. Heng has become a breeding ground of nascent cults, this cult of the Protectress among them. Even among the devoted of Hood some are turning to his champion, the Mortal Sword. And then there is this worship of the so-called "Shadow Throne".'

'The Shadow Throne? What in all the Realms is that?'

Sessin peered about as if wary. He whispered, 'No one knows. I've only just heard of it myself.'

In truth Heboric was not overly concerned. New cults came and went every day. No doubt this one too would go the way of its countless ilk. He crossed his arms. 'I had hoped to take counsel with you holy men and women here on this matter.'

Sessin nodded his understanding – Heboric was beginning to suspect that the man simply nodded to everything in order to appear knowledgeable. 'And yet you find us in turmoil. I am sorry. But, perhaps I may suggest the very exhortation the Kynie sent to us. Perhaps one must face the unrest. Perhaps one must journey to Heng itself. The city many here name the Whore on the Idryn.'

* * *

Gregar knew he was no officer-trained military genius, but the disposition of the Bloorian League's lines left him rather puzzled. It seemed to him that the weakest troops occupied the most vulnerable positions, while the strongest troops – the armoured heavy cavalry – held the *least* vulnerable points.

The Yellows contingent for example, all four companies, held a length of line near the end of the left flank just where Gregar would expect to see a cavalry troop – positioned to strike to any opening near the centre. Meanwhile, the various nobles' personal cavalry units dominated the centre of the League's lines – poorly positioned, it seemed to him, for manoeuvrability.

When Leah next passed by inspecting the troops, he caught her eye and gestured her over. 'What are we doing way out here?' he whispered. 'We're *infantry*.'

Their newly promoted sergeant peered round to make certain none nearby were listening, and answered, low and fierce, 'What we are is *unimportant*, okay? Nobodies. The lords choose pride of place, right?'

'But that's not effective.'

'Says who? That's the way it's done. Remember your place.'

Gregar clenched his lips against saying any more – it wouldn't get him anywhere. After one last warning glare Leah continued on her tour.

'These kings and knights, they have a lot of experience at this sort of thing,' Haraj assured him.

He nodded, rather sullenly. 'Yeah. At fighting on and on just for the fun of it. And nothing ever gets settled – sounds like great job security to me.'

Haraj cast him a quizzical look. But he'd returned to waiting, leaning on his tall spear with its limp colours. It was a chilly winter's morning; a mist was burning off and everything glistened with a melting overnight frost. Gregar stamped his feet for warmth; cloth covered them up to his knees and over this went leather wraps. A thick padded leather haubergeon hung down below his waist, belted, its leather sleeves laced with iron lozenges down to leather-backed gloves. As colour-sergeant this was his promotion in armour – making him one of the most well-accoutred members of his company. Which said a lot about Baron Ordren of Yellows' resources. To make things even worse, he'd not yet managed to scrounge any sort of cap or helmet.

Haraj, for his part, wore only a plain leather jerkin. But then he could prance naked through both lines and no one could touch him, so that didn't matter.

Across a lightly rolling field of dry stalks, fallow fields, and pasture, lay a treeline where the Grisian forces were making final deployments. This field of battle had been mutually settled upon after some degree of jostling and skirmishing between the forces' scouts and advance light cavalry.

No ambush or surprise attack by either side was even a possibility, as both forces knew this region well. In fact, lords on both sides pressed long-standing claims to this border area, and several earlier wars had been fought over it.

Though distant, the Grisian lines appeared thin to Gregar. He imagined they must be quite spread out over there, both to disguise their poor numbers and to match the wider front the League could muster. That would only invite a cavalry charge from Vor or Bloor, he was certain. And there across the fields they must know that as well, and have planned for it. At least that's what he'd have done.

Drums rolled then, announcing an advance, and Gregar straightened.

Light skirmishers and crossbow units advanced to harass. These would be met by similar forces from the Grisian allies and they would probe and press one another for some time while the lords watched and searched for weaknesses in the opposing lines.

Squinting into the gathering light, he made out the pale blue favours of Gris, the green of Bloor, the burnt orange of Vor, and the dark blue of Rath. These favours were sometimes nothing more than armbands, or ribbons on chests. Some knights wore no discernible heraldry at all – usually the hireswords – and he understood this often led to a great deal of confusion as to just who was on what side.

It all seemed too much of a free-for-all to Gregar – but again, he was no expert. The lords and knights obviously preferred this system, or lack of system, as each no doubt considered her or himself the equal of any other lord present, and aimed to prove it by bashing their heads in.

After a few hours of skirmishes and light contact, the manoeuvring began. Troops of cavalry came thundering back and forth as lords sought advantageous positions, or angled to match up against a perceived soft target, or long-standing enemy. The lords of Nita and Athrans, for example, were great rivals, and each asserted ancient family claims to Jurda – however tenuous. These two troops now faced off.

Gregar caught sight of the flowing red cloaks of the Crimson Guard as they went cantering towards the extreme left flank and again he was frankly rather puzzled. Why send them so far from the main action? Perhaps the lords Vor or Rath were loath to share any of the glory of victory with mere mercenaries.

The ground shook then as a massive charge suddenly broke from the Bloorian League lines. It looked like a collection of the lesser barons and knights hoping to win some distinction before the total chaos began.

It was premature, as it was met with a withering fusillade of arrows and crossbow bolts from the opposing lines, and they reined aside before being completely decimated.

Gregar was then surprised as the entire Crimson Guard contingent, which had been trotting parallel to the lines for the left flank, now dived in straight for the Grisian front – a feint! They made contact with the opposing position, an unlucky contingent of medium infantry from Fools, and appeared to be delivering ferocious punishment.

Down the distant treeline, Gregar noted columns of crossbowers running double-time in support. One such large unit wore black tabards, which surprised him mightily; no one had dared wear black since the hated Talian hegemony.

Seeing a possible opening, the Rath heavy cavalry – including King Styvell of Rath and his personal troop of sworn bodyguards – went thundering for the opposing lines.

At that commitment of forces, the Abyss itself seemed to open up across the entire valley as every unit now surged into sudden movement. Gregar lost track of who was going where and he gave up any hope of knowing who was winning or losing. Orders came down the Yellows lines to double up and that at least made good sense to him. He levered his spear outwards to signal that he was expecting a charge any time through the flying mud and churning ground mists.

Complete disorder only increased as broken bands of cavalry now came charging back and forth, all but destroying any idea of set lines – it was now a milling melee of massed cavalry circling and shouldering one another. And to Gregar's gathering horror the main bulk of the press was now heaving their way.

Yellows infantry peered about in a panic for instructions as the wall of horseflesh came lurching towards them. 'Lower spears!' Gregar bellowed, but the command was lost under the cacophony of clashing weapons and screaming wounded horses.

The melee was so disordered that knights actually unintentionally backed over the Yellows line, presenting their mounts rump-first to the flinching infantry who frankly did not know what to do, as the chaos included lords and knights from both sides all milling together and bashing away at each other.

Gregar was not so discriminating as he jabbed at any horse that came close. The Yellows lines were effectively cut in two as the melee rolled over them, and Gregar wanted to throw down his spear in impotent frustration. Once the main scrum passed, he called in the surviving Yellows troopers to form a small defensive circle. From here, colours still raised high, he watched in growing confusion as through the chaos he perceived Gris cavalry pursuing Nitan forces across the field – though they were supposed to be allies.

This left the rest of the opposing allies in utter and complete disarray. Even to Gregar's inexperienced eye the immense gap it opened among the enemy forces was glaring. The largest remaining cohesive body of knights and nobles, the main Vorian contingent including King Gareth, now commanded the centre of the field. But instead of pressing the advantage and scattering the dis-ordered Grisian allies once and for all, to Gregar's complete disbelief horns sounded a recall and the entire mounted force curved round and charged in the opposite direction, abandoning the field.

He watched them go with his mouth hanging open, completely stunned.

Next to him, even Haraj grasped the significance of this betrayal. 'We are so fucked,' he announced.

'We have to retreat,' Gregar answered. Frantically peering round, he spotted a copse of woods to the south and pointed in that direction. 'South!' he half bellowed and half screamed. Urging, shouting, clapping shoulders, he managed to get the defensive circle of remaining Yel-lows lights lurching that way.

Their path took them over a trampled portion of their original position and here he had to step over the broken remains of Sergeant Leah, among so many others. He gently pressed closed her wide staring eyes, and crossed her hands over her bloodied breast. As to the fate of Master-sergeant Teigan and the rest of the far distant Yellows lines, he had no idea.

As they went they gathered up stragglers from other broken elements, a few unhorsed knights, stray skir-mishers and such, and gradually, from these sources from distant disparate portions of the field, a picture slowly emerged of just what in Hood's name had actually happened.

It seemed that out of nowhere Nita had suddenly turned on other Grisian allies positioned next to them, opening up a section of the lines that Bloor surged through. Yet it seemed that Gris was not entirely surprised, as they immediately abandoned that flank and surged round to take Bloorian allies on the opposing side. From then on it was complete and utter chaos.

Gris heavy cavalry sought out the Crimson Guard across the field, trampling every force in their way, friend or foe. Nita kept after the Duke of Athrans, pursuing his personal mounted troop entirely off the field, while for some inexplicable reason Rath elements lost all direction and order and became field ineffective.

And after all this, when Vor, as the last remaining even slightly cohesive force, was poised to win the day, at the decisive moment King Gareth sounded the recall and the Vorian cavalry and supporting infantry suddenly, and unaccountably, abandoned the field.

Crouched in the woods, Gregar, Haraj and a surviving Yellows sergeant watched the mopping up. Word came to them then, via survivors, explaining the inexplicable twists and turns of the engagement. It seemed that in the middle of the battle Baron Ranel of Nita had gone over to the Bloorian forces – and his price was Athrans, whom no one did anything to defend. On top of this, Styvell, the king of Rath, was very nearly mortally wounded by a crossbow bolt and everyone blamed Nita, which made no sense to Gregar but meant that that noble was now reviled by both sides of the dispute, and everyone wanted his head.

The worst news, however, came last, explaining the otherwise bizarre behaviour of King Gareth of Vor.

Word had come at noon that very day that some damned pirate force out of Malaz had besieged and taken Vor itself by stealth two nights ago. Gareth, of course, immediately withdrew his forces to return with all haste.

'I can't fucking believe it,' another Yellows sergeant kept repeating, over and over, where they crouched at the treeline. 'We'll have to surrender.'

'Surrender?' Gregar asked, astonished.

The man held out his hands in a shrug. 'What choice do we have? Gris has the field. It's five days' march to Yellows. We're outnumbered. No food. What are we going to do?'

Gregar motioned to the west. 'Then get started, damn you.'

The sergeant looked Gregar up and down, sneering. 'To Hood with you, fool. I'll not end up with my head split open because of your pride.'

Gregar tossed him the spear with its colours. 'Take this with you, then. It suits you.'

The man raised his fingers in an insulting gesture and waved the troops to him, withdrawing west. Gregar and Haraj watched them go.

The pale mage rubbed his hands up and down his stick-thin arms, shivering. 'What're we gonna do? There's nowhere to go. I don't want to be captured'n'sent to the tin mines, or the galleys.'

Gregar peered to the north, the last direction in which he'd seen the Crimson Guard withdrawing, and drew a heavy breath. 'There's one place we can try.' He waved Haraj down. 'We'll wait till dark.'

Chapter 19

THE NEXT NIGHT KELLANVED AND DANCER walked the main marshalling grounds of the Napan palace cum garrison in Dariyal. Kellanved made a vague waving motion with his hands. 'Where are all the troops?'

'I understand all the recruits have been sent to Malaz for training under Dassem,' Dancer replied.

'Ah. Of course. Well – have ships sent to take them to Cawn with us. Now, this very night.'

Dancer frowned. 'Raw recruits? Is that wise?'

The mage waved again, dismissively. 'The Cawn merchants will have no fight left in them, I assure you.'

Dancer had to admit that after a visitation from the Hounds, this would probably be quite true. 'Very well.' He raised a hand to beckon a courier to him. It occurred to him that half these messengers attending Kellanved were probably Surly's Claws in disguise, but this did not worry him overmuch as he knew he had Talons working among her own that even she knew nothing of.

'How many?' he asked.

'All,' Kellanved answered. 'Every single soldier available.'

Dancer paused. 'Really? I'm sure that would be

thousands.' The mage nodded, apparently unconcerned. Troubled, Dancer pressed the issue. 'Why so many? As you say, Cawn should be prostrate. A garrison shouldn't even be necessary.' He knew his friend well, and the furtive look the falsely aged fellow got in his eyes made him suspicious. 'What's going on?' he demanded.

Kellanved twisted his fingers together and hummed and hawed, until finally admitting, after a deep breath, 'I want Cawn cowed because I want the Idryn open.'

'The Idryn? Why would you . . . oh, *no* . . .'

'It's time,' the mage asserted, nodding.

They had been pacing, but now Dancer stepped before him to face him directly. 'You don't mean to head *back* there, do you?'

Kellanved raised his chin, defiant. 'It's time. They have it coming.'

A courier arrived and Dancer bit his lip against speaking in front of the woman. Kellanved gestured her close. 'Order all available vessels to Malaz to pick up all troops in training there for transport to Cawn. Dancer and I shall accompany them. We leave at dawn.'

The woman bowed and raced off.

Dancer waited until they were alone once more. 'They do not have *anything* coming – especially from us. They broke the back of the strongest army on the continent. This is foolish, Kellanved. Truly foolish.'

The mage raised his hands, his walking stick in one. 'Do not worry, my friend. All is in hand. We have an answer for the Five now. Myself, Tayschrenn, Nightchill, and the rest. We are a match for them. All that remains are the walls. It's the walls that defeat their enemies, not their wretched troops. The walls. And I have an answer for that now as well . . .'

Dancer looked to the night sky. 'Oh, so you have some

army that can ignore the strongest walls in Quon Tali? What? You think they're just going to—'

He froze in mid-step and faced Kellanved, who waggled his greying bushy brows. 'Oh no . . .'

Kellanved raised his walking stick in emphasis. 'Oh *yes*, my friend.'

Dancer shook his head. 'No. Don't do this. I mean it. Don't.' Peering right and left to make certain they were alone, he leaned close to hiss through clenched teeth, 'Remember Jadeen!'

Kellanved disparaged that with a wave. 'As I said – do not worry yourself, my friend. All is in hand. I have a plan!'

Dancer wanted to groan, but the little mage ambled off, humming to himself and tapping his walking stick. Why was it that every time the fellow said that he was less and less reassured?

In the midst of the preparations for departure Urko came stomping off the gangway of the *Sapphire* to face Kellanved. 'What's this about a raid?' the huge fellow demanded.

The mage nodded to him. 'Indeed. Cawn. But first we leave with the morning tide for Malaz to pick up troops.'

Urko snapped his fingers. 'Right! Surly wouldn't let me go to Vor, but we're all refitted now. I can meet you at the Bay of Cawn.'

Kellanved nodded indulgently. 'Very well. Two days hence. The Bay of Cawn.'

'I'm short of captains I can trust – can I dragoon my brother?'

Kellanved waved him off. 'Yes, yes. Whatever you think appropriate.'

The huge fellow tramped down the gangplank, chortling to himself.

Dancer watched him go, then turned to Kellanved. 'We're leaving Surly shorthanded.'

'No we're not,' the mage answered, and he pointed his walking stick up to the shrouds. Dancer looked up to see a female sailor come descending the ratlines, handhold over handhold, to thump down barefoot to the deck to face them, hands clasped at her back.

Surly. She eyed them the way Dancer's old teacher used to eye him when he'd been careless. 'You're up to something,' she said. 'What is it?'

Kellanved laughed, a touch nervously. 'Why, we're taking possession of Cawn, of course!'

She shook her head. 'Cawn's a smokescreen. What are you really after?'

The mage pressed his steepled hands to his lips and nodded. 'Very well. Divide and conquer, Surly. I intend to take control of the centre of the continent. I will isolate east from west. They will be divided, unable to coordinate against us. Divide and conquer.'

The woman let out a long taut breath – clearly she'd been dreading, or anticipating, this moment for some time. She nodded to herself. 'I see . . . and if you fail I will still hold Nap. Yes?'

Kellanved waved his accord. 'Oh, of course! Nap shall always be yours. Just as Malaz shall be mine.'

Surly snorted to show what she thought of Malaz, but nodded her agreement. 'Very well.'

Dancer eased out his own breath and loosened his shoulders. *That was the hard part.* Now, we shall see. This is it. The throw for the mainland. At least it wouldn't be *him* summoning their eldritch friends.

*

366

The task force sailed for Malaz. There they picked up all the recruits and trainee marines, together with further Malazan vessels, and sailed immediately for the Bay of Cawn. On board the *Sapphire*, Dancer was surprised to find that damned stuffed-shirt cultist Dassem Ultor himself present.

He looked the young man up and down, resenting, only slightly, those wind-blown curly black locks. 'What're you doing here?'

'You've come for my soldiers,' the fellow asserted. 'You'll not have them without me.'

Dancer looked him up and down again, than glanced to the surrounding lads and lasses crowding the deck, all of whom had eyes only for Dassem, as if hanging on his every whim, and he had to shrug his shoulders. 'Fine. It doesn't matter. We doubt there'll be any resistance.'

'None the less, I'll not have the life of one man or woman in my care thrown away on some wild scheme of your partner.'

Dancer fought the urge to slap the fellow down. 'As I said . . . we don't anticipate any major resistance.'

'Let us hope so,' the swordsman answered, his hand going to the grip of his weapon.

Dancer almost – but not quite – rolled his eyes to the sky.

In the Bay of Cawn they rendezvoused with further vessels from Nap, including those under the command of the brothers Urko and Cartheron Crust. Then they swung inland for the harbour of Cawn itself. It was night when they arrived – they were twelve hours late out of Malaz – and Dancer knocked on the main cabin door of the *Sapphire* and let himself in. He found Kellanved behind a desk, feet up, snoring.

He resisted smacking the fellow, settling instead for noisily slamming down a chair and sitting. The mage gasped, his feet falling, and he blinked about. 'Yes? What?'

'Is it done?' Dancer asked.

'Is what done?'

'The Hounds! Did you loose them?'

The mage nodded his greying wizened head. 'Oh yes, last night.'

Dancer rubbed his neck, almost wincing. *Gods. Just like that.* He shook his head. 'So. They should be pretty damned cooperative.'

'I should think so.'

Dancer shifted uncomfortably in the chair. 'I have to say, I don't understand. Why Cawn? Why now? The Hounds are a devastating weapon . . .'

The mage nodded, sat back and steepled his fingers before his chin – a gesture Dancer loathed as too self-aware and affected. 'I see. But tell me, what use a weapon none know? This way stories of the harrowing of Cawn will spread to serve as a warning to all. Also,' and here the mock-elderly mage gave a wink, 'you did tell me to throw them a bone . . .'

Dancer felt his shoulders slump in surrender. Yes. He did say that. 'Still, Cawn?'

'One could say the same of anywhere, my friend. It had to be. Better here than elsewhere.'

Dancer cocked a brow. Well, maybe that was true. After all, no one gave a tinker's damn about Cawn.

At dawn they drew up to the broad wharf of Cawn's harbour. Lines were thrown and the gangway was wrestled into place. A troop of soldiers debarked first, then Kellanved and Dancer came down. A contingent from the city awaited them. Peering up past them, Dancer noted smoke rising here and there across the city, as from disparate fires. Trash and broken carts and barrels littered the broad cobbled way as if some sort of demolition had been taking place.

The Cawn representatives themselves bore witness to the night's terrifying ordeal; dishevelled, their eyes dark and sunken, hair a-tangle, they all kept bowing to Kellanved, hands clasped, eyes downcast.

Kellanved raised his hands in benediction. 'You have had a taste of my ire, citizens. It would not be well to try me once more.'

The merchants threw themselves down to their knees, hands raised. '*Never*, lord. We are yours. How may we serve?'

Kellanved gave a deprecating wave. 'Just one small thing only. Your boats. All your trading river craft. I have need of them.'

The merchants glanced amongst themselves, mystified. 'River boats, my lord? Truly?'

Kellanved rapped his walking stick to the cobbles. 'Indeed. Now. Immediately.'

The representatives of the merchant houses scrambled to their feet. 'At once, m'lord!' They backed away, bowing over and over. Dancer watched them go, half shaking his head. Doing so, he saw among the gathered Malazan and Napan troops the scowling figure of Surly, arms crossed, lips compressed, a frown between her eyes. He crossed to her.

'River boats?' she asked quizzically.

'Transport.'

'So we *are* headed upriver.'

'Indeed.'

She snorted. 'I'd half doubted it. What about the Five?'

'We have Tayschrenn, Nightchill, and the rest. We can match them.'

Now she appeared more worried than vexed. 'It's been hundreds of years since a confrontation on a scale like this. Who knows what might happen?'

'Don't worry. It may not come to that.'

Now she appeared truly puzzled, and she opened her mouth to ask, but Dancer pulled away, motioning after Kellanved. 'Have to go. Don't worry. You'll see.'

Over the course of the morning every Napan and Malazan trooper was transferred to a river craft of lesser draught. Joining Dancer and Kellanved on board the first vessel were Surly, Tayschrenn, Nightchill, Hairlock, Calot and Dassem. Thankfully, the Idryn was a shallow and wide river of sluggish current and so sails served to take them on the first leg of the journey.

Dancer sat back against the low railing while the vessel tacked its way north. Tayschrenn, who had been on board another ship out of Malaz, came to stand next to him. The lean mage drew a hand down a patchy beard he was growing, eyeing him on and off. Finally, Dancer sighed and motioned to him. 'What?'

The High Mage nodded and cleared his throat. 'So, you succeeded?'

Dancer didn't have to ask what he meant. Peering at the passing low farmlands, he nodded. 'Yes. After a fashion.'

'And Jadeen?'

'She . . . failed.'

The High Mage nodded again; clarification was unnecessary. Both understood what failure meant at these stakes. 'And?'

'And . . . what?'

The High Mage smoothed his thin beard. 'Will we . . . see?'

Dancer drew his hands down his thighs, let out a long breath. 'Let's hope not.'

The mage's brows rose in understanding. 'Ah. I . . . see. Indeed. Let us hope not.' And bowing, he took his leave.

Dancer returned to watching the flat farmland pass. So, Li Heng. The one city he wished never to see again. Still . . . once all this was over, perhaps he should go by to see how she was . . . But no. Better not to draw any more attention to her – he'd brought enough misery into her life as it was. In three days and nights – if the winds were with them – they should make Heng. As far as he was concerned this was it. Taking a no account pirate haven named Malaz was one thing. Overcoming an entrenched cabal on the mainland was another entirely. There would be no going back after this. Every hand would be raised against them. Quon and Tali would march. Perhaps even Unta, noble haughty Unta, would be forced to wade in.

It would all be different from this point onward – should they succeed.

And if they failed . . . well, both he and Tayschrenn understood what failure meant at this point. It was what they had put down as a stake – and this was the toss of the bones.

*   *   *

Two weeks into her captivity, the mage Gwynn came to see her in her room, or cell as she called it. She was of course blind at this point. The cell had a window, but

371

only rarely did a bird ever come by and she refused to command any to remain, being a prisoner herself.

The mage sat in the one chair while she sat up on the rope and straw pallet of her bed. He sighed, and she imagined him knitting his fingers together across one knee as he regarded her. The few times she'd seen the mage he'd struck her as curiously old in his dress and mannerisms, as if he were in a hurry to age; or perhaps trying to compensate for his youth.

'You have not been out for some days now,' he said.

She ignored him.

'Sister Lean is offering lessons on the dulcimer. Would you be interested?'

Ullara resolutely continued to stare in the direction she was fairly certain the window lay.

'Or literacy, perhaps?' Gwynn asked. 'I am teaching reading and writing. It is a rare and valuable skill.'

She had to turn her head to him at that. 'In case you hadn't noticed, I'm blind, you fool.'

'Ah. About that.'

She heard him rise, heard the door open. Then, instantly, miraculously, she could see. It took her a moment to get the perspective right, but it appeared the man was carrying a small wicker cage within which a tiny bird darted and fluttered. He offered it to her. 'A chickadee. They overwinter here. A hardy bird. Surprisingly resourceful and resilient for its size – rather like you.'

She clutched the cage to her chest. 'Thank you,' she managed, her voice thick.

'Not at all. Can you read and write?'

She shook her head. 'No. Our family couldn't afford the tutors.'

'Ah. Well, then. Lessons?' She nodded. 'Very good.

The commons, at noon.' He clapped his hands to his thighs and rose. 'Until then.'

Ullara proved an avid student; more than once Gwynn expressed his astonishment at the speed with which she advanced. Soon she was pursuing her own studies and her room became cluttered in scrolls and rare texts. She read with her bird, Tiny, on a hook just over her right shoulder.

A month and a half passed and more and more often, despite the diversion of worlds of written histories Ullara had never even guessed existed, she found herself peering up at the window for long hours. Her appetite faded and it seemed to her that she would never escape this new prison.

Late one night her door opened, waking her, and Gwynn entered holding a dimmed lantern. Ullara sat up, alarmed – twice before a stable-lad and then a hired hand had come pushing their way into her attic room in Heng – but back then she'd had her pets to protect her. Both times she'd had to rescue *them*.

This time the intruder sat in her one chair and regarded her. She pulled her blankets up her chest, blinking suspiciously. 'Yes?'

'They say some birds never take to captivity,' the mage said. 'They simply give up the will to live and fade away.' He tilted his head, regarding her. 'I fear we are tempting the same fate with you.'

'Are you going to force me to eat?'

Gwynn just smiled. 'I've decided on a much more radical solution.' He got up and pulled something into the room. Ullara straightened on her pallet; it was a large backpack. He pulled out two long objects, tall boots of oiled hide. 'Sheepskin lined,' he told her. Then he tossed her a bundle of clothes. 'Woollen trousers, sheepskin jacket and mittens. A fur hat.'

She immediately began dressing, while he averted his head.

'Why are you doing this?' she asked as she dressed.

'I believe it was wrong of us to interfere with your journey and I am sending you on your way. In the pack you'll find dried meat and grains. Flint and steel and tinder for fires. Tiny here will be your eyes.'

Once she'd finished dressing he rose and shouldered the pack. 'This way.'

She lifted Tiny from his hook and followed.

He led her through narrow back passages, almost always downwards. The halls became ever more chill, until hoar frost glittered on them in the golden lantern-light. He stopped at a thick door bearing a layer of ice that he began hammering at with the pommel of his dagger.

After some work he was able to edge the door open a crack wide enough for her to slip out. Frigid winds blew into the corridor. Outside, the deep blue of starlight reflected from snow. He handed her the backpack. 'Fare thee well, little bird.'

She didn't know what to say, could only gasp, 'Thank you, Gwynn.'

'Please do not think too badly of us,' he answered. 'Our commander believed he was doing the right thing.'

'I understand. Fare well. And thank you again.'

'Thank me by surviving.'

She waved and turned away to the snowy slopes.

Gwynn watched her go until her path took her from his sight, then pushed closed the door. He returned upstairs, and here, in the common room, he found Seth waiting for him at a table next to the low embers in the stone fireplace. He sat at the table and poured himself some wine.

'You've sent the girl to her death,' Seth said. 'I'll have you drummed out of this company. You are no better than a murderer.'

'We were wrong to interfere.'

'So *you* say.'

'So the cards said.'

Seth scowled. 'Whatever do you mean?'

'The Dragons Deck. I am no talent, formally. But I have some small ability. Every night this last month I have consulted the deck. And every time the connotations have been the same. I've tried all the arrangements and permutations I am familiar with. The Southern Arc. The Old *and* the New House. The Great Circle. Every time it has been clear. The girl has a Fate. A Wyrd. And we were wrong to come between her and it.'

'Regardless. I will take this to Courian and have you dismissed.'

Gwynn shrugged. 'Go ahead. Cal-Brinn will support me.'

Seth pushed himself from the table and stood. 'Damned mages. Consider yourself under house arrest.' He snapped his fingers and two guardsmen came forward. 'Take this man to his room and hold him there.'

Pursing his lips, Gwynn slowly swirled his wine in the glass and finished it.

* * *

Orjin had the word spread through the ranks that come the dawn they would be making a break west. He knew he was taking a fearful chance in trusting the word of this agent and normally he would never have done so.

Frankly, he would not have done so this time either, save for the support of his Dal Hon shaman Yune.

That night Arkady came to him with a band of hill tribe youths. 'We will fight with you,' their spokesman said.

Orjin shook a negative. 'You shouldn't. There'll be retribution against your people.'

The youth laughed. 'They sneer at us. Push us into poorer and poorer ground. Starve us. What worse can they do?'

'I'm sorry,' was all Orjin could say. 'We will be honoured to have you with us.'

This lad inclined his head and the youths withdrew. Arkady remained, peering after them, and, to Orjin's eyes, appearing troubled. 'What is it?' he asked.

'It's the same story among us Wickans,' Arkady said. 'And the Seti tribes. Encroachment. You coastal people with your city states creeping over the land.'

'Surely you Wickans are too strong to be threatened.'

The scout shook his head. 'It will happen. In time.'

Personally, Orjin didn't think any force could subdue the Wickan tribes, but perhaps the same had once been said of the Seti. He lifted his shoulders. 'We shall see.'

The Wickan lad gave him a wintry smile and followed the tribal youths.

This left the thorny matter of a rearguard. Orjin, of course, considered himself part of it. But so too would his lieutenants, and this was a problem as he needed them up front to bull through any strong resistance they might encounter.

So he ordered them all to take the van, while they, in turn, ignored his order.

Even as troops were filing out of camp he was still arguing the point. 'I mean it,' he told them. 'Get going.'

'You must take the van,' Orhan answered.

'No – I'll take the rear, make certain everyone gets out.'

'This time rearguard's mine,' Terath said. She motioned Orhan forward. 'Guard him.'

The huge fellow nodded. 'Very good. Orjin and I shall lead the charge.'

Orjin gave the Untan ex-officer a hard look. 'You're certain?'

She waved him off. 'Get going or the fight'll be over.'

He let out a hard breath, rolled his shoulders to loosen them. 'Fine. This time. But next time it's mine.'

'Whatever. Go.'

He gave her a nod, then clapped Orhan on the shoulder. 'Let's go.'

As Orjin suspected, breaking through the encirclement was the easier job – for now. Of course the Quon Talian troops were expecting a desperate last-minute break for freedom, but not to the west. The west was their stronghold, firmly in their grip, and of course beyond lay the coast. An insurmountable barrier. A dead end.

And they would be right – should no relief arrive from these erstwhile new allies.

In a squall of blowing snow he and Orhan came crashing through an encampment of cookfires and lean-tos of fresh spruce branches over frames, scattering the Quon Talian infantry. While shock and surprise were on their side he paused here to wave his troops through.

A small victory, but the infantry would reorganize and then it would be a chase. The last unit through was Terath's; she urged him up the path while arranging her troop behind cover.

'We'll hold them up for a while,' she told him.

'Unnecessary. Let's go.'

She pushed him on. 'Get back to the front, dammit!'

He pointed for emphasis. 'Do not delay.'

She waved him onward. 'Yes, yes.'

Orjin jogged off up the path.

The rest of that day was something of a game of hide and seek with the Talian infantry. Orjin's hill tribe youths scouted ahead, chose routes, and sent them by roundabout paths, cliff-side walks, and down the rocky spillways of frigid mountain streams to avoid strong-points and ambushes.

Come nightfall, once it was too dark to travel safely, the scouts had them hole up among the bare boulders of a gorge. All day Orjin had seen nothing of Terath and the rearguard, but with night the last units came jogging in, accompanied by Terath on a makeshift stretcher carried by two of her troops.

Orjin knelt next to her, took in the ghostly pale face, the blood soaking her wrapped torso. He clasped her bloodied, cold hand in his. 'We'll fix you up.'

She shook her head. 'Lost too much blood.'

Prevost Jeral appeared and knelt next to the stretcher. 'She shouldn't be moved,' she told Orjin.

Terath shook her head again, and weakly motioned Jeral closer. The prevost lowered her head, and her brows rose in astonishment as Terath planted her mouth on hers. 'Always loved those . . . braids,' Terath whispered, and her head fell back.

Jeral sat on her haunches, seemingly stunned. Orjin pulled his hand down the Untan swordswoman's face to gently close her eyes.

The next morning they headed onward. Orjin ordered there would be no more rearguard actions; everyone was to keep moving, never engage, always pushing forward.

He and Orhan kept moving up and down the lines, ready to act should any group get pinned.

So they wound their way up and down steep valleys, following circuitous routes known only to the locals, always a few bare steps ahead of pursuit, but always returning to angle westward.

Sunrise was a victory by Orjin's count.

Two days, he kept repeating to himself as he staggered, exhausted, along narrow rocky paths. Just two.

Then, finally, *one*.

Chapter 20

SURLY FACED KELLANVED AND DANCER ON BOARD their cargo boat and gestured upriver. 'I'm told that a few turns through those wooded shores and we should see the walls. So, let me reiterate.' She raised a finger to Kellanved. 'If this goes south – if you fail to deliver – I'm ordering a full retreat and I will happily leave you two swinging in the wind. Is that clear?'

The Dal Hon mage waggled a hand to dismiss her concerns. 'Do not worry yourself, my dear.'

Dancer gave her a nod of understanding.

They tacked upriver further and eventually the walls of the Outer Round of Li Heng hove into view above the treetops. For his part Dancer could hardly look at them – this was the last city of Quon Tali he wished to return to. A crowd of archers manned the walls over the river gate, which was closed, blocking their advance.

Kellanved looked to Hairlock and Calot, then motioned to the walls.

The bald Hairlock raised his hands, gesturing. Above the walls the archers suddenly turned to face one another and began loosing their arrows point-blank. The burly mage chuckled to himself as they fell one after the other. He next made a puppeteer-like motion with his hands, as if pulling unseen strings, and the remaining guards flung themselves off the tall parapets to their deaths.

Dancer winced. He caught Kellanved's eye, and the dark-hued mage motioned to the grinning Hairlock. 'That's quite enough, thank you.'

The squat mage's frog-like mouth turned down and he lowered his hands. 'Fine. We're pretty much done, anyway.'

'Trouble,' Calot announced, pointing.

A Dal Hon woman with a huge mane of kinky black hair now stood at the shore; she pointed to their lead boat and the deck beneath Dancer suddenly bucked. But Calot snarled under his breath, gesturing, and the vessel levelled. 'Damn she's strong,' he gasped, straining.

'Keep her busy,' Kellanved told him. He motioned ahead to the closed river gate. 'Nightchill, if you would be so kind?'

Leaning against the side, Nightchill raised her eyes to the sky in disgust. 'I told you – I'm not one of your hirelings.'

'Just the gate. A mere architectural feature now cleared of any people. This is all I ask.'

'All?'

'Yes. All. I swear.'

The woman sighed and straightened. 'Very well.' She reached out and clawed at the gate, as if she would draw it towards her.

Dust appeared, bursting from the blocks of the stone arch above the gate, and a high keening screech of tortured metal reached Dancer. Even as he watched, the entire arch, including the gate, came tilting towards them, tumbling, fracturing, to crash down into the river with a gigantic blast of water. Spray showered the boat as it rocked and bucked over the resulting wave.

Kellanved had a handkerchief out and was mopping his face. 'Thank you so very much, m'lady.'

Nightchill leaned back against the side of the boat, looking away, as if to ignore him.

Kellanved tapped his walking stick in one palm, clearing his throat. 'Ah, yes, well . . .' He turned to Dancer. 'Now then, you and I have an errand to run.'

Surly stepped up, 'What's this? You're not taking off, are you?'

'Regrettably, yes. Unavoidable.' He urged Surly away. 'Go and establish your foothold here in the Outer Round. We are off to move against the Five.'

'We don't have the troops!' she snarled, but Dancer was no longer listening as the world darkened around him and he recognized a shift through Shadow. The darkness faded and with the slightest half-step he recognized where he now stood – in the catacombs beneath Heng. He even knew where: in the precincts of the mage Ho. 'What are we doing here?' he asked Kellanved, keeping his voice low.

The mage was tapping his walking stick to his lips now, squinting at the many cell doors lining the hall. 'Now, which ones were they . . . ah! Here we are.' He rapped on a thick door.

'Lar!' came a yell from the cell beyond, startling Dancer. 'Lar, Lar, Lar!'

Kellanved nodded to himself. 'Yes. These three here, if you would, Dancer.'

A touch anxious, Dancer unlatched the three doors then stood, hands on weapons, waiting. Three men poked their heads out to peer round, then stepped out, and he was astonished to see three near identical individuals, all clearly brothers to the mage Ho – save that each was even shabbier, in dirty torn clothes.

Kellanved waved them to him. 'Your freedom, friends,' he announced, 'for one small errand.' The three exchanged eager glances, and Dancer was a touch unnerved by their strange, empty half-smiles and wild eyes. 'Your brother,' Kellanved continued. 'Find him and bring him to me. I would have a word with him.'

The three grinned even more broadly, nudging one another, and tramped off with a lumbering, flat-footed stride. Dancer watched them go, then turned to Kellanved. 'So, that's Ho, then?'

The mage nodded. 'Yes. And my, ah, agents tell me Koroll is no longer in the city.' Dancer raised a brow – apparently one or more of Kellanved's young lads and lasses had actually returned to Heng to spy for him. Courageous, that. 'The rest of the Five alone are not a worry. That leaves Shalmanat.'

Dancer had to steady himself. Ah. This was where things were going to get ... difficult. The mage peered round the tunnel and shook his head. 'No. Not the right place.' He gestured, and darkness enveloped Dancer once more.

When the shadows dispersed he found himself atop one of the ring-walls of Heng, the Inner Precinct wall surrounding the palace and the tall towering spire itself. He looked to the short hunched mage. 'You're getting much better at this.'

Kellanved dipped his head in acknowledgement. 'My thanks.' Letting out a long hard breath, he tapped his walking stick to the flagstones of the walk and announced, 'Tem Benasto, Bonecaster of the T'lan Imass! I call you! Come. It is I – occupant of the throne.'

Dancer whipped out his blades, peering round. 'Don't compel them!' he warned Kellanved.

'I'm not *compelling* them – I'm just calling them ... Ah!'

Dust swirled about the mage as if in a whirlwind. When Dancer's vision returned there stood not just Tem Benasto in his huge hunting cat headdress, but the other Bonecasters of the Logros clan, along with the sword-bearing Onos T'oolan.

Hengan guards who had been closing upon them halted, jaws agape, and began scrambling away. Dancer ignored them for now.

'You summon us away from our work gathering our brothers and sisters?' Tem demanded. 'Here? To what purpose? You waste our time.'

The mage raised his hands. 'Please! Hear me out. An enemy is near.'

'Enemy?' Onos T'oolan grated breathlessly, his flesh-less hand moving to the wrapped grip of his flint blade. 'We care nothing for your pathetic scramblings for power. I consider this call . . . unworthy.'

Dancer half drew his heaviest parrying blades, leaning forward.

'No, no,' Kellanved pleaded. 'Really. A true enemy. I swear.'

Tem Benasto extended a withered hand to Onos T'oolan to check him. 'Speak,' he told Kellanved.

'Here,' Kellanved stressed, 'in this very city. I have seen him with my own eyes in the flesh. Not longer than one year ago . . . a Jaghut!'

T'oolan's blade whipped free of his belt in a motion too swift for Dancer to follow. '*What!*'

Tem Benasto pointed a bony finger at the Dal Hon mage. 'This is impossible. We ourselves cleansed these lands many ages ago. No Jaghut remain on this continent.' He tilted his head sideways, as if confused by the little Dal Hon mage. 'You do understand that if you are lying you will be judged . . . unworthy.'

Kellanved rubbed his neck, then dipped his head in acknowledgement. 'None the less, I saw what I saw.' He opened his arms. 'Prove me wrong.'

Tem Benasto turned his wide cat-jaw headdress to his brethren. 'Summon our brothers and sisters and search the city.'

*

Silk and Smokey had taken up post at the Eastern Inner river gate when a wash of major sorcery made them both stagger. Moments later a rumbling came and dust rose over the Outer Round river gate.

'What in the name of the Nine was that?' Silk demanded.

Smokey was rubbing his forehead and wincing. 'Don't know. But – *damn.*'

'This is no two-bit raid,' Silk growled.

'The Cawnese did warn us that it looked as though that Dal Hon runt was bringing mages.'

Silk nodded at that. Yes. But he'd been expecting a few ship's mages, or a drunken hedge wizard – not *this.* He backed away from the wall, thinking, *Hood take it, if they got through I know where they will be headed. And that damned assassin is with them . . .*

He turned and ran for the nearest stairs.

'What about the defence, man!' Smokey yelled after him. 'The walls!'

But in Silk's eyes there was only one thing worth defending.

He found the palace in a panic. Functionaries and servants ran every which way. He grabbed one's arm, demanding, 'What's going on?'

'Creatures!' the woman gasped. 'The dead walk!'

Silk curled a lip. 'Really? Did you see these?'

'Well, no. But everyone's saying—'

Snarling, he released her. He knew it; that damned Dal Hon sneak was up to something.

He pushed further into the complex. Curiously, just where he'd expect to see barricades or wall-to-wall palace guards, he found none. Yet neither was there blood, or corpses, or the ruin of battle. It was as if everyone had simply upped and run away. It troubled him greatly, but he made for the central cynosure, hoping to find Shalmanat.

Heaving open the door of the domed inner sanctum, he froze, absolutely shocked as he faced the backs of four individuals who, frankly, fitted perfectly the description he'd been given of dead walking. Without a pause he threw out his hands and gave them every ounce of summoned Warren power he possessed.

The conflagration of energies left the floor glowing and crackling and through the smoke he saw Shalmanat limping away through a distant door. Of the interlopers nothing remained, just smoke and charred ash.

He hurried forward only to be yanked backwards off his feet and lifted by an iron-hard grip at his neck. He was turned to stare into a face that was, frankly, death incarnate: dried, aged flesh stretched over bone, dark empty eye-pits and bared tannin-stained teeth. And round this head, the opened fleshless skull of a wolf, jaws agape.

'Do not interfere,' the apparition told him, and he was unceremoniously flung aside through the air to land tumbling.

Blinking, dazed, he squinted while the things seemed to disintegrate into dust before his very eyes. He blinked again. Dust. *Dust?* And bones? The Army of Dust and Bone?

So – they were here for her. Well, not without a fight. He clambered to his feet and staggered after Shalmanat. The door opened on to a narrow hall that led to the spire. Here he started up the circular staircase. He lost his breath about halfway but grimly carried on, teeth clenched, gasping in air.

He gained the top landing to find himself once more facing the rear of the four members of the Army of Dust and Bone. Two turned to face him, bony hands going to the grips of flint weapons thrust through twisted hide belts.

'Leave her alone!' he demanded. Shalmanat stood at the balcony of the spire, her chin raised, defiant. The wolf-headdress creature turned at his call. 'She is not your enemy,' Silk told it.

'No. This is why she still lives.'

'Then what do you want!' Silk yelled.

Wolf-headdress raised a pole-thin arm of dried flesh over bone to her. 'We are displeased to find one of her kind ruling here over you humans. This is distasteful to us.'

'She has been our benefactor!'

'None the less.' The creature faced Shalmanat. 'Liosan calls. It is time for you to return to your kind.'

Shalmanat shook her head, pushed her wind-tossed thin white hair from her tear-stained face. 'No. You don't understand. They would not have me.'

The creature drew a flint dagger. 'Choose. Return to your kind . . . or face us.'

She snarled then, straightening. 'Damn you pitiless Imass!' And, grasping the ledge, she rolled herself over the top to disappear, her white linen shirt and trousers snapping in the wind.

Silk lunged forward, '*No!*'

He half leaned over the ledge, only to be blinded by a great flash of light from below, and he turned away, blinking. 'What have you done?'

'She chose wisely,' the Imass said.

And with that the four suddenly dispersed into dust that quickly blew away. Silk slid down the wall of the balcony to hunch, head in hands, somehow still unable to understand. Was she gone? Really truly gone?

What ever would he do now?

Resistance in Li Heng collapsed as the account spread of witnesses seeing monstrous creatures flinging the Protectress to her death from the top of the spire. This, plus the apparent routing of the Cabal of Five, completely ended the hostilities.

Kellanved and Dancer entered the central palace unopposed.

They found it a littered mess vacant of all functionaries, guards and servants. Kellanved peered round at the overturned furniture and scattered scrolls and vellum sheets, then eyed Dancer. 'Not the welcome I was expecting.'

Dancer suddenly pushed his companion back as dust gathered before them in a thickening gyre to coalesce into the forms of three T'lan Imass: Ay Estos in his wolf headdress, Tem Benasto in his sabre-toothed cat skull and the lean figure of Onos T'oolan. Tem Benasto grasped the leather-wrapped grip of the flint dagger at his waist. 'You lied. No Jaghut can be found here. Only one woman of the Tiste Liosan – whom we dealt with.'

Kellanved spread his hands wide. 'But I assure you—'

'Too late,' Ay Estos answered, like a sentence.

The Bonecasters nodded to T'oolan and he clasped a

hand to the grip of his long two-handed flint blade. 'You have been judged unworthy,' Onos announced.

Dancer stepped between them, his blades drawn. He eyed the creature, saying, 'First let's see how we compare—'

A new shape appeared then: Ulpan Nodosha in his headdress of a gigantic cave bear. He raised a hand for a halt. 'Vestiges of Omtose Phellack have been detected.'

T'oolan's weapon fairly flew up and he spun. '*What?*'

Dancer saw then the speed of this Imass swordsman, and despaired. He knew nothing like it, save for the Dal Hon half-breed, Dassem.

'Impossible,' Tem answered. 'We ourselves cleansed this land millennia ago.'

Ulpan Nodosha gave a nod of his gigantic bear skull headdress. 'None the less. Along the river. And very recent.'

Tem turned to regard Kellanved. 'This is . . . troubling. If true, you were right to bring it to our attention. We must pursue this.'

And with that all four sloughed away into dust. Kellanved waved his hands. 'Wait! Are you going? *Really* going?' He looked to Dancer and threw his hands in the air. 'A little consideration – that's all I ask!'

For his part Dancer resisted rubbing his neck in relief. That had been far too close. Fortunately, the little Dal Hon mage had been on top of things, but what of next time? If there ever was one, which, if he had any say, would be never.

Kellanved gestured aside with his walking stick. 'Ah, here we are.'

Dancer glanced over and flinched, as there stood Ho. But it was not Ho, for that mage never possessed such an empty half-grin. It was one of the doppelgangers he and Kellanved had released. The quadruplet urged them to him, his grin twitching, and disappeared into a side room.

'This way,' Kellanved invited, and followed. Within, they found all four identical burly men. Three held the fourth subdued: one with a headlock, the others on each arm. The constrained one grunted, struggling and glaring. Kellanved approached and nodded to him. 'Ho. You worried me the most. How was I to get the better of one such as you?' He gestured to the other three. 'Thankfully, you yourself provided the means.

'Wrap him in chains,' he told them, 'and take him to the waterfront. A riverboat is waiting to take him to Cawn. There, a Napan vessel is provisioned and waiting for a long journey. A journey all the way to the lands of the Seven Cities.'

Ho, the cords of his neck straining, his lips drawn back, cut in: 'Idiot! No prison can hold me.'

'Oh, but this one can, I assure you. It is a prison perfectly suited for one such as you.' He nodded to the three and, grinning, they proceeded to drag their brother away. 'But watch out for the dust,' Kellanved called after them. 'It is a very dusty place.'

The Dal Hon mage offered Dancer a smug smile and motioned him onward. 'There we are. The Protectress dealt with, as you heard. All that remains is to take possession.'

Dancer was not so sanguine. 'I doubt anything could be as all settled as that.'

Kellanved headed out to the main hall, waving Dancer's reservations aside. 'You'll see!'

The long hall led to the formal throne room where Shalmanat used to receive petitions and lower judgements.

Here, Kellanved pointed to a robed functionary running past. 'You there! Come here!'

The man gaped, scrolls and vellum sheets clasped to his breast. 'Don't kill me, m'lord!' he pleaded.

'Nothing of the sort, I assure you,' the mage said soothingly. 'Gather the court, please. These are my orders, yes?'

The fellow nodded jerkily. 'The court, my lord?'

'Yes. All those who wish to witness the change of rulership here in Heng. All interested parties. Yes?'

The palace clerk kept nodding. 'Very good. Yes, m'lord. At once. As you order.'

'Excellent.' Kellanved bade him go with little shooing gestures of his hands. The fellow ran, sheets flying.

'And what will this accomplish?' Dancer asked, brows arched.

'Witnesses, my friend. Vital.' He raised a crooked thin finger. 'Nothing happens unless it is witnessed.'

＊

When Heboric arrived in Li Heng he immediately asked about the location of the main temple to Fener. Not surprisingly, it was located in the main garrison of the city, Fener being not only the Boar of Summer, but one of the acknowledged gods of war. Entering, he was surprised to find himself rather quickly assuming the role of High Priest of the temple, as none of the local adherents wore blessings of the boar beyond small tattoos upon their cheeks and wrists.

As such, he was entitled to attend court here in Li Heng, which he did at the earliest opportunity. Yet it was a disappointment; the legendary Protectress did not appear. The mundane dispensing of justice fell that day to some overly groomed mage who Heboric was

391

surprised to discover was the moderately famous mage of Telas, Smokey.

He turned instead to questioning the gathered court of wealthy merchants, high functionaries, nobles, and other such flunkeys and hangers-on. Eventually he found what he was searching for: a self-important sycophant eager to prove how close he was to power by voicing all the many secrets he was privy to.

'The Protectress is not in attendance?' he asked the fat fellow.

The hanger-on laughed indulgently. And, glancing left and right, leaned closer. 'I happen to know for a fact that she is unable to.'

Heboric made appreciative noises, 'Indeed ... And why would this be?'

The man nodded as if in secret accord with him. 'Well, Brother Fener, you are new here, yes?'

'Yes.'

'Well, the Five have things in hand – let us just say that, yes?'

Heboric raised his brows, impressed. 'You are implying ...'

The man peered right and left once more, and winked. 'Let us just say that I am now in such a position that no action is taken at all by the Cabal of Five without my consultation, yes?' And he patted Heboric on the arm, conspiratorially.

For his part, Heboric struggled to make sense of what the fellow was insinuating. That he was, or was not, currently consulted? He decided that unctuous buttering-up would smooth over any confusion and so he made more rapt noises, adding, 'Indeed!'

The court hanger-on nodded profoundly. 'Indeed.

You are obviously incredibly observant yourself. I can tell, as I myself possess an acuity that is uncanny.'

'Amazing!'

'Absolutely. Believe me. This so-called "retreat" by the Protectress is a completely false cover-up. The Five now rule in all but name. Take it from me, for I am never wrong.' And raising a fat finger in emphasis, the fellow strode off.

Heboric was left blinking in a fog of confusion, until, with some mental effort, he managed to dismiss ninety per cent of the blow-hard verbiage to distil the conclusion that plots and rumours were now rife here in the power vacuum of the court of Heng.

Familiarizing himself with the city, walking the rounds, he found very little to worry him regarding the purported rampant cult activity. True, the cult of the Protectress was on display in shrines and votary offerings at crossroads and marketplaces, but as a scholar of religion and history he understood that such was the normal ferment of beliefs and competing factions. Time would be the test here. And it would be interesting to find out if any of these new creeds or personalities would ever actually amount to anything.

A week later he was attending to the dutiful in the temple when a guard entered and ordered everyone to post. Heboric stepped out on to the main training grounds to find guards rushing about and reinforcements being assembled. He set off to find a ranking officer to question.

He found a lieutenant of the garrison attached to the palace across the grounds. This woman inclined her helmeted head to him in respect. 'Priest,' she greeted him.

'What is all the activity?'

'A raid. A rider arrived yesterday from Cawn, warning us. The pirate ruler of Malaz heading upriver. We were ready for a minor raid, but things are heating up. Seems they came ready to take on the Five.'

Heboric nodded. 'Ah. So a mage battle.'

'Unfortunately for the rest of us, yes. Now, if you would excuse me?'

He bowed. 'Of course.' The officer jogged off.

As priest of one of the gods of war, Heboric chose to walk the walls of the palace grounds to witness this attack. Hengan guards came to ask his blessing, which he gave freely as he sought out a position from which to see the action. Eastward, apparently.

Reaching a viewpoint on a corner barbican of the palace walls, he leaned on the stone crenel and peered out along the Idryn. He saw nothing in particular, save for thick traffic on the roads, a great many citizens rushing this way and that in panic and confusion. Some smoke and dust in the air over the city far to the east.

The raid, such as it was, didn't seem to have penetrated very far into the city proper. The Five must have repelled these pirate adventurers. Still, he remained for a few hours as noon approached, and then, to his surprise, the Boar suddenly came to him.

It was as if a shadow of the beast himself reared up over him; the hair of his neck and arms bristled just as any boar's would. He raised his nose to scent the air as the shadow-boar did over him and what it sensed made it chuff and stiffen. The power of the Boar burst upon him then, as an aura, sizzling the air, and his head turned to the inner palace walls within the compound, and what he saw there through Fener's eyes staggered him.

Lean and ragged shapes stood the walls, some wearing archaic headdresses and tattered hide cloaks. Yet through Fener's senses Heboric saw them for what they were: entities fairly blazing with power, and he recognized them from ancient accounts: the undying army of the Imass themselves, and even the Boar within him was staggered.

He understood now why he was here. This was far more epochal than the mere transfer of authority from one ruler to another. An ancient and implacable power had been raised anew and nothing would be the same again.

He headed for the palace. Had these Elders now taken charge?

The court was a mass of panicked functionaries, bureaucrats, merchants and city aristocrats, all jostling and exchanging whispered news – awaiting their fates, in fact. Later that afternoon the doors opened and in came a short, wizened Dal Hon elder with a walking stick, accompanied by a lean youth and a Napan woman. These three walked to the front and the Dal Hon seated himself on the formal throne of Heng, flanked by the other two.

The elder raised his hands for silence. 'Calm yourselves, please, citizens of Heng. Nothing shall change. All shall remain as before. The Protectress may be gone, but you have a new Protector.' The ancient pressed a hand to his chest. 'Myself.'

'And you are?' some brave soul shouted from the crowd.

The ancient appeared quite startled. He planted his walking stick between his feet, announcing, 'I am Kellanved, ruler of the isles of Malaz and Nap – and the ruling authority over the city state of Cawn, and now of Li Heng also.'

Heboric squinted – the fellow might look old, but he

appeared startlingly quick and vigorous for one of such apparent age. He had to wonder: was this the one responsible for the summoning of the Elders?

This 'Kellanved' now stroked his chin. 'And thinking on that ...' he turned to the blue-hued Napan woman with him, 'does that not make me emperor? After the Talian hegemony? Ruler of more than one kingship?'

The woman's lips tightened, and she murmured from the side of her mouth, 'Now is not the time ...'

The fellow banged his walking stick to the flagged floor. 'Now is absolutely the appropriate time! This is momentous! It must be witnessed!' He scanned the court, peering all around. 'Is there no historian present? None qualified to record these events for posterity? For the ages to follow?'

Heboric looked about him, as did the hunched Dal Hon elder upon the throne. No one stirred to raise a hand, and so, driven by the demands and dictates of his training as scholar and historian, Heboric very slowly, reluctantly, lifted his arm into the air.

The ancient, Kellanved, perked up. 'Ah!' He pointed his walking stick. 'Here we are. Fener is with us! Welcome, priest. Please approach.'

Heboric edged his way through the crowd to reach the fore. The elder urged him even closer. Hesitantly, he advanced, but quite warily, as the slim fellow on the elder's right now leaned forward, hand on a dagger, and he knew that one false motion, one shift too close, and that weapon would be lodged in his throat. 'Yes m'lor – that is, your excellency?'

The elder's brows climbed in appreciation of this address, and he shifted to look to the woman. 'There! You see? Our priest of Fener understands. 'So ... am I not entitled to style myself emperor after the historical precedents?'

Heboric bowed his head. 'Indeed. If one is the ruler of more than one kingdom, principate, or protectorate, then one may claim the title emperor or empress.'

The elder opened his arms wide. 'There we have it. Emperor Kellanved.'

The Napan woman, Heboric noted, looked to the ceiling at this announcement. But he was obliged to continue. 'However, after these ancient precedents, the date of assumption of said emperor or empress must be set at their birth.' He raised his gaze to address the fellow directly. 'Therefore – may I enquire as to the year you were born?'

The Dal Hon ancient snorted at this, glancing about rather as if he'd been cornered. He gestured peremptorily. 'What a ridiculous request! As if I can remember! And who knows which dating system to follow?'

'Nevertheless . . . ?'

The elder huffed, puffing and shifting uncomfortably on the throne. 'Whatever! Very well. The fifth year of the rule of Gorashel of the Eastern Dal Hon savannas – if you must!'

It just so happened that Heboric had been briefed on all the dynasties of the continent. He eyed the wrinkled elder and could not help but raise a brow in scepticism. 'Are you saying that you are less than twenty years old?'

The presumed ancient gaped at him, astonished, only to recover quickly and wave a hand in dismissal. 'That is not what I meant at all! Absurd! No – what I meant was one hundred years *prior* to that year, of course!'

He may have been mistaken, but the slim youth with him, presumably the purported assassin Heboric had heard of, covered his mouth, perhaps to disguise a smirk.

'That was not what you said,' Heboric persisted.

Now the grey-haired Dal Hon mage urged him closer, leaning in, and whispered, 'Very well – what say you we split the difference? Seventy? Yes? Can you work with that?'

Heboric could not drop his lifted brow. 'I'm sorry, but I heard what I heard.'

The presumed elder threw himself back into the throne, gesturing aside. 'Guards! Take this fool away! He is wilfully misinterpreting my meaning.'

The only guards present were Malazan troops. These respectfully motioned Heboric away, he being a priest of Fener after all.

'Find a deep cell!' Kellanved shouted after them. 'Where he may reconsider his wilfulness, and recant his errors.' Addressing the gathered court, the wizened Dal Hon announced, 'Seventy! Did you hear that? The official *imperial* count shall be seventy years! So begins the rule of Emperor Kellanved! Now, any other historians or scholars present? Anyone?'

On his way out of the throne room with the guards, Heboric was hardly surprised when no one else spoke up.

*

Close to the river gate of the Inner Round, Smokey dug through the wreckage of the raiders' passage, heaving aside planks, a shattered cart, dust and rubble of broken rock to pull a woman from beneath the heap. Dust sifted from her thick mane of wild kinky hair as she staggered upright, clutching his arm. 'I was doing fine,' she insisted, 'until that Kartoolian waded in.'

398

Smokey nodded, guiding her to the gates. 'They came with more than five.'

'And Shalmanat?'

'Stories are the T'lan Imass themselves returned to murder her.'

Mara spat blood and grit from her mouth. 'The T'lan Imass, in truth? Hard to believe. So this dark wizard cut a deal with these Elders?'

'So it would seem.'

She touched gingerly at a bleeding cut along her scalp. 'Fucking bastard!'

'We're all that's left,' Smokey said.

'Silk?'

'Probably cut down by the Imass – he was with her.'

'Ho?'

'Witnesses say he was dragged down by replicas of him. Sounds unbelievable, but there you are.'

She held her head. 'None of this makes any sense! Why here? Why now?'

He shrugged as he dragged her along through the ruined gate. 'Had to strike somewhere, I suppose. As good a place as any. Now we have to go before those mages return looking for you.'

'Did you see that gargoyle Hairlock among them?'

Smokey scowled his disgust. 'Wanted from coast to coast, that one.'

She limped along, blinking, perhaps trying to focus her eyes. 'Find a cart or a mule – I can't walk. That Kartoolian is a powerful bastard.'

'Don't worry. We'll find something.'

'Then what?'

'Don't know. Wasn't joking earlier when I said I was thinking of joining the Crimson Guard.'

Mara laughed her scorn at that. Laughed, then held her head, groaning.

*

Silk didn't remember descending the tower and making his way out of the palace. Everything seemed blacked out, an unreal blur, but now that he was at the waterfront he realized that he was about to be captured. These raider mages, their Warrens raised and sizzling, were still hunting for the last remnants of the Five, himself included.

Frankly, he didn't care what happened to him any more. It was all over. But the idea of submitting to these murderers repulsed him. He kept ducking away, moving on, and his retreat brought him to the wharves and piers crowded by the invaders' riverboats. Here Silk spotted one of the hunting mages, a squat and hairless nut-brown fellow, his Warren a bright aura about him, scanning the crowds of milling citizenry, and he jumped down to a lower floating dock where a mass of men stood jammed together, their clothes just as dirty and torn as his own. A fat fellow armed with a truncheon pushed through the crowd to wave him off.

'You're not allowed here!'

Hand at his side, Silk turned his cupped palm to show his coin-purse. The fellow's thick black brows narrowed as he peered right and left, then he brushed past Silk, taking it. 'Name?' he demanded.

'Yusen,' Silk offered, borrowing a friend's name.

The fellow pointed his truncheon. 'Get in line . . . Yusen.'

The line filled a long twisting gangway up on to one of the larger riverboats – a trireme galley. Here armed sailors pushed the file of men down into the narrow alleys of its rowing benches. Silk held back, alarmed, but he could not resist the long line of men behind him, pushing him forward, and so eventually he ended up next to an empty berth and his companions gestured forcefully that he should sit on the filthy bench.

The last thing he wanted to do at this point was bring any attention to himself and so he complied, all the while straining for a glimpse of the pier through the oar-port, searching for his pursuers. He spotted the squat, scowling fellow now talking with another mage, this one tall and lean, in dark severe robes, his raised aura particularly intense. He hunched back down among the ranks of rowers.

'This is a Cawnese vessel, yes?' he asked the fellow next to him.

'A privateer vessel,' was the answer. 'Under hire.'

Silk studied the interior once more, a touch confused. 'We are not fettered?'

His companion on the bench appeared quite startled. 'Of course not. We made our agreements, signed our papers.'

'Papers? Agreement?'

His companion looked him up and down. 'Are you all right? Did you take a fall?'

Silk touched his head to find there dried crusted blood. He didn't remember falling, but he must have at some point, probably on the stairs. 'It's nothing. Please – papers, you say?'

'Yes. Service to cover your debts in Cawn, of course.'

Silk stared, though somehow he managed not to gape. 'So,' he said, nodding, 'this vessel is contracted to the Cawnese.'

'Oh, no,' the fellow answered. 'It's not. It's contracted to the Malazans. You are in their service now.'

This time Silk did gape. Then he burst out with a high laugh. Somewhere the gods were holding their stomachs in hilarity; they had done their job and completely and utterly destroyed the complacent, prideful, comfortable and recently getting fat Silk. He was frankly almost in awe of their thoroughness – right down to the poetic end.

He just laughed, and kept laughing, chuckling on and on and shaking his head, until the point when all those around him exchanged knowing looks and touched fingers to their temples in pity.

Chapter 21

WHAT ORJIN AND HIS REMAINING TROOP WERE doing now could no longer be described as fighting. Fleeing was more like it. Whenever they encountered a column of Quon Talian soldiers they ran westward, and the enemy commander Renquill, no fool, was happy to drive them onwards towards the coast.

The word 'remaining' was the one Orjin adopted as his force dwindled before his eyes. Understandably so, as exhaustion and hunger became unbearable, and injuries worsened. Desertions increased as well, admittedly, as hopes faded.

Still, those remaining jogged onward, and Orjin constantly checked in with the hill-tribe guides, who would shake their heads, rather embarrassed. 'Found it?' he constantly asked, and they would look away, lowering their gazes.

'It is a very narrow opening. Difficult to locate.'

'Well . . . keep looking.' And they would nod and run off to search anew.

That night, the western ocean in sight from the slope occupied by Orjin and his troops, word came of the sighting of the gorge entrance. He signed for everyone to move out.

Word also came that the rear elements were in

running contact with Talian forces. Orjin and Orhan both jogged for the rear, but Prevost Jeral intercepted them, urging them forward and running ahead. Cursing, Orjin turned for the front.

He found the Wickan, Arkady, together with the guides guarding a slash in the steep slope less than two paces across – more of a hole than any sort of gorge.

'This is it?' he demanded of the hill youths, incredulous.

'No one ventures here any more,' one explained.

'Fine! I'll go.' Orjin started forward.

But Arkady edged down ahead of him. 'We will explore – wave down the troops.'

Orjin snarled his frustration, but complied, waving the men and women forward. Below, Arkady struck a torch and its light blossomed. Orjin urged the stragglers onward.

Arrows now came flying out of the darkness surrounding them, and he hunched. More and more of his remaining troops emerged from the dark and he pushed them on and down, clapping shoulders, pressing them forward.

Last of all came Prevost Jeral with a band of some twenty. 'The Talians are hot on our heels,' she announced, panting, her blade bared.

He gestured her down the crevasse. 'Get going!'

'After you.'

'No. No rearguard. They won't come chasing after us into this cave. They'll think us cornered. Now go on!'

'Fine.' She waved her band down among the brush-choked rocks.

Torches now waved about them and Orjin caught the glint of starlight from blades and armour. He pushed Jeral down and followed, backwards, feeling his way.

Within, the ground continued downward in a slope of

loose broken rock. He could hear it clattering and sloughing underfoot as the men and women descended. Torches shone below, showing a narrow stone throat.

After some stumbling and sliding on the loose debris, he reached the bottom to end up standing ankle-deep in frigid water along with everyone else. Arkady was waiting here, together with one of the hill-tribe lads.

'This is an old underground riverbed,' the lad explained. 'We follow this for a time.'

Orjin nodded. 'Fair enough. Let's take the van.' He turned to Jeral nearby. 'Will you watch the rear now?'

She nodded – a touch sourly, as both knew the danger now resided ahead. Renquill would no doubt take his time above, calling for them to surrender, perhaps even tossing combustibles down.

Orjin now passed the long file of his surviving troops to the fore, where three of their guides waited together with the giant Orhan. He was uneasy to see these habitually sombre and guarded youths appearing nervous. He nodded a greeting, took a torch, and advanced up the narrow course of the waterway.

The bone-chilling water rose at times to their waists, while at other times the chute lowered or narrowed to the point where Orjin had to slide along sideways, or hunched double. Poor Orhan had to crawl nearly on his stomach through these choke-points. The way continued ever onwards, however, without any dead end or impassable barrier – so far.

Eventually, they did come to something of a dead end: a cliff where the waters cascaded over, arching downwards into misted darkness.

'How far?' Orjin asked over the roar of the falls.

The youths appeared uncertain. 'We do not know. Beyond is the cavern of the . . . of it.'

Orjin looked to Orhan. 'Throw a torch.' The huge fellow tossed down his torch and everyone watched it tumble to land amid rocks. Some ten fathoms, Orjin reckoned it. 'Do we have any rope?' he asked of the troop at large. Heads turned, peering round, but no one spoke up. Wonderful, he thought. No one held on to any rope. 'Fine. I'll try climbing down.' He handed Orhan his weapon and knelt at the edge, feeling down over the cliff.

At least it was solid rock and not rotten crumbling sandstone or shale. He found handholds and slowly, his way lit from above, he felt his way down the cliff face to piled fallen detritus, the talus slope. 'Not too difficult!' he shouted up. 'Did you see that?'

'Yes,' Arkady answered. 'We will follow. Do not move!'

Orjin remained where he stood – feeling rather foolish standing unarmed in the lair of some sort of reputed eldritch horror.

When perhaps half of his troops had descended, Orjin turned to the hill-tribe youths. 'Thank you, but you needn't go on from here. Just tell us the way.'

'No one alive knows the way from this point onward,' one said. 'We will come.'

Orjin nodded his gratitude. He glanced to Orhan and Arkady. 'Let's take a look.'

They explored the cavern. At one point starlight streamed downwards from some hidden crack above. The bones of animals that had tumbled into the gap above lay broken amid the rocks here. Listening, Orjin thought he could almost hear the surf rolling against the rocky shore. The cavern narrowed here, the water rising to their knees.

He might have been fooling himself, but he thought he saw the glint of light just above the water level far ahead. 'Is that an opening?' he asked Arkady.

The Wickan did not answer. Glancing at him, Orjin saw the fellow staring aside, hand white on the grip of his curved long-knife.

What Orjin had taken for a pile of pale rocks off to one side now shifted, rising, climbing ever higher until he found himself staring upward at a great upright lizard standing at some four fathoms of bones and withered flesh. Yet it stood awkwardly, tilted, and he saw that the bones of one thick leg were broken.

The hill-tribe youths all gaped, frozen.

Yune came, pushing forward. 'Not a dragon!' he yelled. 'Though I understand the confusion. A K'Chain Che'Malle warrior.'

Orhan had given back Orjin's two-handed sword and now he drew it. 'I don't give a damn what it is – can it be killed?'

'It appears preserved against rot somehow. Undying. Perhaps it fell from above ages ago,' Yune told him. 'It will have to be dismembered.'

'Dismembered!' Orjin snarled, appalled. 'Fine. Orhan, you distract it and I'll go for the other leg.'

Prevost Jeral had pushed forward. 'No! All at once! Too many targets, yes?'

The creature struggled to advance upon them, dragging its shattered rear leg.

Orjin cursed again. 'Right! All at once – we overpower it.' He raised his sword overhead, bellowing, 'All who would dare . . . draw your weapons and attack!'

He did not wait to see how many actually took him up on his challenge and charged in. The creature took great wide sweeps with its forelimbs, knocking soldiers flying aside. With his two-handed sword and brute strength, Orjin managed to deflect one such sweep, but it took far too much out of him to be worth it, and he ducked from then on. Some few managed to reach the good leg and they hacked at the bone and withered dried ligaments. The beast brushed them off, and too many of the tossed men and women did not rise again from where they'd fallen among the rocks.

Incensed by these losses, just on the cusp of escape, Orjin charged in for that side. He ducked a sweep and hacked with all his strength, chopping deeply. But the blade caught and he could not dislodge it. The next thing he knew he was flying through the air, the wind punched from him. He crashed into rocks and was sure he heard and felt ribs crack.

Gasping, rising, he staggered in once more, meaning to retrieve his blade from where it stood jammed into the main joint of the beast's leg. It was pawing at the blade now, and from the opposite side the giant Orhan came charging in, two-handed mattock raised high above his head. He brought the weapon down on the creature's skull with a bellowing yell that echoed from the rocks around. There was an audible crunch and the creature staggered, but not before turning upon Orhan, snapping its jaws round him and tossing him aside.

Orjin saw his chance. The beast seemed stunned, its skull crushed, and he darted in, rolling, to grasp hold of his blade. He yanked it up and down, severing ligament and tendon, and the creature came tumbling, nearly crushing him as he threw himself backwards.

Down, thrashing amid the dust and broken rock, the thing could hardly defend itself and all the troops piled in, chopping and hacking. Orjin limped to where Orhan lay, Yune cradling his head.

'No beast too large for us, hey, Orhan?' he said.

The huge fellow chuckled, blood at his lips and chin. 'Indeed. No beast too large.'

'We'll carry you out.'

But Orhan shook his head. 'No. I am all broken inside. Leave me here with my defeated enemy.'

'Yune here will fix you up and then we'll be off.'

Prevost Jeral came to Orjin's side. 'It's done,' she murmured, her eyes on Orhan.

'Very good. Explore ahead. Is there a damned way out?'

The woman nodded. 'At once.'

Orjin caught Yune's eye and the shaman shook his head. He nodded then, holding his side. 'A fight to remember,' he told Orhan, who nodded his mute agreement.

He mouthed what might have been *A fight to remember* before his head fell slack.

The gods were not so fickle this time as to deny them an exit, and the hill-tribe youths found a gap in the rocks that one could reach in neck-deep water to emerge beneath starlight and a gathering pink glow to the east. Wincing, holding his side and swimming one-handed, Orjin emerged to be helped up by nearby troops. Arkady was already with others, waving torches towards the ocean where answering lights flickered far out at sea.

Cradling his side, Orjin eased himself down on to a boulder draped in dry seaweed and wished he had a flask or a skin of wine to raise.

As the light of dawn gathered over the cliffs behind them, launches appeared amid the waves, oaring in towards the shore. Orjin rose and limped out to join his troops wading into the surf.

The launches brought them to merchant cargo vessels that had been converted into troop-carriers. Orjin couldn't climb the netting and so a sling was lowered for him. On board, he peered round, rather bemused to see armed marines wearing black jupons.

'Who commands you lot?' someone called from the stern.

Orjin limped over to the bearded Napan captain. 'And you are?' he asked.

'Choss,' the fellow said, extending a hand. 'Admiral Choss.'

'Orjin,' he answered.

'That's Greymane,' Prevost Jeral said, now at his side. 'Commander Greymane.'

'Very well,' Choss said, shrugging. 'Welcome to service with Malaz, Greymane.'

* * *

Gregar and Haraj made their way through the mixed forest and farmlands north of Jurda. They hid from soldiery from all sides roaming the woods and fields. Some of these units pursued legitimate orders from Gris or Bloor, hunting deserters, or harassing the enemy. Others were plain broken elements or bandit bands, intent on raiding hamlets, or each other, and disappearing. Uncertain which was the case, Gregar hid from everyone. On wooded paths they did occasionally come across locals; these he questioned for news of the Crimson Guard.

Contrary stories reached them via these crofters. It seemed no one was certain what happened that day on the field east of Jurda. Regardless, everyone agreed that Gris and its allies had won the day. The Bloorian League was in complete disarray; King Gareth of Vor had withdrawn to attack the pirate raiders who occupied Castle Vor, while Styvell of Rath was dead – assassinated, so everyone said, at the orders of Baron Ranel of Nita.

This struck Gregar as a particularly foolish action as, having deserted the Grisian lines, the Nitan forces now found themselves hunted on all sides with all hands raised against them. A few elders Gregar and Haraj spoke to speculated, like Gregar, that just because a Nitan weapon was used to kill the king, that didn't mean it was done at the baron's orders. In any case, Ranel did not make himself available for questioning, and now it was too late, as reportedly two days ago his forces were run down by King Hret of Bloor and exterminated to a man and a woman.

Meanwhile, Gregar and Haraj kept northwards, trudging through the chill rains and sleet along muddy cart-trails through woods and fields. After five nights farmers directed them to a military encampment in a fallow meadow just shy of a large northern forest. They tramped onwards, Haraj having long given up complaining about the cold, the rain, and his hunger.

Here, in the darkness and icy rain, they were met by two pickets in oiled cloaks.

'Move along,' one told them.

Gregar lifted his chin, drops of chill rain falling from it. 'We're here to join.'

The guard – one Gregar didn't recognize – waved them on. 'Cadge a meal somewhere else, deserters.'

'We're mages,' Gregar said. The pickets exchanged looks beneath their hoods. 'Get Red. He knows us.'

The spokesman raised an arm, as if to cuff him. 'We don't take orders from some damned—'

But his companion reached out and lowered his arm. 'Wait here,' he said, and disappeared into the driving sheets of rain.

Some time later the guard returned with another figure in a shapeless oiled cloak, his mussed dark hair flattened wet: the mage, Red. He looked them up and down then nodded to himself and motioned them to follow.

Once more Gregar found himself in the wide central tent of the Crimson Guard that, he supposed, passed as their mobile main hall. Within, a long central trench glowed with a blazing fire, while at the head of the main table Courian sat as before – almost as if no time had passed at all.

But it wasn't entirely the same. Gregar noted how the commander sat slumped in his chair, quiet now, and that he used only his right hand to drink and eat while his left lay immobile on his lap. Red approached Cal-Brinn, on Courian's left, and they spoke in low tones. Then Cal-Brinn waved them forward.

Rather reluctantly, Gregar approached, Haraj in tow.

Cal-Brinn leaned in to whisper to Courian, who cocked his head, listening. Closer now, Gregar noted how one corner of the man's mouth hung slack, and how his one good eye now drooped half open.

Courian looked them up and down, blinking, then snorted. 'You two. So, reconsidering our offer, hey?'

Gregar made an effort to straighten beneath the man's glower. 'Yes, m'lord. Yellows was destroyed in the battle.'

Courian nodded. 'I understand. Well . . . your timing is impeccable. We, too, endured unacceptable casualties in that fiasco. So we are recruiting. Therefore, remember, I am no lord. I am your commander.' He waved them off. 'Now get something to eat.'

'Thank you, sir!' Haraj gushed.

Gregar nodded. 'Yes. Thank you indeed.'

Courian waved them away. 'Yes, yes. Go on with you.'

Later that night Cal-Brinn showed them to a tent.

Inside lay a change of dry clothes. 'As mages,' he explained, 'you get private quarters. Now rest. We'll speak tomorrow.'

Both Gregar and Haraj started babbling about how thankful they were, but the Dal Hon mage raised a hand for silence. 'Tomorrow. Rest now.'

Gregar nodded and sat on one of the pallet beds. Almost immediately, he fell backwards and closed his eyes.

The next day K'azz welcomed them and introduced them around. They ate in the main tent, along with all the other guardsmen and women who were off duty at the time. Listening to the talk, Gregar gathered it was true that the Guard had suffered a great number of losses in extricating itself from the chaos of the field of Jurda.

Courian, however, that evening at dinner was more jovial, though his arm remained immobile. He spoke of more recruits expected, and winked his one half-lidded remaining eye.

Two days later the recruits arrived. It started with the noise and tumult of a great number of horses arriving at the camp: the stamping of hooves and the jangle of equipage. Everyone within peered up, surprised, save for Courian who straightened eagerly, motioning to the guards at the wide tent-flap. 'They are here! Let them in!'

The flap was pushed aside and in came a tall, powerful-looking fellow in a long mail coat, belted, with a two-handed sword at his side. His hair was a dirty blond, long and thick, and curled, as was his thick beard. He looked round, and Gregar thought his expression a touch too self-satisfied and smug as he approached the main table.

Courian struggled to his feet to reach out for his hand. 'Skinner! Welcome! You are most welcome indeed.'

K'azz appeared quite puzzled. 'Father,' he asked, 'what is this?'

'Recruits!' Courian announced. 'Four hundred swords! Skinner here has agreed to join under my command.'

Gregar was surprised; whenever anyone wished to condemn mercenaries out of hand it was always Skinner's troop they pointed to; the worst of the worst, was the common perception. Nothing more than hired bloody-handed murderers and killers.

K'azz rested a hand on Courian's arm. 'Father, a word, please . . .'

Courian shook him off. 'No. There's nothing to talk over. Open war is upon us. We must gather strength to survive. Skinner has the swords, but most importantly the will to use them. That is what we need now.'

The blond mercenary commander inclined his head – a touch sardonically, it seemed to Gregar. 'Four hundred blades are yours, Courian,' he said.

The commander nodded, giving a battle-grin, but the grin turned to a grimace as he clutched his side, kneading it. 'Excellent, Skinner,' he gasped. 'You are welcome. Cal-Brinn! See that they settle in!'

The Dal Hon mage bowed, rising. 'At once.' He motioned to the entrance. 'This way.' He and Skinner went out.

Gregar, however, noted the troubled expression upon K'azz's face, which he tried to hide by lowering his head, and the now hardened features of Surat, sitting at the far end of the table. Then he recalled: Surat was the Guard's champion, while Skinner was regarded as a champion himself.

Courian, it seemed, had nearly doubled the Guard's strength. But at what price?

Then he almost shook his head himself; in joining the Guard he thought he'd left behind all such concerns. Growing up, he had always held the mercenary company to be the paragon of merit and reward: be good enough, and you will be rewarded. Now it seemed that even here personalities and politics played their roles. Well, human nature, he supposed. We drag it with us wherever we go.

He looked to a worried Haraj at his side, now coughing mutely into a fist in a way that bespoke his anxiety, and whispered reassuringly, 'Well . . . at least we joined before they did, hey?'

* * *

Once the novelty of her new position as chief bouncer in a high-class bordello wore off, Iko became bored. Guiding drunken nobles down halls and into carriages was, frankly, not a challenge to her abilities. Neither was arm-locking rowdy young bravos who thought they were tough.

Still, it was an engagement that allowed her to remain close to the palace, and she spent every spare hour haunting the roof-top garden, peering out across the city to the precincts now forbidden to her.

She was, she knew, an odd bird in a menagerie of exotics and misfits, and she was, rather against her better judgement, getting to know them. The lad she met the first night went by the name of Leena and preferred to be addressed as a woman. Fair enough. Likewise, there were women who catered only to women – it was a come one, come all establishment. Iko didn't judge, because, after all, she was perhaps the oddest of the lot.

415

She was in the kitchens having breakfast, on call as usual, when Leena came rushing down the narrow servants' stairs to announce breathlessly, 'There's fighting in the palace.'

Iko set down her tea. 'Fighting? What do you mean?'

Leena pulled her dressing robe more tightly about herself. 'Talk on the streets. The gates and doors closed. Perhaps even fires!'

Iko surged to her feet and charged up the stairs. She did not halt until she gained the roof and here she gazed, shading her eyes. There was indeed smoke over the palace grounds, and there was a much louder than usual clamour rising from the streets and markets all about. She stormed down to the exit and headed straight for the walled palace grounds. Citizens were milling about, talking of the clash of weaponry from beyond the walls, and seeing new, unfamiliar armed guards in the grounds. Iko ran even faster.

She charged for one particular stretch of wall, a low section that sided on the wildest portion of the gardens. Here she cast about and found what she needed: a streethawker's cart. Marching up, she yanked it from him and drove it against the wall, climbed on to it – ignoring the yelling owner – and jumped to grip the top of the wall. From here she pulled herself up and over, and dropped down.

That, she congratulated herself, went well. But then in her thoughts she'd been rehearsing just such an action for several weeks. She ran for the Sword-Dancers' quarters.

A column of marching troops forced her to take cover behind a pavilion. She was astonished to see that they wore gold and black favours – the colours of the Fedal family, who had held the throne before the Chulalorn

416

dynasty. And with them was a detachment of Dal Honese, armoured, but showing no colours. An alliance.

A dread such as she'd never before known gripped Iko now, and an iron band closed around her chest. She ran on, not able even to breathe.

The smoke was thickest around the Sword-Dancers' quarters, and rounding a building on the square Iko saw why: the barracks still burned, collapsed, timbers still in flames. She slowed then, as if in a daze. A heap of the fallen lay before the smouldering ruins of the main doors: her lifeless sisters. Some in shifts and trousers only, many with their hair burned away, their flesh seared, but one and all pierced by countless arrows.

Bending, she took the whipsword from the still warm hand of one, and turned her head to the palace. She tightened her two-handed grip and ran for the nearest entrance.

A knot of Fedal troops guarded the door. Hardly one yell of surprise left their mouths before she was upon them, slashing and spinning. All fell in an instant. Then she was in, running for the king's private quarters. Here the rooms showed the wreckage of a sacking. Fine ceramic vases lay shattered, desks overturned, sheafs of vellum records everywhere. And, here and there, fallen royal guards.

Passing one entrance she paused, and returned. Here lay a great number of Fedal and Dal Hon troops; they'd met strong resistance from a knot of Kan family guards. And among the fallen lay the Kan of family Kan himself, Leoto. He lay panting shallowly, his chased-iron hauberk only half done up, but sword in hand. Iko knelt next to him and his rolling eyes found hers.

He shook his head, chuckling. 'So . . . couldn't walk away, hey, Iko?'

'Who?' she asked.

An effort at a weak shrug. 'The Fedal – and allies.' He chuckled again. 'It's never where you're looking, hey?'

'The king?'

He nodded, his teeth clenching in effort. 'Save him,' he snarled, then slumped back, limp.

Iko pressed his eyes shut then ran for the throne room.

Entering, she found a press of Fedal family troops and Dal Hon allies, probably elite infantry. Before the empty throne stood a heavy-set woman Iko knew from official functions. The woman wore her long black hair piled high on her head in a complicated arrangement and favoured loose flowing silk robes; the Marquessa of family Fedal.

'Who are you?' the marquessa called, one thick black brow arched.

Iko turned and calmly locked the doors behind her, then retightened her two-handed grip, readying the weapon. 'Where is the king?'

'Do you really know how to use that blade?' the marquessa enquired sceptically.

'Where is the king?'

The marquessa merely waved her troops forward. 'Oh, please kill the fool.'

Iko charged to meet them all.

They closed on all sides – which was exactly what Iko wanted as she spun, the blade whirling about, spinning with her. Fighting now, she became suddenly quite calm as she eased into her so-familiar battle presence. Blood splashed the walls as the whipsword slashed and lashed about her. In moments all were down, the Fedal troops and the Dal Hon elites, though these were the last to fall. The marquessa stared dumbfounded as Iko closed upon her. Backing away, the woman tripped over the raised dais and fell.

'*Where is the king!*' Iko bellowed.

'Taken away,' the marquessa stammered.

'Where?'

Her eyes flicked north – the river – and Iko straightened. Taken by boat, no doubt.

'You cannot kill me!' the marquessa almost squeaked, a hand at her breast.

Iko peered down at her. 'Yes I can.' And she slashed her throat.

She charged straight for the riverfront where naval vessels docked, and the royal barges and pleasure-craft could be found. She scanned the docks, spotted one such royal craft readying to depart, and ran for it.

The lines had been slipped and a mixture of sailors and troops on the broad deck were poling away from the pier. Some stared, pointing.

Running, Iko leapt and slammed down hard on the stern-piece. The barge's pilot reached for her, one hand on the tiller. She slashed his arm and he stared, gaping, at his severed wrist. Releasing the tiller, he clamped the stump between his legs, screaming.

The sailors flinched from her but the troops closed, drawing their weapons.

As the barge lazily curled its way downriver towards the harbour, Iko stalked the deck, killing. These men and women proved the most resilient. She could tell they were veterans – probably cashiered or deserted Itko Kan infantry. They parried and counterattacked, but her own training was that of an expert and these veterans, though competent, fell one by one as Iko advanced upon the bows.

Here the obvious leader awaited her, shortsword held negligently in one hand, no doubt an officer herself. The barge spun rudderless now, as most of the sailors had jumped ship.

'Who are you?' the woman called.

'Where is the king?' Iko demanded. 'Tell me, or I will kill you!'

The woman nodded as if considering, then drew back a tarp at her feet, revealing the lad, gagged and wrapped in chains. Chulalorn the Fourth stared up at Iko, his eyes huge.

'Don't worry,' she told him soothingly. 'It will be all right.'

'They told me to get rid of him,' the veteran officer said. 'No trace. No burial site. No cairn or tomb for remembrance . . . and now you want me to give him to you.'

Iko nodded, her whipsword held ready. 'Do that and I will let you live.'

'I can think of a third option,' the officer said. And she took hold of the lad's chains and raised him up to set him on the edge of the barge. 'I think that you will let me live . . . if I do *this*.' And she pushed the boy over the edge, where he disappeared with a splash into the river.

'*Nooooo!*' Iko dived off the barge.

The waters of the Itko river were dark and silty. Abandoning her whipsword, Iko felt about, grasping at the muddy bottom until her screaming lungs forced her to surface for one desperate gulp of air before submerging once more to search again.

Again and again she did so, her breathing ragged, coughing on the dirty water, squeezing mud between her fingers as she searched on and on. But she found nothing. The weak current had drawn her some way past where the lad had fallen and she just floated now, almost unconscious, limp, pulled along towards the harbour.

She lay staring up at the cloudy sky as she drifted along. Then, resolutely, she threw her arms back and ducked her head under, exhaling all her breath. Holding herself under, lips clenched, eventually she could resist her body no longer and her lungs convulsed, drawing in a great spasm of water. She flailed then, her body clawing towards the surface where sunlight rippled so close above, in a last desperate bid to save itself against her will.

But her vision darkened. Her arms weakened. And she hung motionless under the surface and knew nothing more.

*

She awoke amid nets on board a small fishing vessel. It was night, and two old men peered down at her, a lantern between them. One was scratching his head, the other stood with hands on hips.

'You are perhaps a mermaid?' one asked, rather hopefully.

Iko just let her head fall back.

'She is, I think, one of those sad suicides,' the other said. 'A lover betrayed her, perhaps.'

Iko threw herself for the side, but she was so weak that even these two scrawny elders were able to pull her back.

'By Chem!' the first said, 'I think you are right!'

'Bind her,' the second said, and the first did so.

'Let me die,' Iko croaked, and she could not help it or resist it – she started to weep.

The second elder patted her shoulder. 'Later,' he said, as one might soothe an infant. 'Plenty of time for dying later.'

* * *

Once there was no more wood for fires – or bare rock to set them on anyway, only ice – Ullara was beginning to suspect that she'd pushed her luck past the breaking point. That night she sat wrapped in blankets in the lee of a crag of ice, trying to gnaw a portion of dried meat from a frozen strip. Chewing, she decided she'd gone too far to turn back now, and she lifted a portion of the blankets to study Tiny in his wicker cage and feed him a few bits of seed from a dwindling pouch.

In the morning she set out northward once more. The only birds she could reach inhabiting these icy wastes were large snow-white owls, and these she drew near her occasionally to serve as her eyes. Other than these broader views, it was Tiny who provided her vision.

So it was a blow when she awoke to find she could not see. Whether it was the cold, the improper feed, or perhaps plain loneliness, she wasn't certain. She couldn't help but sit and cradle the basket, thinking that it was now fairly certain that it would not be long before she followed.

And if that were to be the case, she decided, then she might as well get a move on. Feeling about, she grasped her long probing stick and stood, sensing about. She found a hunting owl not too far off and urged it her way. After a short wait she was peering down at herself, and she set off.

With the aid of the hardy snow-owls, she crossed many more leagues of the wind-scoured ice wastes. Now she began to despair. Was there nothing here to come *to*? Why the drive for such a journey? To what end? Was it all just a delusion, or childish wilful foolishness, as that Crimson Guard commander Seth had suggested?

Yet there was no turning back now, so she hunched her shoulders against the driving wind with its stinging jabbing needles of ice, and struggled on.

As the days passed, the owls became more and more

difficult to find or call. Eventually, one morning, she found herself blind, her allies gone. She knew she couldn't just sit still and freeze, so she set out, probing the ice and crusted snow before her, advancing one step at a time.

Later that very day, the sun's heat sinking where it touched upon her cheeks, she pushed her stick down before her, testing, and relaxed her grip momentarily, only to have the stick slip from her hands and disappear. She heard it, for a few moments, banging and rattling as it fell hundreds of paces, striking the edges of whatever deep crevasse of ice lay before her.

Now she did find herself fighting back tears, but they flowed anyway, freezing to little beads of ice upon her cheeks. She sat hunched. Now what? Who knew how far across this canyon was, or how far to either side? What could she do now, other than just sit?

She decided to send out as strong a call as she could, for who knew? Perhaps one of the snow-owls, or some other bird, would answer before it was too late.

She called and called as she sat, wrapped in blankets, rocking. Night came, then day, and as she sat, her legs and hands now numb and useless, she thought she sensed some sort of answer. But no doubt her imagination, desperate for life, was playing tricks upon her, for it was too late. Her head was drooping for longer and longer. Her face was completely numb, and she couldn't feel anything. In fact, it was becoming rather pleasant – she wasn't feeling any pain at all.

But she could still hear, and what she heard over the constant howling of the winds alarmed her: the crunching of footsteps on crusty snow. She struggled to rise – and hands aided her to her feet. And suddenly, like a blessing, she could see.

Four individuals faced her, squat, wrapped in furs,

with wind-darkened wrinkled features and narrow slitted eyes. One held a cage that contained a large bird of prey of some breed unfamiliar to her. The four bowed to her. 'Welcome, priestess,' one said – a woman by her voice.

'Priestess?' Ullara mumbled through her numb lips. 'I am no priestess.'

'Our last priest is old, dying. He cast forth a summoning for new blood and you have answered.'

'Answered? But who are you? I don't know you.'

'We are the Jhek. The beast-blood is strong in us, and you have been called to be our new priestess.'

Ullara's head sank in exhaustion and she struggled to hold it up. 'But I don't . . .'

'No matter, come.' The woman gestured to some sort of sledge they'd brought with them. 'You are welcome. We thank you for answering our call.'

She sank then into the layered warm furs, just happy to be out of the punishing winds.

* * *

Sitting on the gilded throne in the audience hall of Heng, Kellanved shifted uncomfortably. He drummed his fingers on the gilt armrests, sighed loudly, and slumped as if exhausted. Standing next to the throne, arms loose at his sides, Dancer listened as the local official guild of merchants presented their greetings, their authorizations, and began probing Kellanved as to the status of prior agreements and other such understandings.

Finally, Kellanved waved a hand, interrupting, to sigh, 'Yes, yes. All old arrangements shall be honoured – for now. Thank you.' He waved the contingent away. 'Thank you!'

424

The merchants eyed one another, confused and uncertain, but all bowed and backed away. Once they were gone, and the hall was empty but for guards, Kellanved set his head in one hand. 'The duties and obligations of rulership are crushing, Dancer my friend,' he complained. 'How I long for our old carefree times.'

Dancer cocked a brow. 'It's only been two days.'

'None the less! Every throne is an arrowbutt! Uneasy rests my bottom! Everyone is plotting against the emperor!'

'Of course they are.'

The wrinkled and spindly mage waved a hand. 'Oh yes. Of course.'

The doors at the far end of the hall opened and in walked Surly, accompanied by Dassem. They stopped before the throne and Surly crossed her arms. 'We need to talk privately.'

Kellanved rolled his eyes but waved away the guards. The walking stick appeared in his hands and he leaned forward, resting his chin upon its silver head. 'Yes?'

'Strategy,' she answered, nonplussed. 'What is our next move?'

Kellanved nodded thoughtfully. 'It is to our advantage that this city is used to being ruled by a cabal of mages. We will merely replace it with our own – for the time being.'

Surly nodded her agreement. 'And beyond that?'

Kellanved looked to Dassem. 'Then we recruit and train for as long as our neighbours will give us. Consolidate.'

The Dal Hon swordsman nodded his agreement.

'And the neighbours?' Surly asked.

He glanced significantly to Dancer, then back to her. 'We'll need good intelligence as to their moves and intentions.'

Dancer eyed Surly and she inclined her head in agreement once again. 'Do we have a target?' she asked.

Kellanved sat back, tapped his fingers on the armrests. 'I was thinking south first. There is much unrest currently in Itko Kan. We can exploit that.'

For an instant the woman appeared quite startled; then her eyes narrowed as she regarded him, and Dancer could imagine her wondering how he could possibly know such things. 'As I have heard as well,' she finally admitted, a touch resentfully.

Kellanved slapped the armrests. 'Very good. That is a plan.'

'Can we count on your . . . allies?' Dassem asked.

The mage shook his head. 'No. We cannot. They come and go of their own accord. However – that needn't leave this room.'

Dassem gave a knowing smile, and nodded. 'I understand. Deception is the first weapon of any duel.'

'It's my main one,' Kellanved muttered, and Dancer saw Surly tilt her head at that, as if filing the offhand comment away for future reference.

Now the mage raised his hands and waved them as if shooing everyone off. 'Very good. You know your duties. Get to them.'

Surly drew a hard breath, but bowed, if shallowly. Dassem gave a curt bow from the waist.

Once the two had left and the tall ponderous doors banged shut, Kellanved slumped back in the throne and pressed a hand to his brow. 'Gods! It's exhausting! Endless duties and obligations. It will be the death of me, I tell you, Dancer.'

Now the assassin couldn't help but crook a teasing smile. 'And just how long *has* it been? Twenty years? Seventy? Over a hundred? I get confused.'

The mage pressed both hands to his hanging head as if in despair. 'Oh, shut up.'

However, as Dancer knew it would, the moment passed. Suddenly, Kellanved raised his head and turned to him with a certain impish glint in his eyes. 'Don't you think, my friend,' he said, 'that it is high time we explored Shadow?'

DANCER'S LAMENT
Path to Ascendancy Book 1
Ian C. Esslemont

It was once a land ravaged by war.

But then the rival cities of Tali and Quon formed an alliance and Quon Tali came into being. And with it a peace of sorts. However, that was a long time ago.

At the heart of Quon Tali lies Li Heng. Under the iron rule of the sorceress called the 'Protectress' and her cabal of five mages, the city has enjoyed relative stability for centuries. And that is about to change . . .

Two young men have arrived at the city's gates. One is determined to prove he is the most skilled assassin of his age, while the other is his quarry – a Dal Hon mage who is, it appears, annoyingly difficult to kill.

And marching from the south are the forces of Itko Kan, led by their ambitious new king. His assassins have already entered Li Heng, and with them come rumours of inhuman, nightmarish forces at his command. It seems chaos now stalks the city streets. But – as a certain young Dal Hon mage knows – in chaos there is opportunity . . .

'Brilliant . . . filled with rooftop knife fights, devastating magery and underworld evil, this book hits all the right notes at all the right times'
FantasyBookReview

'Great storytelling, brilliantly entertaining characters . . . a must-read'
CriticalDragon

DEADHOUSE LANDING
Path to Ascendancy Book 2
Ian C. Esslemont

Out of ruins an empire will rise, but first
let chaos reign!

Recently arrived in Malaz City, Dancer and Kellanved
intend to plunge straight into the increasing conflict
between the island of Malaz and its neighbour – the
equally piratical isle of Nap. But their plans go awry
when Kellanved develops a strange and dangerous
fascination for a mysterious, dilapidated structure at
the city's heart – a place avoided by locals at all cost.

As powerful entities start to take an interest in the
Dal Hon mage, Dancer wonders whether it's time he
abandoned his partner-in-mischief – especially when
Kellanved's obsession with shadows and ancient
artifacts brings them alarmingly close to death and
destruction. Because who would willingly enter the
Deadhouse of an Elder?

Continuing his chronicling of the genesis of the Malazan
Empire, this second chapter in Ian C. Esslemont's
thrilling epic fantasy takes readers back to the time
before it all began . . .

'Tremendous . . . for fans of anything Malazan,
this is an absolute must'
FantasyBookReview

'Truly impressive . . . addictive and engaging . . . if
you're looking for a new epic fantasy read, I strongly
recommend taking a look at *Deadhouse Landing*'
Rising Shadow

Have you read Ian C. Esslemont's first foray into the world of Malaz?

NIGHT OF KNIVES
Ian C. Esslemont

'The first instalment of the shared world that
we had both envisioned'
STEVEN ERIKSON

Malaz gave a great empire its name, but now this
island and its city amount to little more than
a sleepy backwater. Until this night.

Because this night there is to be a convergence, the
once-in-a-generation appearance of a Shadow Moon – an
occasion that threatens the good people of Malaz with
demon hounds and other, darker things.

Also it is prophesied that the Emperor Kellanved will return
this night, and there are those who would prevent that
happening at any cost. As factions within the Empire draw
up battle lines, an ancient presence begins its all-out assault
upon the island. Witnesses to these cataclysmic events
include a thief called Kiska, and Temper, a war-weary
veteran. Although they do not know it, they each have a
part to play in a confrontation that will determine not only
the fate of Malaz City but also of the world beyond . . .

Drawing on events touched on in the prologue of Steven
Erikson's landmark fantasy *Gardens of the Moon*, *Night of
Knives* is a momentous chapter in the unfolding story
of the extraordinarily imagined world of Malaz.

'A hugely promising start . . . Esslemont triumphs'
Death Ray

'Telling a story set largely over just one terrifying
night, it pulverizes you with an economy
that is rare in fantasy'
SFX